RIVER KISS

"Please wake up, Philip," Anna pleaded. She pulled his shirt loose from his trousers and opened it wide at the yoke, then wiped the cloth down his neck and chest. She pressed her cheek against his forehead and laid her palm over his heart, feeling the rise and fall of his chest as he breathed. "Can you hear me, Philip? Tell me you're not going to die."

His fingers wrapped around her wrist and pulled her hand up from his chest. Anna jerked her head from his forehead and her startled gaze locked with intense gray eyes that held not pain, but hunger . . . sweet, tormented longing so compelling that she couldn't look away . . . could not, in fact, even raise her face further from his.

"Dying is the absolute *last* thing on my mind right now, Anna," he said huskily.

He released her wrist and cupped his hand around the back of her head, bringing her mouth the last few inches to his. He instantly ignited a fire in both of them that had started as a warm glow of concern and was kindled into a flame of desire the instant their lips touched. He moved his head under hers, deepening the kiss as he heated their passion. He reached under Anna's robe and stroked her back with a seductive rhythm that had her squirming to get close to him.

Lost in the spell of his hands and lips, Anna's desire soared with the pounding of her heart and the tantalizing of her senses. Her hunger rose to meet and satisfy Philip's, and she felt his need almost as strongly as her own . . .

BOOK YOUR PLACE ON OUR WEBSITE AND MAKE THE READING CONNECTION!

We've created a customized website just for our very special readers, where you can get the inside scoop on everything that's going on with Zebra, Pinnacle and Kensington books.

When you come online, you'll have the exciting opportunity to:

- View covers of upcoming books
- Read sample chapters
- Learn about our future publishing schedule (listed by publication month *and author*)
- Find out when your favorite authors will be visiting a city near you
- Search for and order backlist books from our online catalog
- Check out author bios and background information
- Send e-mail to your favorite authors
- Meet the Kensington staff online
- Join us in weekly chats with authors, readers and other guests
- Get writing guidelines
- AND MUCH MORE!

Visit our website at
http://www.zebrabooks.com

RIVER
SONG

CYNTHIA
THOMASON

Zebra Books
Kensington Publishing Corp.

http://www.zebrabooks.com

ZEBRA BOOKS are published by

Kensington Publishing Corp.
850 Third Avenue
New York, NY 10022

First Printing: September, 1998
10 9 8 7 6 5 4 3 2 1

Printed in the United States of America

*This book is dedicated to the memory of
Esther Burkhart Collins and to Barbara Collins Brackett,
and to all mothers and daughters who bridge
the generation gap with books*

I would like to thank Ona Bustos, Nancy Cane, Charlene Newberg and Ann Reynold for helping me keep this book on track. And a special loving thank you to Bert Brackett, my dad, for being such a wonderful story-teller

PROLOGUE

Missouri, 1872

Anna stared at the unshaven man in front of her. *I guess he could be my uncle,* she thought, though she hadn't seen him since she was nine years old. All she could remember for sure was that he had made her laugh with his tall tales and uncommon behavior. Now that she looked at him through the eyes of a twelve-year-old, it was hard to believe this heavyset, unkempt man in the loose-fitting clothes could be the brother of her tall, handsome father.

"Anna, say something to your uncle," the headmistress prompted, giving her a push toward the man. "Have your wits left you altogether? You do remember him, don't you?"

To admit there was very little she recalled about this man she had only seen three or four times in her life would not have been wise. If there was one thing Anna Rose Connolly did know, it was that she wanted to get out of this place, and she hoped and prayed this man would take her.

"She may not remember me at all, ma'am," the man said with a sympathetic glance toward Anna. "I'm afraid we've never had a chance to get to know each other very well." He peered at his niece from under the brim of his dusty gray bowler. His upper lip was hidden completely by a mustache gone wild with neglect, but he smiled at her, and his face was kind.

"Of course I remember you," Anna stated with pretended certainty. "How have you been, Uncle?" She wanted it to seem as though she inquired about his health on a regular basis.

He removed the bowler and revealed a crop of coarse, graying hair that stuck out in all directions from the indentation left by the hat. "Well, I'm fine I guess," he said, "though I'm grieved to hear of your mama and papa's passin'."

"It's all right. You don't have to say that. After all, it happened so long ago now."

He cocked his head to one side and eyed her suspiciously, as if he doubted her stoic composure. "Still, your papa was my brother and a fine man. I was quite fond of your mother, too. And, Anna, I'm sorry about how long it took me to get here. I only got to Hannibal last week and picked up my mail. It's been months since the fire. I would have come sooner—"

"All that doesn't matter does it, Anna?" the headmistress interrupted. "You're certainly grateful that your uncle came for you today, aren't you?" She put her hand on top of Anna's short blond curls and coaxed her to nod.

Anna willingly went along with the coaching. After all, the headmistress was right. Anna was grateful to see anyone who would take her away from Miss Brockman's. "Let's go then, Uncle," she said, reaching for a small, worn carpetbag by her feet.

"Anna, are you sure this is what you want to do?" he asked. "Maybe we should talk about this." He stared at her resolute face for a long moment before he picked up her bag. "I guess you are sure at that."

"You're all she's talked about for months, Mr. Connolly," the headmistress said, nudging Anna toward the door.

Anna jumped back to a safe distance, certain Miss Brockman would be struck down by a thunderbolt for telling such an outright lie. But, as usual, the headmistress escaped divine retribution.

"You'd best get started soon," she said. "St. Louis is no place to be after dark since gold fever started. The city is a den of thieves."

Mick responded to the authority in the woman's voice as nearly everyone did, and Anna watched him move to the door. He waited for her to precede him outside, and they walked wordlessly down the cobblestone sidewalk. Only when they reached the iron gate did Anna turn to look back at the gray stone orphanage which had been her home for months. She had said her good-byes to her few friends inside, and now it was time to move on. The headmistress had already shut and latched the heavy oak door. Anna Rose Connolly might never have lived there at all, so final and unceremonious was her leaving.

Mick cleared his throat, and Anna looked at him with clear, dry eyes. "My wagon's just outside," he said. "I hope you know I travel around most of the year. I don't really have any roots to speak of—just that general mail delivery in Hannibal and a little place I hole up in for the winters."

No roots . . . yes, that's what Anna's father had said about his brother. "Deep down Mick's all right, but he's sure not like the rest of us. He's never believed in roots or having a place to call home." But Anna remembered the fondness she'd heard in her father's voice whenever he'd talked about this strange relative who'd never really been a part of their lives.

"Traveling is just fine with me," she said, raising the latch on the gate. "In fact, the farther we go from here, the better I'll like it."

They walked to the street where Mick had left his horse-drawn wagon. The weather-beaten, whitewashed contraption had been decorated at one time with letters that retained very little of their original splendor. Anna went up to the wagon and was able to discern the words Connolly's Housewares, Hardware, and Notions. She traced her fingers along the worn letters. "Is this what you do? Travel around and sell things?"

There was something oddly pleasing about the man's vagabond life.

Mick patted the rump of the patient horse harnessed to the wagon. "This is it. At least till somethin' better comes along for Irish and me." He walked around to the back of the wagon and tossed Anna's bag inside. "I guess it ain't much of a life for a pretty young girl like you."

"It's a whole lot better than being in this place," she answered.

He helped her up on the wagon bench. "You know, Anna, I was wonderin', did you tell that ol' biddy in the orphanage that I was your only relative?"

"I did, yes."

"You do know that you have grandparents in Boston, don't you? As I recall, they're fine and fancy people. They'd prob'ly be much more suited to raisin' a young lady of quality than the likes of me. I'm curious as to why you didn't mention your ma's folks to the orphanage lady."

"I've never once heard from my mother's parents, sir, and neither did my mother. They might even be dead. And if they are alive, then I think they are mean and only care about themselves."

Anna paused a moment and decided this man would appreciate an honest opinion. She gave him one. "Now, *you* do not seem mean at all. Maybe you're a little strange, and you haven't been around much for most of my life, but I'm willing to forgive that."

Mick stepped back a few feet and scratched the gray stubble of beard on his chin. "Fair enough," he finally said. "I guess kinships have been built on less than that." He walked around and climbed up beside her. "I don't know how this is goin' to work out, Anna, but I'm ready to try if you are."

She smoothed the worn skirt of her thin cotton print dress and sat up straight next to him. "Let's go then, sir."

"Land's sake, Anna, call me Uncle Mick, or at least just Mick. Maybe I ain't earned the right to be called 'uncle,' but I know for certain I don't deserve to be called 'sir!' " He quirked an eyebrow at her, and she couldn't hide an answering grin.

Mick gave the horse a coaxing slap with the reins, and the wagon pulled away from Miss Brockman's Home for Girls. Anna Connolly never looked back.

CHAPTER ONE

Illinois, 1880

Anna stood in the wings of the River Flats, Illinois, Opera House and once again tugged at the ruffles on the waistband of her new green satin dress. Her uncle had picked this particular gown for her premier performance on the stage. "It'll be perfect, darlin'," Mick Connolly had said, convincing her the gown would have "just the right fanciness" when illuminated by the latest in incandescent lighting at the foot of the River Flats Opera House stage. But the new dress and even a leisurely lilac water bath that afternoon at the hotel had done little to calm Anna's jitters.

She glanced at her uncle, who was standing near the entrance to the stage. She couldn't remember a time in the eight years she'd been with him that Mick had been flustered by any situation, but this night, he acted as if his nerve endings were prickling on the surface of his skin.

He held back the red velvet drapery that framed the proscenium and looked out at the two hundred seats available for patrons. A low mutter of disappointment, barely discernible to Anna, hissed through his lips. She figured that meant hardly any of the seats were occupied, and it was getting close to showtime.

She touched his elbow and asked, "How many people are out there?"

"Enough, darlin'." He let the drape fall back into place. "Don't you worry. We still have almost a half hour till you go on. It'll fill up."

"I'll never know why I let you talk me into this," she grumbled, although, in truth, she did know. Her uncle Mick could charm a mudfish out of the Mississippi and convince him he was better off on land . . . for the five minutes he lived anyway. She clasped her hands at her waist so tightly her knuckles turned white. "What if I can't sing a note? What if I can't remember the words?"

"Then I guess the Mississippi Songbird's handsome and charming 'father' will have to do the singin' for her, and I'll be the one who gets all the applause. If that doesn't scare you into singin' the right words, I don't know what will."

Mick's teasing came across as only halfhearted. Anna glared at him. "It won't work to make a joke at a time like this, Uncle Mick. Can't you see I'm scared to death?"

"I know ya' are, but don't be," he said, with only a fraction of his usual confidence.

Anna suspected he was worried they wouldn't collect enough in donations to even pay the rent. He paced around the small area offstage and passed his hand over his hair several times, a habit he had when he was thinking seriously. Suddenly his mustache twitched, and his gray eyes flared with the sparks of a germinating plan. He stopped in his tracks and faced Anna. "I've just had the most amazin' idea!"

She saw the look on his face and cringed. Most of Mick's inspirations over the years had exploded with the intensity of a lightning strike instead of taking shape slowly, guided by sound reasoning. Recognizing the familiar fire in his eyes, she sighed, "Oh, no, not again."

"It's a good idea this time, Anna. I know how to win over every single person in that audience tonight and even ensure a full house for tomorrow."

She shuddered. "I know I shouldn't ask, but how?"

"Sympathy," he said. "I don't know why I didn't think of it before. A little pity warms the coldest of hearts, and the best part is, it works wonders to loosen up the pockets."

"And who are these people supposed to feel sorry for?" she asked, afraid of the answer.

"Why you, a' course." He grasped her arms and locked his eyes on hers. "Anna, do you think you could fake a little affliction of some kind—nothin' too serious. I was thinkin' that maybe you could pretend you're blind."

For a long moment she could only stare at him in shocked disbelief. "Blind!" she finally blurted out in a hoarse whisper. "Have you lost your mind? First of all, I can't do it, and second, it's dishonest. I can't cheat good people out of their money."

"Good people! Good people!" Mick echoed, his voice raising an octave. "You mean like the mean-spirited people of Unity, Illinois? Like that crooked lawyer who took practically all of Laura's money? Or do you mean that withered old thief, Miss Brockman, at the orphanage?"

Dumbfounded by Mick's tirade, Anna shook her head. She hadn't liked the headmistress, but she had no reason to think the woman was a thief! "What's Miss Brockman got to do with this? I'll admit that honey didn't exactly drip off her tongue, but she was at least an honest woman doing an honest job."

"Ha! That's what you think! What about that gold necklace you got from your mama and papa when you were nine years old? I was there when you got it, and, as I recall, you said you'd never take it off. Where is it now?"

"One of the other girls in the orphanage took it when I was sleeping. I never found out who."

"Is that so? And who told you that?"

"Miss Brockman told me when I woke up the next morning."

Mick shrugged his shoulders as if to say 'I told you so,' and gave her a smug grin. "You see, darlin', the truth is, people are basically out for themselves, and it's time you started thinkin' of yourself first. What harm can it do if you make these folks feel good tonight by givin' from their hearts to a poor blind girl who sings like an angel?''

Anna set her lips in a firm line and planted her fists on her hips. ''You can try to talk me into this until the show starts if you want, Uncle Mick, but I'm not going to do it. I just won't knowingly cheat people. This isn't Unity, and I don't have anything against any of these people in the theater, if there even *is* anyone here,'' she added, feeling her tentative confidence slip away.

''Land's sake, Anna, you're just like your father, rest his soul—so full of stubbornness that there's no room left for common sense. I tried to tell your papa it would come to no good if he defied ol' Pat Sullivan and set his cap for Kathleen, and just like you're doin' now, he paid me no mind.''

Anna winked playfully at him. ''And it's a good thing he didn't, too. If my parents hadn't followed their hearts, I wouldn't be here now listening to your crazy ideas.''

''But, Anna, my plan makes good sense. We'll get the money so much faster and catch that ship in New Orleans lickety-split.''

''No, forget it! I told you in the hotel today that you should charge admission instead of asking for donations, but you didn't, and now we're just going to have to work harder and longer to get to Boston.''

Mick looked as if he might continue his argument, but the longer he looked at Anna's stern face, the more his shoulders sagged in defeat. ''Okay, you win,'' he gave in reluctantly.

''Good, now go away for a few minutes. I've got to calm down and think about what I have to do out there or the only donations we'll get will be a few rotten eggs.''

Mick started to walk away, but stopped and gave Anna an encouraging little grin. ''You know, darlin', even if you get out on that stage and don't sound any better than an old saw cuttin' through tin, we'll still get to Boston. I'll just figure out another way to go about it.''

''I think that scares me more than facing a crowd of strangers!'' As usual with this man, she let her smile take the sting out of her words.

"You just remember why we're doin' this, Anna, and you'll do fine out there."

She walked over to the single chair available backstage and sat down. Laying her hands in her lap, she took several deep breaths and concentrated on Mick's words. *Just remember why we're doin' this . . .*

How could she forget the reasons why Anna Connolly, normally so sensible, had agreed to paint rouge on her cheeks and fresh whitewash on Mick's old peddler's wagon? Or why they'd taken to the road with the colorful words, The Irresistible Miss Anna Rose, the Mississippi Songbird garishly proclaiming her identity on the side of the wagon?

Anna and Laura Harper, the loving, patient women who waited every fall for Anna and Mick to return to Unity, both recognized one significant truth about Mick Connolly. Once he had worked his way into a lady's heart, there was no way she could ever let him go again, and when he talked, no matter how outlandish his words seemed, she still listened.

"So here I am," Anna mused, feeling a calm settle over her as she looked at the rafters in the ceiling. "Laura, you understand don't you? You know why I'm probably about to become the 'gullible Anna Rose,' with her make-believe father contributing to her foolishness." Anna realized that she should no doubt question her sanity at this moment, but never the reasons why she was here.

It had been a gray, mist-shrouded day the previous fall when Mick and Anna came home to Unity, as they had for all the years Anna had been traveling with her uncle. She was looking forward to spending the winter in Laura's cozy little house. The last thing she expected to see was a new grave on the back hillside.

Seeing Laura's name on the simple ground marker, and facing a profound sadness once again, Anna realized that her life had taken another unalterable turn. Laura had been their anchor, and her death left Anna and Mick adrift on a sea of pain and loss.

That winter in cheerless Unity was the longest, dreariest season Anna had ever known, but as she sat in the wings of the River Flats Opera House facing an uncertain future, she had to smile when she recalled that cold night, two months before, when Mick told her about his plan to put her on the stage.

She had found an assortment of notions and fabrics in Laura's attic and was stitching whalebone buttons to the placket of a shirt she'd made for Mick. She was singing an Irish lullaby she remembered from her childhood in St. Louis when Mick suddenly bolted up from his rocker by the fireplace and looked at her with an old familiar sparkle back in his eyes. "You sing like an opera star, you know that, Anna?"

She questioned him about his unexpected interest in lullabies when the only tunes he ever sang were dance hall ditties. It was then that he spoke of his plan. He admitted he'd been writing to her grandmother in Boston, because with Laura gone, he wanted Anna to assume her rightful place in society.

He went to a shelf and retrieved a wooden box that held all their savings and removed a small stack of letters. "I never told you about this, Anna, because your mind was always so dead set against hearin' anything about your ma's folks, but Ophelia Sullivan has written me back." He tapped the envelope which was on top of the stack. "This last one I got this past week."

Anna had been furious, and perhaps she still was a little. Some hurts were nearly impossible to forget.

"Your grandfather died this past year, Anna," Mick explained, "and your grandmother wants to make peace with you. I think that's a good idea. It's time you had a permanent home and a chance to meet a nice young man who'll take care of you. And Ophelia with her fancy Beacon Hill address can give you respectability, so people will stop lookin' down on you. All that's important to a young lady."

Anna had tried to argue with him, but it was obvious his mind was already made up. "Ophelia can give you a future, darlin'," he said. "A grand one befittin' her station in life, a station that you've rightly inherited. You can have it all, and I want to see that you get it.''

In the end, Mick persuaded Anna to read her grandmother's letters, and she discovered compassion and sincerity in Ophelia's words. When she pointed out that they didn't have nearly enough money to get to Boston, Mick was prepared for her objections.

''Our peddlin' days are over for this summer, Anna. We're goin' into show business. That's where the money is on the Mississippi. His hand swept in front of his eyes, painting an imaginary sign. ''The Irresistible Anna Rose, Songbird of the Mississippi. I'll paint it on the wagon for everybody to see. And I'll say I'm your father . . . a proper chaperon.''

It had been the glow in his eyes that had finally persuaded her. She felt the same confidence begin to shine in her eyes that was in his. Maybe it was because they'd lost Laura; maybe it was the bleak, cold winter in Unity; maybe it was the first spark of life she'd seen in her uncle since Laura died; probably it was all of these things. But finally, Anna began to believe in Mick's dream.

She pictured her mother, the beautiful and serene Kathleen Connolly, and she wanted to believe that just maybe this other woman, this Ophelia Sullivan, could help fill the void that a tragic fire and the death of Laura Harper had left in Anna's heart.

On April 1, 1880, just two weeks after Anna's twentieth birthday, Mick loaded the freshly painted wagon with their possessions, including the wooden box which contained the several hundred dollars they had received from the sale of Laura's house. They left Unity at dawn and headed west toward River Flats, for the first time without the bittersweet parting from someone they loved. The last sight Anna remembered of Unity and the life she was leaving behind was the soft new grass carpeting Laura's grave. Sprouts of spring flowers were already peeking through the loose rich soil surrounding a brand-new tombstone.

* * *

As hard as it was for Anna to believe, just two weeks had passed since then, and in moments she would walk out on the River Flats Opera House stage and sing her heart out to an audience of strangers. But, oddly, it all made a sort of cockeyed sense. Going to Boston seemed like the right thing to do, and Mick's extraordinary plan seemed like the quickest way to get there. She settled comfortably back in her chair, believing for the first time that she could do this.

Mick settled his formal top hat over his neatly combed gray hair and tapped it into place. He motioned across the stage to the piano player who had just arrived, and the man walked onto the platform and sat down on the piano bench. "Here we go, darlin'," Mick said. "How do I look?"

"You've never looked better," Anna answered with a teasing grin, "and I know that because I'm not blind!"

"Very funny." He ran his fingers around the brim of his hat. "But you're right. I do look dapper for a scruffy ol' Irish wharf rat."

Anna agreed. Normally not the least concerned about his appearance, Mick was impeccably groomed in his black frock coat and dress trousers. When he stepped on stage, he spoke his first words in a strong, controlled voice very much like a circus ringmaster's. "Ladies and gentlemen, you are indeed in for a rare treat tonight as I welcome you to the premier performance of Miss Anna Rose, the Mississippi Songbird!"

Mick's enthusiasm did not have the effect he intended. There was no applause. Instead, the audience hushed to an almost morbid silence, and backstage, Anna fidgeted once more with the ruffles of her dress. She listened as her uncle continued in a clear voice.

"For those of you who have not heard of Miss Rose, I guarantee you will enjoy her rare gift. Direct from the finest music conservatories in New York and the East Coast, Miss Rose and I, her adoring father, have selected this very opera house to begin the Songbird's tour of the Mississippi valley as she returns to her roots in America's heartland, in this great state of Illinois!'' Mick paused for effect and raised his hands in the air in an exaggerated imitation of P.T. Barnum, but instead of hearing the anticipated cheers, Anna heard only restless mumbling coming from the audience.

He cleared his throat and proceeded anxiously. "As you all know, tonight's performance is completely free of charge. If, at the end of the show, however, you would like to express your appreciation of Miss Rose's talent, we will be happy to accept donations.''

Offstage, Anna cringed at the disgruntled murmurs and rude catcalls that came from some of the patrons. She heard Mick's voice falter as he added, "This is, of course, entirely up to you."

He glanced to his side, too quickly for Anna to mask the trepidation she knew was written all over her face. *Oh, Uncle Mick, we're never going to be able to win them over,* she thought, but when he looked back again, she was ready. She gave him an encouraging little wave that urged him to go on.

Swallowing hard and wiping his palms on his trousers, Mick croaked out a plea that caused Anna's heart to pound with alarm. "Forgive me, darlin', for what I'm about to do.'' Then he faced the audience once more.

"Folks, before I bring Miss Anna Rose on stage, there is something I think you ought to know. My lovely daughter doesn't like for me to talk about this, and I figure I'm goin' to get huffed at plenty for talkin' out of turn, but I sense a warmth and a carin' in this audience the likes of which I've never seen before.''

An attentive pause settled over the crowd as the patrons silenced each other and looked at Mick. In the wings, Anna stopped smoothing the imagined wrinkles in her skirt and listened to his next words with panic rising like a lump in her throat.

A look of intense sadness came over Mick's face, and he walked to the very edge of the stage to be closer to the audience. In a voice dripping with melancholy, he said, "Several years ago, Miss Anna Rose was in a terrible accident that left her totally blind.''

Exclamations of both surprise and sympathy came from the patrons, and Anna froze in horror.

"Yes, ladies and gentlemen,'' he continued without looking at her, "it was an untimely and tragic consequence for the sweet, young songstress you are about to meet, so please let your warmth surround her on the night of her premier introduction to the stage and welcome her with your generous applause, since my poor courageous Anna will not be able to see that carin' in your kind faces.''

At last Mick glanced at Anna, and a sheepish little grin played at his mouth. He shrugged with boyish innocence as she mouthed the words, "What are you doing?''

"So, without further ado,'' he said, ignoring her anger and sweeping his arm toward the wings in a grand gesture, "I present the Mississippi Songbird, Miss Anna Rose!''

He walked over to where she stood, refusing to move, as the applause beckoned her. "Why did you do that?'' she hissed.

"I was losin' 'em, Anna. Hell, I never had 'em in the first place! You can do this. You have to. If you don't playact like you can see about as much as you could in a west Texas duststorm, then we're gonna get tar and feathers all over our fancy duds.''

Mick took her arm and pulled her on stage as the polite applause merged with expressions of sympathy and admiration. "They're goin' to love you, Anna,'' Mick whispered as he pretended to place her exactly in the middle of the stage. "You look like a goddess of spring on this stage, and these folks are sittin' in the palm of your hand right where we want 'em.''

He stepped to the side and left Anna standing in front of a backdrop of stately elm trees and diapered cupids. "Goddess of spring,'' she muttered angrily, remembering the silly, painted cherubs behind her. She imagined them fluttering ridiculously around the upper limbs of the trees, caught forever in the whimsy of an artist's brush just like she was caught in her uncle's ruse.

To control the panic building inside her, Anna focused her

gaze on the footlights dancing over the emerald sheen of her dress and the blond tresses which curled above the scooped neckline. Drawing a deep breath, she finally raised her face and leveled a controlled stare over the heads of the audience.

Though her heart hammered in dread, the response she heard from the patrons was astounding. It seemed as though everyone in the River Flats Opera House reacted with the same sympathetic awe to the vision of those beautifully clear, yet tragically sightless blue eyes.

Mick nodded to the piano player. "Maestro," he said, and the introductory notes of "I'll Take You Home Again, Kathleen" drifted across the stage. This was Anna's favorite song since Kathleen had been her mother's name. She knew it so well she could have sung it in her sleep, and when her first notes rang out true and clear, she experienced an overwhelming sense of relief. Maybe she could keep them out of jail.

Amazingly she was able to concentrate on her singing while still keeping up the pretense of blindness. Believing she could actually pull off Mick's outlandish scheme at least this night, she answered the audience's applause with a deep curtsy at the end of her third song.

It was when she was rising from her bow that a slip-up occurred which might have cost them the game. Her eyes locked with the intense gaze of a man looking up at her from the front row. She stared at him for just an instant too long as she became lost in the soft backwash from the footlights reflected in the spellbinding charcoal of his eyes. While she remained so entranced, an amused smile touched the man's lips and he winked at her.

She blinked hard in surprise before she resumed her rigid posture and remembered to stare over the audience. She recognized the introductory strains of her next song and cleared her throat, which she found much easier than clearing her mind.

At the end of an hour, Anna closed her performance with a hymn while Mick walked among the theater seats with his top hat turned upside down in his hand. She could hear the jingle of coin hitting coin as he gathered the donations.

When she finished her song, Mick came to escort her offstage, but just before she disappeared behind the curtain, she stole one more quick look at the possessor of those remarkable smoky eyes. He placed a black Stetson on his thick, dark hair as his long, lean body seemed to unfold from his chair. That was the last Anna saw, because Mick wisely pulled her into the wings.

Later, in the wagon, Mick dumped all the coins onto the floor and spread them out. He immediately reached for a large coin imprinted with a double eagle. "Will you look at this, Anna. A twenty-dollar gold piece! I wonder who gave you this?"

She shrugged her shoulders as she momentarily forgot her anger at Mick and remembered a bold wink and a knowing grin. "I don't know, Uncle Mick," she lied, "but it was awfully generous."

"It was more than that. Whoever it was just paid our entire rent and bought us dinner tonight!"

An hour later, Mick and Anna waited at the entrance to the River Flats Hotel restaurant. Before the hostess came to seat them, Mick whispered in Anna's ear, "Remember now, darlin', you're blind."

"Don't remind me," she snapped. "Are you sure you don't have a pair of crutches hidden under your coat you'd like me to use?"

"Don't be mad, Anna. You've got to admit the plan worked just like I told you it would."

"Yes, and I told *you* that I wouldn't do it, remember that?"

"It doesn't really matter now, does it? I've got thirty-three dollars in my pocket to prove it." He poked her gently in her ribs. "Aren't you just a little bit tempted to admit I was right?"

"Any time I admit you're right, I'm admitting that the rest of the world is wrong," she shot back in an angry whisper, "and I don't happen to believe that's a fact!"

"Just give me time, darlin'," Mick snickered.

He motioned for the dining-room hostess to escort them through a maze of crowded tables and purposefully drew atten-

tion to Anna's 'disability.' She listened to the pitying comments
from patrons who had obviously been at the theater.

"The poor little thing . . ."

". . . sings like an angel, too."

"What a tragedy at such a young age . . ."

Mick pinched her elbow. "Do you hear that, Anna? Tomorrow night we'll have a packed house for sure." He jingled the
coins in his pocket. She struggled to keep her pasted-on smile
from fading.

Anna shrugged off her cape and Mick draped it over the
back of her chair. With calculated awkwardness, she felt for
her napkin at the side of her plate and placed it in her lap,
which allowed her to keep her gaze away from the people
around her. Only when the waitress came to take their order
did she look up from her lap expecting to level a blank stare
over the heads of the diners. Instead, her gaze was drawn to
the center of the crowded room where a pair of teasing gray
eyes captured hers.

She was aware that Mick was talking to her but she didn't
hear what he was saying. Transfixed in her seat, she didn't
blink, and until she began to feel strangely light-headed, she
didn't even breathe. And she most definitely didn't look away
from those intense eyes staring back at her.

"What do you want to eat, Anna?" Mick asked impatiently,
at last causing her to break free from the force which held her
from across the room. "This young lady is waitin' for your
order."

"I . . . I don't know. I haven't thought. Order for me, Uncle
Mick." He rattled off his choices from the menu, and the
waitress walked away.

"What's the matter with you, Anna?" Mick asked. "Are
you feelin' ill?"

She had been concentrating on her hands twisting her napkin
into a thin spiral, but at Mick's question she looked up again,
hoping that the man would be gone, and at the same time
stifling a desire that he wouldn't be.

He was still watching her, only now his full lips curved in
a taunting grin that brought faint lines to his temples, framing

a teasing gaze. He leaned back in his chair, raised his hand to his brow and boldly greeted her with a two-fingered salute that made her sit up sharply and gasp. Her skin flushed hot from her neck to her cheeks.

A worried frown pulled at Mick's mouth. "Anna, what's wrong with you?" he asked. "Let me get you outta here. You look like you've caught a fever."

She gripped his arm. "No! Don't get up. I'm all right. It's just that man over there. He was at the theater." Mick scanned the crowd for the object of Anna's distress. "He knows I'm not blind!"

"Well, land's sake, Anna, so will everyone in this restaurant if you don't watch what you're doin'! You're as red as a beet and about to give us away." He waited for her to calm down and her color to return to normal before he said, "Who is this fella anyway? Where's he sittin'?"

Anna's gaze darted to the center of the room once more, and she squeezed Mick's arm until he winced. The man had stood up and was coming around the tables toward them! "That's him," she croaked out. She stared at the silverware on the table in front of her and sensed, rather than watched, his approach. He stopped at the corner of their table, standing between her and Mick. She did not turn her head, but out of the corner of her eye she saw his finely tailored black pants which fit snugly to his thigh. She judged him to be tall, over six feet.

"Excuse me," he said, the deep, mellow baritone of his voice sending unfamiliar shivers down her spine. "I was at the young lady's performance tonight, and I just wanted to compliment her on her lovely singing voice."

She felt his eyes upon her and noticed the easy grace of his movement as he turned toward Mick.

"I would say that your lovely daughter was born to the stage, Mr. . . . Rose, is it?"

"Er . . . yes, Michael Rose, and this, of course, is my daughter, Anna."

The man took Anna's hand from where it rested on the table and held it in his own warm palm. "Philip Brichard, Miss

Rose. I'm delighted to meet you. Your talents as an 'actress' and singer are quite remarkable.''

She didn't know if the heated blush on her face came from her acute embarrassment or from the warmth generated from the man's hand covering hers.

Mick was quick to correct Philip's statement about Anna's talents. "Oh, my daughter is not an actress, Mr. Brichard; she's a singer only."

He released Anna's hand, but she knew instinctively that his gaze was still on her bent head. "I guess after watching her tonight, I just assumed her capabilities were equally great in both areas, despite her unfortunate handicap."

Anna trembled under his knowing scrutiny. Drat this man! He was doing everything he could to make her squirm and enjoying every minute of it.

"You're aware of course, sir," Mr. Brichard continued, "that modern medicine has come a long way in treating diseases and traumas to the eyes. You *have* taken your daughter to a specialist about her problem haven't you?"

Right at that moment, Mr. Brichard was Anna's problem! What kind of game was he playing? A cold fear shot through her. Could he possibly be working for the River Flats sheriff?

"Of course, Mr. Brichard," she heard Mick say through the rapid heartbeat drumming in her ears. "In fact, that's exactly why I'm taking donations during Anna's performance. She's going to have an operation in New Orleans as soon as we get the money together. We hope that her vision can be brought back."

An operation! Anna wished a trapdoor would open up in the floor and swallow her whole. Mick was only making a horrible situation worse!

"In New Orleans! How fortunate," Philip Brichard said as if the information truly delighted him. "New Orleans is my home." He leaned down very close to Anna's ear and asked, "What's your doctor's name, Miss Rose? Perhaps I know him."

Anna could feel his breath on her neck and smell the tangy pine scent of his cologne. She shifted to the very edge of her chair. "I'm blind, Mr. Brichard, not deaf! And I'm quite sure you don't know my doctor. He . . . he's only recently moved to New Orleans." *Now, please just go away!* she pleaded silently.

His voice edged with amusement, Philip said, "I see, well, your doctor must be competent or you wouldn't have chosen him. You're obviously a very clever young woman, as well as an extremely lovely one. In any case, remember my name. I live at Frenchman's Point in St. Gerard's Parish, just north of the city. Please call on me if you need anything."

Though she couldn't look at him, Anna could well imagine the taunting expression on Philip Brichard's face. How much longer must she endure this man's brash behavior? "We won't need anything, Mr. Brichard," she shot back angrily.

"What brings you to Illinois?" Mick blurted, covering Anna's curt response.

"I'm here on business, Mr. Rose. I'm leaving tomorrow morning for Chicago."

"What business are you in?" Mick asked, dragging the encounter tortuously.

"I'm a merchant, a trader in foreign goods."

"Is that so? I used to be a pretty fair trader myself," Mick said cheerfully. "Who knows? Maybe someday we'll have dealin's."

"Someday we just might," Philip said, turning back to Anna. "I've taken up enough of your time. Enjoy your dinner, Miss Rose, and good luck to you."

Anna raised her head slightly but resisted the unexpected temptation to take a long look at Philip's face so she could commit it to memory. *This is a man you'd best forget,* she told herself. Suddenly she lunged forward in her chair. She had just been given a firm jab to her leg from the toe of Mick's boot.

"Tell the man 'thank you,' Anna," Mick prompted as if she were a child who forgot her manners.

She thought she heard a low chuckle come from Philip Brichard's mouth, but she forced her lips into something resembling a smile. "Of course, Father," she said. "Thank you for your kindness, Mr. Brichard."

"You're welcome, Miss Rose," he said with exaggerated politeness. "I'll say good evening then."

After Philip left, Mick tapped his fork thoughtfully on the table, "Unless I miss my guess, that was our twenty-dollar gold piece, Anna. He prob'ly hails from some high-falutin' blue bloods in New Orleans. I'm sorry he won't be at tomorrow night's performance."

What was wrong with her uncle? Was he being purposefully addle-brained? "Well, I'm not!" she declared.

"What's eatin' you? You're wrong about him bein' on to us. He was a perfect gentleman."

"Then you're the one who's blind, Uncle Mick. Mr. Brichard was just playing with us!"

"Maybe so," Mick conceded, removing the double eagle coin from his pocket and turning it slowly in front of his eyes. "But I'll say this for him. He plays, but he pays!"

The waitress brought Anna's food, but she was too nervous to eat a bite. Was it because she feared she might see this man again while she played out her little confidence game to New Orleans, or because she feared she wouldn't?

CHAPTER TWO

Cape de Rive, the southernmost river town in Illinois, was actually a small city situated partially on a spit of land that jutted out into the Mississippi and formed a natural dock for numerous riverboats and barges. It was the largest, most active town Mick and Anna had visited in the two weeks since leaving River Flats, and once they passed through the outlying residential areas, Anna regarded the bustling business district with almost childlike excitement.

Because her face was practically hidden by the large brim of her bonnet, she felt she could safely look at the buildings along the main street through town without revealing to anyone who might notice the wagon that she was not blind. They passed through a section of fashionable shops and nice hotels and restaurants on their way to the livery stable which they were told was located in a less desirable part of Cape de Rive.

As they neared the levee, which separated and protected the town from the river, the more substantial brick buildings gave way to clapboard cafes, saloons, and gambling houses, but Anna was no less interested in the sights around her. In fact, she found this seedier side of town more fascinating than its respectable counterpart. "Look at the colored lanterns in that window,'' she said to Mick, indicating one brightly decorated building. ''In the middle of the day no less.''

Mick hid a grin behind his hand. ''Looks like you've just seen your first bordello, darlin'.''

Anna's gaze drifted to the second-floor balcony where three ladies leaned over the wood railing watching the passing scene. They were dressed in loose robes that fell open to reveal scanty camisoles and ruffled bloomers.

''Quit gawkin' now,'' Mick warned. ''Some busybody will see you, and our game will be up before we've even got a lease to perform!''

''Are we going to set up here?'' Honkytonk pianos and boisterous shouts from saloons didn't seem like the right atmosphere for the Mississippi Songbird.

''Not hardly!'' Mick assured her. ''I asked that fella back uptown where we could put on a respectable show, and he said the Methodist church rents out the main meeting room. I figure we'll get Irish boarded and walk back up there to settle things.''

Steering the wagon through the bustling downtown traffic, Mick watched the activity around him with a wistful longing in his eyes. ''I must admit, though, I wouldn't mind settin' down in one of those gamblin' halls for a spell. I'll bet they get some poker pots in these houses that would make those in the little backwater saloons I'm used to look like pocket change!''

They turned onto a side street and pulled into the livery. Anna knew Mick would be a while discussing the details of Irish's board, so, leaving her bonnet firmly in place, she walked to the corner where she could casually watch what was happening on the main thoroughfare.

Drawn by the sights and sounds around her, she stepped off the wooden sidewalk and into the street. She was craning her neck toward the noisiest of the gambling parlors when she heard the rumbling of horses' hooves behind her. She whirled around to see a speeding brougham pulled by two sleek black horses racing down the street. The driver of the conveyance cracked a whip over the horses' backs and shouted, ''Give way!''

In a whirling cloud of dust, the coach careened wildly toward Anna. She stood rooted in terror, unable to command her feet to run, as precious seconds ticked by. Crippling fear kept her from escaping, though she knew the driver could not possibly stop in time to avoid running her over. She raised her arms to cover her face.

The horses thundered closer, but Anna never felt the impact. She was suddenly dragged away from danger in a pair of strong arms. Then, locked in someone's tight grasp, she fell, rolling over in the street, with her body held firmly against her protector's.

When the coach passed by, Anna coughed and sputtered to clear the dust from her mouth. She ached in places she didn't know she had. Her bonnet had come off and its ribbon was choking her. She spit tangled hair out of her mouth and shook her head to clear her mind of the dizzying effects of her fall. She needed to make sense of the miraculous event which might very probably have saved her life.

When full awareness of what had happened returned to her, Anna realized that she was lying at the base of the sidewalk underneath the hard body of a man who had apparently accomplished the brave deed. She looked into the face of her savior, who was leaning on his elbows above her and smiling down into her eyes with unmasked amusement.

"So we meet again, Miss Rose," Philip Brichard said as casually as if they'd just sat down next to each other on a park bench. "You really didn't need to go to such lengths to prove to me that you are truly blind. I believe you, for only someone who is blind or a damn fool would wander out into a busy thoroughfare in the middle of the day!"

Anna shoved at his chest and he stood up, offering his hand to help her rise. She refused, struggling clumsily to her feet and attempting to brush the dust from her dress. "So I'm a fool, am I?" she said, slapping at the enormous bonnet which was blowing about her face and neck in the breeze. Still shaken from her near brush with death, and humiliated to have this man, of all men, see her in this condition, she muttered, "I suppose I should thank you."

He shrugged his shoulders. "Well, the thought had crossed my mind."

"What are you doing here anyway?" she demanded, a sinking sensation crashing to the pit of her stomach. Had he followed her deliberately, just waiting for an opportunity to expose her and Uncle Mick? She stole a look at his rugged, tanned features. The smoky eyes that she'd been unable to forget were unreadable. "Are you following me?"

"I assure you, I'm not," he said, "although I'm quite certain it would be a most interesting pastime! I just arrived at Cape de Rive this morning by boat."

"So it's just coincidence that your boat arrives at Cape de Rive on the exact same day that I get here?" *That sounds unlikely to me.* "I'll tell you what I think—I think you're a detective and you're checking up on us. I figure you're planning to arrest us and . . ."

She never finished her sentence. Philip grabbed her arm and pulled her toward the levee a few hundred feet away. She struggled against his grip, but he pulled her up the steps as if she were weightless and stood with her on top of the earthen barrier. "Look around you, Miss Rose," he ordered. "What do you see?"

The dock was crowded with all manner of river crafts from the most elegant steamboats to freighters, barges, and rafts. Philip turned Anna around to face him after she had taken a good look at the bustling scene below them. "No less than six passenger steamers came into this harbor today alone, Miss Rose. That number and more arrive every day, and it's my belief that not one of them is following you!"

"All right," she snapped back at him. "You win. I'm sorry, I apologize, thank you for saving my life!" Her face flushed with mortification, she jerked out of his grasp and started down the steps, leaving him alone on the levee.

Watching Anna hike up her dusty skirt and head toward the street, Philip shook his head in bewilderment. "She's not your concern," he warned himself, though he still followed her progress with his eyes. He saw her father approach the levee, his arms flailing about in frustration. Probably, Philip thought, because his little 'songbird' was strutting down the main street with obviously perfect vision! A moment later, Philip assumed Anna was relating the details of the incident with the carriage, for she pointed to the corner and then to the brougham which had stopped in front of a gambling parlor.

He recognized the carriage from his previous trips to Cape de Rive and was tempted to warn Miss Rose and her father about its disreputable owner. But he realized that the ungrateful lady probably wouldn't appreciate his interference any more than she had his life-saving attempts. "Forget about her," Philip muttered. "Inside that beautiful vixen beats the heart of a swindler who obviously thinks she can take care of herself!" He crossed over the levee toward the river and the *Duchess of Orleans,* the largest and brightest of the steamboats tied at the dock.

As soon as Mick Connolly heard the harrowing tale of his niece's near demise, he marched off toward the sleek, polished brougham to find its owner. Anna followed behind him, tugging at his elbow in an effort to keep up with his determined stride. "Stop, Uncle Mick!" she cried. "What will you accomplish by storming off like a vigilante after this man? Besides, I'm all right, you can see that!"

None of her arguments worked, and as Mick approached the carriage, he issued a warning to Anna. "Stand away now and let me handle this." She backed up a couple of steps and stood on the sidewalk while Mick went up to a man who was leaning against the carriage door. "Who owns this vehicle?"

"Who wants to know?" the man answered with a smirk.

"Mick Connolly, that's who! And I want to see the face of a man who'd run a lady down in the middle of a street without so much as a backward glance."

"Then you must be lookin' at it now," the man said, pushing his bulky frame away from the carriage and squaring off with Mick, " 'cause I'm Jake Finn, Mr. Stuart Wilkes's driver."

Mick glared at the man without flinching. "It's a cowardly face you have, too, and as ugly a puss as I've ever seen. What kind of a mean snake would do what you just did to this poor girl?''

Mick inclined his head toward Anna, and she braced herself for what she feared would happen next. *Oh, Uncle Mick, you never know when to keep your mouth shut!*

The man raised bushy eyebrows at Mick, and a belittling little snicker sputtered through his thick lips. Then his fist shot out and slammed into Mick's chin. ''The same one who'd do that! Now get outta here while you can still walk away!''

Mick fell back against the wall of the gambling house, and Anna rushed to his side. He brushed her away and charged at the carriage driver with his head aimed at the man's midsection. Just before he made contact, two pairs of beefy arms grabbed hold of him and held fast, causing his feet to slip out from under him. One of his captors looked over his shoulder and said, ''We got 'im, boss.''

A tall man clad in a black waistcoat and high-necked black shirt lounged in the doorway to the gambling house and watched the confrontation as if it were a play staged for his personal entertainment. ''What's the problem here?'' he asked Jake Finn.

''There's no problem, boss. Leastways nothin' we can't handle.''

The man pointed at Mick. ''Bring him over here to me,'' he instructed. Mick was lifted up and set down before the man's narrow, hawklike eyes. ''Do you have a complaint against my driver, sir?''

Words came tumbling out of Mick's mouth in spite of the two burly men holding him. ''You bet I do. You and your driver just came barrelin' around that corner nearly runnin' my niece over, and I aim to see that at least she gets a proper apology. There isn't any man who's too big or too powerful to show respect for a lady!''

Mick looked at Anna, and the man's hawk eyes followed. ''Please,'' she said, ''there's no need for an apology. I'm fine, really. Just let him go and we'll leave. We don't want any trouble.''

As narrow eyes roamed over her, Anna clutched the yoke of her blouse, holding the material tightly over her chest. She didn't like the situation they were in one bit and waited breathlessly for the men to release Mick.

The tall man licked his lips, and with a blatant stare fixed on Anna, he ordered, "Let him go."

She expelled a long, slow sigh of gratitude and muttered, "Thank you." She reached for Mick's arm to pull him away, but long, thin fingers wrapped around her wrist like an iron bracelet. She looked up into slits of eyes that bore down at her from under the brim of the man's wide hat.

"Your uncle is right, miss," he drawled in a low, deep voice edged with such malevolent tones that Anna shivered. "What happened to you is unforgivable, and I apologize for my driver."

Anna's instincts told her that this man rarely apologized for anything, and when he did, he didn't mean it. "It's all right. Just please let us go," she said, avoiding his eyes and twisting her hand to free it from his grip.

Instead of releasing her, he pulled her to him and seized her hand in both of his. Using a guise of utter politeness he said, "Allow me to introduce myself. I am Stuart Wilkes, owner of this establishment and others on the street as well. I would like to make up for the unfortunate circumstances which brought us together today by inviting you to have dinner with me tonight, here at the Lucky Chance. You will join me, won't you?"

A ribbon of fear crept up Anna's spine as Wilkes's lusting gaze swept over her. The rigid set of his thin lips only increased her dislike of him and her apprehension about his intentions.

Mick wedged his body between Anna and Wilkes, forcing Wilkes to drop her hand. She prayed that her uncle wouldn't antagonize this dangerous man any more.

Thankfully, Mick said in a calm voice, "She can't go to dinner with anybody, Mr. Wilkes, because . . . because we're leavin' town this afternoon. Isn't that right, Anna?"

She nodded her head vigorously. "Yes, that's right."

"I'm sorry to hear that," Wilkes said. "I just wanted to make up for what happened to you."

Anna wanted to hold on to Mick and get away as fast as she

could, but Wilkes prevented her from doing that with a totally
unexpected proposal. "Do you play cards, sir?" he asked Mick.

Mick shrugged his shoulders noncommittally, though his
eyes peered longingly over the swinging doors and into the
interior of the Lucky Chance. The corner of Wilkes's lip curled
into a triumphant sneer. "I see that you do. Let's find a friendly
game where we can enjoy a few hands then. Perhaps if you
leave town today with some of my money, you'll think more
fondly of Cape de Rive."

Mick looked at Anna, but the scowl of warning she gave
him obviously didn't lessen his desire to accept Wilkes's offer.
"Excuse me," he said, taking her arm and walking out of
Wilkes's hearing. "Anna, this could be our big chance!" he
argued. "I could get enough in one afternoon to get us to New
Orleans and set us up for Boston in fine style!"

"Or lose everything we have!" she reminded him. "I don't
like it, and I don't like him. He could be a cheat."

"Anna, we're not goin' to play head to head. He said we'd
join a game. It's broad daylight, and this is a big-town gamblin'
hall. Nothin's goin' to happen. Besides, this is the first time
I've ever had any kind of a stake to play with."

"You're talking about *my* stake, too, you know!"

"I haven't forgotten that. Just give me half of what we've
earned . . . sixty dollars, and I promise I'll bring back ten times
that amount."

"And if you lose it all?"

"I'm not gonna lose it all," Mick said, glowering at her.
"Land sakes, Anna, I never knew anyone to always look on
the dark side like you do!"

Anna studied his face for a moment. He really wanted to do
this. Maybe it was just his ego striving to get the best of the
haughty Mr. Wilkes. Maybe it was his eagerness to play a game
of cards for gentlemen's stakes for a change. Whatever it was,
Anna couldn't argue with him any longer. She ducked into an
alleyway and lifted the hem of her dress above her pantalettes
to take out sixty dollars. She put the wad of bills into Mick's
palm and closed his fingers over it. "I'll wait for you down at
the livery," she said, "but win or lose, don't be too long. These

people and this town give me the willies, and the sooner we leave the better!''

Mick had underestimated his luck when he promised Anna that he would turn their sixty dollars into six hundred. Three hours after he sat down at a poker table with Stuart Wilkes and three other citizens of Cape de Rive, he counted his winnings with unbridled mirth. Even though he knew Anna was waiting for him, the desire to stay for just one more hand kept him in his seat.

''The game is five-card stud,'' Wilkes announced as he dealt the first card down. The betting progressed rapidly as the next two cards were placed face up to each player. Wilkes had a pair of queens showing, Mick had two low spades, and the other players had cards of lesser consequence.

''Fifty dollars on the queens,'' Wilkes announced boldly as he slid two double eagles and ten silver dollars into the growing pot.

All of the other players except Mick turned their cards over in admitted defeat. Mick looked once more at his hole card to reassure himself that it was, indeed, a spade. The possibility of a flush existed, though the odds were long. But Mick let his previous streak of good luck dictate his actions. ''I'll see you and raise you fifty,'' he declared optimistically. ''I have a feelin' I'm goin' to catch this flush.''

''Well, I'm betting you won't,'' Wilkes replied. His eyes scrutinized Mick's face for telltale signs of a bluff. He called the bet and dealt the fourth up card—another spade to match the two showing for Mick, and a queen to match his own pair. A self-satisfied sneer tugged brazenly at Wilkes's lips as if he thought a win was definitely going to be easy. ''You won't beat three of a kind, my friend,'' he proclaimed, sliding two hundred dollars into the center of the table.

''Now, it's still too early to tell, isn't it, Mr. Wilkes?'' Mick responded. He slid the appropriate coins to the pot, matching the bet and boldly raising another two hundred.

The normally raucous sounds of the gambling parlor had

hushed to indistinct murmurs and gasps of surprise as the patrons gathered around the table to watch. With swaggering confidence, Wilkes taunted his opponent, "A fool and his money are soon parted, Mr. Mick." Wilkes called the two-hundred-dollar raise without so much as a blink of his hooded eyes.

The last up card Wilkes dealt to Mick was another spade while an ace joined the three queens. An anxious silence fell over the crowd as every man looked at Stuart Wilkes to see his reaction to the potentially dangerous card which had fallen to his adversary. With cool certainty, Wilkes removed his wallet from his vest pocket, counted out five hundred dollars and placed the money on top of the pot. "My three ladies say you don't have the fifth spade in the hole."

"Sorry, Stuart, but your ladies are wrong," Mick said, a wry grin finally altering his perpetually calm countenance. "But since I've never been one to beat a man when he's down, I'll just call you instead of raisin' that bet." He slowly rolled over his fifth spade. "Now, if you don't mind, I'll just take my pot."

Wilkes's hollow cheeks flushed red as he grabbed Mick's hand. "How do you know I don't have a full house?" he challenged.

"Because I've studied too many faces across a poker table not to know when a man's hole card will make him a winner . . . and Mr. Wilkes, yours won't."

Wilkes picked up his cards and slammed them down on the table without revealing his fifth card. Mick stood up, pushed his chair under the table, and replaced his bollinger on his head. As he gathered his winnings, he realized that his meager stakes had multiplied to over three thousand dollars, and most of it had come out of Wilkes's pocket. "Thank you, gentlemen," he said. "It has most definitely been a pleasure doin' business with you."

"Sit down!" Wilkes thundered. His mouth curled into an angry grimace. When nearly everyone in the room looked at him, he managed a twisted half-smile. "You have to give us a chance to win some of it back."

"Sorry, mates," Mick said with a satisfied grin. "Not today and not in this town. I've given you all the time you're goin' to get." He folded his stack of bills in half and put it in his jacket pocket. "It seems like this was just Ol' Mick's lucky day, and from the looks of all your finery and gold watches and money clips, I'd say you gentlemen will recover quick enough from the loss. I'll be leavin' Cape de Rive now, but I guarantee I'll remember my visit!" He touched his fingers to his hat brim and sauntered off, chuckling delightedly.

"Obsequious toad," Wilkes muttered. "That's not the way I wanted this game to end."

"For heaven's sake, Stuart," one of the other players said, "you can't expect to win every time."

"I don't care about every time. I wanted to win *this* time!" Wilkes turned to face one of his men who had just come around the table. He cupped his hand around his mouth and demanded in a low voice, "What was wrong with you? I told you to watch his cards and signal me."

The man bent down to Wilkes's ear. "He played too close to the chest, boss. There wasn't anything I could do."

Wilkes stood and forced a smile as he regarded the other men at the table. "Count me out, gentlemen. I've lost my appetite for the game today." He strode out the door of the Lucky Chance with his three men following closely behind, then signaled to Jake Finn. "Jake, you and Sam watch which road that bothersome moth and his pretty butterfly take out of town. I'll get my horse and meet you. 'Ol' Mick,' as he calls himself, is about to discover that he's only borrowed my money, and it's time to give it back, with interest!"

Anna threw her arms around Mick and squealed into his ear, "You won! You actually won! And all this money. It's all we'd ever need for the rest of our lives."

"You're breakin' my eardrum, Anna," Mick admonished with a grin as he disentangled her arms from his neck. "And it's not hardly that much, but it'll do to get us to Boston and set Ophelia Sullivan to rights." He tapped the pocket where his winnings were secreted. "You won't have to play like you're blind anymore, darlin'. As a matter of fact, you can lay back in a stateroom and stare at that pretty money all the way from St. Louis to New Orleans."

Riding the little peddler's wagon out of town, Mick and Anna made their plans. They would book passage on a steamboat in St. Louis after they had bought all new clothes. Anna didn't even try to hide her excitement. "With bustles on the backs of the dresses and hats with great white feathers. And satchels and handbags and large brass-trimmed trunks!"

"All of it!" Mick said, laughing along with her. "And we'll leave Irish in the poshest stable in Missouri so she can munch on soft new grass and oats and barley till I come back."

A desolate gloom suddenly settled over Anna at the realization that Mick would leave her in Boston, and the thought marred the joy of the past few minutes. "But you won't leave until I say you can, right? You promised you'd stay as long as I need you."

Mick looked at her and saw again the face of the little girl he had taken from Miss Brockman's. He pictured her as she had been then, in her plain dress with a mop of curls around her face and a proud set to her mouth. "I won't leave you, darlin', until you say I can go, and even then I'll keep turnin' up in your life for the rest of my days. You've been tellin' me what to do for eight years; I don't see any reason to change things now!"

CHAPTER THREE

About two miles southwest of Cape de Rive, Mick turned the wagon off the main road and into a secluded stand of oak trees that bordered a clear lake. Though the afternoon temperature was cool, the water looked so refreshing that Anna jumped down from the wagon seat, ran to the lake, and plunged her hands in the water. She couldn't wait to immerse herself fully in the sparkling ripples and wash away the last of the dust and grime of Cape de Rive. "This spot will do nicely, Uncle Mick," she said, and with her expression of approval, Mick went about the tasks of setting camp and tending to Irish.

Satisfied that their campsite was completely hidden from any traffic that might pass by on the road, Anna stripped off her clothes and waded into the cold water. She paddled around to keep from shivering and quickly bathed and washed her hair.

She could hear Mick through the trees. He talked to Irish as was his custom, letting the horse know what she was having for dinner and where she'd be taking them tomorrow. When it was just the three of them on the road, Mick conversed almost as much with Irish as he did Anna, and she always had a suspicion that the horse communicated back to him.

Soon the sounds of Mick's twig gathering and the promise

of a warm dry campfire lured Anna out of the lake. She took her dress from the tree limb where she had hung it and put it on over her head. Then she went by the fire and began cutting up potatoes and carrots for Mick's smoked pork stew.

It was going to be a clear, cool evening, a fitting end to their years of making camps, since this might be the last night ever that Anna and Mick would spend under the stars. From now until they boarded a steamboat for New Orleans, the Connollys would stay in hotels.

As darkness settled over the campsite, Anna put the dinner dishes away and sat in front of the fire. She held her hair over the last remaining embers and shook the still-dampened ends to dry them.

Mick lit the lantern that hung on the side of the wagon, and a soft glow illuminated the cozy camp. "I guess you won't miss sleepin' in that old wagon, will you, Anna?" he said.

"I never minded, you know that. You're the one who'll have several sleepless nights getting used to feather beds instead of cold hard ground under your back!"

"I'll look forward to the sufferin'," he teased, and poked a stick into the fire pit to stir the last of the burning twigs to ash.

Red sparks flew upward from the dying embers, illuminating four horsemen who rode out of the trees and halted in front of the fire ring. An ominous red-gold glow outlined the men's shapes. Anna was momentarily spellbound by the eerie crimson reflected off their faces.

Mick stood up and stepped between Anna and the riders. "Who are you?" he demanded.

Stuart Wilkes cut boldly in front of his men and pulled on the reins of his straining horse. Mick's eyes lit with recognition at the same time Anna realized who the intruders were. She rose to her feet, and Mick stepped back, pushing her into the shadows behind him.

"You remember me, don't you, Ol' Mick," Wilkes said. "We've come to collect on a debt."

"What debt? If you're talkin' about that poker game, I won that money fair and square!"

"I think you're a cheat, Mr. Mick," Wilkes stated flatly, "and these men can back me up. They saw everything."

"That's a damn lie and you know it." Mick inclined his head toward Anna and spoke out of the side of his mouth. "Stay back. If there's trouble, make a run for it." Then he took two steps away from her and faced Wilkes. "I don't know what kind a' game you're playin', Mr. Wilkes, but there's plenty of witnesses back at the Lucky Chance that'll swear I never cheated anyone at that table out of a dime."

"But they're not here, are they?" Wilkes said, sweeping his hand around the campsite. "It's just us, and I say you cheated and I want my money back—all of it!" Wilkes waited, tapping his riding crop against his boot, and when Mick didn't move, he shrugged his shoulders and nodded to his men. "I guess Ol' Mick doesn't want to cooperate, boys. He must need some convincing."

While Wilkes remained on his horse, the other three riders dismounted and approached Mick. He spread his legs wide in a fighting stance and clenched his fists. "Go on, get outta here," he warned Anna.

She walked up beside him. "No, I'm not going anywhere," she said, hoping her determination to stay and an ounce of logic would keep her uncle from losing his temper. "Give them the money, Uncle Mick, please. It's not worth getting hurt."

"Listen to her, Mick," Wilkes taunted. "She's a lot smarter than you are, and while a few blows to your homely face might not make a lot of difference, the same treatment could certainly damage hers."

Mick looked at Anna and again at the threatening trio of assailants. His shoulders sagged in defeat. "All right. I'll give you the money, and then you damn well better ride off and leave us alone!"

"Why wouldn't we?" Wilkes responded with a thin smile. He turned his palm up and wiggled his fingers at Mick. "Give it to me, now."

Mick removed the folded bills from his pocket. He walked to Wilkes's horse, handed up the money and returned immediately to Anna.

Wilkes fanned through the bills and put them in his vest pocket. Then he spoke to his men. "While we're here, boys, you might as well see what these folks have in the wagon we can use. Check it out, Jake."

"Now, just hold on a minute!" Mick shouted as Jake climbed up on the wagon seat. "That wasn't part of our bargain. I gave you the money, now clear out!"

Anna held Mick's arm to prevent him from moving, but he brushed her hands away and strode angrily toward Wilkes. He never made it, because one of the men grabbed his arms and held them locked behind his back while another of Wilkes's henchmen landed a powerful punch along Mick's jaw and another in his midsection. Mick's head slumped to his chest while his hands clutched his abdomen. When the men released him, he crumpled to the ground.

Anna rushed to her uncle. "How could you be so cruel?" she cried at Wilkes. "He couldn't have hurt you, and he gave you the money." She took Mick's head in her lap and urged him to speak to her. "Are you all right? Please, please, be all right."

"I'm okay. Quit fussin' at me, Anna."

She tried to prevent him from looking at the wagon, but he managed to steal a sideways glance. Jake Finn was climbing out of the back carrying the wooden box which Mick kept hidden under the wagon seat. When he saw the last of their money was being taken, Mick bolted up from Anna's lap and charged head first at Jake, sending him sprawling to the ground. The box flew open, the contents scattering around the campsite. Wilkes's men immediately gathered up the bills and coins.

"Well, look what we have here," Wilkes said, a self-satisfied smirk curling his lips and gleaming in his dark eyes. "You've been holding out on me, Mick."

Anna watched her uncle's muscles tense for battle. "Don't do it, Uncle Mick," she pleaded.

There was no stopping him now, not when he and Anna were about to lose everything. "Run, Anna," he said before turning blazing eyes on his adversary. "You low down bastard!" he spat out and charged the cocky Wilkes.

For the rest of her life, Anna would remember the glint of the barrel of Wilkes's pistol when he pulled it from his holster and fired point-blank at her uncle. In the span of an instant, as long as it took for the flash of gunpowder to send a deadly missile to its target, Mick Connolly was silenced. The bullet tore a gaping hole in his chest. The impact lifted him from the ground. He landed at Anna's feet as his last breath passed through his lips in a groan of agony and shock.

Anna screamed, a terrible, shrill sound that she didn't even recognize as her own. She covered her mouth with her hands and fell to her knees before her uncle's body. She looked down at his face, at the lifeless eyes staring back at her, and felt a pain so great, it was as if the bullet had ripped through her own heart. "No, no, no," she repeated mindlessly, her gaze frozen on the stricken form of the man who, for eight years, had been father, brother, and friend.

Her eyes stung with tears of grief, then burned with the fire of contempt as she raised them to Stuart Wilkes. He looked down at her with a smug indifference that spawned a rage in Anna she'd never known she possessed. It began as a volcanic boiling deep inside her, blocking out all sense of reason and leaving only an unquenchable need for revenge.

"Wouldn't it have been easier if you had just accepted my dinner invitation and Ol' Mick here had stayed in the game a little longer?" Wilkes asked.

His words, void of remorse or sympathy, and the taunting lift of the lips that delivered them, ignited the fuse of Anna's fury. "Murderer!" she ground out at him, her breath coming in short, quick gasps as her rage seethed at the surface of her consciousness. She ran at him until her tight fists made contact with his legs and arms. She pummeled his thighs and clawed at his hands while his horse reared up on its hind legs.

"Get her away," Wilkes ordered as if he were being disturbed by a bothersome insect. Two of his men tried to grab her, and she turned her fury on them, clawing and scratching at their eyes and faces.

Finally Jake Finn subdued her from behind by wrapping his arms around her chest in a painful grip, but she continued fighting with her feet, kicking wildly at the other man. One foot found its target, and the man doubled over in pain. Anna and Jake fell backward to the ground, wrestling each other and rolling over and over through thick brush.

Suddenly the ground sloped precariously, and Anna and Jake began to slide in an avalanche of loose dirt. She slipped out of Jake's grasp and tumbled headlong into a narrow ravine. Like a rag doll, she whirled with clods of earth in an unstoppable downward spiral. Rough outcroppings of stone and limbs cut and scraped her skin as she fell helplessly into total darkness. Finally she landed on a solid ledge. Her breath left her lungs in a painful whoosh as her head struck a rock. The blackness around her was shot with searing stars in the instant before she lost consciousness.

Anna couldn't make herself move. She tried lifting her arm. She attempted to wiggle her toes. It was as if she'd lost control of her body ... a body that mocked her with pain in every joint and muscle. Yet she was dimly aware that she lay on a soft surface. She wished she could sink lower into its soothing cushion and just float away from the pain.

Distant voices penetrated her consciousness, but she was unsure where they came from. Perhaps if she could open her eyes. Her lids felt like leaden weights, but she raised them enough to determine that she was in a room. She looked across a narrow space to a door. It was shut, but the voices seemed to originate from the other side.

"I coulda' killed myself goin' down in that ravine, boss," a man said. His voice was vaguely familiar, in an unpleasant way. "I shoulda' just stayed up top and shot her. It woulda' been easier."

Shot her? Was he talking about her?

"Stop whining, Jake." It was another voice, and it was lower, threatening. "If I'd wanted her dead, I'd have killed her myself. No, I have plans for Miss Anna. I suppose we'll have to kill her eventually, but as long as my wife is visiting her sister in Moline ... well, a man must have his diversions."

The vision of a tall man in black attire pierced the shooting pain behind Anna's eyes. She pictured hooded eyes raking over her. The glint of moonlight on steel, the harsh crack of a gunshot, the fall of a body at her feet. Oh, God, she remembered. The horror of it slashed through her mind like a knife blade, and for a moment, Anna truly wished she were dead.

"Did you dispose of Ol' Mick's body?" Stuart Wilkes asked.

"Yeah. I did what you told me."

Anna raised her head. A buzzing sound drowned out Jake's words but not the pounding at her temples. Not the ache in her heart. If only the agony of what had happened at the campsite could be blocked out as easily as the explanation of what Jake had done with her uncle's body.

"No one'll ever find him, you can bet on it," Jake boasted.

"And the wagon?"

"I'll go back tomorrow and take care of it. It's hidden in the trees tonight. And that old nag should still fetch a dollar or two from a farmer. Ought to be able to plow a few fields with her."

Poor Irish! Everything Anna held dear had been wrenched from her life in one terrifying night. And here she was, in a place she didn't know, with the vilest creature on earth on the other side of that door. She managed to raise herself up on her elbow and scan the interior of the small room. If she was to have any chance against Stuart Wilkes, she had to arm herself with the details of her surroundings. Suddenly Anna didn't want to die anymore. She wanted to live to see Wilkes pay for what he'd done.

The room was sparsely furnished with a bed, a single chair, and an old oak nightstand which held a kerosene lamp. The wick was turned low, but it wouldn't have mattered if it were bright enough to illuminate each corner of the room. There obviously was nothing here Anna could use as a weapon to defend herself.

The doorknob turned in the latch, and Anna sank back down into the mattress. She closed her eyes and pretended to be sleeping. Perhaps the element of surprise was the only weapon she could count on.

"She ain't moved, boss," Jake said.

"But she's not . . . dead?" A maudlin quality to Wilkes's voice suggested that he would indeed be disappointed if she were.

"No, sir. Fact is, I don't think she even has any broken bones. She just took a bad blow to her head."

A bright glow permeated Anna's eyelids. Someone had turned up the lantern. She felt fingers brush hair off her forehead, and it took all her willpower not to flinch from the touch.

"A few cuts and bruises. Such a shame to see exquisite beauty marred." It was Wilkes's voice. He was standing directly over her, his fingertips coming in contact with sensitive areas on her cheeks and jaw.

His hand moved away from her face and settled first on her shoulder, then snaked down her arm to her rib cage. If she hadn't still been covered by her dress, Anna wouldn't have been able to stand his intimate explorations of her body.

"You may go, Jake," Wilkes said.

"I'll stay on the landing like you told me. Remember what you said, boss, about me gettin' the chance to—"

"I said you can go," Wilkes stated impatiently. "I'll see that you get what's coming to you."

The door closed, and Anna heard the click of a lock. Footsteps approached the bed. There was a rustle of fabric and the snap of a belt buckle. Then Wilkes's voice broke the silence. "So, Ol' Mick, which was your most valued possession? The three thousand dollars which is already locked in my safe, or this rare beauty whom I intend to have before many minutes have passed? No matter, both are mine now. Stuart Wilkes always gets what he wants."

He ran his hand down Anna's body, pressing the dress against the mounds and valleys of her still form. It was all she could do to resist striking out at him, but it was too soon. Bile rose to her throat, but she forced it back down.

Wilkes next undid the three buttons at Anna's bodice and slipped his hand inside. When he found the soft peak he sought, he groaned.

Anna's stomach lurched violently. She willed herself not to

be sick. She was almost thankful for the pain in her head, and concentrated on it. Anything was better than thinking about what Wilkes was doing.

He fondled her breast and pressed his lips to her mouth. It was more than she could bear, and she choked back a gagging reflex.

"Don't cry, pet," he said, misinterpreting the sound. "It's much too late for tears. Mick can't help you now, but I know what you want." He lowered his head to the open bodice of her gown. His parched lips grazed her skin.

Anna's head throbbed in time to the wild beating of her heart. Now was the time, now when he would least expect her to fight back. Fear coursed through her veins. How would she ever find the strength to beat him? In her mind's eye she saw the stark planes of the face she loathed. But out of the nightmare of what was happening to her she heard Mick Connolly's voice. It broke through the pain like a beacon in a sea of anguish. "Fight, darlin'," the voice of her uncle urged. "Kick and claw. Do whatever you have to, but don't let this snake win."

She snarled like a cornered animal.

"So you like that, my little pet," Wilkes snickered. His lips moved over her, seeking her other breast, and his hands sought new territory. "I have a hunch that Ol' Mick was your pitiful lover and not your uncle at all. One thing is for certain— whatever he was, he was a fool, and you are about to discover that I am not."

A low, tortured scream tore from Anna's mouth as she twisted her fingers in Wilkes's hair and jerked his head up. His startled glare locked onto her eyes. She had raised her consciousness from hurt and fear to a cold, enraged sanity, and it empowered her. Her fingernails dug into the sides of his face, leaving bright red tracks down his cheeks. She drew her legs to her chest and pushed him away with a sudden thrust of her feet.

"Whore!" Wilkes screamed, lunging for her throat.

Anna rolled away from him and tumbled to the floor. "Don't you touch me," she hissed. "I'm going to tell everyone what an evil, murdering devil you are!" She stood up, her head reeling from sharp stabs of pain. She backed toward a window, her hands searching frantically behind her for something to hang on to.

"Oh, no you aren't," Wilkes stated in a calm but threatening tone. "You're not going to utter one sound." He took a handkerchief out of his pants pocket and pulled it tightly between his hands. Then he advanced toward her. "First of all, I'm going to shut up your pretty face, and then I'm going to finish what I started."

"Boss! Boss!" Jake's voice came from the other side of the locked door.

"Go away, Jake!" Wilkes shouted. "I said I'd call you if I needed you." His eyes snapped back to his prey and he came closer, holding the cloth up to Anna's face.

Her fingertips found the rough wood of the windowsill, and she craned her neck to estimate the size of the opening. She ran her hands around the frame and edged closer and closer until she was sitting on the window ledge.

Wilkes laughed at her. "Go ahead, Anna, jump. It's only three stories, and you'll land on a thicket of my wife's prize rosebushes. Let the thorns do to your lovely face what your fall in the ravine only started."

She looked down, and through her blurred vision she saw that he was right. Even if she survived the fall, the rough branches would cut her to ribbons. But it was too late to think of another plan. Wilkes was upon her, grabbing for her arm.

She leaned back, ready to strike one last time when out of the corner of her eye she saw a tree branch a few feet away. Instinctively she kicked out at Wilkes, forcing him back while at the same time she propelled herself out the window and across the space that separated her from the branch. Her hands felt shaggy bark, and she clawed, scraping her fingers until her palms closed around solid wood. She looked over her shoulder to see Wilkes leaning precariously out the window, reaching for her, his arms flailing madly in the air.

Catlike, she scrambled onto the branch just as his hands brushed her gown. She felt the fabric slip through his fingers at the same time she heard his startled cry. Then he was falling, as if in slow motion, tumbling head first toward his wife's bloodred roses. Anna clung to the branch as the sickening thud of Wilkes's body resounded in her ears.

She didn't have long to contemplate what had happened, because once again Jake pounded on the bedroom door. ''Boss! Boss, answer me!'' She could see the door strain against the frame as Jake attempted to break in. She shimmied down the tree, landing just inches from Wilkes's crumpled form. She stared at the oddly misshapen body, the head angled crazily away from the shoulders. Her lips turned up in a narrow, fleeting sneer of victory before a cold fear washed over her. She turned away from the mansion and ran down the hill toward the bright lights that beckoned her from the river, the ones blazing from the *Duchess of Orleans*.

CHAPTER FOUR

Anna crossed the levee that separated the town of Cape de Rive from the Mississippi River bank. A loud clanging of a bell from the area of the Wilkes's mansion alerted her that news of Stuart Wilkes's death must be spreading. Soon the entire town would know, and she had to act fast. Already there was a soft illumination in the sky on the other side of the levee, which meant the citizens of Cape de Rive were rousing from their beds and lighting their lanterns to see what all the commotion was about.

She crouched low and crept silently toward the gangway of the largest steamboat at the harbor, hoping it would offer more places to hide. She had no idea what time it was, but she sensed there were still several hours of darkness left before daybreak. The only people around the quiet dock were lamp boys feeding kindling to the torch baskets which lit up the riverbank. She was grateful for the thick black smoke which rose from the baskets and concealed her flight across the gangway.

Once on board the *Duchess of Orleans,* Anna pressed her back against a wall and drew a long, fortifying breath. Laughter and conversation came from the grand salon, and she had to make certain she wasn't spotted by any late-night revelers. She crawled under the windows of the salon, avoiding the light from the brass lanterns mounted every few feet to the outside walls. Finally she reached the staircase at the end of the salon and climbed to the third deck where dimly lit areas of the promenade allowed her to proceed more confidently.

From the third deck, Anna could see over the levee to the streets of Cape de Rive. Citizens had come out of their homes and were congregating on corners and under streetlamps. She imagined the story Jake Finn could be telling at this moment, and knew *she* was no doubt portrayed as the villain, not Stuart Wilkes. She knew she only had a short time before a search for Wilkes's murderer would be under way. Desperate to find a place to hide, she tried the door handle of each stateroom, praying that one of them would be open and, more importantly, vacant, giving her a temporary safe haven. At last, a handle turned easily. She pushed open the unlocked door and peered inside.

Enough light came through the window for Anna to see the room was empty, and she crossed the threshold. Her relief was brief, however, because she soon concluded that the stateroom was indeed occupied. An assortment of toiletries were arranged neatly on the polished mahogany bureau, and a man's suit of clothes had been left on the double bed. She crossed to the wardrobe cabinet and looked inside. Men's and women's garments were hanging side by side.

Although she was safe for the moment, Anna realized that whoever occupied this room would return soon, and she had better leave immediately. She would have fled right then, except footsteps outside the door forced her to stay in the room. She crouched beside the bed and waited for an end to the activity on the promenade.

Philip Brichard tucked his leather wallet inside his waistcoat pocket as he left the grand salon. Four other men accompanied him through the large double doors that led to the deck, and Philip turned to one of them and smiled. "A pleasure as always, William," he said.

"It was for you, young man," the man answered good-naturedly, "but I'm afraid my coffers were severely depleted."

Philip chuckled. "This just makes up for the last trip when, as I recall, you cleaned me out pretty well."

"I guess I did at that. I'll be getting off at Hannibal, so I won't have a chance to win my money back. Be sure to give my regards to your mother. I'm sorry she didn't accompany you this trip."

Philip paused at the stairs where he would part company with his friend. "Mother thought she would be bored by all the business I had to tend to, but even though she didn't come, she still had me bring back several gowns she'd ordered in Chicago for her and Claudette." Philip grinned at the thought of all the dresses he'd carried on board the *Duchess of Orleans*. "It was a bit of a nuisance," he said, "but I'm sure there would have been many more parcels had the ladies come along!"

"Right you are about that. Good night then, Philip."

The men shook hands and Philip climbed the stairs to the third deck where his stateroom was located. He passed several passengers who were lined up along the deck rail and looking toward town. "What's going on?" he asked one man who was dressed in a nightshirt and trousers.

"I don't know," the man answered, pointing toward the center of Cape de Rive. "I know that building yonder, though. It's the constable's office, and it's lit up like the Fourth of July, so my hunch is that something big happened."

"It would seem so," Philip agreed, wondering if what had occurred would delay their leaving at daybreak. "I suppose we'll hear soon enough." He yawned, flexed his shoulders to relieve the tension of sitting too long, and went into his stateroom.

Anna heard only one pair of footsteps cross the threshold. She pressed herself to the floor and looked under the bed ruffle hoping to get a glimpse of the person who had come in the room. It was definitely not a woman, for all Anna clearly observed was a pair of polished black leather boots fit snugly around gray broadcloth trousers. She lay very still, afraid that even her shallow breathing would alert the man to her presence.

She watched as a charcoal velvet waistcoat was draped over the back of the small desk chair. She heard a soft metallic clink as a piece of jewelry was set on the bureau. Then the bed slats creaked and the foot of the mattress depressed as the man sat down on the end of the bed and sighed wearily.

He bent over to pull off his boots, and Anna realized with mounting panic that his hand was dangerously close to a slip of white fabric protruding from under the bed. His finger actually brushed against the hem of her dress!

He hesitated for just an instant and continued to remove his boots. Then he stood up, crossed to the bureau and lit the kerosene lantern.

Anna drew in a quick, panicky breath. Oh, no, not a light!

He went back to the foot of the bed, which was under the single window, and drew the shutters closed. Then in one swift, sudden motion, he reached down by the side of the bed, caught Anna's wrist and dragged her to her feet.

Her head reeled with the unexpected, abrupt movement, and her knees started to buckle under the painful pressure of his grip on her wrist.

In the low light produced by the kerosene lantern, his gaze raked knowingly over the tumble of blond hair tangled around her face. He dropped her hand, thrusting her arm so violently that she stumbled back a step. "You!" he hissed, his eyes shooting sparks like steel splinters.

She choked back a startled cry when she recognized Philip Brichard. She could do no more than stare at him through eyes partly covered by wild strands of unkempt hair. Her head ached so badly it was all she could do to remain standing in the heat of his angry gaze.

"Well, now I know why my instincts told me to be sure and bring all my money with me to the salon tonight," Philip declared. "Deep down I must have known that thieves would be prowling around!" Anna opened her mouth to speak, but no sound came out. "What's the matter, my little 'blind friend'?

Are you mute now as well? Isn't your other con game working out well enough for you?''

He folded his arms across his chest and appraised Anna's disheveled appearance, including the dress which was still gaping open at the bodice. "Now I have it," he said as his gaze returned to her face. "Your father has come up with another little game for you to play . . . one that is much older and more proven." He looked away from her, disgust evident in his cold eyes. "Is there nothing your father won't have you do to get money?''

"No, no, it's not what you think," she finally managed to say. The pain in her head was almost unbearable, and she pressed her hands against her temple to stop the throbbing.

"It is *exactly* what I think, Miss Rose, or whatever your name is!" He cocked his head to one side, and his steely eyes brightened with alertness. "Where is your partner in this scheme anyway? Hidden in my wardrobe perhaps?" He strode to the cabinet and pulled open the doors. Satisfied that Mick wasn't there, he slammed it shut again. "Waiting for you on the shore, then?''

Anna shook her head, unable to think clearly through the haze of pain. She trembled as hot tears came to her eyes.

Philip stormed over to her and grabbed her arms. "I want some answers from you or I'll march you into town right now and turn you over to the authorities." He shook her so forcefully her hair fell away from her face. All at once the anger died in Philip's eyes and was replaced with something else. It could have been either pity or disgust, Anna wasn't sure which.

She tried to extricate herself from his grasp, but he pulled her nearer the lantern and held her close to the light. He grabbed a handful of her hair and held the thick mass of tangles at her nape. With his other hand he cupped her chin and turned her face toward the lamp. "These cuts . . . what happened to you?" he demanded in a gentler voice. "Who did his?''

She couldn't answer him. She could no longer think at all, but could only feel the pain as it pounded mercilessly in her ears. As blackness overtook her, Anna blinked once before she slumped against him.

* * *

The next time she woke, Anna was aware of sunlight diffused through her eyelids. She was lying between sheets that smelled vaguely woodsy, like pine. She floated on a down-filled mattress. There was a sensation of heat radiating from deep inside her, but something cool and damp was being stroked along her face and neck. Since her head still ached, she resisted the temptation to open her eyes until she felt the soft cloud she was lying on move slightly, like a gentle wave. She realized with a start that she was not alone, that someone was with her on a bed, and she heard the sound of a cloth being wrung over a dish.

Slowly Anna opened her eyes, and the face of Philip Brichard undulated into view. She smiled, and a subtle sigh of contentment whispered through her lips. It was such a pleasing face to look at, rugged and square with high, fine cheekbones on either side of a straight, chiseled nose. A frown pulled at the corners of his full lips, though, and lines of worry creased his brow.

Philip held a glass of water to Anna's lips while his hand cupped the back of her head urging her to drink. "Are you feeling better?" he asked.

His voice caused the first flicker of a confusing yet bitter remembrance to dawn in Anna's mind. "What am I doing here?" she managed to say. "Am I in your bed?" With trembling hands she lifted the covers and saw that she was wearing a man's shirt instead of her dress. She looked back at Philip. "How?"

He shrugged his shoulders. "You're still wearing your undergarments, so you can quit looking at me like that, but your gown was filthy." He raised an eyebrow at her. "Were you tumbling about in the mud with someone, Miss Rose?"

"Stay away from me," she ordered. Grief over the events of the last hours and anger over her current situation warred within her. She knew Philip Brichard was taunting her and, more importantly, he was in a position to exert power over her. With the recurrent image of her uncle's violent death came the bitter realization that she was completely alone now. She was grief-stricken, hurt, and now vulnerable to the whims of a man she barely knew.

Philip stood up and set the glass of water on the bedside table. "Since you are strong enough to issue orders, then I assume you can now tell me what happened last night."

"I don't have to tell you anything!" she declared, throwing back the bedcovers. "In fact, I'm getting out of here right now. Either return my gown or give me the rest of your clothes so I can leave!" She sat up and spun around so her feet were dangling over the side of the bed, but they never reached the floor. The throbbing in her head forced her to lie back against the pillows again. She moaned with pain and frustration and covered her face with her arm.

"You're in no condition to go anywhere," Philip said, pulling the sheet over her once more. "You're feverish, bruised from head to toe, and you probably have a concussion from that dazed look I see in your eyes. I'm going to send the cabin boy into town for a doctor."

"No! No doctor. I'm fine. I need to rest a moment, that's all. Just leave me alone."

Philip frowned and sighed with exasperation. "Where is your father, then? I can at least send for him to care for you."

"He's not my father."

"Big surprise," Philip muttered. "So who is he anyway, and how can I locate him, assuming he isn't the one who did this to you."

She turned her face away. "He is . . . *was* my uncle. He was murdered last night." When Philip didn't say anything, Anna looked back at him. His eyes were cold and gray and indifferent to her distress. "You don't believe me?"

"I don't see any reason to believe you, Miss Rose. I only know you as a fake and a swindler who accused me of being an investigator looking into your less than honorable schemes. I find you in my stateroom in the middle of the night suffering from the effects of what must have been a terrible struggle. On top of that, bells and sirens have been sounding in Cape de Rive since three o'clock this morning because I hear that one of its foremost citizens was scratched and clawed about his face before being hurled out a third-floor window to his death. Oddly enough, the dearly departed is the very same man who nearly ran you over in his carriage yesterday afternoon. Call it a hunch, my dear Miss Rose, but my logical conclusion is that you had a very busy evening before showing up here.''

Despite her best efforts, Anna couldn't keep the panic from her voice. "You haven't told anyone else about your ridiculous hunch, have you?''

"Not yet, but can you give me one good reason why I shouldn't?''

She didn't have a chance to respond, because they were interrupted by a loud knock at Philip's door.

"Who's there?'' Philip called over his shoulder.

"Beggin' your pardon, Mr. Brichard, sir, but it's Captain Cruthers. I need to search your room; it's orders from the constable himself.''

"No!'' Anna shouted in a terrified whisper. "You can't let him see me!''

Philip regarded her skeptically. "You're awfully nervous considering you think my theory is 'ridiculous.' ''

"Please, you have to help me! I promise I'll explain everything later.''

The captain called through the door. "Mr. Brichard, I'm afraid I must insist, sir.''

"I'll be right there, just give me a moment.'' Philip looked at Anna one last time, apparently appraising the desperation in her plea. She waited for his decision without taking a breath.

"All right,'' he said finally. "Get under the covers completely and stay there.''

She yanked the sheet over her head but peeked out to watch Philip with one eye while he went to the wardrobe and removed an elegant gown from among the dresses inside. He tossed it carelessly across the desk chair so that the wide skirt ballooned onto the floor. Then he raked his hand through his hair, pulling several strands onto his forehead. He opened the stateroom door about halfway and spoke to the man on the other side. "Good morning, Captain. What can I do for you?''

"I have to personally check every room, sir. There was a murder in town last night and we've been ordered to search the boat from stem to stern."

"I can assure you, Captain, that I did not murder anyone, unless of course one of the men I beat at cards blamed me and jumped overboard!"

"Oh, no, sir," the captain said. "It wasn't you. It was a young woman that did it. She murdered Mr. Stuart Wilkes up at the big house, and she may have had an accomplice."

"Oh? And just how did this woman do away with the unlucky Mr. Wilkes?"

"Mr. Wilkes's man, Jake Finn, said she came up to the house lookin' for food. She was with another man, an older fella, and they were drivin' a peddler's rig with some sort of theatrical nonsense written all over it. Mr. Wilkes let her in and somehow she lured him up to the third floor and pushed him out a window. Broke his neck, he did."

"How dreadful!" Philip said, voicing appropriate shock.

"The constable figures the old man ran off when he heard trouble, but Jake says the woman's likely to be still around. We also found out that those same two people have been seen up north along the river runnin' a confidence game."

"They sound like tough characters all right, and the woman must be strong as an ox to have overpowered Mr. Wilkes!"

"I hear she's a powerfully built woman all right."

Philip cleared his throat and spoke seriously. "Well, I can tell you, Captain, that I've seen no muscular women around my room tonight, no one suspicious at all."

"Just the same, sir, I gotta check your room myself."

Philip spoke in the way men do when they think another man is their co-conspirator in matters of indiscretion. "I'm afraid I have a little problem, Captain. You see, I am not entirely alone in my stateroom at the moment. See for yourself."

Anna heard the door creak open a little more and surmised that Philip was allowing the captain a view of both her body outlined by the sheet and the fashionable gown on the chair.

"I have a lady guest who would be embarrassed beyond measure if anyone knew she were here," he explained. "She's the . . . well, the wife of one of your most prosperous and most frequent passengers, and if her husband caught wind of this, she would surely be a scorned woman and I would be a dead man.''

The captain chuckled. ''I can see there's been some entertainin' goin' on in here, sir. Mind if I just get a peek at the lady and I'll be on my way?''

''The lady does not want anyone to know, Captain, and her husband's influence is great enough that if you value your position with the steamboat line, I think you should leave it alone.''

''Oh, I know who she is then,'' the captain said, obviously trying to impress Philip with his deductive powers.

''I thought you would.''

''Anyway, the woman I'm lookin' for was wearing a simple sort of dress, not a fancy ball gown like that one.''

''There you have it then,'' Philip said, concluding the matter. ''Good luck with your search, Captain.''

Philip shut the door and Anna popped her head out from under the sheet. ''I'm impressed. That was quick thinking,'' she said.

''You and your uncle aren't the only ones who can tell a convincing lie, Miss Rose.''

''Don't call me that. It's not my name. I'm Anna Connolly, and my uncle was Michael Connolly. We just used the name Rose for . . .''

''Professional reasons?''

''Something like that. Thank you, Mr. Brichard. I owe you a great deal for what you just did.''

Philip hung the dress back in the wardrobe and pulled the desk chair over to the bed. He straddled it backward, his arms resting on the top rung. ''You can start to repay me right now, Anna, by telling me exactly what went on in Cape de Rive last night. If I'm helping a murderess to escape, I've got to know all the facts.''

* * *

It was apparent that Philip would not let her rest until she told him. Besides, hadn't he just proven that he was an ally of sorts, albeit one who bore close watching. Anna propped herself against the pillows and began her story. Philip sat very still, intent on every word. When she related the events that occurred in the campsite, his eyes darkened and the muscles in his jaw tensed.

When Anna was nearly finished, a resonant brass bell mounted somewhere above Philip's room on the *Duchess of Orleans* sounded several times. Within minutes, a steady vibration began in the stoked boilers of ship's bowels and quaked through the great engines to the piston that turned the paddle wheel. The shudders were eventually felt on the third deck, just before the engineer's whistle sounded three times. Shortly thereafter, the grand steamboat pulled into the calm waters of the Mississippi River.

"What's happening?" Anna asked. "Where are we going?"

"To our next stop, of course," Philip explained. "Thanks to the misdeeds of the late Stuart Wilkes, however, we're leaving later than we should."

Anna had just finished her account of Wilkes's fatal fall from his third-floor window. She glanced out the window next to the bed. With conflicting emotions she watched the disappearing shoreline of Cape de Rive. While she realized that she could never be safe in the town where the authorities were searching for her, she hated the thought of leaving behind the last traces of her life with Mick Connolly.

So many unanswered questions plagued her and demanded resolutions. Where was Mick's body? What had happened to the wagon and all their belongings? And what about Irish . . . what would become of her?

She didn't have long to contemplate these concerns because she felt Philip's intense gaze on her face, and she worried that his stern scrutiny meant he didn't believe her story. Even though he acted as her ally, she still didn't know if she could really trust him. She avoided looking at him and focused on her hands folded in her lap. "Do you believe me?" she finally asked.

"Yes, Anna, I do," he said, and a flood of relief washed

over her. "I know about Stuart Wilkes's reputation, and I have no doubt that he could have committed the crimes you have charged him with. The question now is, what are we going to do with you?"

"I don't want to be a bother to you, Mr. Brichard. I know you've already compromised your principles by lying to the captain."

Philip chuckled, and his eyes, which just moments before had been dark and foreboding, now held an amused glint. "I wouldn't worry too much about my principles, Anna," he said. "I've had to compromise them any number of times on this river in the past. You'll notice the captain didn't have a difficult time believing my story this morning!"

That was true enough, Anna had to admit. The captain acted as though he almost expected such outrageous behavior from Philip Brichard, the man whose charcoal eyes still made her decidedly uneasy. She looked out the window again and watched the tree-lined riverbank on the western shore as the *Duchess* drifted down river. "Where are we headed?" she asked as a plan began to take shape in her mind.

"Our next stop is Hannibal, Missouri," he revealed. "Even with our late start, we should still be there well before dark."

"It's not far, then, from Cape de Rive."

"No, not too far, but still close enough for me to believe that the authorities will be actively searching for you." He looked at her with keen, suspicious eyes. "You're not thinking of getting off the boat, are you?"

"How could I do that? I feel horrible, I haven't any money or clothes." She leveled her most innocent look on Philip, and he relaxed. Hopefully she had convinced him she wouldn't do anything so foolish as to strike out on her own and return to Cape de Rive.

He nodded once and smiled at her. "The thing you need now is rest," he said. "And you must be starving. What do you feel like eating? I could probably bring you some soup and bread."

"That would be nice. And some tea perhaps. But what I'd really like is a hot bath."

"I'll see what I can do," Philip assured her, "although convincing the chef that I've suddenly developed a fondness for tea might take some doing!" He walked to the door, but turned back to her before opening it. "Keep the door locked," he warned. "Don't open it to anyone but me."

She nodded and settled back against the pillows once more. While Philip was gone, she decided to try very hard to just think of the luxury of a warm, cleansing bath, perhaps the last one she would have for a while.

He returned shortly and opened the door just enough to poke his head inside. Anna looked over at him and he mouthed the words, "Get down."

She scrambled to the floor on the other side of the bed as Philip came in followed by a boy dressed in a blue-and-white uniform. The young man dragged a wooden tub through the door and left it in the center of the room.

"I'll be right back with your buckets of hot water, Mr. Brichard," the cabin boy said.

"Just leave them outside, Jim. There's no need to keep coming in the room. I'll get them all at once from the promenade."

The boy agreed, and after he left, Anna stood up and walked to the bath. It was a polished golden oak tub with a high, round back complete with a brass headrest. Brass handrails were mounted to the inside of the tub, and a basket etched with the words *Duchess of Orleans* was attached to the outside. Inside the basket were bottles of scented oils and colognes, a thick soft sponge wrapped in floral paper, and a new bar of soap. A big thirsty towel was draped over the end of the tub where Anna imagined she would soon be wiggling her toes in the warm water.

"It's wonderful," she sighed. "I've never seen such an elegant bath."

"A good soaking is the best thing for aches and pains like yours," Philip said.

At the mention of her injuries, Anna shivered, and the

momentary delight she had experienced seeing the welcoming bath was overshadowed by the reality of her dire situation and her grief over Mick's death. "I guess it can help some pains, Mr. Brichard, but not all," she said.

Philip's lips pulled down in a frown, and his eyes softened. "I'm sorry, Anna," he said, reaching his hand out to touch her arm. "I didn't mean to remind you . . ."

She stepped back, wary of letting him get too close, and his hand dropped to his side. "It's all right," she said. "I'm all right, really." She knew it was a lie, but she was determined to keep her distance from him.

There was a knock at the door and Philip turned away. "Ah, the water has arrived." He seemed grateful to have something to do and busied himself by carrying in buckets of steaming water and filling the tub. "There you go," he said at last, smiling at her. "Enjoy it."

She hesitated, waiting for him to leave the room, but instead he began unbuttoning his shirt. When he had stripped to his waist, he sat on the bed and took off his boots.

Anna stared at him in bewilderment. "What are you doing?" she asked.

"Going to sleep for a while. I'm exhausted."

"Now?"

"Yes, now."

"But, you can't!"

"Why not?"

"Be-because I'm taking a bath!"

"I know that. It won't bother me. I'll be asleep in two minutes."

His insensitivity confused her, especially since he'd seemed to have such compassion for her just a few minutes before. "You can't think that I would undress with you in the same room!"

"I think that if you're going to bathe, you'll have to. I haven't been to bed in thirty-six hours, Anna, so as tempting as you must imagine it would be for me to gaze upon you in your bath, I must tell you that I'm just not interested at the moment."

Giving her a devilishly improper wink, he added, "Perhaps some other time."

Anna stood glued to one spot, staring at him. Her emotions wavered between indignant fury and abject humiliation. Seemingly unconcerned, Philip lay down on the bed facing away from her and drew the satin coverlet up to his waist. Anna watched as he rolled his shoulders in relaxation, flexing the taut muscles in his back. Then he was completely still. Just as he had predicted, within two minutes his breathing became shallow and steady, and Anna knew that he was indeed asleep.

She began to unbutton the large shirt she was wearing, stopping often to peer over at Philip. When she had freed the last button she let the shirt fall to the floor. As quickly as possible, she removed her undergarments and stepped into the tub without even time to look at the bruises on her sore body. The delicious warmth of the water slowly enveloped her, inch by glorious inch, until she finally laid her head against the smooth headrest.

If it were a breach of morality to be in this room with this man just a few feet away, Anna didn't care any longer. After all, she had learned in the last year of her life that the world was full of sinners whose crimes were much worse than hers. She picked up a glass bottle inscribed with the word 'lavender' and poured a few precious drops into her water.

She looked over at Philip. The dim light coming through the slats of the window shutters was enough for her to watch the gentle rise and fall of his back as he breathed. She saw, too, the way the ends of his thick hair brushed the pillow at his nape. He was snoring softly, and Anna thought there was something oddly secure about the steady sound. Though his mind may have been far away, his breathing reminded her that he was indeed near. She shook her head to clear it of the troublesome notion and sank all the way down until the water covered the top of her head.

After the bath, Anna would initiate the scheme that had been forming in her mind. She could not stay with Philip Brichard. She had to rely on her own wits, and the sooner she set out to do this, the better. She would disguise herself, leave the *Duchess of Orleans* in Hannibal and return to Cape de Rive, to all the precious treasures she had left behind at the little camp by the lake. She would go back to the place where the person she loved most in the world had been taken away from her.

She hoped Philip Brichard was a sound sleeper. The supplies she needed to disguise herself from the authorities had to come from his stateroom.

CHAPTER FIVE

An hour later, when the water in Anna's bath had become tepid, and her hair, hanging over the back of the oak tub, was almost dry, she roused herself from a relaxed drowsiness into which she had fallen. Glancing over at Philip to make sure he was still asleep, she stepped out of the bath and wrapped a towel around her. Though her cuts and abrasions were still tender, at least the soreness in her muscles had been alleviated by the long soaking. And while her head still ached, she was able to think clearly enough to execute her plan.

Remembering the dresses hanging in Philip's wardrobe, she set about finding something to wear. The cabinet door squeaked on its hinges as Anna opened it, and her gaze darted to Philip. She sighed with relief when he didn't even move, and she realized that he truly was a deep sleeper.

The dresses in the wardrobe appeared to be two different sizes, small and smaller still. Anna looked forlornly down her own five-foot-six-inch frame and frowned. Oh, well, she thought, one of these dresses would just have to do.

She picked out what looked to be the largest garment and held it up to her chest. It was made of copper-colored silk, and had a large draped gather across the abdomen which would hide any telltale wrinkles of snugness. The neckline was low, but a two-inch stand-up ruffle at the bodice would cover her breasts and hopefully hide the bruises on her chest.

She turned the dress around and spied the label sewn to the neck lining. "Especially made for Claudette Brichard" it said. Proud of her own abilities as a seamstress, Anna admired the quality workmanship of the dress and felt a twinge of guilt that she was "borrowing" it without having much hope of ever bringing it back. She hung the dress on the outside of the wardrobe and began to look for a bonnet. "So sorry, Claudette, whoever you are," she muttered as she reached for a hat box on a high shelf.

When she was completely dressed, Anna turned in front of the full-length mirror mounted to the inside of the wardrobe door. The dress was too short to be fashionable and too tight to be comfortable, but it would have to do. The three-quarter-length puffed sleeves covered the scratches on her arms, and the flat bonnet with its flared brim and large ostrich feather would effectively hide most of her face.

Anna set the bonnet on the floor and ran her fingers through her hair, removing as many of the tangles as she could. Then she ripped a gold sash from the waistline of the dress and used it as a makeshift snood to hold her heavy hair at her nape. When the hat was in place, she pulled on the ostrich plume attached to the crown and maneuvered it until it hung almost like a mask over her eyes. "There," she whispered to her reflection. "I look like a totally different person." But the persistent headache at her temples reminded her that she was, after all, the same girl who had recently tumbled down a ravine while wrestling with Jake Finn.

The sun was low on the western horizon when the *Duchess of Orleans* pulled alongside the riverbank at Hannibal, Missouri. Philip had been asleep over six hours. Anna leaned over him and noted that his breathing was still steady and slow. The muscles in his face were slack, and a shock of dark hair fell across his forehead. With the tense furrows absent from his brow and the faint lines around his mouth in repose, Anna thought he looked almost like a little boy, with a child's dark lashes feathered on his cheek.

"Forgive me for taking the dress," she whispered, "and for what I'm about to do now." She picked up a valise from inside the wardrobe, and after removing Philip's things, she tossed in her own soiled dress which she had found at the bottom of the cabinet. Then she tucked the valise under her arm.

At the last moment before Anna left the stateroom, a glittering object on the bureau caught her eye. She had seen the diamond stickpin for the first time when she noticed Philip in the restaurant in River Flats, and she had subtly admired it then. Now, as she saw it again among a casually tossed pile of coins, she picked it up and held it to the light coming in the window. She could not even begin to imagine what such a fine piece of jewelry would be worth, but she knew it had to be plenty.

She knew, too, that the pin, whose monetary value probably meant very little to Philip Brichard, would go a long way in helping her accomplish her goals in Cape de Rive. If luck was on her side, and if she maintained a clever enough disguise, Anna intended to find Irish and as many of her belongings from the wagon as she could. This might mean she would have to buy her things back.

Anna, you know you shouldn't do this, she told herself. She put the pin back on the bureau. *You're not a thief, despite what Mr. Brichard may believe.*

She tried to walk away, but the diamond seemed to beckon her with a tempting wink from the dresser top. *Oh, what's the use!* She went back and retrieved it. *Mr. Brichard's address in Louisiana is right here on his valise tag, and I can always send him money for the pin later,* she decided. *What is probably only a meaningless bauble to him could mean the difference between life and death for me.* She slipped the pin under the elastic of her sleeve and let it fall into the ballooning material at her elbow. *It's not as though I can damage my reputation where Philip Brichard is concerned anyway,* she rationalized. Then, for good measure, she tossed several coins into her sleeve as well.

Watching Philip's back to make certain he wasn't moving,

Anna slowly opened the door. She peeked out to the promenade and was relieved to see that it was empty of late-afternoon strollers. Most of the passengers had probably gone into town. Just as she opened the door wide enough to accommodate her exit, a cloud which had been covering the setting sun drifted away and a bright shaft of golden light speared into the open door. Anna hastily stepped out on deck just as she heard confused mumbling coming from the bed.

Philip blinked hard, attempting to adjust to the unwelcome light. He looked at the door to his stateroom. The sheen of copper-colored silk caught in a beam of sunlight captured his attention. Before he could react, however, the fabric was yanked out of sight, and the door was quickly pulled closed. Realizing what had happened, he sat up and reached for his boots.

"Damn! What the devil does she think she's doing?" He pulled a shirt from the wardrobe, and even while he was thrusting his arms through the sleeves, he was reaching for the stateroom door. With his shirttails flapping behind him, Philip rushed to the deck rail and peered onto the bank. He clearly saw Anna, wearing his sister's new gown, as she crossed the gangway heading for town.

He ran down three flights of stairs, taking the steps two at a time. When he reached the bank, Anna was nowhere in sight, but he remembered seeing her turn north onto a street of businesses that ran through the center of town. Darting among the citizens coming and going from shops and restaurants, Philip kept his eyes peeled for a glimpse of copper dress.

He craned his neck and stretched to his full six feet two inches in an effort to see over the people crowding the main street of Hannibal, but Anna had vanished into the throng. There was no sign of Claudette's gown or the mass of wavy blond hair he would have recognized at a glance. The people of Hannibal stared at what they no doubt perceived to be a half-crazed man scrambling around them, uttering a series of mindless "excuse me's."

Philip was aware that the *Duchess of Orleans* would be

sounding the bells of departure soon, and that made his search all the more urgent. He entered doorways of shops and scanned the interiors; he pressed his face to restaurant windows, and he looked down narrow alleys, but he did not see a copper dress or golden hair.

It was the great white ostrich feather that finally caught his eye—that ridiculous feather attached to the over-wide hat that had brought an odd, indulgent smile to his lips when he had watched the milliner in Chicago pack it in tissue paper in the hat box. He saw the feather through the window of the Hannibal Emporium, and it bounced up and down over the face of Anna Connolly as if it were still attached to the wing of a nervous, fluttering bird.

Philip watched as Anna removed an object from the sleeve of Claudette's dress and handed it to the store clerk. She received a stack of clothing in return and put it in . . . What was it? He strained to see . . . his valise!

She headed to the store entrance, and Philip dashed around a corner and flattened himself against a wall. Determined not to lose her this time, he remained hidden while she crossed the busy street and walked another two short blocks to the Hannibal Livery.

The game had gone on long enough. Before he allowed Anna to enter the livery, Philip caught up with her. He took her arm, ignored her startled cry, and drew her against his chest. Then, to avoid a scene in which he might be interpreted as the villain, he pulled her into the alley which separated the livery from the rest of the shops.

"Who . . . what . . . !" Anna started to scream, but Philip clamped his hand over her mouth until they were at the end of the alley. Then he spun her around and backed her against the livery wall.

Her eyes blazed, first with recognition, then with indignation. "What do you think you're doing?" she demanded.

"What am *I* doing?" he shot back. "That's a question that defies answering! I'm not the one standing here in a stolen dress with a man's valise under my arm!"

"Well, I could hardly walk through town in a stolen shirt,

could I?'' she justified with a defiant spark in her eyes. "I thought it much more appropriate to steal your dress instead!''

Philip scanned the length of her, and frowned. "It looks ridiculous on you by the way.''

Anna dropped her gaze to the hem of the gown which hung several inches above the tops of her slippers. "Don't look at me like that!'' she warned. "I can't help it if I'm not the same size as the tiny Brichard women.''

"No, you certainly aren't,'' he mused, raising his gaze from the tight bodice to settle on a safer part of her body. "You have definitely tried to squeeze the figure of a woman into a dress made for a fifteen-year-old tomboy.'' When he saw that she was about to lash out at him again, he quickly diverted his attention to the hat. "And that silly feather,'' he said, flinging the bobbing plume away from her face. "Are you *trying* to draw attention to yourself? Hey, Sheriff, here I am . . .''

"Stop it. It suited my purpose, that's all. If you're concerned that I've borrowed some of your property, don't be. I have your address, and I'll send you the money for the dress when I'm settled in where I'm going.''

She started to walk away from him, but he blocked her exit with his arm. "And just where might that be?'' he asked, although he already had a good idea of her destination.

"That is none of your business. Now, get out of my way.''

"If you're planning to go to Cape de Rive, then it most definitely *is* my business,'' he declared.

"Oh? And why is that?''

"Consider this: You are returning to a town where you will most certainly be apprehended immediately and convicted of murder, a town from which I helped you escape just a few hours ago, and Captain Cruthers will no doubt remember the 'mystery woman' in my stateroom. Add to that the fact that you're carrying a valise with my initials and address engraved on the latch, and you're wearing a gown with my family's name sewn on the label. I think all of this makes your next *breath* my business, not to mention your travel plans!''

Anna's eyes ignited with fury. "You and your high-handed

spouting of facts! I'm getting darned tired of your logic all the time.''

Philip smiled indulgently even though he could tell it only fired her anger. "Isn't it only *logical* that I wouldn't want my own neck stretched along with yours from a gallows, Miss Connolly?"

"All right," she consented reluctantly. "I guess it was rather shortsighted of me to take your things."

"Shortsighted? I think a better word would be criminal, or perhaps witless."

"I was desperate. I had no intention of involving you." Dropping the valise to the ground, she opened it up and removed her new clothing from inside. She held the garments to her chest. "Here," she said, scooting the empty case at Philip with her toe, "you can have it back, and as soon as I find a place to change, you can have this dress as well."

He looked at the items in Anna's arm. "Where did you get the money for all those things?"

A guilty blush crept up her cheeks and she avoided his eyes. "I borrowed it . . . from a friend."

"I see. Then you won't mind if a friend asks you if that bump on your head destroyed your ability to think like a rational human being, because what you are about to do is insane. You can't go back there, Anna."

She stared defiantly at him and stomped her foot in frustration. "Why do you care, Mr. Brichard? Don't you have a pleasant little life somewhere that you're going back to? Can't you just forget about mine?"

His eyes remained locked with hers as he considered the various implications of her most appropriate questions. Why was he so concerned about her? Why had her problems become so important to him? He managed a little half-grin as he said, "No, I guess I can't. I can't go back to my pleasant little life knowing that you are making such a big mistake with yours." He wrapped his hands around her arms demanding her full attention. "I believe your story, Anna; otherwise I wouldn't have helped you so far. Now you've got to trust me. If I let you go now, you won't stand a chance in Cape de Rive."

"If you 'let me go'?" she echoed angrily. "How can you not? It's not up to you to make decisions for me, and, besides, can't you see that I would only complicate your life? You could end up being arrested for your part in my escape. Is that what you want?"

"I'll take my chances."

After a long moment, Anna exhaled a pent-up breath and relaxed in his grasp. Philip released his hold on her, believing that she was at last being reasonable. They remained staring at each other, separated by just a few inches, as three loud clangs from the ship's bell rang through town.

"Let's go, Anna," Philip said. "There isn't much time. I'll take you to New Orleans with me, and then we'll figure out what to do."

She looked at his face, the bundle of clothes in her arms, and finally the entrance of the alleyway. Philip could see the wheels of decision-making churning in her eyes.

"You don't understand," she said at last. "I've got to go back. My whole life is still there by that lake, all our things ... and Laura's." A choking sob forced her to stop and take a long breath. "And Irish, our horse. I've got to go back. If I don't, I'm afraid that I won't be able to remember all the things I need to about Mick Connolly, just like I can barely remember the little things about the others, and I can't let that happen."

Tears began to roll down her cheeks and she trembled. Philip reached out his hands tentatively. He was used to the independent woman, the one who fought back despite her pain, but the girl before him now was vulnerable and afraid and mourning a loss that had left her hollow inside. And Philip was not at all sure how he could comfort her. But he did know that if he let her pursue this dangerous journey to reclaim what she'd lost, she could very well lose her life as well.

He placed his hands on her back and urged her gently to his chest. Slowly, hesitantly, she leaned into him, and the brim of Claudette's hat grazed his chest. Philip untied the ribbons at her chin and tossed the bonnet to the ground. Then he put his arms around her and she stepped into his embrace. She rested her cheek on his shirt, and her tears dampened his chest.

They remained that way until Anna's sobs became whimpers, and her shaking lessened. When he sensed she had stopped crying, he placed his finger under her chin and coaxed her to look up at him. But before she did, a sound at the entrance to the alley distracted them.

They turned to see a boy pounding a nail through a poster on the livery wall. Even though they were several yards away, Philip read the names Anna and Mick Connolly on the poster. There were also two crude likenesses of their faces. And worst of all, the poster proclaimed in bold figures that a five-thousand-dollar reward was being offered for their capture by Stuart Wilkes's widow.

The bell on the *Duchess of Orleans* sounded again as Philip indicated the poster with a nod in its direction. "Look there, Anna. If nothing else convinces you, then that should. Come with me to New Orleans. My brother is a lawyer. I know he can help you, and maybe I can get some of your things back."

The poster had been her undoing, and Philip sensed the fight ebbing out of her. She acquiesced with a slight tilt of her head. He picked up the valise, put her things inside, and started to take her left elbow. He hesitated at the last minute, stepped around to her other side, and placed his hand on her right arm to lead her down the alley. She looked up at him, a question in her eyes.

"I've already been stuck once," he said. "If I'm not mistaken, I think my cravat pin is in your other sleeve, and I feel safer on this side."

"Oh, dear." She closed her eyes as her cheeks flamed pink. "I . . . I . . ."

"I know . . . you were going to mail it to me."

That evening, Philip went to the salon to play cards while Anna promised to remain in the cabin. She was so exhausted she wouldn't have argued even if she had wanted to. But she didn't. She slid between the clean, white sheets and fell asleep almost instantly. And when she awoke in the morning, she found a tray of muffins and cheese on the desk. She munched on her breakfast, gazing quietly at Philip who slept soundly on a pallet he had made for himself on the floor.

While Anna waited for him to awaken, she stared out the window while the *Duchess of Orleans,* known more for opulent luxury than for speed, steamed south on the river at a leisurely pace. She knew their next stop was St. Louis, the town she had been born in, though she hadn't been there since she was a child. In fact, the last view she'd had of St. Louis was from the seat of Mick Connolly's wagon after he picked her up at Miss Brockman's Home for Girls.

She might have been apprehensive about her return to the city where her parents had died and she had spent long months waiting to be rescued from Miss Brockman's orphanage, but that was not the case. She listened to Philip's steady breathing and suddenly realized that she was experiencing a rather pleasant sensation, one which she had doubted she would ever know again. She was actually feeling hopeful. For the first time since her ordeal in Cape de Rive, Anna felt she might actually have a future, and she owed this incredibly satisfying conclusion to Philip Brichard.

She looked over at him as he moved in his sleep. His arm reached out from under the coverlet and extended along the floor. The tendons of his lower arm stretched and released as he flexed his fingers. She remembered how that arm had felt when it circled her back and held her to his chest, how that hand had stroked her hair. And she remembered how his soothing words had comforted her.

And what had she done for him? Involved him in her escape, stolen his belongings, and had at the same time been generally unpleasant and demanding. Anna wished there were some way she could repay his kindnesses and convince him she wasn't the harridan he must believe her to be. But what she really wanted, she decided as a totally unexpected thought came to her mind, was for Philip Brichard to like her!

All at once, Anna thought of a small way to repay her benefactor. She decided to repair the damage she had done to Claudette Brichard's new dress. She had ripped the sash from the waistband and had no doubt stretched the gown's seams to near tearing. If she couldn't find a needle and thread, then she would ask Philip to get her one in St. Louis. She went to the wardrobe to get the dress.

When she opened the cupboard door, Anna slid the hangers to locate the copper-colored garment. Seeing the two sizes of clothes hanging side by side, she became curious as to the name on the labels of the smaller dresses. She chose one and examined the neckline. The designer label was written in the same fine script that Anna had seen on Claudette's dress, but this one said, "Especially made for Madame Monique Brichard."

At first Anna simply shrugged and pushed the dress aside, but as her mind interpreted the obvious meaning on the label, she pulled the gown back and stared at the name again. "*Madame* Brichard!" she whispered hoarsely. "He's married!" The pieces of the puzzle that made up Philip Brichard suddenly fell into place. She remembered his reference to the mysterious Claudette as a fifteen-year-old tomboy. "She must be his daughter," Anna concluded miserably.

She walked away from the cabinet and sank onto the desk chair. No wonder he could so easily make up a story for Captain Cruthers about a married woman coming to his stateroom, Anna thought. He was a philandering spouse himself, so marital indiscretions meant nothing to him. He had even bragged to Anna about his noble principles being compromised many times. While her anger at Philip Brichard flared anew, it was the disappointment she felt that gripped her even more, and she hated herself for feeling it. And to think that just minutes ago she had actually cared if he liked her!

Philip's desire to keep Anna on the *Duchess of Orleans* suddenly became very clear to her. Of course he didn't want her to return to Cape de Rive. He had a wife and daughter to protect from his scandalous reputation and ill-advised decision to help a murderess. He as much as told her so when he reminded her that she was risking his family name if she returned to the lake with his belongings.

So why was he taking her all the way to New Orleans? Anna questioned his motives. There was a chance he truly meant it when he said he would help her and take her to his brother.

Philip had, after all, shown her he was capable of being kind, and he admitted that he believed her story. It was entirely possible that he wasn't a total cad. He could keep her from ever seeing his home or family, and at the same time, if she were lucky, he might actually assist her in proving her innocence.

If that was his plan, Anna would be a fool not to accept any help he chose to give her. What did she have to lose? St. Louis was certainly too far from Cape de Rive for her to consider going back now. If she were to have any future at all, she had to depend on Philip Brichard for the next few days at least, and she would have to make the best of it.

As Anna made this decision, Philip mumbled and squinted his eyes. She looked at him again in the brief moment before he awakened fully, and she experienced an unexpected disappointment that his tenderness toward her was nothing more than a brief moment of concern for a downtrodden, lonely girl.

She mentally scolded herself for having indulged in useless daydreams about Philip Brichard. Mick had been right about him. He probably was a "high-falutin' blue blood," and she was the niece of a peddler. She dismissed all thoughts of mending Claudette's dress. It no longer seemed important for Philip to like her; it only mattered that he didn't *dis*like her enough to go back on his promise.

CHAPTER SIX

"You want to take me into St. Louis?" Considering the fact that she ought to be hiding from crowds, not joining them, Anna found the idea preposterous. She focused on Philip's back as he shaved.

It was nearly noon and he had been up for almost an hour. In that time, he had washed and was dressed, except for his shirt. A towel was slung over his shoulder, and he wiped his straight razor on the end before looking at Anna from the mirror. "Yes, I do. Why? Don't you want to go?"

She most definitely wanted to go. She had been staring out the window of the stateroom since they had docked over an hour before. The harbor was alive with activity, and all of it beckoned to her. There were dozens of vibrantly decorated booths in a bustling dockside marketplace. She could smell gingerbread cakes and wharf pies and sizzling barbecued ribs. She heard the vendors' voices ring out in a colorful medley of the streets as they offered their wares to passengers of the *Duchess of Orleans* coming down the gangway.

Anna could hardly believe this was the same town she had lived in as a child, but then her parents rarely brought her to the harbor, claiming that too many unsavory characters dwelled around the riverbank. They didn't look unsavory to Anna this day, for over the years she had learned a new respect for a man who peddled his goods, and she longed to be among them. "Of course I want to go," she answered honestly, "but do you think it's wise? What about the posters?"

"I don't think it's safe to go into the market down there," Philip said, "but where we're going, the buildings are not likely to be papered with wanted posters, and the lady I want you to meet will not even have heard of Stuart Wilkes or care that he was sent to an early grave."

"What lady is that?"

"It's a surprise for now" was all he said as he thrust his arms into the sleeves of a starched white shirt and fastened the buttons. He covered the shirt with a handsome brown vest interwoven with fine gold threads. "Why don't you get dressed while I walk around the deck. As I recall, you like your privacy. I'll be back to get you in a half hour."

Philip looked splendid in tan trousers that hugged his muscular thighs and tapered into his midcalf leather boots. He left the collar of his shirt open, and the small ruffles at the yoke opened over the vest and revealed a few dark hairs on his chest. She nodded to show her agreement with his plan, and he retrieved a brown jacket from the wardrobe. It fit his waist snugly before flaring slightly at his hips.

For a brief instant, Anna imagined herself walking arm in arm with the dashing Philip Brichard down a quiet, tree-lined St. Louis avenue, but she quickly dispelled such a vision from her mind.

As long as there were wanted posters of Mick and Anna Connolly being passed around the river towns, and since Philip was married, she was not entitled to dwell on such fantasies. She told herself the only reason she accepted Philip's invitation was because it would do her good to be away from the confining cabin and out in the sunshine on a warm, spring afternoon.

Nevertheless, when Philip had gone, Anna took a hairbrush, the one extravagance she had purchased at the Hannibal Emporium, and brushed her hair until it gleamed. Then she looked at the two simple, inexpensive dresses she had purchased and tried to decide which one would do for the outing. But since she had bought them because they were practical for a difficult trip to Cape de Rive, she knew that neither of them seemed appropriate for an afternoon in St. Louis with an elegantly dressed gentleman.

Don't be a fool, Anna, she berated herself silently. *After all, you're going into town with a married man who shouldn't be looking at you anyway. He couldn't possibly care what clothes you wear or how you fix your hair!* But she couldn't forget the feel of Philip's arms around her at the Hannibal livery or the way his intense gaze had lingered above the bodice of the ill-fitting copper dress.

"Stop it, Anna!" she said aloud. "You'll remember also that in spite of what you wanted to believe, he said you looked ridiculous in that gown." She grabbed one of the dresses without any further consideration. It was a plain cotton frock with a round neck and elbow-length sleeves and a full skirt printed all over with dainty blue cornflowers. It was not nearly the quality of Claudette's gown or even some of her own dresses left in the wagon at Cape de Rive, but it fit nicely, and did not deserve to be termed ridiculous.

When Philip returned to the cabin, he knocked before opening the door. At Anna's invitation, he entered. She stood in front of the window with the shutters open to admit the sunshine. The natural light outlined her figure like a soft halo starting at the top of her golden hair and ending at the bottom of the rippling skirt that just grazed the toes of her shoes. Her hands were folded at her waist, and she gave Philip a nervous little smile that made him realize he was making no attempt to hide his obvious approval of her appearance. She smoothed her skirt and said simply, "This will have to do."

Philip Brichard, who had escorted hundreds of ladies in all manner of fashionable dress, was struck speechless as he gazed upon the remarkably lovely creature Anna had become. True, he had seen her at her worst, with her hair in tangles and her body sore and bruised. And he had seen her when she was at a disadvantage in a dress much too small, with her heavy hair bound by a cumbersome thick ribbon. But now she looked more like she had when he first noticed her in the soft amber footlights of the River Flats Opera House stage. It was this Anna, the beguilingly innocent yet deceptively alluring woman who had demanded his guarded attention that night and had taken his breath away, just as she was doing now.

Philip leaned against the closed door and folded his arms over his chest. "You are incredibly lovely, Anna, do you know that?" he said.

She looked down the length of her body and frowned. "This seems so plain, not at all like the beautiful gowns in the wardrobe." She met his gaze and waited for him to speak.

Did she want his approval? Did it matter to her at all? Surely she knew his appraisal of her was intense and thorough. Her response was a blush that said she recognized her grooming had brought about a pleasurable reaction. Any man would have thought she was lovely, and any woman would have blushed at such a forthright appraisal as Philip's.

"Almost any woman could look lovely in those gowns," he said, "but you make a little blue flower on a simple country dress look as grand as the fleur de lis on a royal robe."

A warmth crept up Anna's neck to her cheeks, partly because the smoldering gray of Philip's eyes told her he meant every word of his compliment and partly because a modest little voice inside told her she had made a mistake by letting their conversation lead to such personal flattery.

"I'm glad you like it," she said as indifferently as she could. "Anyway, I'm sure it cost you much less than those gowns in the cupboard." She thought that reminding him of his wife's dresses in his wardrobe would create a more suitable, impersonal feeling between them and perhaps even urge him to tell her about his family.

Instead, he chuckled softly and replied, "Maybe so, but whatever the cost, I consider it money well spent. Now, may I take you to lunch?" She nodded, and he handed her the large bonnet she had worn the day before. "Just until we're out of the marketplace," he said. "We don't want to take any chances."

As soon as they walked over the gangway to the busy market square, Philip hired a towncoach to take them across the levee to the business district of St. Louis. When she had settled into the coach, Anna immediately removed the awkward bonnet and looked out the window of the partially enclosed cab to watch the bustling energy of St. Louis.

Soon they were beyond the multi-storied office buildings and had entered a quieter, more refined area of distinctive shops and restaurants. Philip instructed the driver to pull up to a charmingly decorated building with the name Chez Georges printed in black script on each of its front windows. When they exited the carriage, Philip leaned up to the driver to give instructions. The man nodded and touched his fingers to the brim of his top hat before driving away.

Anna hardly noticed the carriage leaving since her eyes were riveted on the elegant appointments of the exterior of the restaurant. Elaborate moldings divided each of the three floors of the building. An intricately carved cornice framed the top of the wide double entrance where a doorman in formal black-and-gold livery waited for them to enter. Each window was bordered with glossy black shutters, looking eloquently simple next to the delicate lace curtains at each windowpane. The top floor of the restaurant was as festive as a top-of-the-cake decoration with a row of dormer windows and an enchanting weather vane sitting in whimsical attention on the peaked roof, its variety of farm animals turning lazily in the breeze.

"I hope you're hungry," Philip said, taking her arm. "Chez Georges has the best French cuisine in the city."

When they entered the restaurant, Anna knew Philip had been right about this visit to St. Louis. There would be no wanted posters on the walls of the elegant Chez Georges.

After a delicious lunch, Philip and Anna strolled down one short block to a section of shops, and he stopped in front of one that announced its ownership with a simple swinging sign over the door, which said, "Lilly's."

"I'm going to leave you in Lilly's capable hands," he said, opening the door and allowing Anna to precede him inside. "I hope you'll forgive me, but I examined your purchases from yesterday, and it occurred to me that you might still be missing several important items." Anna gave him a puzzled look and Philip shrugged his shoulders innocently. "I have to admit that over the years, I have learned a good deal about women's clothing and accessories . . ."

I'll just bet you have! she thought.

". . . but I've always found the ladies at Lilly's to be experts on the subject."

He couldn't have brought me to the same shop where his wife and daughter buy their clothes! Anna thought, her insides roiling. If that proved to be, she could not believe Philip's nerve. He must have coerced the shop owner into keeping silent about any "friends" he might bring to her establishment. Well, Anna wasn't about to be silent. If she was going to endure an embarrassing afternoon at his wife's clothiers, then she was going to get some answers about Philip Brichard!

A tinkling brass bell just inside the door had no sooner announced Philip and Anna's arrival than an elegantly attired matron came out of a back room and approached Philip. Her arms were extended in welcome. She was a tall, middle-aged woman with perfectly coifed gray hair and expertly applied coloring subtly shading her eyes and cheeks. A pair of small wire glasses attached to a gold chain bounced against her ample bosom as she crossed the shop, a bright, wide smile on her face.

"Ah, Philip, it's wonderful to see you," she gushed as she raised slightly on her toes to plant a kiss on his cheek. "Monique and Claudette are not with you," she said, glancing over his shoulder.

"No, not this time, Lilly," Philip said, returning her smile.

The woman stepped back and regarded Anna with kind eyes. "But who is this lovely creature?" she asked. She took Anna's hand in both of hers.

"I'd like you to meet a good friend of mine. This is Anna. Anna . . . Jones. I met her on the *Duchess of Orleans* after all her belongings had been stolen."

"Stolen! Good heavens!" Lilly commiserated. "From the *Duchess of Orleans?* Who could imagine such a thing?"

"We assume it happened when we were docked," Philip said, "and a local thief crept aboard and made off with Miss Jones's trunk. I've brought her here hoping you will help her replace some of the things she lost."

"You poor dear," Lilly said, clucking at Anna with genuine concern. "You are lucky to have such a handsome and generous knight in armor at your service."

"Quite lucky indeed," Anna said with as much sincerity as she could manage, thankful that at least he hadn't led the woman to believe she was his mistress!

"I'll leave you ladies to your fitting and pinning," Philip said. "And, Lilly, don't forget all those little . . ." He maneuvered his hands into several odd shapes, trying to delicately express himself, ". . . you know, dainty things. And brushes and things for her hair." He avoided Lilly's amused gaze and looked out the window where the carriage that had taken them to lunch was just pulling up at the curb. "I've got to attend to some errands, but I'll be back in a couple of hours."

"Go, then," Lilly said, shooing him out the door. "We can manage just fine without you."

Philip went out to the street, but called back over his shoulder to the ladies watching from the window, "And night clothes. I'm sure she needs those as well."

While Anna stood dumbstruck at the magnitude of Philip's order, Lilly waved gaily at him with dainty wiggling fingers. The coach pulled away and she sighed, "Such a dear man he is. If only I were twenty . . . ten years younger!"

Then Lilly whisked Anna off to a back dressing room as she shouted instructions to her assistant. "Claire! Claire! Come quickly and brings lots of gowns in size . . . Oh, dear," she hesitated, appraising Anna. "You are a thin little thing about the hips, but certainly full enough up top, and so tall. Just bring one of everything. We haven't much time."

Anna was pinched and tucked and gathered and hemmed. All the while the two women helping her chattered incessantly about a variety of topics, most of which were interrupted with, ''Ooo's'' and ''Ahh's'' and ''That won't do's.'' Each garment was relegated to one of three stacks: a ''definite,'' a ''possible,'' or a ''back to the shop.''

Anna found their company so congenial that she was beginning to enjoy the afternoon despite the tiresome onslaught of gowns. She decided to test the women's knowledge of the Brichard family to see just how much she could find out.

''So how well do you know Madame Brichard?'' Anna asked casually after Lilly made another complimentary comment about Philip.

''Very well, dear, very well,'' Lilly stated proudly as if it were a mark of honor to know Philip's wife. ''She is such a fine lady, a perfect combination of grace and dignity. And she is one of the kindest women I have ever known. She brightens up my shop whenever she comes in the door.''

''It's no wonder, then, that Philip loves her so,'' Anna said, continuing her fishing expedition.

''That would be understating his affections, my dear. I could easily say that Philip *adores* Monique. And why not? The woman is an angel. He treats her like she was made of French crystal, but don't let that fool you. Monique Brichard is made of much stronger stuff.''

''And the daughter, Claudette, you know her also?''

''Of course. Monique and Claudette are practically inseparable. The girl promises to be a great beauty like her mother.''

''Are there any other children?'' Anna asked.

''You don't know of Henri?''

Anna shook her head. Disappointment inexplicably washed over her again at the mention of yet another limb of Philip Brichard's family tree.

''He's a fine young man. Monique is very proud of him. She is fiercely loyal to her children. She would stand and fight for them even in the face of the strongest enemies; in fact, once she almost had to do exactly that!''

Anna started to believe she had misjudged Philip. She was

convinced that Monique Brichard was a beautiful, kind woman, a loving wife and mother. Perhaps Philip did not stray from their bed as he had hinted. Perhaps his bragging about his supposed exploits had been just that . . . reckless bravado. Why would any man want to sample other pleasures when he had such a virtuous and adoring wife at home?

She decided to ask one more question that might settle the issue of Philip's infidelity once and for all. "And how does Madame Brichard feel about Philip's business trips? He must be gone from home for weeks at a time."

"Months sometimes," Lilly answered. "You know he is a trader, don't you, Miss Jones?"

"Well, he told me he was."

"Don't let him be too modest. Monsieur Brichard is a shipping magnate. He commands a fleet of over a half-dozen ships that sail regularly from New Orleans to the East Coast and the Caribbean. Often he captains the vessels himself."

"I didn't realize . . ."

Lilly nodded with an air of superiority that comes with having knowledge that someone else does not. "But I didn't answer your question. I'm sure Monique misses him, but she never has kept a tight rein on Philip. You've met him . . . you must know that to do so would be a mistake, an utterly fruitless endeavor. A man like Philip needs the freedom of the sea. He needs to roam, and Monique understands that, as do the rest of the Brichards.

"Besides, Monique's life is full. She has Claudette and Henri, and they are always at her side." Lilly's eyes sparkled with amusement as she added, "But when Philip is home, what happy times they must have!

"There!" Lilly exclaimed, setting her needle and thread on a tray by her knees. "That about does it. Do you like this gown, Miss Jones?"

"It's lovely," Anna said absently, realizing that she truly didn't understand Philip any more now than she had before she came into the shop. But she did understand Monique Brichard, and if what Lilly told her was true, and Anna believed it was, then she felt nothing but admiration for Philip's patient, almost saintly wife.

"Good, let's decide then from among these things." Lilly pointed to a mound of dresses that would have kept Anna clothed for the rest of her life. "Or do you want them all?"

"Certainly not!" Anna declared. "Two or three are more than enough."

They compromised on five gowns, two night ensembles, the necessary undergarments, two hats, a pair of shoes, and several grooming implements, all of which were finer and more elegant than anything Anna had ever had in her life. She watched Lilly and Claire pack the garments in boxes, all the while wondering how she would ever repay Philip. But she decided then and there that she would somehow give him back every cent he spent on her.

One of the gowns was an especially beautiful traveling dress made of forest-green brocade and trimmed with shimmering gold braid on the shoulders, buttons, and cuffs. When Lilly took special care with the fashionable bustle, wrapping tissue around the gathers so gently, Anna recalled one of the last conversations she'd had with Mick. He had promised to buy her lovely gowns with bustles, and hats with great white feathers.

If everything had gone as she and Mick had planned, Anna would have worn one of those gowns to Boston when she knocked on the door of Ophelia Sullivan's home and introduced herself as Kathleen and Tom Connolly's daughter. And Ophelia would have opened her arms to the granddaughter she had never known and welcomed her into the Sullivan's Beacon Hill world.

Mick would have stayed with her until she was happy and settled in the life that he said was her birthright. It was all Anna could do to keep fresh tears from falling down her cheeks as she thought bitterly, *Oh, Uncle Mick, if only . . .*

And then, suddenly, she knew what she had to do, what course of action made the most sense for her life, because it was what Mick had wanted for her. But once again her plans were dependent on Philip Brichard's willingness to help. He had ships, and Anna sorely needed one to accomplish Mick Connolly's dream for her.

Somehow, someway, she would convince Philip to let her board one of his ships bound for Boston where her future would be secure, and her debts to him settled. *I hope you meant it, Ophelia, when you said you wanted me,* Anna thought, *because you are my last hope. I just pray my troubles aren't more than you bargained for.*

The last of his errands completed, Philip left the office of St. Louis's most respected detective agency where he had given explicit instructions and a great deal of money for an investigator to accomplish a nearly impossible feat. He had been told to locate one chestnut mare named Irish and the contents of a peddler's wagon left abandoned by the side of a lake two miles outside of Cape de Rive, Illinois. The investigator would, of course, not utter a word about who had hired him and proceed with the search as discreetly as possible.

Once the animal and the items were procured, at any cost, they were to be sent immediately to the plantation at Frenchman's Point, Louisiana. And, as expected, the investigator agreed to Philip's proposal, no questions asked.

When Philip returned to pick up Anna at Lilly's, he did not seem in the least surprised by the number of packages sitting by the door. In fact, he pretended to scout around the shop looking for more. "Is this all there is?" he asked teasingly. "You didn't forget anything? I think I've gotten off far too easily this time."

"Miss Jones has chosen some lovely things," Lilly said, "and she is not in the least extravagant. I hope you will get a chance to see her in all of her new wardrobe."

"I know I would enjoy seeing her in *some* of them for sure," Philip responded with a suggestive twinkle in his eye that made Lilly chuckle, Claire blush, and Anna scowl. Undaunted, Philip went directly to the counter where Lilly was seated and asked for his bill. He put a few extra bank notes in Lilly's hand and pointed to a bottle of French perfume in the glass counter. "Let me have two of those as well, Lilly. It's my mother's favorite fragrance, and I think Anna will like it also."

It took all of Anna's willpower to keep from suggesting that he should buy a gift for his wife as well. But she reminded herself that since she had decided to ask Philip to provide passage for her to Boston, it would be wise to hold her tongue. When the packages had been loaded in the carriage, Philip escorted Anna to the door of the shop.

"Enjoy your new things, Miss Jones!" Lilly called as they left. "I hope your belongings are returned to you, but unfortunately that is not likely to happen."

"You're probably right," Anna agreed. "Thank you for all your help."

As soon as they were in the carriage, Philip tapped the back of the driver's seat and called out, "La Place de Louis, William, if you please." Then he settled comfortably back against the plush seats and rested an ankle on his opposite knee. He gave Anna a lazy grin. "I thought you might have worn one of the new dresses," he said, "but I don't see how you could look any lovelier than you do in that one."

Anna leveled her gaze on the driver's seat of the carriage. "I suppose I should thank you for what you did today," she said. "Though it was quite nice, you shouldn't have done it. There really was no need."

"I disagree, Anna. There was most definitely need, but there was no ulterior motive if that's what you're concerned about."

"Certainly not!" she said, looking back at him and noting the suggestive lift at the corners of his mouth. "I never for a moment thought . . ."

"Not for a moment?" he asked challengingly as he brushed an imaginary speck of dirt off his boot.

"No. Not for a moment. We both know that nothing . . . romantic could ever happen between us."

His eyebrows raised in surprise and he regarded her with a teasing glint in his eyes. "Naturally, we both know that. You won't get the wrong idea then when I tell you that we're staying in a hotel tonight."

Her jaw dropped open, and she gave him a look of such surprise and affront that there could have been no doubt of her opinion of his plan.

"No, of course you won't," he continued, unaffected by her stern gaze. "We've been staying in even closer proximity for days now without being in the least attracted to one another, isn't that right?"

"Yes, that's right," she quickly agreed, "but why are we staying in a hotel? What if the boat leaves?"

"It won't. It always stays in St. Louis overnight to give businessmen and shoppers a chance to visit the city. We'll be back on board in the morning. You're not nervous about this, are you?" Philip struggled to hide a smile. "Because if you are, I should tell you . . ."

He never finished his sentence because the coach driver pulled the horses to a sudden stop, jolting Anna and Philip forward in their seat.

"What's going on, William?" Philip asked, grasping the back of the driver's bench.

"I'll be darned if I know, sir," the driver said from his position a foot above his passengers. "A couple of rough-looking types are causing a ruckus up the block. I can't tell exactly what they're doing, but they've stopped a few carriages and are only letting them go one at a time."

"Can't you go around?"

"No, sir. The street is much too congested here, but it shouldn't be too long. They're almost up to us. They're handing out a paper of some sort. It's got a picture on it."

Every joint and muscle in Anna's body tensed with alarm. "Philip, it couldn't be," she whispered urgently. They both leaned forward at the same time, and Anna choked back a terrified scream. "It's the one they call Jake! He worked for Stuart Wilkes." She could plainly see the paper Jake was passing out. It was the wanted poster offering Mrs. Wilkes's five-thousand-dollar reward.

Jake Finn and the one called Sam approached the front of the coach and demanded William's attention. If they found her on the busy thoroughfare, Anna knew she couldn't escape. She grabbed Philip's hand, and he acted quickly to conceal her identity.

"Well, my darling," he said loud enough for William to hear, "we might as well take advantage of this little interlude." In a sudden impulsive move, Philip pushed Anna into the tufted back of the coach seat and covered her body with his. "Kiss me, Anna, now!" he ordered.

She obeyed without thinking, for her fear was much greater than her instinct to resist. Philip's lips moved to hers and he pushed her further down on the seat. His legs straddled her and he shifted his head, deepening the kiss, at the same time keeping her face completely hidden.

Jake's gravelly voice filtered through the glass and canvas of the coach as he spoke to the driver. "My partner and I . . . we're looking for this woman. She's wanted for murder, and we're the ones gonna bring her to justice."

"And collect a neat five thousand dollars, I see," William said scornfully. "Well, I haven't seen her, so you'd best get out of my way."

Anna felt a warm rush of air on her face as Philip expelled a breath of relief. Like her, he must have counted on the fact that the driver would not be able to connect the woman he had driven around town with the crude likeness of Anna on the poster.

"Mind if we talk to your passengers?" Jake asked, leaning toward the cab.

"I certainly do mind!" William answered. "I've got a fine gentleman and lady in my coach, and I won't have them bothered by the likes of you two!"

A raucous laugh splintered the air as Jake exclaimed, "It looks like they're already bothered! If that's the way a gentleman behaves and he doesn't get his face walloped, I've a mind to buy myself a fine suit and get me a lady."

Keeping his head perfectly in place over Anna's, Philip raised his face just inches from hers, tossed a few bills onto the street by Jake's feet and shouted, "Go on then and get your suit and your own woman and let us be on our way!"

Then he did something that completely startled Anna, considering the gravity of the situation they were in. While Jake and Sam cackled and scrambled for their unexpected good fortune, Philip smiled at her, a large, broad, mischievous grin that broke through her fear and apprehension and brought a matching smile to her own lips. And even though Jake and Sam were walking away, Philip lowered his mouth to hers once more, taking her lips in a playful, teasing kiss that stifled an impetuous giggle.

Assuming that he was just making light of a desperate situation, Anna was unprepared for the mounting urgency of Philip's kiss. His tongue moved against the crease of her mouth, sliding along the soft contours, demanding and insistent. His fingers twisted through the hair at her nape and he caressed her neck. Then his hand slid around to her face, and he laid his palm gently on her cheek, while his thumb massaged the tender hollow at her temple.

Anna's arms crept around his shoulders. She abandoned all reason and gave in to the emotions fired by the wonderful, exciting things he was doing to her mouth. She had only been kissed a few times in her life, and these were merely awkward fumblings in the dark at county fairs by inexperienced farm boys. But at that moment, as she was being kissed in a carriage by Philip Brichard, she realized that she had never really been kissed before, because she never would have imagined that it could be like this.

She opened her mouth to his demanding thrusts and his tongue found its haven. He groaned as a tremor shook him, and at the same time, the carriage lurched forward, tossing them both against the soft squabs.

Philip raised his face and looked down at Anna through eyes dark with arousal. "I think we fooled them," he said, "but I don't think we can go on fooling ourselves."

The sound of his voice and the jostling of the carriage brought Anna back to a shattered reality, and she pushed against his chest. "Stop it, Philip!" She was now fully aware of what she had allowed to happen, perhaps what she had even *willed* to happen because of her foolish imaginings. "Don't say that. I don't want you to ever kiss me again!"

He sat up against the seat and regarded her with confused, still dark eyes.

"And I don't want to stay in any hotel with you," she continued, "especially if you expect . . ."

"I don't expect anything, Anna," he said, his voice chillingly calm. "I've had my suite booked in the hotel for weeks now since I knew I would be playing cards in the poker room tonight with some old friends. I only booked your suite adjacent to mine this afternoon so that you would not have to return to the *Duchess of Orleans* alone tonight. I thought it was the safest place for you to be since I had no intention of altering my plans for this evening . . . for anyone."

There was such a cold indifference in Philip's voice and such a granite set to his chin that Anna wilted into her corner of the coach seat in an effort to get as far away from him as possible. In the short time she had known him, Anna had experienced Philip's anger, his gentle teasing, even his tender caring, but she had never before seen this remote impassivity, and she found this side of Philip the most difficult to bear.

"I'm sorry," she said. "It must have sounded as though I were blaming you when, in fact, what happened just now was as much my fault as yours."

His eyes remained fixed forward as he said, "Isn't it odd, Anna, that you find a simple kiss something for which someone must take the blame rather than the credit?"

A simple kiss! Anna's heart was still pounding at the rush of emotions he awakened in her. She wondered how he could interpret what they had just done as "simple" when to her it was at the very least unforgettable, and it was this realization that troubled her deeply. "Even so," she managed to say, "you must admit that it should never have happened."

"If you want me to admit that, Anna, then I will, and I promise to behave with decorum and restraint whenever I'm around you."

She sat up straight and smoothed the bodice of her dress. When she risked a look at Philip out of the corner of her eye, she saw that he had been stealing a glance at her as well. As he leveled his gaze forward again, she said very softly, "Well, you don't have to make it sound as if it will be all that easy to do."

His lips turned up slightly at the corners, but he refused to look at her. "I didn't say it would be."

"Here you are, sir," the coach driver called over his shoulder, "La Place de Louis."

Anna looked out her window at the elegant facade of the multi-storied hotel. In the shimmering motes of afternoon sun, the impressive building looked as if it were fashioned of gold blocks. A red marquee ran the width of an elongated sidewalk where a doorman clad in red and gold waited to help her from the carriage.

Philip followed Anna out of the carriage and instructed the doorman to bring her packages to her room. Then, after stopping briefly at the registration desk, he escorted her up two flights of stairs and down a luxurious hallway to the last two doors on the floor. He opened the door to her suite and stepped aside as she entered.

Anna fully expected him to follow her into her room, giving her a chance to thank him for his generosity, but he didn't. He leaned against her doorframe, both of his feet planted firmly in the hallway. "Aren't you coming in?" she said. "It's all right." Her invitation sounded insincere and forced even to her own ears.

"I don't think so. My suite is right through there." He gestured to a dividing door with a gold doorknob and keyhole lock. "I was told the key is on the mantel. I quite understand if you feel the need to lock it."

"Don't be ridiculous . . . I wouldn't . . ."

"I'm sure you'll be safe here, Anna," he said. "I can't imagine that Jake and Sam would have the nerve to distribute posters at La Place. I'll be in my room for an hour or so, and then I'll be gone for the evening. I'll see that the dining room sends a menu up soon for you to select your dinner. And a red cap will bring up your clothes. Other than that, it would probably be wise not to answer your door. It must be hard for you to know just who you can trust."

Anna cringed inside at the ill-disguised commentary on her

insecurities with regard to Philip. Well, what did he expect? He was absolutely right. How was she to trust anyone, when Philip Brichard, married to the saintliest of women, had just spent hundreds of dollars on a wardrobe for Anna Connolly, and then taken her to a hotel. Trust, indeed!

"I'll say good night then, Anna," he concluded. "I'll knock on your door at first light tomorrow morning. We don't want to miss the *Duchess*." He pulled the door shut behind him, leaving her alone.

She heard him enter his own suite, and though she pressed her ear against the door that divided them, she could hear nothing. She assumed he was resting.

Her clothes arrived, and she opened all the packages again and admired the lovely things from Lilly's. But all the while, her gaze kept wandering to the door that separated her from Philip. This went on for about an hour until she heard his door open and close and the sound of his key in the lock, then his muffled footsteps on the carpeting as he passed her door.

CHAPTER SEVEN

When Philip left the card room of La Place de Louis at two-thirty A.M., he was enjoying the good-natured ribbing of his companions. He slipped his wallet, now ten thousand dollars fatter, into the pocket of his brown jacket.

"Do you need help carrying that to your room, Philip?" one man asked him.

"Can you lend me a quarter eagle for a cab ride home, Brichard?" another quipped as he patted Philip on the back.

Not one of those from the poker room noticed the trio of men who had been sitting for hours in the grand lobby. Though their suits were shabby and worn, the men were still dressed appropriately enough to avoid suspicion by hotel personnel. As soon as the three men ascertained who the winner was from among the players talking jovially outside the card room, they moved to the bottom of the stairs without drawing attention to themselves. Since they knew ahead of time the names of all the players, they were certain that their target was New Orleans shipper, Philip Brichard, and they knew as well that his room was at the end of the hall on the third floor.

After saying good night to his friends and promising to give all the money back at a later date, Philip trudged with a weary but satisfied step up two flights of stairs to his room. He blinked his blurry eyes to guide the key into the lock of his room.

As soon as he opened the door he was pushed inside. Burly arms grabbed his own and held them locked behind his back. He felt the first real sensation of pain when a beefy fist crashed into his stomach, leaving him gasping for air.

While Philip tried to extricate his arms from his captor, several more blows fell to his rib cage and abdomen, accompanied by a string of moans which he came to realize were his own. Finally he shook his head to clear away the cobwebs of weariness and pain and lashed out at his attackers. He kicked one of the men firmly in the stomach and the man reeled backward, swearing profusely.

A second man, however, barreled at Philip with both fists flying and hitting their target, leaving stinging welts next to Philip's eyes and upper lip. When he saw both men coming at him at once, Philip jerked himself free from the ironlike grip on his arms and met his circling combatants with a firm stance and fists poised for striking. If he was going down, and he supposed he was, he was going down fighting.

In the adjoining room, Anna had not been sleeping soundly, so she was easily awakened by the noise from Philip's suite. She covered her head with a pillow and attempted to go back to sleep, but the muffled sounds penetrated even that barrier, and at last her curiosity got the best of her. She went to the door separating her room from Philip's and listened.

She heard what sounded like the shuffling of feet and low groans, and her first thought was that Philip was entertaining a lady in his room. She backed away from the door, repulsed by what she assumed was Philip's infidelity to his saintly wife, but she also experienced a totally unwelcome and unexpected attack of jealousy that Philip could so easily forget her and move on to another conquest.

It was this latter emotion and the sudden loud crash of a piece of furniture hitting the floor that caused Anna to give in to temptation and peek through the keyhole into Philip's chamber.

What she saw horrified her as she witnessed the beating being inflicted on Philip by three assailants. Philip had been slammed up against a wall, but he was still battling his attackers. Anna knew, however, that he could not last much longer against such unfair odds, and she desperately sought a way to help him.

At the same time, the object of Anna's worry and concern recognized the grim reality that he would not win his fight with the three thugs. But he had convinced himself that if they did get his ten thousand dollars, they would have to take it from the body of an unconscious man, because there was no way he would give in to them while he was still able to do battle. And it gave him some satisfaction to know that while the odds were against him, he had at least caused serious damage to his opponents with a few well-placed punches and kicks.

Too dazed and weak to fight back with effectiveness, Philip slid down the wall and fought to hang on to the last vestiges of consciousness. A thick hand groped into the pocket of his jacket searching for his wallet. As his eyes began to droop, and he tasted his own blood, Philip knew it was over.

He almost slipped into blessed oblivion when the door between his and Anna's room burst open and she entered wearing a long white nightgown and robe. She stared wildly around the room and held her arms out in front of her face at eye level.

"Philip!" she called in a trembling voice. "Where are you? What's going on? Who's in this room?" She waved her arms in all directions as if she were feeling her way in utter darkness instead of pale moonlight.

Struggling to keep his eyes open and make some sense of the sudden new commotion around him, Philip squinted at Anna in confusion. He didn't know what she was trying to do, but the realization that she had entered the room enabled him to shake off the numbness which had nearly overtaken him. "Anna, get out of here!" he ordered in a loud tone. "Go back to your room and lock the door!"

She heard the coarse laughter from Philip's attackers and saw the looks of surprised amusement on their faces, and she knew that she, and not Philip, was suddenly the object of their attention.

All three of the men gawked at the image of the fragile, trembling creature coming slowly toward them, her arms criss-crossing in front of her as her blue eyes gazed vacantly into the room.

"Who are you? What are you doing to my brother?" she cried.

"She's blind as a bat," one of them said.

"Is this your protector, Mister New Orleans gentleman?" another laughed. He kicked at the lapel of Philip's coat with the toe of his boot.

"Philip, answer me," Anna pleaded as she neared the three men who stood over him. Out of the corner of her eye she could see that the skin around Philip's eyes was already turning black and blue, but she saw, too, that at least his eyes were open and he appeared alert. She counted on him being able to react quickly.

"Anna, go back!" he shouted once more as she came close enough for one of the men to reach for her outstretched hand. Just as he did, she turned both palms up, and with perfect aim, she emptied the contents of two bottles of fine French perfume into the faces of the two men nearest her.

Both men screamed in shock and pain as they gouged at their smarting eyes. Anna reached for a crockery pitcher on a nearby washstand and broke it over the head of one of the men, sending him sprawling onto the water-soaked carpet. The third man lunged for Anna, but he missed his target because Philip grabbed his ankle and jerked him to the floor with a bone-cracking jolt. The injured man cried out in pain.

The second man afflicted with the shower of perfume had crawled to the door and was clawing for the knob. Philip opened the door, and with a swift kick to the man's posterior sent him hurtling into the hallway. It was an easy matter for Philip to propel his two cohorts after him, and the last he saw of the three would-be thieves, they were nursing their wounds, cursing vehemently and hobbling toward the fire exit at the end of the hall.

When Philip closed the door, Anna was already hurrying

toward her room. "Wait a minute," he said. "Where are you going?"

"I'm going to put my dress on and go down to the front desk and report those criminals!" she said over her shoulder.

"Don't bother," Philip said weakly. "By the time the authorities get here, those villains will be a mile away and lost in the city."

"You can't just let them get away!"

"They already *are* away," Philip observed, leaning on one of the tall posters of his bed, "and thanks to you, without my ten thousand dollars!"

"Is that all you can think about? Ten thousand dollars! You could have been killed. We have to tell the police."

"We?" he repeated incredulously as he rested his head against the wooden post. "Anna, Anna . . . think this over. Do you really want a couple of constables up here talking to the notorious Anna Connolly about someone else's crime? Don't you think that would be rather . . . idiotic?"

She shot him a warning look to tell him she did not appreciate his choice of words, but she had to agree he was making a valid point. "I guess I didn't think about that."

He turned his head and looked at her with pain-clouded eyes that still held a glint of amusement. "I notice you didn't think before wasting forty dollars worth of Lilly's best French perfume, either!"

At the teasing in his voice, Anna flashed him a self-satisfied smirk. "That's the best those rotters have smelled in years!"

Chuckling weakly, Philip said, "You were crazy to come in here, you know that don't you? But it was an inspired performance, Miss Anna Rose, truly inspired, and I am forever in your . . ." He never finished, because his hands slipped slowly down the bedpost as his knees buckled under him. He fell unconscious by the foot of the bed.

"Philip!" Anna rushed to his side. "Oh, my God, what do I do now?" She looked down at his prone form, then ran to the bed and grabbed a pillow which she slid under his head. She struggled to get his jacket off and loosened the buttons of his shirt. "Wake up, wake up, please, Philip," she repeated over and over while fanning her hand in front of his face.

When he didn't respond, she ran into her room for her own pitcher of water. Then she took a washcloth and began sponging Philip's face and neck. She smoothed the hair away from his temples and forehead and gently stroked his brow, eyes, and cheeks. She brought the cloth down around his jaw and swollen lips. She almost cried when she saw the cuts around that wonderfully soft, sensitive mouth, and she wiped away the blood that had begun clotting at the corners.

"Don't die, Philip, please don't die," she whispered urgently. "I've been so awful to you, I know I have, and I'm sorry. That thing that happened between us in the carriage, I'm sorry I got so angry. You were just trying to help me. I know you didn't mean anything by it. I've misjudged you all along. Please don't die, Philip, so I can tell you all this."

Despite his almost overwhelming desire to take Anna in his arms right there and then, Philip remained completely still during her declaration. He had begun to pull himself up from a groggy semiconsciousness when she first applied the cloth to his face, but he had kept his eyes closed, savoring the feel of her soft hands tending his wounds.

She was repeating his name over and over again, and it was as if he were hearing it for the first time. He marveled at the sound of his name coming from her lips.

"Please wake up, Philip," she pleaded. She pulled his shirt loose from his trousers and opened it wide at the yoke, then wiped the cloth down his neck and chest. She pressed her cheek against his forehead and laid her palm over his heart, feeling the rise and fall of his chest as he breathed. "Can you hear me, Philip? Tell me you're not going to die."

His fingers wrapped around her wrist and pulled her hand up from his chest. Anna jerked her head from his forehead and her startled gaze locked with intense gray eyes that held not pain but hunger ... sweet, tormented longing so compelling that she couldn't look away ... could not, in fact, even raise her face further from his.

"Dying is the absolute *last* thing on my mind right now, Anna," he said huskily.

He released her wrist and cupped his hand around the back of her head, bringing her mouth the last few inches to his. He instantly ignited a fire in both of them that had started as a warm glow of concern and was kindled into a flame of desire the instant their lips touched. He moved his head under hers, deepening the kiss as he heated their passion. He reached under Anna's robe and stroked her back with a seductive rhythm that had her squirming to get closer to him.

His skilled hands tingled the nerve endings up and down her spine. She leaned into him, pressing her weight ever so carefully and gently onto his body, needing to be near him, yet still mindful of his injuries. She glided her hand over his chest to the muscled roundness of his shoulder and the taut tendons of his upper arm.

He answered with his own explorations as his hand slipped around to her side where he rested his fingers against the soft swell of a breast, his thumb teasingly near her nipple. A pulsing heatwave rippled through Anna and centered itself under Philip's hand. His thumb moved higher until it had found its mark, circling and tempting.

And his lips continued their magic, moving sensuously under Anna's, his tongue probing and thrusting against the yielding line of her mouth. She opened her lips to him and he explored the softness beckoning him, moving his tongue over her teeth and into the sweet dark recesses beyond. He moved his hands to her shoulders and pushed down the silken fabric of her robe. It slipped slowly down her arms, allowing his hands access to her bare skin.

He returned to her breast, laying his hand above the low bodice of her nightgown and slipping his fingers inside to cup the fullness now hidden by only one thin layer of material. Anna moaned softly when Philip's hand covered her breast and his finger and thumb claimed her nipple, sending a rush of awakening passion through her body.

Lost in the spell of his hands and lips, Anna's desire soared with the pounding of her heart and the tantalizing of her senses.

Her hunger rose to meet and satisfy Philip's, and she felt his need almost as strongly as her own.

A low, throaty sound came from Philip's throat. Anna sat up, certain she'd caused him pain. "I've hurt you," she said. "I'm so sorry."

"No, no, you haven't." He tried to pull her back.

A warning signal sounded in Anna's mind and dimmed the passion of the past few minutes. She concentrated on drawing a calming breath and looked down into the smoldering flame in his eyes. "Philip, don't," she said. "You know this isn't right."

"This *is* right, Anna," he responded hoarsely. "Surely you can feel it."

She turned away from him, and Philip reached for her hand. "What is it?" he asked. "What's wrong?"

His innocent charade only added to her frustration. She pulled her hand away and cried out, "I saw the labels on the dresses, Philip. I talked to Lilly. I know you are married, and Monique Brichard is your wife!"

"What?" He bolted forward and pinned a startled glare on her face.

"There's no point denying it. Lilly told me what a kind and loving woman Monique is, what a wonderful mother. Any man would be lucky to be her husband."

"I quite agree," Philip stated as a smug little smile curled the lips which had just worked magic with hers. "And so would my father, rest his soul. He *was* the man lucky enough to be her husband. I was only lucky enough to be her son." The grin he had been holding back suddenly spread across his face. "Monique Brichard is everything Lilly told you, Anna, and I do adore her, but she is my mother, not my wife."

"But that can't be." Anna's thoughts raced back to the conversation in Lilly's shop. "Lilly said there is a daughter . . ."

"My sister, Claudette," Philip said, matter-of-factly.

"And a son, Henri . . ."

"My brother, the attorney. Remember, I told you about him?"

"And Lilly praised Monique for her wisdom in allowing you your freedom and not demanding much of your time. And Lilly said Monique is fiercely loyal to you . . ."

"She is a good mother, Anna," he said, his grin still taunting her. "When we get to New Orleans and you meet her, I hope you will see that all the praise is well deserved."

Anna stood up, walked to a window and looked down at the street below. She was too humiliated to face Philip's teasing gaze. Of course, now that she thought about it, she realized that Lilly hadn't actually said in so many words that Monique was Philip's wife. Anna had simple inferred it because that was what she had set out to believe. She had never felt more foolish than she did at this moment.

"She also forgives the passionate excesses she suspects are in my life and loves me in spite of them," Philip added. He seemed completely unaware of her mortification. "And since I believe we were in the throes of possibly the most passionate encounter I can remember in a long time, why don't you come back here so we can resume where we left off? You don't need to concern yourself with Monique Brichard any longer."

Being relegated to the most recent of Philip Brichard's long list of lovers did nothing to lighten Anna's mood. In fact, her humiliation was fast turning to hurt and anger as she whirled around to face him. In her haughtiest voice, she said, "I don't think so, Philip. I'm really rather tired. I apologize for jumping to what was a completely inappropriate conclusion."

Just please don't open your arms to me again, she pleaded silently, knowing that she would not be able to resist. She turned away from him before his gaze could draw her back and walked toward her room.

Struggling to his feet, Philip groaned through a very real pain that had just penetrated his lower back. "Anna, don't go." He winced as another stabbing pain pierced his rib cage. "I want you to stay."

There was no way Anna could ignore the suffering in his voice, but she suspected it had much more to do with the beating he had just received than from her decision to return to her own room. "I rather doubt that you really want me to stay, Philip,'' she said, ''but, even so, as someone once said to me, 'Perhaps some other time.' ''

Feeling the sting of his own words thrown back at him, Philip could only stare at the door long after she had closed it.

CHAPTER EIGHT

Anna returned to her own room and lay down on her bed, but sleep did not come easily. Images of the last half hour tumbled wildly in her head. She tossed and turned, shivering when she thought of the danger she and Philip had faced with the robbers. She trembled even more when she recalled the passionate embraces she had shared with Philip.

Discovering that he was not married did little to calm her frayed nerves. At least when she believed he was unattainable, she could talk herself out of the unrealistic fantasies that crept so often into her mind. Now, knowing he was unattached, she still had to accept that the "blue-blooded Frenchman," as Mick had called him, was far beyond the reach of a poor Irish immigrant's orphaned daughter. Her heart, however, would not let her forget the sweet hunger of his kiss or the tingling caress of his hands on her skin.

She rolled over in bed and punched her pillow in frustration. "I would have been much better off if I had never met him," she grumbled, even though she knew it was not true. She owed her life to Philip's quick thinking and generosity. He had risked his own reputation and even faced the threat of being captured and accused of helping her escape, and still he was taking her to New Orleans where he promised his brother would help her.

And what had he asked in return? Until tonight, nothing, but Anna remembered his touch sending shivers down her spine and his husky voice asking her to stay the night. If that was a condition he expected in return for his help, then he was asking too much. He was offering one night in his arms, not a future with him, because Philip Brichard could never love Anna Connolly. The differences between them were simply too great, and she had to be careful not to confuse Philip's hunger and her own answering passion with love.

But what if Philip refused to help her get to Boston because she had turned him down with a haughty dismissal? Anna couldn't let herself think about that possibility. After all, Philip was fair-minded and reasonable. She would just have to convince him that putting her on a ship bound for the East Coast was in the best interests of all of them—Philip, the entire Brichard family, and most of all herself. Definitely herself.

What she needed right now was distance. She had to get as far away from Philip as she could. Otherwise she didn't know how long she could resist the very real, and completely dangerous, temptation he represented for her. If it took going half a continent to separate them, then that's what Anna would do.

As a gray dawn peeked through the heavy damask draperies in her room, Anna finally fell into a restless sleep. But she had decided what she would say to Philip. She knew how she would convince him that the best place for her to be was Boston, and the wisest and fairest thing he could do was help her to get there.

At seven-thirty in the morning, Anna was awakened by a tapping on the door that led to Philip's room. "Anna!" he called in a loud whisper.

She sat up in bed, instantly alert. "Yes? What is it?"

"If you want breakfast, we'll have to hurry. I'll pick you up in a half hour. Can you be ready?"

"Yes, of course." She threw the coverlet back and jumped

up from the bed. She began scurrying around the room picking
out the clothes she would wear and packing her other things
in their boxes.

She selected one of the day gowns that Lilly had chosen for
her. It was a pale peach muslin with a scooped neckline, long
sleeves that widened dramatically below the elbow, and a softly
flared skirt gathered at the rump in lacy frills that resembled a
bustle. She brushed her hair and pulled the sides up to the
crown of her head where she fastened the thick tresses with a
tortoiseshell comb. Then she tugged free a few wavy strands
that fell to her shoulders and framed her face.

She was ready five minutes early, and she sat down to wait
for Philip and to try and calm her nerves and quiet her pounding
heart. Drumming her fingers on the wooden arm of her chair,
Anna scolded herself for anticipating Philip's arrival with the
anxiety of a skittish schoolgirl afflicted with her first crush.

He arrived exactly when he said he would, and when she
heard him knock, Anna crossed the room slowly, drawing a
fortifying breath before she opened the door. He stood in the
hallway appearing much more rested than Anna would have
believed possible.

It occurred to her that she had not been the only one who
had shopped for new clothes yesterday, because Philip looked
strikingly handsome in charcoal gray breeches and new white
long-sleeved shirt with inch-long ruffles at the wrists. In spite
of a bruise next to his eye and a slight puffiness on his lower
lip, he seemed amazingly fit and comfortable as he leaned
against her doorframe . . . and alarmingly, temptingly attractive.

"You look well," she understated, "especially considering
the way you looked at three o'clock this morning."

His gaze started at her slippers and slowly rose to the top
of her wheat-colored hair, then lingered on her full, slightly
parted lips. "And you look wonderfully well," he said. "Every
bit as good as you looked at three o'clock this morning."

Anna turned away from the seductive, intense perusal of
those gray eyes. She stepped back into the room and inclined
her head toward her packages. "I'm all ready, just as you

asked.'' She was angered by the tremor in her voice . . . a testimony to her nervousness.

He only nodded and stood away from the door. An almost imperceptible wince shook his shoulders, and he squinted his eyes for just a second, but it was enough for Anna to know that, despite his cool exterior, he was indeed suffering from the beating he had taken.

He massaged his shoulder discreetly and said, ''I've sent for a boy to retrieve your things, so we can go on ahead to the dining room.'' Then he stiffly offered his arm to her.

She slipped her hand through his elbow and looked up at him with a smile meant to show sympathy. ''Are you sure you wouldn't rather lean on me?''

''Never mind,'' he said tersely. He walked her to the stairs with a step that was noticeably less authoritative than his usual gait.

At breakfast, when Anna sensed an easy familiarity existed once again between them, she decided to bring up the subject of her desire to go to Boston. She set her coffee cup on its china saucer and looked across the table at Philip. ''About how long will it be until we arrive in New Orleans?'' she asked.

''Today is Sunday. We'll be at Frenchman's Point by Thursday afternoon. The *Duchess* travels slowly, allowing time for gaming and shopping at its stops.''

''We've never really talked about what will happen once we get to your home. You certainly can't keep providing for me indefinitely as though I were some helpless waif you found on the street. But I'm sure you know that.''

Philip shrugged his shoulders. ''I hadn't thought of helping you in those terms exactly. Until we talk to Henri, I don't know what course of action would be best for you. I promised you I would consult with my brother to see what he advises from a legal standpoint, and I intend to keep my word.''

''I appreciate that, Philip, really I do, but I wonder if involving your family in my problems is the right thing to do.''

He regarded her with a fixed stare and raised his eyebrows questioningly.

"What I mean is, do you think your family could be put in danger because of the trouble I'm in?"

"My family is strong, Anna. We can, and have, taken care of ourselves, and we never back down from 'trouble,' as you put it . . . ours, or a friend's."

Anna looked down at her plate and pushed her eggs around with her fork. "That's what you tell me now," she said, "but it's not the impression I got at the livery in Hannibal. Then you were terribly concerned that my actions might reflect on the Brichard name."

Obviously recalling the way he had chastised Anna about taking his valise and his sister's dress, Philip regarded her across the table with a guilty smile. "True, but that was when I was trying to stop you from doing something dangerous and extremely ill-advised. Foolish, in fact," he added for good measure.

If he expected her to argue, she was determined to disappoint him. This situation demanded sweetness and accord. "And you were right that day," she agreed. "Going back to Cape de Rive would have been a foolish thing to do, but I'm afraid that staying long at Frenchman's Point with your family would be just as foolish."

Philip shifted in his chair and steepled his hands under his chin. "You're trying to tell me something, Anna. Why don't you just come out with it?"

"All right, I will." She clasped her hands together and placed them on the table, then squared her shoulders so she was almost Philip's height. "I've made a decision about what I should do, but I can't do it without your help. What I'm about to ask you is going to sound like a very big favor, perhaps bigger than you will feel I deserve."

"By all means, ask."

"First, I want to point out some things to you. I have been indebted to you on several occasions. In Cape de Rive you saved me from Wilkes's carriage, and twice you have kept me from being recognized and taken into custody."

He shrugged without speaking, but his eyes widened, alert and ready for what she would say next.

"I appreciate all you've done for me, and I'm grateful that last night I was able to repay you in a small way for your many kindnesses. I came to your rescue when you needed help and possibly saved you from a worse beating, or even . . . well, who can say what could have happened? It's dreadful to think about."

"Yes, who can say," he echoed. His voice was already edged with suspicion, a bad sign.

Anna plunged ahead. "And then there's the matter of money. You've spent a great deal on me. You have fed and clothed me, and I can't even imagine what my room in this hotel cost. Plenty, I'm sure. And then there's the *Duchess of Orleans,* by far the most luxurious boat on the Mississippi . . ."

"Am I supposed to be adding this up?"

"No, but my point is that last night I saved your winnings from the poker game. I believe you said it was ten thousand dollars—a lot of money. That amount certainly repays my debts to you with much left over . . . wouldn't you agree?"

"I would agree that I haven't spent nearly ten thousand dollars on you."

"Exactly. And if it weren't for me, the whole ten thousand would be gone."

Philip lowered his hands and sat forward, leaning toward her. Anna shrank back when his piercing stare leveled on her, and he said coolly, "I wasn't aware we were keeping score."

She hastened to correct the calculating impression she must have given him. "I don't mean to suggest that we are. It's just that what I'm about to ask you might seem like much more than I should ever expect, but I want you to consider that perhaps, just maybe, it's not."

"I suggest that you go ahead and ask me, then I'll decide if what you want is beyond my ability . . . or inclination to provide."

Anna flinched at Philip's frigid tone. She was afraid she'd made a mess of her attempt to create a businesslike arrangement with him. Still, it wouldn't do to put off what had to be said. She steeled herself against a likely rejection and blurted out her request. "I want one of your ships to take me to Boston as soon as possible."

"You *what?* Boston?" His outspoken reaction to her demand drew the unwelcome attention of several diners around them, and he lowered his voice to a startled, frustrated whisper. "Do you realize what you're asking?"

"Yes, of course I do, but please hear me out. I have a grandmother in Boston, but I don't have the means to get there."

"And this . . . grandmother," he said skeptically, "she wants you to come?"

"Well, she did at one time, but that was before . . ."

"She couldn't possibly know of your recent troubles."

"No, but she has money, and she can help me, at least I think she can. Her husband, my grandfather, recently died, but I understand that he was wealthy and no doubt left his fortune to her. My grandmother can pay you back for any expenses, I assume she can anyway . . ."

"You don't sound very sure."

"No, I'm sure. I am. I promise she'll pay you back."

Philip's eyes narrowed to slits under his furrowed brow. "How long has it been since you've seen your grandmother, Anna?"

This was the one question she'd hoped he wouldn't ask. She looked down at her lap and muttered under her breath, "I haven't actually seen her . . . in a long time."

"Have you *ever* seen her?"

"No."

"But you correspond?"

"Not exactly. But my uncle wrote her a few times."

"And your uncle was convinced that this sweet little old lady, who's never met you, sitting in her well-appointed parlor in Boston with piles of money around her, would be willing to part with it to help you?"

"Yes, he was." This was not going at all like Anna had hoped it would. She suspected her cheeks were flushed scarlet with embarrassment. She felt warm enough to melt icicles.

Philip Brichard certainly had a knack for making her uncomfortable.

"I know it sounds crazy," she said, "but Mick and I were trying to get enough money to go to Boston when you first saw us that night in River Flats."

"I remember your little scheme," he said with the cool exactness of an accusation. "As I recall, you were attempting to get an unsuspecting public to pity you enough to give you money. Now I find out you did it so you could arrive on the doorstep of an equally unsuspecting wealthy relative in Boston. I'm beginning to see the picture quite clearly."

"No, you're not! It wasn't like that. It wasn't a scheme. Well, the act in River Flats was, I guess, but not the part about my grandmother. She really wants me to come."

Now Anna was having to defend herself, and that's not at all what she wanted to do. Perhaps it was time to become more aggressive. Obviously sweetness and humility wouldn't work with this man.

"It's not up to you to judge me," she snapped. "I just want you to agree to get me to Boston, that's all. It's not so much to ask, especially since . . ."

"I know . . . especially since I'm in your debt for something like . . . nine thousand, five hundred dollars? Is that a fair estimate of what I owe you, Anna?"

She truly believed he was going to deny her request if she didn't do something fast. She immediately softened her tone and tried a different argument. "Philip, please, think of your family. How safe can they be with my picture on hundreds of reward posters? We've already seen Jake in St. Louis. Who knows where he'll show up next? You don't want to put your family in danger. Getting me out of New Orleans is the best possible plan. Once I'm gone, you and your family will be safe."

In truth, Philip had no worries about his family's safety. The plantation at Frenchman's Point was practically a fortress, considering the number of servants and employees who lived on the grounds who had been loyal to his mother and family for years. But he could see that it would accomplish nothing to tell Anna this.

She wanted to go to Boston, and he truly had no right to stop her. And perhaps she was right. His life had been turned upside down since he found her in his stateroom. She was independent, stubborn, and, considering just the little he knew of her past, probably not very trustworthy. Besides, what other course of action did he have? A decision had to be made about her future, and perhaps this was the best one.

He tried not to notice the morning sun slanting through the dining-room windows and casting golden highlights on her luxurious hair. He looked away from her momentarily so as not to be lost in the deep aqua of her glorious eyes. And mostly he tried to erase from his mind the memory of her gentle touch tending to his wounds, and the feel of her skin under his hands while her lips were pressed to his.

"All right, Anna, if this is what you want, then I will see to your passage when we reach New Orleans."

She expelled one long, tremulous breath. "Thank you, Philip."

He nodded and stood abruptly. "We'd better go. We don't want to miss the *Duchess.*"

When Philip escorted Anna back to the boat, she wore Claudette's large bonnet. He walked with her quickly and quietly across the gangway and up the little-used staircase at the bow of the boat. As far as he knew, they hadn't attracted any attention, even when he went back to the hired towncoach to retrieve Anna's packages. After all, it wasn't the first time Philip had carried boxes from a women's clothiers onto the *Duchess of Orleans* .

When he saw Anna was safely in the stateroom, he left almost immediately, saying he had to attend to a pressing errand. She was left to wonder at his sudden, mysterious departure. He returned later and announced he'd made arrangements for her he was sure she would appreciate, "under the circumstances." She looked up curiously from the desk where she had been reading a newspaper.

"I've gotten you a new identity for the rest of the trip," he stated.

"Oh? Did you manage to get me a new face as well?"

"No, I'm afraid not, but I've invented a complex enough background for you, so I doubt anyone will question whether or not you are truly 'Jennifer Saxton.' Besides, you're going to remain reclusive for the rest of our journey. No one will even think it's odd that you stay to yourself all the time."

"And why have I chosen the life of a hermit? Did you invent a reason for that as well?"

"Because you have recently been widowed." Philip chuckled at the bemused expression on her face. "You're an old family friend of the Brichards. Your grief is so great you felt the need to retire to a more relaxed environment where you can be among people who will care for you and help you get your strength back after a lingering malaise. Thus, I'm taking you to Frenchman's Point. *Voilà.*"

For a long moment there was only silence, the last reaction Philip expected from Anna. Finally she graced him with a delicate arch of her brows and an admiring nod of her head. "And you accuse me of being a schemer and a liar?"

"Since I've met you, I've improved my lying skills," he said with a wry grin.

"There's just one little question of morality that you seem to have overlooked," Anna said. "Why would the grieving, but no doubt virtuous, Jennifer Saxton be sharing a stateroom with the son of an old family friend . . . especially one whose exploits with women, married and otherwise, have become legend among the boat captains?"

"You underestimated me, Anna. I didn't overlook a thing. This is the part of the surprise I think you'll like best." He reached into the pocket of his breeches and pulled out a brass skeleton key attached to a *Duchess of Orleans* medallion. "I've arranged for you to have your own room where you may rest peacefully in the knowledge that you are abiding by all the rules of proper decorum and etiquette befitting your station in life."

"My own room?" Her voice had raised a notch. "Why would you do that?"

"Really, Anna, why wouldn't I?" he said, taking her hand and pressing the key into her palm. "Isn't this what you want . . . a safe, secure place for you to await your arrival in New Orleans and your passage on a Brichard ship to Boston? I thought you'd be pleased."

"I *am* pleased, and grateful, most definitely," she said without looking at him. The extent of that gratitude was questionable if only because of the forcefulness of her response. "It's better for you, too, isn't it? You can have your bed back, and your privacy. It's for the best all around."

"I'm sure that it is," he quickly agreed. "You'll have nothing to worry about. I'll check on you every day and order your meals sent to your room. You don't even have to see the cabin boy. When he knocks, you can just instruct him to leave your tray outside the door. You'll be absolutely safe . . . from everything that threatens you."

She stared out the window, though he couldn't imagine what she found so fascinating about the river on this gray morning. In the last few minutes, a thick mist had descended over the water, blocking the sun. The room was gloomy. "It will be very nice, Philip," she said without turning around. "Thank you."

Philip was better than his word. Instead of checking on Anna once a day, he came to her stateroom several times daily to make sure she had everything she needed, that her meals were delivered according to his instructions and that fresh linens were provided each morning. If she desired a bath, he made certain one was brought to her room. Often he stayed with her longer than was necessary until she assured him that she was comfortable and lacked nothing.

His attentiveness did not stop with his obligations to her physical well-being. He seemed overly concerned about her mental state as well, apologizing unnecessarily for her hours of confinement in her cabin. To offset her boredom, he began bringing her little gifts from the towns where the *Duchess* docked.

After a three-hour visit to Memphis, he presented her with several copies of local newspapers, a Jane Austen novel, and the latest edition of the *Farmer's Almanac,* just in case she wanted to "investigate the weather conditions predicted during her voyage to Boston."

While in Natchez, he bought her a musical glass globe with a replica of a grand southern mansion on the inside, complete with stately oak trees housing miniature meadowlarks in their branches. When she turned the globe upside down, crystal "snowflakes" tumbled around the mansion. Anna had been delighted with the gift and laughed when Philip remarked, "It's pretty but not very realistic. It doesn't snow very often in southern Mississippi."

When he went to Natchez-Under-the-Hill, Philip stopped at a dress shop that catered to the notorious "ladies of Under-the-Hill" and picked up a red satin garter belt trimmed in black French lace. It was emblazoned with the town's name on a round satin ribbon. "I wish I could have taken you there, Anna," he said when he presented her with the garter. "Seeing Natchez-Under-the-Hill should be part of every young lady's education."

"I can well imagine." She held the gaudy thing up to close scrutiny. "And I can assume you've had quite an education there yourself," she accused with a mischievous grin.

He pretended an innocence he knew she'd never believe. "I would never do anything ungentlemanly so close to home," he said.

He then told her about an encounter he'd had in the city, one he knew would frighten her. "There is something about my visit today you should know, Anna."

"What is it?"

"I saw Jake Finn."

Her eyes widened, and she set the garter on the bed. If she was alarmed, her voice did not convey it. She seemed more resigned than afraid. "What was he doing?"

"I learned he's been following the river with a couple of

raftsmen and distributing his posters at nearly every dock. It seems he's not going to give up easily.''

"No, I guess he isn't. We'll be at Frenchman's Point tomorrow afternoon at least," she said. "I think it would be wise for me to set sail for Boston as soon as possible."

Philip nodded. "I suppose you're right. Still, I would like to talk to Henri. Even if you do go to Boston, it would be nice to know that your name can been cleared.'' He walked to her door and turned the handle. "Keep your door locked, Anna. I'll see you tomorrow."

At his good-bye, she looked so forlorn that Philip hated himself for having given her the bad news about Jake, but he believed that she had a right to know the man was so close on their trail. He hesitated before leaving her room, knowing that he would have been content to just stay with her that night and hold her in his arms and make her feel safe.

He raised his hand to touch her face, but when he looked into her eyes for a sign she wanted him to stay, he saw that grim determination existed where just moments before there had been desperation. Was she thinking ahead to her journey to Boston? Was she suddenly gaining confidence since she would not need him to protect her much longer? He dropped his hand to his side and said, "You'll be all right?"

"I'll be fine," she said, and he had no reason not to believe her.

The next afternoon, the *Duchess of Orleans* rounded a wide bend in the river four miles north of the French Quarter in New Orleans. Philip and Anna leaned against the rail of the observation gallery on the Texas deck watching the landscape change from wild, untended riverbank to the majesty of oak trees draped in Spanish moss.

Philip had seen this view of Frenchman's Point many times, but it never failed to inspire him with a pride of heritage and the joy of homecoming. He took Anna's hand and pointed to the lush green arm of rich delta soil jutting out into the river. At the end of this projection of Brichard land there was a wide dock. Frenchman's Point had its own stopping place for riverboats.

The steam whistle on the *Duchess* sounded two long blasts, telling other river craft to give way to the southbound *Duchess of Orleans* as she gracefully drifted across the river to her destination. Philip knew his family would hear the whistle and know he was home. From the colorful bunting draped along the Frenchman's Point dock, he knew they were expecting him.

Anna adjusted the prim little hat that perched on the side of her head, its dramatic pointed brim dipping onto her forehead. A black veil covered her eyes and nose, but did not hide the downward curve of her mouth that said she was nervous about seeing his home. She was wearing a green traveling dress with a fashionable bustle and shining gold braid, and Philip had a hard time keeping his eyes off her as they traveled the last few hundred yards to Frenchman's Point.

"You look lovely, Anna," he said, taking both her hands in his to keep them from trembling.

She managed a tentative little grin. "I don't know why I'm so nervous. Well, yes, I do. I'm hardly the perfect houseguest."

"Oh, I don't know. You should have seen the pirates, plunderers, and thieves they tell me my grandfather used to entertain here. You seem incredibly innocent by comparison."

She shot him a quick, sharp look of skepticism and frowned. "I'm afraid your family will think that times haven't changed much."

Philip chuckled. "Once you meet my family, you'll see that a little excitement is just what they like! Would you please just relax. Everything will be fine."

He walked her down the stairs as the gangway was lowered onto the dock at Frenchman's Point. After their luggage, packages, and Monique and Claudette's parcels were carried to the landing, Philip and Anna crossed over to the riverbank.

She looked back one last time at the *Duchess of Orleans*, and Philip let his gaze follow hers. He saw the grand steamboat as she must have, and gained a new appreciation of the multistoried red paddle wheel, the gleaming white walls of the salons and staterooms, and the glistening black smokestacks joined together with banners of colorful flags.

Holding tightly to Philip's arm, Anna was indeed overcome with a sense of sadness that the *Duchess of Orleans* would only be a memory from now on. The boat had been her shelter from a past that had grieved her with its violence and loss, while, at the same time, had thrilled and excited her with a rush of new emotions. She looked up at Philip with a hesitant smile as the grand steamboat pulled away from the dock.

"Good day to you, Mister Brichard, Mrs. Saxton," Captain Cruthers called, touching the brim of his hat. "Hope to see you again soon."

"Isn't it odd?" Anna said. "I'm going to miss being on that boat."

Philip smiled and covered her hand with his. "Not so strange, really," he said. "She's a grand old girl."

He urged Anna to turn around, and when she did, she faced a wide green lawn that stretched for hundreds of yards on each side of a wide driveway meandering through a canopy of magnificent oaks. At the end of the drive she could just make out the outline of a large imposing structure sitting atop a low rise. Her attention was then drawn to an open carriage pulled by two high-stepping dapple-gray horses coming toward them down the middle of the drive.

"Huckabee is right on time," Philip said.

CHAPTER NINE

Anna watched the polished teakwood landau pull up beside the dock. She smiled at the white-haired Negro driver who was sitting on the plush leather bench seat issuing practiced commands to a pair of Tennessee Walkers. He nodded a greeting at Anna as he set the brake on the carriage.

Philip met the driver as soon as his booted feet touched the ground. "Huckabee!" he said, wrapping his arms around the older man. He patted the back of the Negro's form-fitting red vest which covered a gleaming, starched white shirt.

"Welcome home, Mistuh Philip," the black man said. Anna caught a glimpse of his wide smile over Philip's shoulder. "It sho' is good to have you back. The womenfolk been talkin' of nothin' but fo' days."

"It's good to be back. Come here, I want you to meet someone." He motioned for Huckabee to come near Anna, and he introduced them. "Anna, I'd like you to meet one of my oldest friends. He's been at Frenchman's Point since before I was born." Philip's fond smile indicated that the word "friend" was certainly appropriate. "This is Huckabee Johnson. Huckabee, meet Miss Anna Rose Connolly. She'll be our houseguest for a while."

Anna offered her hand to the man and he took it in a firm, pumping grasp. "How do you do, Mr. Johnson?" she said.

"You jus' call me Huckabee, now, miss," he said with that same warm smile. "Oh, but won' the missus be pleased to lay eyes on you! We're havin' comp'ny at the big house tonight!" He shook his head and chuckled softly at Philip. "You've done brought a nice surprise home this time, Mistuh Philip."

"Well, then, let's get these packages in the carriage and go up to the house." Philip began collecting the parcels. "I see you brought the two-seater. Very wise of you, Huckabee. We're going to need the extra room."

"I shuly 'member how the ladies 'specs lots o' dresses whenever you go to Chicago. Looks like this trip wasn't no diff'rent."

"No, it wasn't," Philip admitted, tossing the boxes one by one to Huckabee who loaded them into the carriage. "Is Mama home?"

"Where else would she be, Mistuh Philip? Been waitin' all day fo' the *Duchess* to roun' the bend. She was watchin' from the third floor, an' when she see the smoke curlin' up, she done hollered for Miss Claudette, and the two of 'em took to shoutin' and carryin' on. Miss Claudette was saddlin' her horse when I left the carriage house."

When the packages were all stowed, Philip opened the carriage door for Anna. She ran her gloved hand along the gleaming tan surface of the door, noting the forest-green scrollwork on the outside which had obviously been hand-painted by an artist. The ends of the flourishing design met in the center of the door to form the initials, *CFB* in elaborate script. The four wheels of the landau were painted a matching forest green, the same color as the plush leather seat which Anna occupied next to Philip.

Huckabee mounted the driver's bench and snapped the reins on the backs of the eager horses. They immediately set off at a perfectly matched brisk gait, their iron shoes snapping brightly on the oyster-shell drive.

They had only gone about halfway to the house when a

rider appeared around the north wing of the mansion, galloping toward them at breakneck speed.

"It looks like a tornado is descending upon us," Philip quipped to Anna.

The rider was bent low to the horse's flying mane, and a long, dark braid tossed like a whirlwind behind the daredevil female who commanded the horse like she was born to it. "You'd better pull over and stop, Huckabee," Philip warned. "Otherwise I'm afraid she'll barrel right into us!"

The carriage pulled to a stop just as the galloping horse reached them. Philip stepped down at the same time the young rider dismounted and flew at him.

"Philip!" she squealed, jumping into his outstretched arms and wrapping her legs around his waist. "I've missed you so."

"My, my, little sister, as usual, a remarkably graceful entrance." He bestowed a brotherly kiss on her cheek and set her on the ground. Then he stepped back and regarded her with a disapproving glare that was unsuccessful in hiding his affection. "I've missed you, too, *ma petite,* though I see you haven't learned the art of genteel manners yet. But mostly I'm amazed you haven't broken your neck riding the way you do."

The girl placed her hands on her hips and shot back a retort that blended her southern upbringing with her family's native French dialect. "I can be just as genteel as the next lady, Philip, and you know it just as well as you know that there isn't a horse at Frenchman's Point that would throw me."

She grabbed her horse's reins from the ground and gently tugged the Arabian mare toward her. Then she stood on her toes and kissed the animal on her soft nose. "See? She loves me."

"Don't we all," Philip said, rolling his eyes to the sky. "I think it's the curse God gave us to bear."

"Anyway, quit harping at me and make your introductions." Claudette strode ahead of him to where Anna sat in the landau, completely enthralled with the scene that had just taken place before her delighted eyes.

"Anna, this, as you might have guessed, is my fifteen-some-times-going-on-ten-sometimes-going-on-twenty-year-old sis-

ter, Claudette Marie Brichard. Claudette, Miss Anna
Connolly.''

Claudette rubbed her hand down the front of her riding skirt
before offering it up to Anna. A smile lit up her face as she
said, ''It's a pleasure to meet you, Miss Connolly. Any friend
of my brother's is a welcome guest at Frenchman's Point, and
despite what Philip may have done in the past, the rest of us
here will try to make your stay a pleasant one.''

Anna laughed at the girl's outgoing manner. She warmed to
Claudette Brichard instantly. ''Please, just call me Anna, and
I assure you that your brother has only shown me great kindness
and consideration.''

''I'm glad he has remembered his 'genteel manners,' '' she
mimicked, casting a sideways look at her brother.

''I think you'd better hightail it back to the house, Claudette,''
Philip said. ''Besides, I'm sure you can't wait to tell Mama
I've brought a guest.''

''Did you bring my dresses?''

''Of course.''

''All right, then, I'll go. I'll see you in a few minutes, Anna.''
Grabbing the Arabian's mane, Claudette jumped on the horse
and turned her around. She galloped away at a slightly more
moderate pace.

''She sho' keeps your mama jumpin', Mistuh Philip,'' Huckabee chuckled as he watched her ride back up the drive.

''I know that's true.'' Philip climbed in beside Anna and
threw his hands up in pretended frustration. ''There you have
it—the tempest of Frenchman's Point. I hope she wasn't too
much of a shock.''

''I think she's wonderful. I would love to have her for a
friend.''

''Before the evening is over, I'm sure you will.'' Philip
tapped the back of the driver's bench. The carriage started up
the drive and continued through a canopy of magnolia trees
and live oaks, until the entire mansion was revealed in its stately
grandeur.

The first thing Anna noticed about the great house was its
unusual design. The entire first floor, where she learned the

kitchen was located, was built of red brick to insulate the big room from the oppressive Louisiana heat. It was covered by a wide veranda surrounding the main floor of the house, which was actually situated on the second story.

A high, peaked roof rose above yet another story and extended beyond the boundaries of the house, providing an enormous gallery around the entire second floor. A row of dormer windows with graceful arched panes marched across the roof and accentuated the four substantial chimneys. The entire roof structure was supported by eight Doric columns that spanned the first and main floors and alternated between the dormers.

Wide brick steps led to a double entrance door on the main floor. When the carriage pulled up to the house, Anna noticed that both doors were opened wide to admit the spring breeze. The main floor was ventilated with a series of doors, not windows, leading to the veranda. When she saw the thin, gauze curtains rustling in all the open doorways, she assumed this open-air feature must be a common architectural detail in the hot climate of Louisiana.

As soon as the carriage stopped at the foot of the stairs, a petite gray-haired woman in a burgundy linen day gown descended from the entrance to the circular drive. "Philippe!" she called, reaching her arms out.

Philip nodded to Anna and whispered, "I'll be right back to get you."

She urged him down from the carriage with a wave of her hand. "Go, go on."

He kissed the woman on her pink-tinted cheek, and she hugged him close. *"Mon cher,"* she said, *"Je t'adore, mon fils."*

"Bonjour, Mama. You look beautiful as always."

"And you are a hopeless flatterer," she said, smiling up at him. She stole a look at Anna in the carriage and asked with a mischievous wink, "So how was your trip, Philippe?"

"I think it will prove to be profitable, Mama," he answered, as though he didn't comprehend the true meaning of her question. "The purveyors in Chicago signed a contract for two thousand pounds of Saint Sebastian coffee, and that was in addition to getting top dollar for Brichard sugar and rice . . .''

"That's all well and good," she said, "but not what I meant and you know it."

"I think Mama wants to know about . . . you know who."

Philip and Monique turned toward Claudette's voice as she came down the steps toward them. She was smiling impishly, and with her finger hidden behind a cupped hand, she pointed toward the carriage.

"You don't say, little sister," Philip said, shaking his head and walking toward the carriage. "I'm lucky to have you as an interpreter for Mama."

Philip opened the carriage door and took Anna's hand. She stepped to the drive, and he escorted her to where his mother waited. "Mama, I'd like you to meet a friend of mine, Miss Anna Connolly. I met her on the *Duchess*. She was traveling to New Orleans to procure passage on a steamer to Boston. I persuaded her instead to sail on a Brichard ship. If you don't mind, she will be staying with us for a while."

"Of course I don't mind," Monique said as a smile very much like Philip's lifted the corners of her coral-colored mouth. "It will be lovely to have you here, Miss Connolly. How long can you stay?"

Anna looked at Philip. "Well, that depends on your son, actually . . .''

"Anna wants to sail as soon as possible, Mama."

"Then we'll just have to make the best of the little time we have," Monique said, taking Anna's elbow. "You must be hungry and thirsty. Come inside and we'll have refreshments." Monique led Anna up the stairs to the house. By the time they reached the front door, both women were chatting easily, and Claudette was following closely behind them listening to every word.

Anna was brought into an enormous entry hall that was open from the front door to the back of the house. A breeze wafted through the foyer, tinkling the sparkling crystals of a chandelier mounted from the third-floor ceiling. Sitting opposite each other along the walls of the hallway were two French sideboards each holding a large crystal vase of fresh-cut flowers. A pair of delicate cabriole leg settees covered in pastel brocade sat next to the sideboards under ornately framed landscapes in muted shades of tan and green.

Anna followed Monique to the back entrance. Along the way, she admired several portraits of people who must have been Brichard ancestors. The intricate oils lined the wall of the wide staircase leading to the upper floor.

"You have a beautiful home, Madame Brichard," Anna said.

"Thank you, Anna, and please call me Monique. Ah, now we are coming to my favorite part of this house." They walked out the back door to a wide veranda that looked out across a perfectly manicured garden whose elaborate flower beds were bordered by tall hedges of vibrant green holly.

Monique took Anna to a group of white iron chairs surrounding a large table under a balcony extending from the floor above. Pots of ivy, ferns, and philodendron hung from brass hooks all along the veranda ceiling. "This is where I spend the long afternoons of summer," Monique said. "It is always cool and nice here."

Colors and aromas of the wide variety of flowers that stretched for almost as far as she could see brought an appreciative smile to Anna's lips. "It's wonderful here, Monique."

"You like flowers, Anna?" Monique asked as she sat between her and Claudette. "I have to admit they are my passion."

Anna thought of the patches of wildflowers she and Mick used to pass on the road in the peddler's wagon and the bright geraniums in Laura's little window boxes, and she smiled, remembering how they had cheered her in the past. "Yes, I guess I do, though I've never seen any garden as magnificent as this one."

"There is as much beauty in a single bloom as in a whole garden," Monique said. "Even the smallest bed of roses feeds the eyes and the soul as well as a field of yellow dandelions or the gardens of a king."

"Can I get something for you, madame?"

"Ah, Darcine," Monique said to a young Negro woman

who had just arrived on the patio. "Meet our guest, Miss Connolly. Anna, this is Darcine Johnson, Huckabee's daughter. Darcine will be seeing to your needs while you're here."

Seeing to my needs? The concept was as alien to Anna as was this marvelous house. No one had ever seen to Anna's needs but Anna herself.

She said hello, and Darcine acknowledged with a smile and a slight curtsy. "Anything I can do for you, miss, jus' let me know."

"Will you bring us a pitcher of lemonade and some of Maizie's orange marmalade and meringues?" Monique asked, and Darcine nodded before going into the house. "Now, Anna, tell me all about your trip down the river and just how you met my son."

Anna bit her lower lip. How was she going to find the right words to explain how she and Philip met? By anyone's standards, the events were bizarre. If she were honest, she wouldn't blame Monique Brichard for tossing her out of her home. And if she lied . . . well, everyone knows the truth comes out sooner or later.

"H-how we met?" she began. "Let's see . . ."

Thankfully Philip appeared on the veranda. "So ladies, can anyone join this conversation?"

"Of course, *chéri,*" Monique said. "Sit down."

Philip straddled one of the patio chairs and skillfully guided the conversation away from Anna. "And just when is that paragon of Louisiana law in the three-piece vested suit due home?"

"Your brother will be here for dinner," Monique answered. "He said there is no way he would miss your homecoming."

An hour later, Darcine took Anna to her room. Deciding to free herself of the constrictive stays and buttons of her traveling dress before admiring the fine appointments of the Brichard guest room, Anna tossed her hat and jacket on the bed. Next she untied the bow on her blouse, and fanned the collar open at her neck. Then she pulled the pins out of her hair, and raked her fingers through the top knot she'd fashioned on her crown. Her thick tresses fell down her back.

Rid at last of the confines of proper garments, and completely in awe of her surroundings, Anna clasped her hands together and twirled in a circle. "This room. It's so beautiful!"

She ran to the armoire and threw open the doors. Her dresses had already been neatly hung on the inside. She ran her hands over the polished wood surface of the butler's table which held a crystal decanter full of a sparkling red liquid. She sat down on the edge of the bed and bounced on the pink-and-green floral coverlet. She noticed it matched the billowing curtains at the French doors and the wallpaper border at the ceiling.

When she lifted the cut-glass cranberry drinking glass from the matching pitcher on the bedside table, she watched the play of light refracted through the finely chiseled pinwheel design. "I never knew people really lived like this," she said.

Replacing the glass, she went to the marble mantel over the fireplace and examined the collection of Brichard family photographs bound in etched silver picture frames. "How handsome he looked even then," she said, picking up a miniature of a young Philip. "But he looks so uncomfortable in that high collar."

"And he was, too," Philip said. Anna spun around at the sound of his voice. He was leaning against the open French door, but when he'd captured her attention, he stepped inside and pointed to the photograph from across the room.

"I remember that day. There was a man from the New Orleans *Gazette* at the river taking photographs of the St. Gerard Parish boys going off to the war. Mama persuaded him to come up to the house afterward and take our photos. She had to practically glue Henri and me to our chairs to keep us from running back to the river to watch the soldiers leave."

"H-how long have you been standing there?" Anna asked, flushing with embarrassment. Still, she was unable to pull her gaze away from him. He, too, had removed his formal clothes and looked relaxed in a loose-fitting shirt that billowed out from his chest in the breeze.

He crossed his arms in a casual stance and stared at her with teasing in his eyes. "Long enough to know you think I'm handsome."

Anna set the frame back on the mantel with a trembling hand. "You should have said something. It's not polite to go skulking around other people's rooms, spying on them."

"I guess it is wrong to enter a person's room without asking first," he said smugly.

She cringed in mortification, recalling how she had entered his stateroom on the *Duchess*.

"I apologize, miss, for havin' the bad mannuhs to intrude on your privacy," he drawled in the manner of a scrupulously polite southern gentleman.

"You made your point," Anna countered. "You have the most irritating way of flinging my indiscretions back in my face. Will you ever forget that first night on the riverboat?"

"No, but not because I found it an unpleasant occurrence. Quite the opposite in fact. It was an opportunity that I regret not taking better advantage of at the time."

Anna smiled in spite of a serious effort to appear insulted at his innuendo. "You're completely insufferable at times," she said.

"And you are utterly beautiful at all times," he said, his eyes darkening. "And I can still say that despite the hard-hearted way you've treated me."

"I haven't meant to be hard-hearted, you know that. It's just that, because of my plans, you know that nothing can happen between us."

"Funny, I thought something already had."

"Well, thank goodness we stopped before it was too late."

"A blessing for sure," Philip grumbled.

Anna walked to the second set of French doors which opened onto the balcony and looked out over the garden. After a moment she said, "This is a wonderful place, your home. So peaceful and gracious."

She expected to hear his voice from across the room, but instead she felt his hands reach under her heavy hair to rest on her shoulders. She drew in a quick, sharp breath, and her back arched under his hands. But she made no attempt to move away from him.

His fingers massaged the curve of her shoulders, sliding the silky fabric of her blouse over her skin, and she relaxed against his chest. She even laid her cheek against his hand for a moment before raising her face to look out over the gardens once more. "Your mother is very proud of her flowers," she said.

"Yes, she is. I'm sure before you leave she will take you on a tour of her little Eden down there and tell you the names of every blossom."

"I would like that."

"Talking about Frenchman's Point is something my mother never tires of, but you've probably already noticed that." His hands slid down her arms to her elbows. He drew her close until her bottom rested against his hips.

"Are you saying your mother talks too much?" she teased. A tug of his fingers urged her to turn and face him. She kept talking even though she now looked into eyes that could make a girl forget the entire English language. "I disagree. She is most gracious. Her friendliness has made me feel right at home, and . . ."

"All I'm saying is that sometimes a person should know when to stop talking and start acting." His face lowered to hers and she leaned back, resisting his advance.

"Still, your mother has every right to be proud of her gardens . . ."

"Like now," he said, placing his hand firmly on the base of her spine and pulling her against him. Their thighs touched. His long legs alternated with hers. His hip pressed against her abdomen. Then, without another word, his mouth took hers in a devastating kiss that banished all rational thought from her mind. The house, his family, the gardens . . . all vanished with the insistent probing of his tongue against her lips.

Her palms splayed on his chest, Anna mumbled a feeble protest, born of obligation, certainly not desire. The sound was smothered by an onslaught of his lips that left her heart racing and her knees weak.

Giving in to her tumultuous feelings, she abandoned her

useless pleading as a low moan of desire escaped her. She reached her hands around his neck and clung to him, moving her head under his, inviting the kiss to deepen.

His tongue pressed against her mouth, forcing it to open and admit his explorations. He pulled her closer until they became a continuous sweeping line of contact, from the calves of their legs to their thundering hearts beating in unison. He cupped the back of her head, holding her immobile to his tongue circling inside her mouth.

Finally he tore his lips from hers and pressed his mouth to her neck, his breath coming hot and quick on the soft skin above her collarbone. "Oh, Anna, how I want you," he murmured. "You must know it. Being apart from you on the boat was torture for me."

"Philip, no. Don't do this to me. I'm not strong enough to resist you forever."

"Then why resist at all?" He returned his mouth to hers in another shattering kiss.

Anna's head spun in a rush of heated passion. The kiss was endless, a sublime mating of mouths. Her heart raced until she was certain she heard it thrumming against her rib cage. Tap, tap, insistently, drumming in her ears. Suddenly Claudette's voice broke through the haze of desire that enveloped her. "Anna, Anna, are you there?"

Philip's sister was at the door!

She broke away from Philip, and he groaned his frustration. "Y-yes, Claudette, I'm here. Just a minute, please." She tugged her clothes into place. Philip stalked to the balcony doors muttering under his breath, "Your timing couldn't have been any better, little sister."

Anna rushed up behind him and pushed him out the door onto the gallery. Her voice came out as a commanding whisper. "Go on, get out of here. How will it look if your sister finds you in my room?"

"Not as incriminating as I wish it had," he returned bluntly. When he saw the bright daggers of warning in her eyes, he held his hands up as if fencing a blow. "I'm going, I'm going."

He retreated slowly down the veranda. "I'll see you at dinner, and then later, we'll remember where we were."

"Just go, please!" Anna ran back into the room and crossed to the door. "Claudette," she said gaily, waving the girl inside. "Please come in. I was just putting some of my things in order." She raced around the room, picking up bits and pieces of her belongings to prove the verity of her statement.

Claudette plunked down on the bed and hugged one of the lacy pillows to her chest. "I just came to tell you that Mama said dinner would be in an hour."

"I'm so glad you did." Anna stopped her pointless chores and calmed her nerves with a soothing breath. "Won't you please help me decide what to wear?"

Dinner at the Brichards' was a formal occasion at Monique's request, and each of her children dressed appropriately to please her. That night, Monique wore a shimmering black brocade gown with a high neck and adorned it with a simple white cameo. Her gray hair was bound at the nape with a thick black net spun with silver threads.

Claudette looked feminine and charming in a yellow silk dress with overvest that flattered her slim figure. Her long, braided hair was wound on top of her head and ornamented with yellow daisies.

Henri, Philip's brother, wore exactly what Philip had hinted at earlier in the day—a finely tailored three-piece black suit with a wine-colored silk cravat at his throat. A gold watch chain looped from one pocket to the other on the form-fitting black vest. His soft-spoken manner and friendly demeanor struck a surprising contrast to his somber business attire, and his alert, intelligent green eyes peered keenly through wire-rimmed glasses. He did not have the masterful presence of his older brother, but it was obvious that a logical mind and a cool head made him an appropriate and necessary foil to the other, more dangerously impulsive Brichard male.

Anna was glad she had chosen a pink satin gown that presented a modest yet elegant appearance. Feminine gathers along the scooped neckline left her chest bare except for a delicate lace trim. Seated across from Philip, she was aware of his gaze on her often throughout the meal. She tried to refrain from looking at him too many times over the eight-armed candelabra on the center of the table.

Oh, but he did look wonderful in a hunter-green jacket that fit snugly over a cream-colored shirt and gold vest. Had he done something different to his hair? she wondered, stealing a glimpse across the expanse of gleaming mahogany. Several touchable strands brushed the collar of his shirt, and dark curls fell onto his forehead. For some reason, that shining raven hair looked especially inviting this night. While Anna imagined her fingers combing it back from his temples and forehead, it was all she could do to keep her mind on the conversation around her.

"Where did you say your family is from, Anna?" Monique asked.

The question broke through Anna's pleasant reverie, and she sat back in her chair with a start. "Boston," she said, reaching for her napkin to cover the abrupt movement. "That's why I'm going there now."

"Will you be seeing your mother and father?"

"No, it's only my grandmother who lives in Boston, and it's her I'm going to see. I don't have any other family."

"I see. How is it that my son was able to persuade you to sail on one of his ships?"

Anna looked to Philip for help and he quickly jumped in. "Anna was traveling with an uncle when I met her in River Flats, Mama. We became friends almost immediately. Her uncle was a merchant much like I am, so we had a great deal in common. He was giving Anna a firsthand education about the Midwest while escorting her to Boston. When we discovered that we were all on the *Duchess,* our friendship naturally grew."

"How interesting," Monique said, looking at Anna. "Where is your uncle now?"

Again Philip answered for her. "Unfortunately Mr. Connolly became gravely ill right after we met, and he died quite suddenly on board the *Duchess.* Since Anna was already acquainted with me, I offered my assistance and persuaded her to come to Frenchman's Point. And you know the rest, Mama.''

"You poor child," she said to Anna. "What a shock it must have been to lose your uncle so suddenly.''

"It was," Anna answered truthfully, "and hearing Philip relate the story over again, I must admit that I am just as shocked as I was when it happened.'' She looked at Philip over the candlelight, and he responded with an innocent shrug.

A mischievous sparkle in Monique's eyes and a hint of a grin on her little mouth suggested that she believed there was more to Philip's relationship with Anna than he'd indicated.

"Dinner was excellent, Mama," Philip said suddenly, rising from the table, "but if you'll excuse us, I promised Anna a brief stroll through your gardens.''

"Go on, then. It's a lovely night for a walk. You will come to my room later and tell me good night?''

"Yes, of course." Philip pulled Anna's chair out, and she stood up.

"If I don't see you again tonight, dear," Monique said to her, "I'll see you for breakfast in the morning. I hope you sleep well.''

"I'm sure I will, thank you.''

Before Philip escorted Anna from the room, he nodded toward Henri and said, "Will you meet me in the library for a brandy in . . . say, a half hour, Brother?''

"Certainly." After Philip and Anna left, Henri looked over at his mother and raised a quizzical eyebrow. "What's going on, Mama?''

"I haven't any idea, Henri, but I expect that before tonight is over, one of us will know.''

"How could you possibly make up such a tall tale?" Anna demanded, staring up at Philip in the garden.

They had stopped under one of the kerosene lanterns that hung from wrought-iron posts along the walkway. Amber light shone down on her from behind, casting her in a pool of irides-cent gold. Her eyes reflected the dazzling shimmer of the night sky, and Philip could not be sure if he were seeing starlight in their azure depths or sparks of condemnation for his blatant exaggeration of the facts at dinner. Knowing Anna, he suspected it was the latter.

"I couldn't believe how you twisted the details about Cape de Rive to your mother," she added. "Really, Philip, you lie too easily."

"You're right, Anna. It was dreadful of me," he said. His hand actually itched to take a strand of gold hair from her shoulder and entwine it around his finger, but he supposed it was bad timing.

"Tomorrow I shall tell her the truth," he declared. "That you, with your overly zealous uncle, had been traveling around for weeks pretending to be blind to collect donations from sympathetic citizens until, as bad luck would have it, you were accused of murdering one of Cape de Rive's most prominent businessmen. Because of that unhappy circumstance, you hid in my stateroom and we traveled together for many miles down the river avoiding the law and dodging bounty hunters who would stop at nothing to collect the five-thousand-dollar price tag on your head. Now, is that better? I think Mama will appreciate that story for its honesty if nothing else."

Anna answered his sarcasm with a scowl. "How easy it is for you to poke fun, Philip Brichard," she said. "If you only knew how I long to erase that little smirk from your mouth."

"Kiss it off, then," he challenged. "Smother it with your own lips until I haven't the strength or inclination to tire you with another discourteous comment. My behavior is entirely in your hands."

Oh, yes, it was working. The scowl was becoming more difficult to maintain. In seconds it disappeared altogether, and a smile as bright as the night sky burst upon Anna's face.

"You are impossible," she said. "I only meant to suggest that a story somewhere between the truth and the one you told might have been more appropriate and less of an outright lie. I just know that I could never have told those lies to your mother."

"Is that so? And what lies *would* you have told her?"

The phrasing of Philip's question caused a ripple of laughter to come from Anna's lips, and she looked up at him with a playful gleam in her eyes. "I would have told her that I was the niece of the Duke of Windsor, and I was traveling through America with my chaperone who ran off with a riverboat gambler leaving me stranded and helpless with only the likes of you to lend support!"

"I like your story much better than mine," he said, "especially because I was worried for a minute that you had gone honest, and I was afraid I wouldn't like the new, virtuous Anna."

"You do imagine the worst about me, don't you, Philip?"

"That's where you're wrong, Anna. You have no idea what I imagine about you, but I can tell you that I have only visions of absolute, vivid clarity where you're concerned, and they are wondrously, excitingly agreeable."

He had rendered her speechless, and he took full advantage of the moment. Before she could react, his hand was around her back and his lips were on hers. It was a quick, hot, hungry kiss that only whetted his appetite for more and left Anna breathless.

Her eyes fluttered open when Philip's hand moved to her elbow. She remained poised on her tiptoes, leaning up toward his face for a telltale moment. He allowed himself to believe it was disappointment he saw in her eyes . . . disappointment that the kiss had ended so abruptly.

"Shall we go in?" he asked, starting back down the pathway to the house. "I don't see how it's possible, but my mother always says a person can catch a chill in the garden at night."

"So that's it, that's all you have to go on?" Henri asked Philip when they were alone in the library.

"I'm afraid so. That's Anna's story at any rate, and I believe her."

"Unfortunately it's not a question of whether *you* believe her. It's what a judge will believe when he hears her story that matters, especially when the grieving widow has backed up the murder theory with a generous reward. Besides that, there's a firm witness ready to testify to Anna's guilt."

"Bah!" Philip snorted derisively. "Some witness! Jake Finn, that misfit of birth, could hardly be called reliable by anyone's standards."

"Maybe so, but he was there, and no one else was, except the victim, of course . . . and the accused."

"So are you saying that Anna has no chance?"

"I'm not saying that at all. I will say that Anna needs a good lawyer, and fortunately for her, she found one."

Philip grinned broadly at his brother. "Once again you haven't let me down. Now what do we need to do?"

"*We* won't do anything. You're much too involved with this girl, and since you're entirely too hotheaded about matters in which you have relatively *little* at stake, I hate to think how you would behave in this case."

Philip opened his mouth to utter a scathing rebuttal to Henri's charge, but Henri stopped him. "I, on the other hand, have a big job ahead of me. As soon as possible, I'll leave for Cape de Rive and do some snooping around. In the meantime, I'll talk to Anna about what happened in the town and at the lake. Even the smallest detail she might remember could be valuable in proving her innocence.

"In Cape de Rive, I'll try to find the other men who were at the poker table that afternoon, and see what they recall about Wilkes's demeanor. Then I'll set about searching for the one thing that could clear Anna's name for good."

"What's that?"

"The body, of course. Uncle Mick has to be somewhere. I'll need to know what he was wearing the night he was killed. After all this time, his body might not be recognizable, but his clothing still could be."

"Excellent idea," Philip agreed, "but what about Anna? Should I try to convince her to stay here for a while?"

Henri appeared to study the amber contents of his brandy glass. When he looked up at Philip, his soft green eyes held the calm and reason that Philip had come to expect from his brother. "I know how you would like me to answer that question, Philip,'' he said, ''and I'm sorry to disappoint you, but I think Anna is right. The sooner she is away from here, the better off she'll be. If she were my . . . *friend*, I'd put her on a boat to Boston as soon as possible, and as her lawyer, I strongly advise it.''

When he left his brother, Philip remembered he still had to fulfill his obligation to his mother. She had summoned him to her room because she had something to say to him, that much he knew, and he suspected she was going to ask him about Anna.

As he climbed the stairs and headed toward the large bedroom at the end of the hall, he made up his mind to tell his mother as little as he could get away with. It was definitely to her advantage to be ignorant of the facts and therefore innocent of any wrongdoing.

He knocked on the door, and Monique beckoned him inside. He crossed the thick Oriental carpet to where she lay in her bed, lounging against her pillows, a book open on her lap. She tapped the edge of her bed and he sat down.

''How long will you be staying home this time, *chéri?*'' she asked.

''Just a few days, Mama. The coffee beans will have been picked in St. Sebastian by next week and I will have to sail to the Caribbean to see that they are packed properly.''

''What about Anna? When will she be sailing to Boston?''

''Soon. I can have the *Seahawk* ready to sail on Sunday, and since Anna is anxious to go, I see no reason to wait.''

Monique nodded her head slowly and then regarded her son with wise gray eyes. ''What is she running from, this Anna of yours?''

''Running? Mama, whatever gave you an idea like that? I told you about Anna . . .''

''I know what you told me, but I also know what I saw. There is much sadness in her eyes, an emptiness. That poor girl has been hurt very badly, Philippe. Tell me it was not by you.''

Philip took his mother's hand in both of his. He should have known better than to try and fool her. Monique Brichard had intuitive powers far beyond his ability to understand. "You see too much for your own good, Mama. No, Anna was not hurt by me."

"I thought not, but it is always best to know. Then what is it?"

"I can't tell you, Mama, for your protection as well as Anna's. Though you don't need me to tell you anything at all. Your intuition is serving you well, as always. Why don't you tell me what you think?"

Monique laid her head back against her pillows as if she were suddenly overcome with an overwhelming sadness. She sighed and turned her face toward Philip's. "The day they murdered your father . . . when I watched from our hiding place in the cellar as he fell to the ground in front of our house, I thought my heart would break with grief, the injustice of that horrifying loss. I believed that no pain could be worse. Yet, later that same day, when the murdering bastards set fire to our home and I came so close to losing all of our precious things, the treasures Claude and I had collected over the years, the pain became even greater, until something inside me died.

"It was as if a light in my soul had been extinguished and could never be lit again. Even today when I look in a mirror, I know that I see Monique Brichard, but it is an older, more sharply honed Monique Brichard, who will never have that certain light of innocence back in her eyes.

"Sometimes, when we lose so much that we almost can't bear it, that loss is forever etched on our faces, and one who has experienced it can see it in another. When I look at Anna, I see a beautiful young woman, but I see, too, that she is missing the same light in her eyes. It should be there, but it was taken from her, and, like me, she will never get it back."

Philip smiled at his mother. He couldn't have explained what Anna had suffered any better than that. "Perhaps you are right, Mama. I know there has been at least one great loss in Anna's life, and perhaps there have been more. Ah, Mama, how is it that you grow wiser every year?"

"Only because I grow older every year as well. Wisdom and age are two lines that move on the same plane. And I believe that my intuition, as you call it, has come close to the mark about Anna, but I will be content to leave it at that. It is all right if Anna keeps her secret."

"Thank you for not asking me to tell you."

"You're welcome, but as your mother, I must say one thing more . . ."

"And that is?"

"You haven't much time, Philippe. You must make up your mind how you feel about this girl. There is something between you, something that goes beyond your pity for her and her gratitude to you."

Philip stood up from the bed and kept his voice void of emotion. "There can be nothing, Mama. Anna is going away. It's what she wants to do."

"And you believe this story about her grandmother?"

A surprisingly cynical sound, akin to laughter, yet different came from his mouth. "I am never quite sure what to believe about Anna, Mama. I think I know her one minute, and then the next I am baffled again, and I realize that I really know very little at all. But, about the grandmother, I'm not entirely certain that Anna believes herself."

Monique reached for his hand. "You will do the right thing, Philippe. In spite of your brashness, you almost always do."

At the other end of the hallway, Anna sat at the antique vanity and brushed her hair with a frenzy born more of frustration than a desire to make it shine. Her eyes darted often to the open French doors reflected in the mirror, the same doors that Philip had used when he entered her room earlier.

His kiss in the garden, though purposefully brief, had been eager and needy . . . for both of them. She knew he would do as he had promised and return to her room that night. She both feared and hoped that her heart would yield to him if he did. But if it did yield, it might very well be shattered.

She set the brush down and buried her face in her hands.

"Oh, Mick, Laura, why aren't you here now? Why did you both have to go away when I need you so desperately? You would tell me what to do."

She paced the room, her gaze hardly wavering from the open doors. Her mind began to wander, returning once again to a past that haunted her with agonizing clarity, though she had tried to block the horrifying visions from her memory.

She recalled her first reaction to Stuart Wilkes, the fear and dislike she had felt toward him when he leered at her on the street in Cape de Rive. That fear had turned to terror and the dislike to loathing when he held her captive in his home. She still fought a sick sensation in her stomach when she pictured his hands moving over her sore body so soon after he had brutally taken the life of the person she had loved most in the world.

That incident should have convinced her that she would never again find pleasure in a man's hands on her body, never enjoy his lips on hers and his breath warm on her skin. But *this man,* oh, God, this Philip Brichard . . . he was noble while the other was vulgar; he offered her passion while Wilkes imposed lust; he was tender while her enemy was savage.

She could clearly imagine *his* hands leading her to new worlds while she willingly followed. She could visualize his lips taking her to heights of desire she never knew existed, if only she would let him.

She walked to the open doors and stepped outside, looking down to where Philip's room opened onto the same veranda. She willed him to come out. While she waited, a breeze cooled her fevered face and swept the hair off her forehead, bringing with it the clear-headed realization of what she was about to do.

"There you go again, Anna, with your fantasies," she whispered into the rustling wind. "Yes, he desires you, but it is not enough, you know it isn't. Philip Brichard doesn't love you, not the Anna Connolly he found in his stateroom with all her problems and all her grief and all that she lacks. Go to Boston, Anna, be what Mick said you could be . . . a fine lady with her rightful place in society. Perhaps if Henri can help you, it

Ophelia will take you in and give you your birthright, perhaps maybe then . . ."

She drew both sets of doors closed and latched them securely. Then she climbed into bed and lowered the wick on her bedside lamp. She lay awake for a while, long enough to hear footsteps approaching down the gallery to her door. There the steps halted, and, through the thin curtains, she saw the achingly familiar shape of a man reflected in the moonlight.

He raised his hand as if he would knock to gain entrance to the darkened room, hesitated for a moment, and then dropped his hand to his side. The last Anna heard were his footsteps fading along the gallery as he went away, leaving her alone.

CHAPTER TEN

The next morning, Anna could barely concentrate on her conversation with Monique during breakfast on the back veranda. It was just the two of them since Henri had gone into New Orleans to his office and Claudette was at her lessons. Anna was determined to find out where the other Brichard male was.

Pretending to be more interested in the contents of her tea cup than her inquiry, she said casually, "Where is Philip this morning?"

"He said he had some accounting to attend to. Sometimes he likes to do his paperwork in *l'école,* the children's old schoolhouse in back of the garden." Monique smiled at Anna over the rim of her coffee cup. "Why don't you go out there and see him? I'm certain he would like the interruption."

"I wouldn't want to disturb him if he's busy."

Monique lifted her index finger in the air, the sign of a sudden inspiration. "Actually, you would be doing me a favor if you would take this light breakfast out to Philippe." She folded a pastry and a piece of ham into a linen napkin and held the package out to Anna. "If I know my son, he rushed around this morning and did not take time for breakfast, and I would feel better knowing he had a little something to eat while he worked."

Anna took the napkin and nodded. "In that case, I would be happy to do as you wish," she said. "Where did you say the schoolhouse is located?"

"Just beyond the garden, *chérie*. Follow the cobblestone path, and don't get lost in the holly maze. *L'école* is the small narrow building you will see among the orange and plum trees in the little grove beyond the garden wall. You can't miss it."

Anna walked through an iron trellis that marked the rear entrance to the garden, and stepped into a grove of fruit trees whose limbs were brilliant with fragrant white blossoms. At first she didn't even see the schoolhouse Monique had described because it was hidden by thick, leafy branches. But after taking a few more steps, she saw an oddly shaped, six-sided white brick building occupying a cozy spot in a clearing bordered by tulips and lavender crepe myrtle. She thought the charming, two-story structure looked like something out of a fairy tale with its shingled roof of cedar topped with a delightful turret and miniature catwalk.

The single door on the first floor was open as were all the green shutters at the windows on both floors. Anna approached the building quietly and began a slow inspection around the six sides, peeking into each window as she went. Three students' desks of varying ages and conditions occupied the center of the first-floor room, and along the walls were shelves holding slates and paper and many books.

What a wonderful place to learn, she thought, imagining the Brichard children studiously bent over their lessons while their tutor watched over them. She did wonder, though, how they managed to keep their minds on their studies with the birds chirping so near in the trees and the aroma of orange blossoms and fragrant flowers floating through the windows on spring breezes.

When she walked around to the back of the building, she saw Philip through the rear window. His shirtsleeves were rolled up past his elbows, and he was seated at what was obviously the master's desk. He appeared deep in thought as he leaned over a stack of notes and papers while his pen scratched across a large ledger. The sunlight streaming in the open windows illuminated the worn desktop and cast golden highlights on the fine hair covering his arms.

Anna peeked around the shutters without announcing her presence. She allowed her imagination to wander back several years, and tried to picture Philip as he must have looked as a little boy in this same room when his tutor was seated at the large desk and Philip occupied one of the smaller ones. The vision would not come readily to her mind, however. Instead, Anna could only see the man he was today, strong and handsome, yet intelligent and pensive, his brows knitted together in concentration. It was difficult to imagine Philip as a boy when, on this morning, he was every bit a man in Anna's eyes.

"I thought you didn't approve of skulking around and spying on a person, Anna" came the low, sensuous voice from inside the schoolhouse.

She jumped back from the window with a startled gasp. The pen had stopped moving and was poised above the ledger, but Philip had not raised his head.

"How did you know I was here?" she asked.

He looked up and gave her a tilted smile. "Anyone who has spent as many hours as I have in this room becomes expert at seeing the movements of even the tiniest creatures outside these windows, and you, Anna, create much more of a stir than a spring moth or a chipmunk."

"You're much too clever for me to ever think of spying on you again," she said, leaning on the wooden sill.

"Did you come out here to see me?"

"I was told Claudette was having her lessons here," she said evasively.

"True, but she finished early and I sent her tutor home. Claudette has gone for a ride to visit a friend at the next plantation."

"I see. I'm sorry I missed her. Oh, I've brought you a

package from your mother." Anna held up the napkin. "She thought you would be hungry."

"So, in truth, you have come to see me after all," he stated with a triumphant grin.

"Well, as I said, only because your mother . . ." She hesitated, her weak excuse trapped in his penetrating gaze, and her voice faded into silence.

"Why don't you come around to the door? As long as you're here, you might as well see the site of my childhood tortures."

When she stepped into the interior of the room, Anna was both charmed and impressed by its utilitarian decor. A large fireplace dominated one wall and four ventilated tin foot-warmers hung beside it on hooks, evidence that there must be some chilly days in a Louisiana winter. Four kerosene lanterns sat on the wooden mantel, and a long board along the next wall held porcelain hooks for hats and coats. She scanned the rows of Latin and French primers, spellers, grammar books, and novels that lined the bookcases. "Have you actually read all these books?" she asked.

"Every one," Philip grumbled as though he were remembering his strict schoolmaster doling out assignments.

"Oh, I think I would have loved learning in a room like this."

Philip's face lit up with a grin. "If you like *this* room, wait until you go up there." He pointed to a narrow, winding staircase that led to a small opening in the floor above.

Imagining the wonders at the top of the stairs, Anna hiked her skirt above her ankles and began climbing. Philip followed her. She stepped up into a world of boyhood delights. It was filled with all manner of toys from wooden soldiers and make-believe muskets and swords to coaches with real turning wheels.

"It's called the *garçonnière*," Philip said with affection in his voice. "It means 'boy's room.' This is where Mama always sent Henri and me to play." His eyes perused the much-loved contents around the room. "I haven't been up here in a long time. Mama always said boys need a special place of their own. She always kept Claudette's toys and keepsakes in the house but said boys should be free to holler and stomp so that when they come in the house at night they are ready to be gentlemen.''

He picked up a replica of a brigantine sailing ship and touched the real canvas sail. A faraway look of remembrance lit his eyes. "It's funny, but I think Mama knows now that Claudette needed this room as much as Henri and I ever did. While they are young enough to play, little boys aren't really so different from little girls.'' He looked at Anna who had sat in the middle of the room. She was admiring a small wooden horse with a genuine horsehair mane and tail. "Someday I would like my own children to know this room,'' he said.

Anna could not have been more pleased to be a part of Philip's private world. "Your children will be very lucky to have you for a father, Philip, but not just because of these things . . .''

He inclined his head toward the pony she was holding. "That was always one of my favorites. See, its legs are jointed so you can pretend he is running.'' He sat beside Anna and turned the pony over in her palm.

The instant his hand touched hers, a warmth began in the tips of her fingers and radiated through her body to a center deep inside her. His eyes locked with hers and she leaned into the magnetic draw of his steel-gray gaze.

Without saying a word, he took the wooden horse from her hand and set it on the floor, then placed his palm against her cheek. When he lowered his head to close the distance remaining between them, Anna drew in a quick, anxious breath. She waited for his lips to settle on hers while her heart beat crazily in her chest.

"Coming up here may prove to be the best part of this day,'' he said before his mouth took hers in a long, lingering kiss.

"Mistuh Philip! Mistuh Philip, come quick!'' Huckabee's voice penetrated the sweet, natural sounds of the grove and abruptly ended the kiss. "It's Miss Claudette, somethin's happened, an' I'm powerful scared, suh!''

Philip jumped to his feet and raced down the winding staircase, taking the steps two at a time. Anna followed him, but he was already at the trellis to the garden when she ran out the door of the schoolhouse. She could hear Huckabee's frantic explanation of what had happened.

"Miss Claudette's horse come back without her, Mistuh Philip. That's never happened befo'. You know the little miss can ride that horse like the wind. I got an awful fear that somethin' bad done happened to that chile."

"Saddle my horse, Huckabee, and see that Grandy, Sparks, and Josiah are ready to ride with me. We'll comb the woods between here and Belle Terre. Does Mama know?"

"I don' know how to tell Missus Monique . . ."

"It's all right, Huckabee, go on now, I'll tell her." Philip ran into the house and came out moments later, racing toward the stable. A groom led a large black horse into the paddock and held the reins for Philip. When he passed Anna, Philip called to her, "Would you go up to the house and stay with Mama?"

"Of course. I pray everything's all right."

"I know."

Four riders galloped around the stable heading north toward the woods that separated Frenchman's Point from Belle Terre, the neighboring plantation.

Anna watched them until they neared the trees and split up in four different directions before disappearing into the woods. As she walked toward the house, Anna saw that Monique Brichard had also been watching the men head out in search of her daughter.

Philip followed the main path through the woods to Belle Terre, holding back on the reins of the black stallion who had fully expected to be galloping at a brisk pace as his master usually dictated. But this day Philip cantered at a slow, steady pace through the forest looking left and right for any sign of Claudette.

He finally saw her about fifty feet off the main road. She was lying absolutely still under a large oak tree whose roots radiated along a gnarled path from its wide base. He rode to within a few feet of Claudette before jumping down from his horse.

She was facedown in a patch of loose soil and leaves. Philip turned her over carefully and saw a jagged cut near her temple. "Oh, *ma petite*," he said, swiping at the clotting blood with his thumb. "Claudette, can you hear me?" He felt for a pulse in her neck and thanked God when it thrummed against his fingers. "Wake up, *ma petite*."

When she didn't respond to his voice, he moved his hands down her arms and legs to convince himself that no bones were broken before he attempted to move her. He saw that her sleeve had been torn from her blouse, and he ripped it the rest of the way and bound the fabric around her wound. Then he picked her up and carried her to his horse. He fired his pistol once in the air to signal the other searchers that he had found her. Then as effortlessly as if she weighed but a few pounds, Philip lifted Claudette onto his horse and laid her against the stallion's neck. He mounted the horse himself and cradled his sister against his chest.

He kept his horse at a smooth, rapid gait back to the house, being careful to keep Claudette as immobile as possible. When he rounded the stable, the others were already waiting for him on the wide veranda, including his mother and Anna. He stopped at the front stairs and motioned for Huckabee to take Claudette. "Carry her upstairs to her room," he ordered. "I'm going for the doctor."

"What's taking so long?" Philip muttered for the hundredth time. "The doctor should have come down to tell us something by now." Anna reached out a hand to comfort him, and he managed to smile weakly at her. "I know I'm raving, but I hate waiting. And where is Henri? Grandy went to get him three hours ago. He should be here by now." Just at that moment, hurried footsteps sounded in the front entrance, and Henri burst into the parlor.

"Good God, what's happened?" he demanded, staring first

at Philip and then turning back toward the stairs as if he weren't sure where he should be. "How is she?"

"We don't know yet. I suppose she rode that horse too hard and the mare threw her. How many times have we told Claudette not to . . ." His words trailed off as the family's doctor stepped into the parlor. "Dr. Lindstrom, how is she? Will she be all right?"

The elderly man took off his glasses and wiped them on his handkerchief. "Relax, Philip, she'll be just fine. I was worried for a while because we couldn't bring her around. She suffered a blow to her head, but just a few minutes ago she opened her eyes and complained of a terrible headache . . . a good sign."

"Thank God," Philip and Henri said together. Philip turned toward the window that looked out over the garden. Though his next words seemed like an angry threat, they were only the expression of a man who felt overwhelming relief. "Wait until I get my hands on her. If she ever rides like a hellion again, I'll . . ."

"She wasn't thrown, Philip," Dr. Lindstrom declared. Everyone in the room, including Anna, turned to look at him. "The facts are still unclear, but apparently a man stopped her in the woods on the way to Belle Terre. He frightened her, and her injuries happened when she tried to run away from him. You'll have to talk to Claudette to get the rest of the story."

"Can we see her?" Henri asked.

"Only one of you at a time, and just for a moment."

Philip strode past the doctor to the parlor door, but Dr. Lindstrom stopped him before he could leave the room. "Don't excite her now, Philip," he warned. "She needs rest more than anything."

Philip glanced at Anna and saw the pain in her eyes, and he knew that the same suspicion was running through both of their minds. "I won't upset her, Doctor. I just need to ask her one or two questions." Then he said to Anna, "You stay right here and don't worry about anything. We don't know for certain if it's him, and if it is, I'll take care of it."

He turned abruptly and headed for the stairs, leaving Henri and Dr. Lindstrom with puzzled looks on their faces.

* * *

The room was in semidarkness when Philip entered, and in the faint light from the setting sun coming through the louvers, he could see his mother sitting on the edge of Claudette's bed, a cup of soup in her hand. As his eyes adjusted, he saw his sister, looking small and frail, propped against a mound of pillows at her back. The large white bandage taped to the side of her face looked somehow grotesque next to her delicate features. His breath caught in his throat as he moved across the room. "How are you feeling, *ma petite?*"

Claudette looked up at her big brother, stuck out her chin, and drew her lips together in a stubborn thin line. "I was *not* riding Mystique too fast, Philip," she stated emphatically, and in spite of his concern, Philip could not hide a grin. She was a Brichard all right.

"I know that, *ma petite.* Dr. Lindstrom already told me. Can you tell me what did happen in the woods today?"

Eager to tell her story, Claudette sat up straighter in the bed. "He was the most awful man, Philip—big and rough and he smelled horrible! He walked right out of the woods and into my path. If I hadn't stopped I would have run him over, and I wish now that I had!"

An image of his sister's attacker was already clear in his mind. "What did this man do, Claudette?"

"He grabbed hold of Mystique's bridle and wouldn't let me pass. Then he said he wanted to ask me some questions. He had a poster with two pictures on it. One of them looked like Anna, and he wanted to know if I'd ever seen her."

"What did you say?"

"I said no, that I'd never seen her in my life. I was afraid he wanted to hurt her, but he didn't believe me. He said he could see in my eyes that I was lying, and he said he saw a fancy gentleman get off the *Duchess* with a woman who might very well be Anna."

Claudette's voice began to tremble and tears gathered in her eyes. "He called Anna a murderer, Philip, and he said only a fool or a guilty man would help a lying, wicked murderess escape! But I knew Anna couldn't murder anyone.''

Claudette's voice had begun to rise in alarm, and Monique stroked her hand along her daughter's forehead. ''Shh, now, Claudette, you must stay calm.'' Monique turned questioning eyes to Philip.

''No, of course Anna couldn't murder anyone, *ma petite,*'' he said. ''The man was lying.'' He waited until his sister had settled back against her pillows again. ''What did the man do then?''

''He said that we would all be arrested for helping her, and that he was going to take her back to Illinois where she would pay for what she did. Only he said I shouldn't tell anyone that he talked to me. He said if I did, I would not go to jail with the rest of you because he would kill me first.''

Philip saw the escalating panic in his mother's eyes, and his anger at Jake Finn threatened to boil over.

''That's when I got really scared, Philip,'' Claudette said. ''He looked so mean!''

It took all of Philip's effort to keep his voice calm as he asked, ''What did you do then?''

''I jumped down from my horse and tried to run, but the man grabbed me and wouldn't let me go. He ripped my blouse and twisted my hand.'' She held up her arm for Philip to see, and his fury increased when he observed the bruises on her wrist. ''His face was so close to mine that I could smell his awful breath as he kept telling me to keep quiet or he would hurt me.''

''And what did you say to him?''

A spark of pride replaced the fear in Claudette's eyes for just a moment as she declared, ''I called him a swamp swilling bayou bat and kicked him you know where real hard!''

Philip heard a strange sound come from his mother's lips and he leaned over to see if she was all right. He was startled to see a smile on her face and pride in her eyes, and he knew that the sound she'd made had been a burst of laughter. He placed his hand on Monique's shoulder and sighed in relief.

''You did just fine, *ma petite,*'' Philip assured his sister. ''I know that man will not want to tangle with you again, and I also know you're tired, but just one more thing . . . how did you hurt your head?''

"I ran away from him and he chased me. I thought I was going to get away, but all at once I felt his hand on my shoulder, and I was falling. I guess that's when I hit my head. I remember him swearing and then my head hurting, and that's all I remember until I woke up here.''

Philip bent and kissed Claudette's forehead. "You get some rest now, and don't worry about that man ever again. I promise you he won't be back.''

Claudette snuggled into her pillows and closed her eyes without ever seeing the veins throbbing at Philip's temple or the sudden narrowing of his dark eyes. But Monique saw everything.

"What are you going to do, Philippe?'' she asked in a whisper.

"I'm going to the Vieux Carré, Mama,'' he said. "Don't let Henri follow me. This is not business for him. I'll take Grandy with me.''

She nodded, knowing it would do no good to try and dissuade him. "Be careful,'' she cautioned as Philip left the room.

"Why is Philip going to the Old Quarter, Mama?'' Claudette asked wearily.

"I don't know, *chérie*, but everything will be fine. You just get some sleep now.''

Anna was alone in the parlor when Philip returned. She stood up and turned toward him when she heard his footsteps. She didn't say a word, but Philip could read the question in her eyes and sense her fear of the answer. How he hated to have to tell her the identity of the man in the woods. "Claudette is fine,'' he began.

"I'm so relieved, but Philip, who . . . ?''

He went to her and put his hands on her shoulders. "It was Jake Finn.''

She couldn't look at him. "Oh, my God. Philip, I'm so sorry."

Philip cupped his hand under her chin and lifted her face to his. "Let me make something clear to you, Anna. You have nothing to apologize for or feel guilty about. Jake Finn is the enemy, not you."

"But if it weren't for me coming here . . ."

"Or if it weren't for me bringing you . . . or if I had handled Jake differently in St. Louis . . . or if Claudette hadn't ridden off by herself today. There are too many 'ifs' and none of them matter. There is a problem and we will face it, understand?" He tried to bolster her courage with a smile meant to convey his belief in her.

"What should we do?" she asked.

"Well, you are going to stay in the house with Mama and Henri. I've already talked to Huckabee, and he has stationed several of our men around the perimeter of the house and grounds. You'll be perfectly safe."

"And you?"

"I have some business to take care of in New Orleans." He kept his voice calm and reassuring, but he read concern in the downward tug of Anna's lips.

She placed her hand against his chest and fought tears that welled up in her eyes. "You will be careful, won't you?" she said.

He wiped away a drop of moisture under her eye with his thumb. "Why, Miss Anna," he drawled, "Ah do believe you are concerned for mah well-bein', and it warms mah heart to know it. A man could slay dragons if he knew you were waitin' at home for him."

His teasing had accomplished its purpose, and Anna responded with a little smile. "I think I'd feel better knowing you were going out to face a dragon. Please promise me you'll be careful."

"I will." Placing his hands on each side of her face, he kissed her quickly but thoroughly. Then he turned abruptly and strode out of the room. "Huckabee! It's time. Bring my horse around and make sure the men are at their stations!" The front door slammed shut, and Darcine rushed across the foyer to fasten the bolts.

There are people in New Orleans who believe that the scurrilous atmosphere of Bourbon Street, the narrow avenue which runs through the center of the Old Quarter, does not change significantly from daylight to dark. Evil is simply evil, no matter whether the sun is shining or not.

Philip Brichard was not one of those people. True, the few blocks of Bourbon Street that Philip visited that night when he left Frenchman's Point had earned a reputation for indecency and meanness that was as well deserved at noon as at midnight. But, in Philip's eyes, the dark shadows of late evening reflected in the pale yellow streetlights and the garish hues of the brazenly lit taverns made Bourbon Street's wretchedness even more apparent.

There was always a varied and colorful array of patrons, from the poorest laborer to the wealthiest French Creole gentleman, who frequented the establishments of Bourbon Street. Therefore, no one that night took special notice of the tall, aristocratic man in the black Stetson who searched the entryways of brothels and taverns. No one seemed aware when he entered the shops of fortune-tellers and practitioners of voodoo.

Walking with this man was a large, muscular Negro whose hair hung in tight braids past his shoulders. The black man's eyes darted in all directions. He watched the street while his companion searched the buildings.

Music and laughter and the raucous claptrap of rowdy citizens spilled out the open doorways and windows of the businesses of Bourbon Street. Philip ignored the barkers who called from sidewalks trying to entice customers to their establishments. He crossed each threshold and looked around each gaudy interior until he determined whether or not the man he was looking for was among the revelers. He finally spotted him in a rundown tavern known for its inexpensive liquor and affordable women.

With his elbows firmly propped on the bar, Jake Finn cradled a glass of whiskey between his hands. A half-empty bottle sat within his reach.

"That's him," Philip said to Grandy. The black man nodded, ready for further instructions. "You go around to the back and wait for me in the alley," Philip said, and after he saw Grandy turn the corner of the building, he went inside.

Palming a small pistol that he had removed from his vest pocket, Philip walked up to Jake Finn. Positioning himself so he was between Jake and the back entrance, he pressed the barrel of the pistol against the thick flesh of Jake's waist.

"Hello, Mr. Finn," he said. The glass of whiskey in Jake's hand stopped midway on its journey to his mouth. "I suggest that you remain quite still while I explain that there is a derringer pointed at your side. It's a small weapon, I know, but chosen because it only makes a little popping sound when it fires, hardly noticeable to this crowd. But at this range it will tear through your abdomen, explode into your kidneys, and very likely kill you. Unfortunately, no one will know for hours whether you are dead or merely sleeping off a nasty drunk."

Though Jake made no attempt to face his attacker straight on, Philip saw his eyes glaze over with fear. "The initials on the handle of this pistol are *P.B.*," he said. "Does that mean anything to you, Mr. Finn?"

"Should it?" Jake croaked. Beads of perspiration formed along his upper lip.

"Well, if it doesn't, it will before long." Philip gripped Jake's forearm and pulled him away from the bar. "We're going outside for a little talk, Mr. Finn. If you're a smart man, you'll cooperate." When they reached the back entrance, Philip shoved him outside into the alley.

Any thought Jake might have had to escape or attack his adversary had to have been abandoned when, in the light from a second-story window, he saw the giant black man across the alley. Grandy stood silently with his legs spread far apart and his huge arms folded across his chest. His black eyes glittered threateningly, and his lips were pressed together in a firm, unyielding line.

"Wh-what's goin' on here anyway?" Jake questioned feebly. Philip slammed him against the outside wall of the tavern and checked his clothing for weapons. He withdrew a knife from Jake's boot and held it up to Grandy. "Would you mind holding this for Mr. Finn?" Philip asked, and the black man walked over and took the knife from Philip. "You can take this, too," he said, passing his derringer to Grandy. His eyes locked onto Jake's with the intensity of his hatred of the man. "Now we are equally prepared for a fair fight."

Philip's first punch to Jake's stomach was as quick and sudden as lightning and almost as powerful, and Jake doubled over with an agonized groan. His jaw, which was slack with shock and pain, was then clamped shut against his upper lip with a bone-rattling crunch as Philip's fist shot into Jake's chin. His head snapped back against the wall, and Philip pressed his arm into Jake's throat.

Through a strangled breath, Jake muttered, "I th-thought you said a fair fight."

"I'm giving you about as much chance as you gave my sister in the woods at Frenchman's Point today," Philip growled.

"Jeezus!" Jake swore as recognition broke through the haze of pain and alcohol. "Now I know who you are. You're the d-dandy who's been squirin' that murderess down the river."

"I'm the man whose sister you nearly killed today!" Philip shot back.

"I n-never meant no harm to that little girl," Jake protested, squirming against the iron clamp on his throat. "I'm just tryin' to get what's rightfully mine."

"That's not the way I see it," Philip hissed between clenched teeth. "When you're in St. Gerard Parish, you play by Brichard rules, and you broke those rules today, Mr. Finn."

"Wh-what do you aim to do?" Jake's eyes darted from Philip to Grandy.

"Have you ever been in a Louisiana prison, Mr. Finn?" Jake shook his head, his frightened stare now fixed only on Philip's face. Philip loosened his hold on Jake's throat. He coughed and craned his neck to clear his air passage as Philip continued.

"The rats are as big as bloodhounds and pick up a man's scent every bit as well. And it gets so hot, and you get so sick of your own stench that you welcome the chance to cut back cypress roots in the swamp for twelve hours a day. But that's where the cottonmouths and moccasins grow to ten feet, Mr. Finn, and the gators will bite your leg off at the thigh just to see if they like the taste of you."

Jake rubbed the back of his hand across his mouth and stared at Philip. From somewhere deep inside, he found a vestige of bravado and snarled a response. "You can't put me in no prison for what I done today. I didn't do nothin' to yer sister. I only talked to her, that's all!"

"You touched her!" Philip spat back. "You put your filthy hands on her, tore her blouse, threatened to kill her, and chased her in the woods. I don't call that *nothing,* Mr. Finn, and neither will the St. Gerard Parish circuit judge who is a very close friend of a New Orleans attorney who just happens to be that little girl's other brother."

Philip gripped Jake's shoulders and leaned so close to him that he could smell the fear oozing from Jake's pores. "You'll be in a Louisiana prison so long that nobody will even remember who you are or how you got there. You will cease to exist, Mr. Finn."

Jake trembled under Philip's hands, but he still managed to squeak out the one question that was uppermost in his mind. "What about the reward money—the five thousand dollars waitin' for me in Cape de Rive? I know you're hidin' that murderin' little—"

"Don't you understand yet, Jake?" Philip said, the forced calm in his voice and the intense fury in his eyes causing Jake to quake more violently. "There's not going to be five thousand dollars, ever, because you and I both know that the whole story about what happened in Cape de Rive is a sham. If I did know this woman you're talking about, and I'm not saying I do, I would also know that the only person who was truly murdered in Cape de Rive was the man whose picture is on that poster you showed my little sister."

"Mr. Stuart Wilkes was murdered!" Jake blurted out. "And that woman done it!"

"Mr. Wilkes had an unfortunate but well-deserved accident, and the facts will bear that out. But we're wasting time here, and you don't have much to waste. You have to make a decision, Mr. Finn. You can spend the rest of your days in prison, or you can take a little trip . . . right now, tonight."

"Where to?"

"I don't care where you end up. It only matters to me that you never come back to St. Gerard's Parish again." Philip glanced over his shoulder and Grandy immediately came to his side. "Grandy, get a good look at this man," Philip said. "If you ever see him around Frenchman's Point, apprehend him at once. As of today, he's a wanted man in Louisiana, so if he gives you any trouble, kill him on the spot, and anyone else who trespasses on Brichard land."

The black man's eyes pierced the last of Jake Finn's tenuous confidence, and he wilted against the rough bricks of the tavern wall. "I'll go, but I ain't got no money," he muttered.

"You won't need any," Philip said. "Your passage has already been arranged on a barge that leaves tonight from Jackson Square. Grandy and I will personally escort you the few short blocks to the dock and see you on board. There's just one more thing I need to know, though. Where is your partner?"

"Sam? He gave up the ghost days ago, and went back north. By now he's prob'ly sniffin' around the widow and askin' for favors."

"He was a smart man not to follow you to Frenchman's Point," Philip said. "Grandy?" Philip motioned for Grandy to take a position on one side of Jake while he remained on the other. Then, with Jake sandwiched between them, the three men walked through the dark side streets of the Old Quarter to where a large steam-driven flatboat, laden with crates of goods for points north on the river, waited at the dock for its only passenger.

* * *

Philip and Grandy lingered until the barge steamed out of the harbor before they, too, left the city to return to Frenchman's Point. It was the middle of the night when they rode around the back of the house to the stable. Philip looked up at the second floor. Two lights were still on at opposite ends of the gallery, which told him that his mother and Anna had not gone to bed yet.

When he dismounted, he saw the slight figure of his mother silhouetted against her French doors. She peeked outside, lifted a hand to say she saw him, and drew her curtains closed. He was aware that Anna remained at her door longer, watching him as he removed the saddle and bridle from his horse. Grandy followed Philip's gaze.

"Looks like the womenfolk been waitin' up for you, Mistuh Philip," Grandy said as the light in Monique's room was finally extinguished.

"I guess so, Grandy. I expect Missy's waiting for you, too."

"I know she is," Grandy said, meeting Philip's smile with his own. "We're lucky to have those sweet souls care so much about us."

"You're right about that," Philip agreed, leading the stallion into the stable. When he came back out a few minutes later, the light in Anna's room was no longer burning, but Philip didn't care. She had waited up, and he knew it, and that was what mattered.

CHAPTER ELEVEN

"Good morning, *chéri*," Monique said to Philip when he joined her and Anna for breakfast the next morning. "I trust you are well."

"Very well, Mama, and happy to be relieved of a troublesome burden." He leaned over and kissed her cheek before taking a seat across from Anna. "Good morning, Anna," he said.

"Good morning," she responded casually, although inside she was bursting to hear news of his exploits the previous night. After taking a sip of coffee, she asked, "Do you mean that this burden, as you called it, is gone for good?"

"As gone as last night's moon, which I understand you were gazing at until quite late."

She looked down at her lap, anywhere but at his knowing grin.

"And, Mama," he said, "how is our little Claudette today?"

"Fighting the doctor's orders, and mine, as you might imagine. She wanted to come down to breakfast this morning, but I wouldn't hear of it. Raising Claude Brichard's daughter is like butting heads with a billy goat most of the time."

"Her headache is gone?" Philip asked, taking a large swallow of coffee.

"I don't think entirely. I saw her wince when I opened her curtains this morning to let in the sun, but she would never admit it. She will need a few more days in bed to be her old self again. But I promised her you would come up to her room and tell her everything that happened last night, minus any details you think would be inappropriate, of course."

"Nothing inappropriate happened, Mama," Philip said, holding his hands up for her inspection. "See? No blood under the fingernails."

Monique gave her son a look of stern reproach. "Do not joke about this, Philippe. *Mon Dieu,* when I think about what happened yesterday . . . what could have happened . . ."

Sympathizing with Philip's mother, Anna glared at him. "Your mother's right. This is not something to tease about." Then she covered Monique's hand with her own. "I am so sorry for what happened, you must know that. I should never have come here and put your family in danger. All this misfortune is my fault, and after I leave tomorrow, I hope you will be able to forgive me . . ."

Monique's face clouded with guilt as she regarded Anna's stricken expression. "Oh, no, *chérie,* I didn't mean . . ."

She never finished her explanation because Philip stood abruptly, scraping his chair across the wood floor. He tossed his napkin beside his plate. "Of course she didn't mean anything, Anna! I told you before that you have nothing to apologize for. When are you going to believe me? The problem is solved. Jake Finn is gone from our lives, and, as a matter of fact, you wouldn't even have to . . ."

Anna could only stare openmouthed at Philip's tirade, while Monique did not seem at all disturbed. In fact, the older woman was smiling!

Philip was prohibited from concluding his outburst, because the door to the dining room opened and Huckabee stepped inside. A heavy, awkward silence fell over the room as everyone turned to the servant.

Huckabee's gray eyes scanned each of their faces, as if he weren't at all sure where he should settle his gaze. " 'Scuse me, Mistuh Philip, I don' mean to interrupt yo' breakfast, but that shipment you been waitin' for jus' came round the bend. I think you might want to go down to the dock.''

Philip cleared his throat. "Yes, you're right, thank you, Huckabee." Then he flashed a quick look at his mother and Anna and excused himself. "Pardon me, ladies, but I have some business to attend to." He strode out of the room without another word.

"What was that all about?" Anna asked Monique.

"I have no idea what the shipment is, *chérie,* but I think the shouting was about the fact that my son does not want you to leave tomorrow."

"Oh, no," Anna disagreed. "He wants me to go, he expects me to go. We've planned it for a long time. I'm sure that Philip will feel he's well rid of me. You don't know everything he's had to put up with ..." She immediately clamped her lips shut, aware that she was about to reveal too much about her relationship with Philip.

Monique regarded her with amusement in her eyes. "My son does not put up with anything he does not choose to, *chérie.* This much I know."

"But we made a deal," Anna offered weakly.

"Ah ... a deal, that's different. My son always honors his agreements, assuming that is what you want, of course."

"It's what's best," Anna said, hoping to convince Monique of this when she couldn't convince herself. "For everyone. We all need for our lives to return to normal, and the simple fact is ... I need to go."

"Then that is what you should do." Monique folded her napkin and placed it neatly on her plate, then rested her chin on her laced fingers. "May I tell you a little story, Anna?"

"Of course."

"Let me begin by saying I believe that when something is essentially good, when it is right, then nothing can spoil it. True goodness prevails for eternity, no matter what forces attempt to corrupt it." Her eyes darkened with sadness, and she sighed deeply before beginning her story.

"The war was almost over when a band of renegade Yankee soldiers came on our land. They rode right up to our house, without warning. When he saw them coming, my husband, Claude, rushed the three of us, myself and our two sons, to the cellar and demanded that we stay there while he went out to face the marauders with only Huckabee beside him.

"Philippe was only sixteen years old, but he thought he was very much a man. It was all I could do with my tears and my pleading to get him to stay in the cellar with Henri and me and do as his papa asked. Through an opening in the cellar bricks, Philippe saw his father killed that day, for no reason that Philippe could understand except that his papa was in the way of a Yankee captain who wanted to get by.

"The soldier shot Claude, and his blood spilled at the bottom of the stairs in front of the house. The Yankees invaded our house, but do you know the strangest thing, Anna? They didn't even take much—a little silver and some wine, and, oh, yes, some chickens and a cow. That was all. They killed my husband for chickens and a cow. And then they set fire to the south face of the house and rode off."

Anna was spellbound with horror at the tragic story of the Brichard family's past. "Why, Monique, why?" She could hardly get the question past an aching lump in her throat. "Why would anyone do such a terrible thing?"

"To this day I have no idea, *chérie,* but that day I believed that the goodness that was Claude Brichard had died with him and I would never experience it again. With Huckabee and the others, my sons and I battled the blaze, and while we saved our house, and put out the fire, we all felt we had lost our light, the center of our universe.

"At least that's what I thought, because I didn't know until later that I had Claude's baby growing inside me. I was forty years old, Anna, and the last thing I ever expected in my life was to have another baby, but I did, and Claudette, with her fire and her spirit and her wit, is every bit the offspring of Claude Brichard. She has grown in his image and has become so much like the father she never knew."

Monique patted Anna's hand. "So you see, Anna, some things are meant to endure; their goodness is everlasting and finds a way to survive." Wiggling delicate fingers at Anna,

Monique smiled. "Maybe I'm becoming a crazy old woman, I don't know, but I think I see something good between you and Philippe. So no matter what you do . . . you can go away for a time if you want to, my son can act as obstinate as a mule, the pair of you can test whatever it is that exists between you, but if it is right for you both, it will win out. You can't stop it." With a sly little grin that wrinkled the corners of her eyes, she added, "Maybe it already has won. We'll see.

"Well," Monique sighed, straightening in her chair, "I have talked enough. Now it is time for me to go upstairs to my daughter and see what I can do to keep her in that bed for another day at least. I will see you later?"

Anna nodded, watching Monique stand and push her chair under the table. Before Monique left the dining room, Anna called after her, "Thank you for telling me that story."

She smiled over her shoulder. "You're welcome. Perhaps one day you can pass it on . . . Well, who knows what lies in the future." Her wide skirt swished softly against the door frame as she left the room.

Philip returned after accepting delivery of the shipment at the Frenchman's Point dock, and tried several times during the morning to see Anna. But each time Darcine told him that Anna was busy with preparations for her journey. "I'm sorry, Mistuh Philip, but Miss Anna is washin' her hair," the servant explained, keeping Anna's door partway closed.

"You'll have to come back, Mistuh Philip. Miss Anna is havin' her bath right now," he was told when he returned later. Once he passed Darcine at the entrance to the clothes pantry off the kitchen. She was carrying a load of garments Philip recognized as Anna's.

"May I see her *now?*" he asked, unable to keep the irritation from his voice.

"I don't know, Mistuh Philip. Miss Anna is packin' her trunk right now. That's why I'm bringin' up these laundered dresses for her."

Philip's frustration was made all the worse because he was

anxious to show Anna something that he knew would definitely please her, and he couldn't even get her to pay the least bit of attention to him. "It's like trying to get an audience with the king of France!" he declared moments after Darcine had climbed the stairs with the gowns in her arms. "I've waited long enough," he decided minutes later. "She's going to see what arrived on that barge this morning, and she's going to see now!"

He strode purposefully up the stairs and knocked once again on Anna's door, perhaps a bit too loudly, because a cautious Darcine opened the door just a crack and peeked out. "What's the matter, you bangin' so hard on the door?" she questioned with narrow, disapproving eyes.

"You know very well what's the matter, Darcine. Is Anna in there?"

"Yes."

"Fine. I'm coming in." Forcing Darcine to step back, Philip swung the door open and went inside. He entered a room littered with a profusion of colors and fabrics. Dresses and other articles of clothing were strewn over the bed, on the floor, and across the lid of the trunk which sat on the floor. Anna was kneeling beside it.

She stood up at the unexpected intrusion. Her hair, still damp at the ends, was hanging loose around her face, and she swept it off her shoulders. She was wearing the white robe she had chosen at Lilly's, the one she had worn when she came into Philip's hotel room in St. Louis. Only this time she did not have the nightdress underneath it, and her tempting curves were clearly outlined through the thin fabric.

"Philip, for heaven's sake!" She pulled the robe tightly around her and crossed her arms over her chest. "You shouldn't be in here!"

His previous irritation all but forgotten, Philip hesitated in the center of the room. The last reaction he'd expected to have toward Anna at this moment was the one that clearly strained in his trousers. With sheer willpower, he called on his pride to maintain an upper hand. "Well, neither should you," he blurted out.

"What's that supposed to mean?"

"It means that I've been trying to get you to take a walk with me all day, but I haven't had any luck getting past your sergeant-at-arms here." He flashed a disgruntled glare at Darcine.

"I know, and I was coming down to find you in a little while," Anna said, "but you must know how many things I have to do."

"Well, stop doing them now," he ordered. "Put something on and come with me, or I swear you'll be marching out in the daylight clad in nothing but that . . . thing!"

For an uncomfortably long moment, Anna stood perfectly still. Only a slight tapping of her slippered foot alerted him that she might actually be considering telling him to go away once again. If that was the case, he decided he was going to make good on his threat and carry her out of the room. Why was it, he wondered, that when a person has something which he thinks is truly wonderful to share with someone else, that other person has to spoil it by not cooperating? He pasted a serious frown on his face meant to dissuade Anna from further rebellion, and she wisely agreed to go with him.

"All right, Philip, I'll come, but please step outside until I can dress." With her arms still folded across her chest, she waved her fingers in a no-nonsense gesture that definitely told him to leave.

He waited outside in the hall for no more than five minutes, and when she came out to meet him, she was wearing the simple cotton dress with the little blue cornflowers she had bought in Hannibal. He remembered how she had looked in that dress when he saw her reflected in the sunlight in his stateroom on the *Duchess*. That day she had been transformed from an unkempt, frightened runaway with a questionable past to a beautiful young woman with an even more uncertain future. She had taken his breath away that morning, and she did so again.

"I'm ready," she said, drawing him back from his reverie, "and I apologize for making you wait. Where are we going anyway?"

"You'll see soon enough." He took her elbow and walked beside her down the stairs.

They went out the back entrance of the house and along the short path to the stable. Neither Anna nor Philip attempted a conversation, each one apparently waiting for the other to alleviate the strangely charged atmosphere evident in Anna's room. After exchanging several cat-and-mouse glances, they reached the entrance to the stable where Grandy was waiting for them.

"Afternoon, Miss Anna," he said.

"Hello, Grandy."

"Is the new arrival inside?" Philip asked.

"Settlin' in as cozy as can be, Mistuh Philip."

"Good. Anna, there's something I want you to see." He led her inside to the stalls.

"We're not going riding, are we?" Anxious words spilled out of her mouth. "I'm not very good at it, I have to tell you, and I'd be especially awkward on any of the horses I've seen around Frenchman's Point. I'd probably fall off first thing."

Philip delighted in the nervous chatter that didn't show any signs of letting up. "I was born in the city, though you would have no way of knowing that. I've only been on one horse in my life, and, truthfully, that's the only one I could ever really trust, though I'm sure these are wonderful animals . . ."

They walked down the row of stalls until they were near the end. "That one horse you say you could trust," Philip said with deceptive calm, "did she look anything like that gentle chestnut mare down there?"

Anna stopped and looked past the remaining stalls to where a shiny auburn head bobbed up and down over the last door. "Irish!" she squealed. "Is it you? Oh, it is!"

The horse answered Anna's greeting with a whinny of recognition, and Anna tore down the brick pathway that led to the last stall. She threw her arms around Irish's neck and buried her face in the horse's mane. "My old girl!" she cried. "My dear, dear Irish."

"How does she look to you after her long trip?" Philip asked, smiling over Anna's shoulder.

Anna stepped back and looked at her horse from every possible angle. "She looks wonderful, fat as can be and as beautiful as ever."

She returned to hug the horse once again. Tears clouded her vision until the present merged with the past. All at once Anna could see Mick as he had been during their last hours together. His words came back to her in a rush of sweet nostalgia.

"We'll leave Irish in the poshest stable in Missouri so she can munch on oats and barley . . ."

"Oh, Philip," Anna breathed, not quite ready to completely let go of the magical spell that had taken her aback. "I just heard Mick's voice as clearly as if he were standing next to me, and all because Irish is here. And I remembered him now without feeling all the sadness and emptiness. I remembered him the way he was when we were happy."

Seeing the joy in Anna's luminous eyes, Philip felt a sudden, almost overpowering sense of affection for her, a feeling that was strangely different and perhaps even stronger than the wild desire he had come to associate with being near her. This new emotion was a need to care and protect and cherish, and Philip was certain he had never felt anything quite like it before.

She put her arms around his neck, and he placed his hands on her waist, content to look into her eyes and allow her emotions to flow through his fingers to his heart. "Thank you," she said softly, and he wondered who felt the greater happiness, Anna or him.

They stayed in the stable for over an hour, and Anna asked question after question. "How did you do this? When did you do it? Where did you find her?"

Philip explained everything by telling her about the private investigator he hired in St. Louis. "I was just fulfilling the promise I made to you in Hannibal, remember? I told you that you couldn't go back, but I said I would try to find your belongings."

"I remember, but I guess I never thought you really would."

"I keep my word, Anna, no matter what." He thought of his promise to send her to Boston and wondered if she were thinking of it as well.

"Do you know if there was anything else at the campsite?" she asked after a moment.

He had dreaded this question, but was prepared with his answer. He led Anna into a storage room where saddles and tack were kept and took a wooden box off a shelf.

She recognized it immediately. "That's our money box!" She took it from Philip and sat down on a trunk to examine the contents. There were scraps of old letters, some torn bits of fabric, and several whalebone buttons.

After she looked at the few things, she rubbed her fingers along the blackened, charred corners of the box. "What happened?" she asked, raising her eyes to Philip.

"When the investigator got there, everything was in ashes, Anna. Someone had taken your horse to a farm and had set fire to the wagon. There was nothing left but this little bit."

Her expression grew pensive and her shoulders sagged with a sudden weariness. "Another fire," she whispered hoarsely. Philip had to lean down to hear her next words. She shook her head with a kind of sad resignation. "Twice my world has been destroyed by flames that left me with nothing."

Philip waited, hoping she would tell him more, but she didn't. Instead she examined the tattered contents one more time. She picked up a piece of fabric, a small square of sooty green satin and held it up for him to see. "You don't recognize this, I'm sure," she said.

"Yes, I do. How could I ever forget that beautiful young lady in the shimmering green gown on the River Flats stage? She was the 'Mississippi Songbird' as I recall, and she was dazzling."

"And you were my most appreciative, and most exasperating, audience. I'll always remember when you winked at me from the front row and I nearly forgot the words of my song." She put the fabric back in the box and closed the lid. "I never thanked you for the double eagle you gave us that night."

"There's no need to thank me, Miss Rose. I got my money's worth," he said, winking at her again.

* * *

That night, dinner was served on the veranda, and Monique agreed that everyone should attend in casual attire. She explained that because Anna was leaving the next morning, the mood around Frenchman's Point was somber enough without asking her family to sit stiffly at the table in corsets and stays, and collars and vests. Claudette was permitted to come to the veranda for a short time, but even her light banter didn't improve the atmosphere.

Henri questioned Anna once more at dinner about the events the night of Mick's murder, and Anna gave him some of the contents from the wooden box, including the whalebone buttons that had been on Mick's shirt. He explained to her that he would go to Cape de Rive as soon as she notified him that she had arrived safely in Boston, and it was his hopeful intention to get the charges against her dropped. He told her to inform his family as soon as possible of her address in Boston in case he had good news to tell her.

Likewise, if his mission failed, she should be deciding if she would want to return to Illinois for a trial to clear her name. If so, Henri promised that he would remain her attorney and defend her in court. If she chose not to return, then her decision to sail to Boston would prove to be the right one, since she could easily "disappear" in the crowds of a large city far from Cape de Rive.

After listening to Henri's advice, and eating very little of her meal, Anna excused herself from the table saying she felt like taking a walk around the grounds. Philip offered to go with her, but she assured him that she would be fine and would actually prefer to be alone to consider everything Henri had told her.

After she left, Monique clucked her tongue and shook her head in sympathy. "That poor child, to be facing such decisions and possibly a bleak future at her young age. My heart goes out to her."

"Tell me the truth, Henri," Philip said, struggling with his own conflicting emotions, "do you think you'll have a chance of clearing Anna's name in Cape de Rive?"

"Honestly, I do. If I find Mick Connolly's body, I feel certain I can get the charges against Anna dropped. If I don't, then, for her own safety, I hope Anna decides never to return to the Mississippi valley again."

Henri's clear, intelligent gaze leveled on Philip's face. "This is something you must consider, Brother, very seriously. Are you going to be able to let her go?"

Philip didn't answer with words. He let a scowl convey his opinion of Henri's question. With both his brother and Anna constantly reminding him that traveling to Boston was Anna's only logical course of action, what choice did he have?

Several minutes passed while each member of the Brichard family finished his meal in silence. Then Philip was the first to excuse himself from the table. "I would have thought she'd be back by now," he said. "I think I'll go see if she's all right."

"Do you know where to look, *chéri?*" Monique asked.

"Yes, Mama, something tells me I know exactly where Anna went."

He saw the lantern glow through the tree branches as soon as he left the garden by the back trellis, and he knew that his hunch had been correct. The first floor of *l'école* was dark, so he carefully picked his way through the desks to the stairs in the rear and climbed to the second floor. Anna was kneeling in the middle of the *garçonnière* with her flowered skirt spread around her. In the soft light it looked as though she were sitting in a meadow of blue flowers.

"I thought I'd find you here," he said.

She looked over her shoulder at him, and he could tell she'd been crying. She was holding the wooden pony with the jointed legs that Philip had told her was one of his favorite toys, and she turned it over in her hands so he could plainly see it. A strained smile pulled at her lips. "I know what you're thinking," she said, "but I wasn't going to steal it."

He smiled at her. "I never thought that for a moment. I think your life of crime is a thing of the past now."

"I was going to ask you if I could have it, though."

"If it will help you to think fondly of me, by all means," he said.

She looked up at him with vivid blue eyes that glistened with moisture. "I don't need any trinket to help me remember you fondly, Philip. No matter what happens, I always will."

Her words pierced his heart, and he smoothed away several folds of her skirt and knelt beside her.

His intense gaze was almost more than she could bear, and Anna looked down at her lap and twisted the pony's mane through her fingers. "I have so little left," she stated matter-of-factly.

It was her way never to ask for pity, no matter how unfairly life treated her. For the first time, Philip understood it was one of the characteristics he most admired about Anna.

"The tokens of my past are all ashes now. I have to build new memories with new treasures." When she raised her eyes to Philip, they were dry. Her lips were slightly parted in a dreamy, reminiscent smile. "It's funny, but all my keepsakes now remind me of you. My wardrobe, the snowglobe, the books, the pony . . ." She tilted her head, recalling a pleasant memory. "Even the red garter. But my gratitude to you goes far beyond these material things. You didn't deserve me, Philip, but in the middle of one awful night I was dropped in your lap, and since then, you've given me the one chance I'll ever have to get my life back."

He took her hand and held it between his. "It has been my pleasure, mademoiselle," he said, his voice husky and low. "Every frustrating, suspenseful, agonizingly wonderful moment of it."

"I'll miss you, you know."

There was a tremble in her voice that told him it cost her dearly to admit it, and her honesty was ultimately his undoing. "Oh, Anna," he moaned, wrapping her in his arms. "Why do we have to talk only about the past? Is a future so unimaginable?"

"It is now," she breathed close to his ear. "There are so many problems."

He pulled the hair away from her neck and kissed the soft skin under her earlobe. She leaned her head back, giving him access to her throat. Thinking only to please and comfort her, he planted gentle kisses on the milky white skin exposed to him. His hands moved on her back and his mouth found hers. He tasted her sweetness and felt her need as she drew his tongue inside the honeyed darkness of her mouth.

He laid her back against the floor until her head rested on the rippling flowers of her skirt. His fingers worked on the tiny buttons at the collar of her dress while his mouth opened wider on hers, his tongue seeking, plundering, taking what he most wanted.

With hands desperate to know every inch of her, he pulled apart the yoke of her dress, revealing the creamy skin of her chest. Tearing his mouth from hers, he groaned, "I don't want you to go, Anna. Don't go."

"I have to . . ." Her words faded to a muffled whimper as his mouth moved to the tops of her breasts rising above her camisole. With his finger and thumb he teased her nipple to a rigid bud.

Her chest heaved with a quick, short gasp when he fully cupped her breast. He kneaded her through the camisole until she groaned her longing. Then he pulled the flimsy under-garment down and let his tongue roam over the tip and the soft mound around it. He experienced a swift, hot pooling of passion in his loins.

Crossing one leg over her thighs, he pulled her closer to his arousal, and held her captive to the thrusts of his hips and the onslaught of his urgent caresses. Filling his hand once more with her breast, his mouth moved upward, sizzling the skin of her throat until he covered her lips again. "I can't let you go, Anna," he murmured against her mouth.

"But Henri says . . ." she protested weakly.

He sensed the escalating fervor of her need, as powerful as his own. Her resolve to resist him melted with each hungry kiss. In his mind, there was only Anna. She was his life force,

he food of his soul. There was no thinking of tomorrow. He
couldn't let her go tonight.

"Henri isn't here with you right now. I am, and I want you
so badly . . ."

"Philip, we can't, we shouldn't . . . we don't know what
trouble still lies ahead."

"We have tonight, Anna, my darling," he said against a
vein pulsing in her neck. "Forget everything else but you and
me and this moment." He slid her dress off her shoulder, and
stroked the smooth plane of her back.

Anna squeezed her eyes tightly shut as if that gesture would
erase the feel of Philip's hands on her skin, of his mouth over
hers. From deep inside her came a low, rumbling groan of
frustration and alarm. His words slashed through a haze of
desire to mock her. *We have tonight. Forget everything else.*
She forced her hands between them and pushed him away.

He raised his head and looked down at her with smoky,
moldering eyes. He started to bend to her again but she stopped
him with her hand on his chest. "What's wrong?" he mumbled.

"This . . . this is wrong. I don't want one night of passion
with you, Philip, yet I know I haven't the right to ask for more,
and I doubt very much that you would give it."

He leaned above her, supporting his weight on his hands.
His breathing was ragged, his face tense. "Oh, I could give
much more, Anna," he said, his voice hinting of a swaggering
persuasiveness that cut to her heart. "I'm quite sure that I
would hardly get my fill of you in one night."

"Stop it!" she cried, sitting up. "This isn't going to happen.
It can't."

He stared at her with a kind of disbelief as she fumbled with
the buttons on her dress. "Are you saying that you don't want
to make love with me?"

She flung her trembling hands to her lap after trying unsuccessfully to refasten all the buttons and looked back at him.
"Yes, that's exactly what I'm saying!"

He leaned up on his elbow, resting his head on his hand and
gazed at her with an expression of bold challenge that had
become temptingly familiar to her.

The scowl on her face dissolved into exasperated surrender. "No, that's not exactly true," she admitted.

"It's not even remotely true," he corrected confidently.

"Even so, I want more than you're offering right now. I may not deserve it, and I know I will probably never get it, but that's what I want. I will not add one night of passion with you to my already growing list of problems."

"That's where we differ, Anna. I don't see it as a problem at all, but if you do, I have a solution."

She stared at him skeptically. "What's that?"

"Don't leave tomorrow."

"But Henri . . ."

"Hang Henri! He's smart, but he doesn't know everything. What difference could a few more days make?"

"To someone hungry for a five-thousand-dollar reward it could make a lot of difference."

Philip shrugged. The prospect of another bounty hunter didn't bother him in the least. "We took care of Jake Finn without much difficulty," he pointed out.

"You're oversimplifying everything. I'm all packed. I'm ready to go. Your family knows I'm going . . ." He started to protest, but she stopped him. "Don't argue with me, Philip. God knows I've been the reason for enough trouble around here. Henri has agreed to certain plans based on my leaving."

She regarded him with a stubborn forcefulness that didn't hide an underlying regret. "I'm going, that's all," she finally concluded. "For once, let me be the logical person in our . . . whatever it is we have!"

He got to his feet and clenched his hands at his sides. She reached out to him, but he backed away. "I'm sorry it has to be this way," she said.

His eyes locked with hers, and his lips pressed together in a thin, obstinate line. "Do you even know what you'll find when you get to Boston?" he questioned angrily. "Do you know where you're going, where this supposed grandmother lives?"

Anna stood up and faced him. Now he was the one being stubborn and difficult, deliberately baiting her with unfounded accusations. "She is not 'supposed,' Philip, she is real, and she has lived on Beacon Hill long enough that I'm certain I can find out how to locate her."

He didn't look convinced, and Anna put her hand on his arm. She didn't want to argue. She was just trying to protect her heart. "Furthermore, I *need* to go, I really do. It's something that you wouldn't understand."

"Why don't you help me to understand, Anna? Tell me why you need to go, aside from the obvious legal aspects? I might understand more than you believe I will."

"All right," she said, raising her arms to encompass the small area of the *garçonnière*. "Look around you, Philip, at all these wonderful things—things that remind you of your youth. Things that tell you who you are, where you came from, and even where you're going." She turned back to him and her eyes pleaded with him to feel her need. "You have this room, that great house, this land, and most of all a family. All of it gives you an identity that no one can ever take away from you. These things are a solid definition of who Philip Brichard is.

"I have none of this, not one concrete bit of evidence to tell me who Anna Rose Connolly is. I feel as if I have no identity at all, and my only chance to get one is in Boston. It's what my uncle wanted for me, and I owe it to his memory to pursue his dream, which has become my own as well. My grandmother, Ophelia, can give me my identity, and I pray that, through her, I will find a connection with my past and a glimpse into my future. I need to feel pride in knowing that Anna Connolly was someone and perhaps might someday be again. Can you understand that?"

His face softened and he drew her into his arms. He wouldn't have had to say a word. Anna had her answer.

"My poor Anna," he whispered. "Life has not been easy for you, has it?"

"Most of it has been good, Philip, so don't feel sorry for me. Just continue to be patient with me as you have in the past."

"What do you suppose will become of us ... of you and me?" he asked, his breath ruffling her hair.

She leaned back in his embrace and looked into his eyes. "I know what is in my heart, and what I fantasize and dream about."

"Do you fantasize about me, Anna?"

"If you only knew," she said with telling sincerity. "It might scare you away."

He smiled before gently coaxing her head to his chest and stroking her hair. "No, it wouldn't do that. It would only make me feel taller and stronger and a far better man than I am right now." He rested his chin on the top of her head and asked, "Do you think, when all this is over, that you might come back here, to Frenchman's Point?"

"I would like to, if the Brichard family, every one of them, wants me to. And besides ..." She trembled with soft laughter instead of tears, "you have Irish!"

His hand slipped to her rump, and he gave her an affectionate and possessive little squeeze. "I never took you for a tease, Miss Rose," he said.

She grabbed his hand from behind her and held it tight, "Just as I never took you for a gentleman, Mr. Brichard."

Philip was still smiling as he took the lantern from the top of a toy box and held it high to guide Anna down the stairs.

CHAPTER TWELVE

As the first rays of morning sun filtered through the shutters of her bedroom windows, Claudette Brichard struggled to force a smile onto her face. "I wish you didn't have to go, Anna," she said.

"I know, Claudette. I feel the same way." Anna sat on the edge of the bed and regarded her new friend with heartfelt affection. Her gaze was drawn to Claudette's clear gray eyes which were a perfect match with her older brother's, a likeness Anna found quite unsettling. "But it's for the best, and who knows? Maybe I'll come back someday. Perhaps sooner than you'd think."

A glimmer of hope flashed across Claudette's face. "Why? Did Philip ask you to marry him?"

"Heavens, no!" Anna corrected at once. "You must not think that. I just meant that the entire Brichard family has been kind to me, and I would like very much to have the chance to see you all again."

Claudette's lower lip quivered and turned down in a frown. She twisted the fringe on her linen bedspread into a tight knot. "I love my brother, but sometimes he behaves like the south end of a horse! Please don't tell me he's sending you away, because if that's so—''

"It isn't so, not at all. All of you have made me feel as if I could stay here as long as I want, but there are so many things to consider.''

"If you're still feeling guilty about what happened to me, then don't, because you can't help what that awful man did.''

"That's only part of it, although I would feel less guilty if when I leave here this morning, I could believe that you are going to follow the doctor's orders and do what your mama says.''

Claudette lowered her head but raised her eyebrows and peered at Anna with charcoal elfin eyes that glittered with stubbornness.

"Will you promise me?'' Anna prompted, suppressing a grin.

"Yes, I promise,'' Claudette agreed reluctantly, "as long as you promise me that you'll be careful and not get caught.''

"I certainly do promise that! And I promise to write you, too, okay? As soon as I know it's safe to do so.'' She kissed Claudette's cheek and stood up from her bed. "I've got to go now. Huckabee was going for the carriage when I came upstairs, and my trunk is already sitting by the front door.'' Anna smiled one last time at Claudette. "I'll miss you,'' she said. "I never had many girlfriends.''

"I'll miss you, too. It's going to be so lonesome around here, and Philip will probably be as grumpy as a gator with lockjaw!''

Anna giggled. "Oh, I don't think his bad mood will last long.''

Claudette's expression became grave. "Stay safe, Anna. Don't let anyone hurt you.''

Anna turned at the door and lifted her hand in a parting wave. When she had reached the stairs, she heard Claudette's angry outburst to a brother who wasn't even there. "Darn you, Philip! You could have done *something* to keep her here!''

*   *   *

When Anna came down the stairs, the rest of the Brichard family were waiting for her. Philip was standing with his elbow propped on the newel post watching Henri and Huckabee carry Anna's trunk to the towncoach. His expression clearly indicated that he might just as well have been staring at a coffin being carried by pallbearers instead of a steamer full of clothing.

Trying to lighten what was obviously a dismal situation, Monique spoke cheerfully to Anna. "What a lovely day you have to set sail, *chérie*. The breeze is gentle and sure, and the sun is warm but not too hot. And I understand the ship is the best of Philippe's fleet." She turned to her scowling son then. "Wouldn't you agree, Philippe?"

He shot a deliberate warning look at his mother punctuated by a grim frown. It was all he could do to refrain from issuing the scathing epithet that trembled on his lips. But he managed to reply with only a hint of sarcasm. "Yes, Mama, the weather is perfect, the ship is in top condition, and Bernard Fitzhugh is the best captain on the high seas. I would say all aspects are perfect for Anna's bon voyage."

"And I would only add that Anna looks lovely this morning," Henri said as he came back into the foyer. He concluded his compliment with a brief glance in Philip's direction.

"Indeed she does," Philip snapped back, though his eyes were fixed on an ornately framed French landscape on the wall and not at Anna.

"Well, then," Henri said, with the controlled demeanor of a skilled organizer, "the trunk is loaded, Anna is ready, we should be on our way."

Philip turned abruptly to his brother. "We? What do you mean by that? You're not going!"

"Oh, yes I am," Henri said. "I've decided to go into the office today. There's no need to tire another pair of horses when I can ride with you."

"On a Sunday?" Philip questioned with more anger than astonishment. "Mama expects you to take her to church."

"Huckabee can go with her."

"But you never work on a Sunday," Philip argued as he saw his last private moments with Anna slipping away.

"I do when I have an important client to consider," Henri said, nodding to Anna, "and I have to clear up some unfinished business before I can devote my full attention to her. I could be leaving for Cape de Rive in a matter of days, you know."

Philip could hardly debate the logic of Henri's argument, but still he thought his brother unbelievably callous not to recognize that he would like this last morning alone with Anna.

He stole a glance at Anna, who appeared not to notice the exchange between the Brichard brothers. She arranged a small velvet hat above the neat chignon at the back of her head. If she was disappointed that she would not be alone with him, he couldn't tell it. Her face was placid and reserved, and tormentingly, unforgettably, lovely.

In his mind's eye, Philip recalled the way Anna had looked sitting across from him at breakfast. The room had been lit by gaslights and candles since the sun had not yet risen. The flames flicked over her cerulean-blue satin dress. He would have recognized the gown as one of Lilly's even if he had not known it had come from her shop. The dress was utterly, temptingly, feminine with its V-neckline and sculpted lapis buttons descending the bodice. The skirt, he had noticed when Anna stood up, was a hip-hugging panel of dazzling azure, perfect for accentuating Anna's delectable curves and enchanting blue eyes.

"God go with you, *chérie*," Monique said, interrupting Philip's thoughts. She drew Anna into an embrace before saying, "You are welcome at Frenchman's Point always, and we will pray for your safe return someday."

Stepping away from Monique's arms, Anna responded, "I am very grateful to you, for so many things. I will never forget your kindness."

"Have faith that all will be well," the older woman said, "and remember that no matter what happens, you can come back to us." Monique's hand remained outstretched long after Anna had released it and gone to the coach.

* * *

They had only traveled a half mile from Frenchman's Point when Henri looked over his shoulder at the two silent passengers sitting behind him in the partially enclosed cab. Philip was staring straight ahead at the well-traveled road with an unmistakable glower, and Anna was looking out her window at the passing river traffic wending its way north from New Orleans.

"So tell me, Anna," Henri said, "did Philip provide you with enough currency to see you through your first days in Boston?"

Philip leveled a warning glare in his direction, but Henri appeared to ignore it.

"Yes, he did," Anna quickly assured him. "As a matter of fact, Philip was more than generous." She patted the cloth reticule that rested on her lap. "I'm sure I won't require nearly so much as he gave me, since I know I'll locate my grandmother right away." She addressed Philip's rigid profile, since his gaze was still fixed on the road. "I'll return whatever is left as soon as I can," she promised.

A dismissive wave of Philip's hand and a curt "There's no need" was the only reaction she got.

"And did Philip see that you were given everything you might require on your voyage?" Henri asked next. "You'll certainly need toiletries and possibly a woolen throw for cool evenings on the deck of the *Seahawk*."

This question prompted Anna to regard Henri curiously. She thought it odd that a man would be concerned with such trivialities as women's necessities, but she tried to answer seriously. "Yes, he had Darcine bring me those things."

"Good. Good. And did he go over all the last-minute details we talked about, like when you should send a telegraph to Frenchman's Point? And what you should do if for some reason you can't locate your grandmother? And when you can expect—"

"Blast it, Henri, of course Anna and I have been over all this, so what's the point of your damned inquisition anyway?" During his outburst, Philip had grabbed the back of Henri's seat and had lunged so far forward in the carriage that the cab swayed precariously on its rockers. Philip's unexpected motion did not startle Anna as much as the fire in his charcoal eyes that blazed at Henri.

Shrugging innocently, Henri flicked the reins on the horses' backs and answered calmly, "I am Anna's attorney after all, Philip. It's only natural that I would be concerned for her welfare."

"I have been watching out for Anna's welfare for quite some time now, Henri, and as you yourself pointed out when we left Frenchman's Point, she doesn't look like she wants for anything! I have taken care of Anna very well up to this point and I intend to do so far in to ..."

Philip stopped short as Henri looked over at him, a knowing grin tugging at his mouth. Anna tilted her head to the side to get a better look at her sullen companion. She waited for him to finish his sentence.

Instead of obliging her, Philip pulled irritably at the ends of his waistcoat, smoothed the rumpled garment over the waistband of his trousers and sat back against the carriage seat. With cool disdain, he muttered, "As I said, I believe Anna is well prepared for her journey today."

"It seems so," Henri agreed. "You haven't overlooked even one tiny detail, have you, Brother?" Henri's seemingly benign statement bristled with sarcasm, hinting that it was a politely disguised insinuation, rather than the compliment it appeared to be.

They rode the rest of the way to the Vieux Carré in silence. Traffic increased on the river road as the buildings of the city came into view. The waterfront was crowded with vessels of all sorts tied to warehouse docks or milling about seeking harborage in the great curve of the Mississippi River, which hugged the shore of the Old Quarter. Anna seemed fascinated with the tantalizing sights of the riverfront, though the enthusiasm in her eyes was tempered with sadness.

The multi-cultural array of New Orleans inhabitants with

their varieties of colorful language and often bizarre customs were commonplace to Philip, as were the elegant and smartly dressed Creole and French citizens who strolled among the gardens of Jackson Square a block away from the river. But as he viewed the city through Anna's eyes, he experienced a renewed appreciation for his birthplace, and he felt an overwhelming desire to introduce her to the wonders of this city and all the others he had seen in his travels. There was so much he could teach her, so many worlds she could explore at his side, and he imagined the childlike wonder he saw on her face this morning repeated with each new threshold they crossed.

She peered out the window at the upper crust of New Orleans society promenading in front of the classically inspiring St. Louis Cathedral. "Look at that beautiful statue," she said, pointing to a sculpted horseman in the center of Jackson Square. The sun glistened off the flared tail and muscled haunches of his rearing steed.

"That's General Andrew Jackson," Philip explained, regarding the work of art as if he were seeing it for the first time even though it had been standing guard over the square for forty years. "The gardens were renamed to honor him after his victory in the Battle of New Orleans against the British. We still consider him a hero even though the occupying Union army added an inscription to the base of the statue that angered many of us. The sentiment, 'The Union must and shall be preserved' still maddens many Confederate sympathizers to this day. The city has to hire guards at night to protect the statue from vandalism."

Henri turned the carriage onto St. Anne Street and guided the horses past the Pontalba apartment buildings that flanked the square. When Anna commented on the intricate iron grillwork on the second-story balconies, Philip explained how the scandalous Spanish baroness, Micaela Pontalba, had built the distinctive buildings thirty years previously, designing the grillwork with her two initials entwined in the iron.

Anna leaned out the cab and craned her neck to get one last look at the buildings as the carriage proceeded to Chartres

Street, where Henri announced his office was located. When she finally settled back in her seat, Philip smiled at her enthusiasm.

"I just want to remember everything before I go away," she said, "in case I never . . ."

Reminded of the purpose of their journey into the city, Philip felt his momentary good humor plummet to despair. "Yes, the city is quite unusual," he said flatly.

In front of a neat two-story brick building on Chartres Street, Henri stopped the carriage and set the brake before jumping down from the driver's bench. For Anna's benefit he pointed to a sign on a second-floor window that said, Henri Felix Brichard, Attorney at Law. "This is where I leave you, Anna." He took her hand and patted it reassuringly. "Don't worry now. We'll get this mess straightened out, the one about Stuart Wilkes anyway," he added with a conspiratorial wink. "I'll wait to hear from you and then advise you when I know something."

"Thank you, Henri," she said. "You've been wonderful."

"Hopefully you'll still feel that way in a few weeks." When he saw that his brother had picked up the reins, Henri stepped away from the carriage, and it lurched ahead down Chartres Street. "See you in a while, Philip," Henri called before disappearing into the stairwell leading to the second floor.

It was only a short drive from Chartres to Canal Street and from there to the center of the shipping concerns within sight of the Vieux Carré. Anna noticed the large two-story warehouse with its high, pitched roof even before she could read the writing on its red brick surface that identified it as the headquarters of the Brichard Shipping Company.

Philip pulled around to the front of the building and allowed a deckhand to tie the reins of the horses to a hitching rail. It was quiet around the warehouse since no business was conducted on Sunday and few vessels ever sailed until Monday morning. Five ships bearing the Brichard name were moored at the dock. Their crews mingled among idle longshoremen resting against wooden crates and bales tied with burlap. Some of the men were playing cards, others rolled dice against labeled cartons. Nearly all were drinking pints.

Philip helped Anna down from the carriage, and nodded toward the largest and finest of the clipper ships sitting in the middle of the fleet, its three mainmasts rising yards above the sister ships surrounding it. "That's her, the *Seahawk,*" he said, his voice an odd combination of pride and regret.

Anna walked over to where the *Seahawk* rested against the dock, her sleek hull pulling against the mooring lines as wakes from passing vessels swelled against the seawall. "It's a beautiful ship, Philip," she said, "though I don't have much to compare it with. You don't see many ships in Illinois." She looked over her shoulder at him. "It's larger than I thought it would be."

Philip chuckled at her obvious relief. "She's plenty big enough to see you to Boston safely," he assured her. "The *Seahawk*'s over two hundred feet long and a full twenty wide at her mid-point. He swept his arm to encompass the other vessels. "Some of the smaller ships here, the schooners, might make the trip to Boston a day or two quicker but with much less comfort. I thought you would choose the *Seahawk.*"

"You know me well," she said, and the simple statement brought a flush of warmth to her cheeks.

"Perhaps I do at that." He took her elbow and led her across the gangway to the deck of the ship. He showed her the four cabins located at the square stern, one each for the captain and navigator with two left over for the occasional paying passenger. He pointed across the open deck space to the sharply angled bow of the ship that ended in a long, graceful point extending beyond the front of the hull. He told Anna that the *Seahawk* had been designed for easy maneuverability and speed. "The cabin area there," he explained, pointing to a more compact, serviceable housing facility, "is for the crew. We sleep twelve men in bunks three high."

"Philip!" Anna and Philip turned toward the robust voice and faced a bullish square of a man in a British naval cap who had just appeared on deck. The man was low to the ground and powerfully built with bulging muscles that created taut lines across the sleeves of his white shirt. A ring of bushy gray hair flared around the band of his cap. The matching coarse hair under his nose and on his chin hid all evidence of the mouth that was speaking to them in a voice clipped with a strong British accent. "So this is to be my passenger," he said, extending a thick arm out to Anna. "What a lovely addition to the *Seahawk* you are, miss."

"Anna, this is Bernard Fitzhugh, captain of the ship," Philip explained while the captain pumped Anna's hand vigorously.

Anna tried to respond to the man's enthusiastic greeting, but he wouldn't let her get a word in. "You'll love the *Hawk,* miss," he said. "She's as fine a ship as sails the seas, and I've sailed plenty o' them. You've a cabin boy assigned to you for the journey, young Kevin O'Toole, a good lad, despite the unfortunate fact that he's Irish. But we can't help what we are now, can we?"

Philip cleared his throat conspicuously to get Fitzhugh's attention. "I neglected to tell you Anna's last name, Bernard. It's Connolly, and she's bound for Boston to see her sweet old Irish grandmother. But as you say, we can't help what we are now, can we?" Philip waited a moment to give Fitzhugh time to consider his social blunder, then he said, "Looks like your foot's found your mouth again, Fitz."

The captain's eyes sparkled with good humor, even though the joke was directed at him, and his mustache twitched from side to side, almost touching his ears. "It has at that, Philip, and, as you say, not for the first time by a long ways."

Bernard Fitzhugh took Anna's hand and brought it to his mouth for a gallant kiss which felt like it was administered by a curry brush rather than lips. "Beggin' your pardon, Miss Connolly. Truth to tell, my opinion of the Irish has just improved considerably."

"Think nothing of it, Captain Fitzhugh. Perhaps I'll come to believe that the Brits aren't the barbarians my father and uncle always told me they were."

"I'll prove it to you myself, miss. Now I'll see to your trunk, which must still be in that carriage." He called the cabin boy to help him and headed to the gangway. "I've prepared number

three for the lady if you'd care to show her, Philip,'' he called
back over his shoulder. ''We'll be leavin' no later than straight
up noon.'' Then, looking at Anna, he added, ''We'll be crossin'
the Gulf by stars tonight on a sea of glass.''

Anna watched the captain lumber toward the coach with a
tall, skinny sailor bounding in his footsteps like an energetic
pup. ''What a funny man the captain is,'' she said.

''And a good, honest man, too,'' Philip assured her. ''If you
need anything, go to him. He'll treat you like his daughter.''

An awkward silence settled between them, and Anna didn't
know how to break it. Finally she said, ''I guess you should
take me to my quarters now.''

He led her around to the port side and unlatched a door that
stood only five feet high. She ducked her head and entered a
cabin furnished with only a narrow oak bunk, a simple mission
desk and chair, and a small built-in wardrobe. The cabin was
dark and gloomy, since the only natural illumination was from
a twelve-inch porthole. She was thankful to see two brass
lanterns swaying on movable wall brackets. The closeness of
the small room and its dim interior made her long to be out in
the warm sun . . . anywhere but here in a tiny cabin on a strange
ship that would soon take her far away from Frenchman's Point.

''It's not a stateroom on the *Duchess*,'' Philip said, ''but by
sailing standards, it's fairly plush.''

''It's quite nice,'' she said, struggling to keep her voice
cheerful in spite of the tears already gathering in her eyes.
Being in this room made her decision to sail to Boston suddenly
seem all too real and final, as if she truly were ending a chapter
in her life. ''I'm sure I have everything here I could ever need
or want,'' she added, knowing her words were a lie, because
what she truly wanted, she would be leaving behind.

The only sounds penetrating the cabin walls were the mumbling of idle deckhands lazing away a warm Sunday morning,
and the steady slap of the river against the hull of the ship, as
low and ceaseless as a widow's sighs of grief.

Only three steps separated Anna and Philip in the still cabin,
yet he stood rooted to the pine planking, feeling as uncertain
and indecisive as he ever had in his life, unable to go to her

and unwilling to leave. One question stood out above all others in his mind: What will happen to stop this madness, for surely something has to.

Captain Fitzhugh's voice cut through the heavy silence. "Leave it here, boy," he said. The thud of Anna's trunk being set upon the deck made Anna jump. "We'll take it to the lady's cabin later," the captain further instructed. "You go on back to the galley now and help the cook. We sail shortly."

Anna removed her hat and tossed it on the bunk, trying to hide her face and her despair from Philip. Her efforts were in vain, however, because, as her thick lashes slid over the glistening aqua of her eyes, one tear fell on her cheek.

Instinctively he went to her. "I don't think I'm going to be able to stand it if you cry," he murmured against her hair.

Before she opened her eyes again, she felt the comfort of his arms around her, the reassurance of his hands on her back. She leaned against him, giving in to the security of his embrace. "I can't help it," she said. "I don't mean to. I'm doing what I want to do, what Mick wanted me to do, what Henri says I should do . . ."

Philip took her chin in his hand and raised her face to his. "What about what I want you to do?"

He bent to her cheek and kissed away the remnant of the tear. The touch of his lips on her face fanned a warmth that simmered in the nerve endings just below the surface of her skin. His mouth sought hers and covered it, more insistent and pleading than any of his words had been. She kissed him back, wildly, needily, pushing into the back of her mind the thought that what she most wanted from him he had still not been willing to give, and she might not even deserve.

Philip tore his mouth from hers and pressed his lips against her ear. "Don't go, Anna," he groaned in a voice edged with the pain of wanting her and losing her. "This is madness." His hands roamed over her back to her hips. He pulled her closer to him and she arched back over his arm. Then he slipped a hand between them and found the blue lapis buttons down the front of her dress.

With one swift movement of his hand, first one then another

of the little buttons fell between them and rattled across the wood floor. The ship pitched against the restraints of the mooring lines, and Anna clung to him. When he had bared her chest, he slipped his hand inside her camisole and found her breast, the nipple already a tight bud.

"You don't have to do this, Anna, we'll find another way," Philip said.

His breath was warm against her ear, sending tingling gooseflesh to her neck and arms. He bent his head to her chest and grasped the fabric which still covered her.

She felt him pulling down her camisole. Then his lips were on her breast, wet and warm, seeking the nipple, while he pushed her dress over her arms. In the last moment before she was swept away with the feel of his hands on her flesh, before she drowned in the waves of her own passion, she pressed her hands against his shoulders. Before she gave in to the delirious sensations he caused her to feel, she needed to know, once and for all. "Philip, stop. Please stop."

He raised his face and looked into her eyes. He took the soft, small hands that held their bodies apart and wrapped them in the warmth of his two large ones. "You're right," he whispered, "this isn't the time or place. Come with me, Anna . . leave the ship with me now."

She opened her mouth partway as a prelude to the question that hung hesitantly on her lips. Without looking away from his intense gaze, she asked in a voice that trembled with dread and uncertainty, "Philip, are you willing to risk everything, the safety of your family, for what you feel for me? Philip, do you love me?"

His gaze flickered away from her for an instant before returning to her face, but in that small gesture, Anna saw the unmistakable trace of doubt.

"I'm trying desperately to love you right now," he evaded. "Let me do that, Anna."

"No, Philip, you know what I mean. Do you love me, really love me?"

He dropped her hands, but his eyes still held hers. "Oh, Anna, how can either one of us know for sure? We've had so little time, but I do know this. Just being near you drives me wild with wanting you, and when we're apart, I can't think of anything else but how badly I want to be with you again. You feel it, too, I know you do."

"Yes, I do, but I feel so much more that I can't explain. You ask how either one of us can know for certain. All I can tell you is that one of us does know, and, because of that, I am desperately afraid of you."

The smoky gray of desire was replaced by a dark anguish in Philip's eyes. "Afraid of me? Anna, you can't mean that. I would never hurt you. All I want to do is protect you, to show you how the thought of you drives me to distraction and how just the sight of you makes my blood boil. That is not something to fear, Anna, darling, it is something to grab on to and feast upon and thank the heavens for. It is something rare and precious."

"It is precious, and indeed rare, for I have never before had the feelings I have for you, but what you offer, though it is all you can give, is not enough, not now at least. Not because of what has happened to me in the past and what might happen in the future. Not as long as the ghosts of Cape de Rive hover between us, keeping us apart.

"You wouldn't mean to hurt me, Philip, but you would. You are a threat to me because of the power you could have over me if my feelings run deeper than yours. I need more than your passion, Philip, and you are unwilling, or unable, to give it, and, after all, perhaps that is best."

Philip watched the heat of desire in her eyes dim to a cool clear sanity as the urges of her heart succumbed to the persuasive reasoning of her mind. The moment had passed, and he did not know how to get it back, for he would not lie to her, could not tell her what he knew she wanted to hear. His own confused thoughts tumbled about in his head like wild stallions refusing to be tamed.

"I'm sorry, Anna. You've asked me to admit to something I . . ." He fumbled for the right words, but for some reason they would not come, and he hated himself for his inadequacy.

Anna smiled at him, a slight rise of the corners of her mouth that said she understood and accepted what he was feeling. "It's all right, Philip, you don't need to explain. But please just go now. It will be easier if you do. Besides, there are so many things I need to do."

He nodded dully, not trusting himself to speak for fear he would reveal a part of himself that had baffled and dismayed him since he had first seen her on the stage at River Flats. He knew that in truth she had nothing to do for the next eight days except to think of him as he would of her, and he was certain that memories of her would haunt his days and nights forever. He was still in her cabin, yet the pain of missing her was already an aching weight on his heart.

"I wish you well, Anna," he said, feeling foolish. It occurred to him that he might just as well have said those words to a distant cousin embarking on a journey instead of the woman who had filled his life with a joy and completion he had never known before. He reached out and touched her hand lightly with his fingertips. "We'll see each other again, I know we will."

"Perhaps," she said. Her gaze was so intent on his face, it was as though she were memorizing every plane and hollow. "Go now," she pleaded, her voice betraying the rigid exterior she struggled so hard to maintain.

He turned on his heel and strode from the cabin, closing the door behind him. He passed Bernard Fitzhugh who had picked up a handle of Anna's trunk and was dragging it toward her room. "Take care of her, Bernard," Philip said without breaking stride.

"You can count on it, Philip," the captain promised.

Philip climbed into the waiting coach and turned the pair of horses around toward Canal Street and the route back to Henri's office. Before he rounded the warehouse and lost sight of the *Seahawk,* he looked at the ship one last time. Instead of seeing the vessel as the pride of the Brichard Shipping Company as he usually did, Philip saw the hulking clipper as something alien and menacing, the one thing that threatened his life and his happiness. Shaking off the shiver that ran down his spine,

Philip slapped the reins on the team's back and raced down Canal Street.

In her cabin, Anna opened the trunk Bernard had just placed on her bunk. She reached among the folded clothes for the memento she had packed at Frenchman's Point. When she felt the little pony from the *garçonnière,* she fought to hold back tears. She removed it from the trunk and saw that it had been wrapped in tissue paper and tied with a ribbon. With trembling fingers she pulled the strings of the ribbon and found an envelope upon which a note had been written in bold, masculine script. ''Your fare back to Frenchman's Point, plus a little extra in case you need it . . . Philip.'' Inside the envelope was a thousand-dollar bank note from the Bank of New Orleans. The phrase, 'a little extra,' struck Anna with its absurdity, since the most elaborate fare possible could cost no more than a hundred dollars. She began to laugh, little sputtering sounds which soon became hysterical sobs. When her legs began to give way beneath her, she sat on the bunk and clutched the bank note to her chest. The tears that had been stinging her eyelids trickled down her cheeks.

Henri Brichard straightened up abruptly as the door to his office was opened so forcefully it hit the interior wall and bounced back again. Philip strode into the office and stopped in front of Henri's desk, his face drawn with lines of distraction and his steely eyes glinting with frustration. He placed his palms on the surface of Henri's polished mahogany desk and stared wildly at his brother, his breath coming in short, ragged gasps.

Henri looked up at the half-mad face staring down at him and asked casually, ''Having a bad day, Brother?''

''You should know. You contributed to it with your ridiculous advice and your silly patter this morning!'' Philip barked.

''Why don't you sit down and we can talk about it,'' Henri suggested calmly. Philip flung his hands from the desktop, sliding the heavy piece of furniture several inches across the walnut floor. He sank heavily into the nearest chair and propped his booted feet where his hands had been.

Henri rose up from his chair and made a show of examining the patina of the desk. "You're ruining the finish, Philip," he said, swiping at a recently inflicted scratch.

"Damn the blasted desk!" Philip swore, removing his feet and leaning forward on his elbows. "She's gone, and I let her go!"

Henri withdrew his pocket watch from his waistcoat and glanced at it. "Really? I didn't think the *Seahawk* was scheduled to sail until noon. It's only eleven."

"Do you have to be so irritatingly literal? She's as good as gone, and I couldn't do anything to stop her."

"She should go, Philip," Henri said in a reasonable voice. "Anna's not safe here. What more proof do you need of that? She won't be safe until I can prove her story is true."

Philip pressed his lips together in an obstinate line, but he did not refute Henri's argument. "I hate it when you're right," he finally mumbled.

"And I hate it when you're miserable. You have a way of spreading your depression like a thick fog, covering everyone."

"And just how would you feel?" Philip challenged, sitting up straight and looking his brother in the eye.

"You mean, how would I feel if the woman I loved was just getting ready to sail out my life? As miserable as you do, I guess."

"I never said I loved her," Philip countered defensively, though his voice hinted of uncertainty.

"And why not?"

"Don't be ridiculous, Henri. There have been lots of women in my life, and I never told any of them I loved them. It never made a difference."

Henri allowed a little smile to betray the amusement he felt. "So, out of respect for all those others, you're refusing to admit you love Anna? How gallant of you, Philip."

Philip scowled at his brother, but he suddenly seemed interested in what Henri had to say. "Just what makes you think I love her anyway?"

"That's the toughest question of all," Henri said. "The truth is, I don't know if you do. Only you can decide that. And since both you and I have reached this mature stage of life without ever professing our love to any female, I would assume that we could only do so now with the greatest trepidation."

Henri stood up and paced around his office. He felt as confident as if he were center stage in a courtroom. "I observed you this morning, however, and the heightened combination of melancholy, irritability, and stubbornness did indicate that you were extraordinarily agitated, even taking into account your normally irascible behavior."

Philip's scowl deepened, but it meant that he was, indeed, listening to every word.

"I might have assumed that you were suffering from a fever or dyspepsia, but you're fit as a racehorse, so I looked elsewhere for your discomfort. And I didn't have to look far. Just to the other passenger in the coach, the woman who I believe is the cause of both your sublime ecstasy and abject pain. At the risk of raising your ire once more, I have to ask . . . I'm right, aren't I?"

Philip sat perfectly still for several long moments. Finally he raised his hand to his chin and rubbed thoughtfully. A quick snort of resignation escaped through his nose and he chuckled softly. "When she asked me if I loved her, I said I didn't know."

"Perfectly in keeping with your character," Henri stated authoritatively.

"I do love her, Henri. I never thought I would love any woman like I do her. I never imagined sharing my life with one woman. I expected to remain single for all of my days, taking pleasure from women when I needed it but giving nothing lasting in return. Anna has absolutely astounded me. She has turned my world around."

Henri nodded wisely. "They say that's what love does. I wouldn't know, of course."

Philip suddenly bolted up from his chair and shouted, "The time! Is it noon yet? I've got to stop her!"

"You have thirty minutes, Philip, but you have to let her

sail. It would be pure foolishness not to. Anna is in danger here.''

Philip pounded his fist into his palm until he came up with the only logical solution to his dilemma. He grabbed Henri's arm and forced their eyes to lock. ''I don't suppose it will hurt the coffee crop in St. Sebastian if the beans remain in barrels for a few extra days.''

''No, I don't think it would,'' Henri agreed as a smile broke across his face. ''I like strong coffee myself.''

''But I don't have any clothes . . .''

''Check under the driver's bench in the coach. I packed a valise for you just in case you'd come around.''

Philip laughed. ''I appreciate your sound counsel today, Henri, but it does worry me that I've recognized my thick-headedness only because I've begun to think like you do!''

''You haven't time to stand here flattering me, Philip. You'll never see Boston if you miss your ship.''

Philip slapped his brother on the back and then quickly pulled him into a tight embrace. ''See you in a few weeks,'' he called as he rushed from Henri's office. His hurried footsteps echoed down the stairs to the carriage.

CHAPTER
THIRTEEN

The sun settled down on a pink-swabbed horizon as the *Seahawk* progressed along a steady course down the Mississippi River to the great southern basin which opened into the Gulf of Mexico. Anna had been on deck for nearly an hour letting the early-evening breeze wash over her. It swept her hair, now loosened from pins and combs, away from her face and down her back in a tumbled riot of honey-colored waves.

She needed the freedom of the open deck since she had been in her cabin for most of the seven hours they had been sailing to open water. When the *Seahawk* left New Orleans, Anna had stayed inside, preferring not to watch the skyline of the city fade into a remote haze, dimming her hopes and dreams at the same time.

Leaning on the deck rail, she looked up at the tall masts soaring above her. Only the mainsail and the lower topsail were opened in a "goosewing" to catch the gentle breeze. All other sails were tightly furled to the yardarms, since the current of the river and minimal sail were sufficient to carry the vessel on its winding course to the gulf.

She had learned a new vocabulary that day by listening to the sounds of activity on deck while she tried to block her last meeting with Philip Brichard from her mind. She had heard Captain Fitzhugh bark orders to his crew to fasten the clew lines to the yardarms, pull the ropes tightly through the halyards, and secure the flying jib. Now she knew that when they reached open waters, all the sails would be unfurled for speed. She was learning a lot about Philip's other life on this gray-green waterway to the sea.

"Excuse me, Miss Connolly," the eager-to-please young Kevin O'Toole said as he came up behind her. Anna turned to face him and raised her eyebrows in question. "The captain is askin' for your presence at dinner tonight."

She nodded her acceptance lackadaisically, for, in truth, she didn't feel like eating anything. She might have thought she was seasick, but common sense told her that her lack of appetite had nothing to do with the gentle motion of the *Seahawk,* and much more to do with a completely different kind of "sickness" . . . one of the heart. But she didn't want to appear rude to any member of the *Seahawk's* crew, since all of them had gone out of their way to make her comfortable.

"Of course, Kevin, tell the captain I'd be delighted to dine with him," she said, managing a small smile.

"He's asked for you to come to his quarters at eight o'clock, miss," Kevin added. "That's only an hour from now."

Anna started to agree automatically to the arrangements when she suddenly realized what Kevin had said. "His quarters?" she repeated, her voice raised in surprise. "I met the captain in the galley for lunch. Why would he request his cabin this evening?"

"It's perfectly customary, miss. The captain usually chooses to eat in his quarters at night. His cabin is quite fine, you see, much grander than the galley where the crew eats. He told me to tell you not to concern yourself with any improprieties. Our captain is a proper gentleman, miss. I myself can vouch for him."

The boy looked so serious that Anna immediately put aside all reservations about meeting Captain Fitzhugh in his room. "If you say so, Kevin, then it must be true. Tell the captain I will come to his quarters promptly at eight."

Anna remained on deck until the sun was just a halo of rose gold above the lowlands bordering the river. With a sigh of regret, she returned to her cabin to prepare for a dinner she didn't feel like eating and a night of polite conversation she didn't feel like pursuing.

She opened the tiny wardrobe in her cabin and removed the first dress the saw, the pink dress with the scooped neckline and softly billowing skirt that she had worn to dinner her first night at Frenchman's Point. She laid the dress on the bed and poured water into a bowl which was inset in a serviceable washstand mounted to the wall in her room. As she washed, she glanced over at the dress, remembering how she had sat across from Philip at the dining table that night and walked with him later in Monique's garden, and how he had rested his hand on her bare arm. She shivered now as she recalled his quick, passionate kiss under the lamp on the brick pathway, a kiss that left her breathless with wanting more and dreaming all night of being in his arms.

She stepped into the dress and pulled it up over her shoulders. "Tonight will be nothing like the last time you wore this dress, foolish Anna," she said to her reflection in the tiny mirror. "Tonight there is no garden, no candlelight, and no Philip Brichard, but unfortunately there will still be dreams." She picked up her brush and swept it through her hair a dozen times, deciding at the last minute not to secure the long tresses into a knot at her nape. "Let the wind do what it will," she said, fluffing the ends over her shoulders. "My entire fate depends on its fickle nature as it is."

She grabbed a knitted shawl Monique had given her and wrapped it around her shoulders. Then she stepped out of her cabin, pulling her skirt free of the door before the breeze slammed it shut behind her.

It was almost completely dark, and the deck was lit by kerosene sidelights as Anna walked around to the starboard side where she knew the captain's quarters were located. She looked up to see clouds the color of light ash blotting out the full moon as they drifted across an ebony sky. The wind blew her hair across her face, and she smoothed the tangles off her

forehead and held the unruly mass at her crown. The breeze
was refreshing. Anna stopped before going to the captain's
door and stood on the deck to let the seaspray cool her face
and revive her from her melancholy so she would at least be
a companionable dinner partner for Bernard Fitzhugh. Drawing
a deep breath and filling her lungs with the fresh, clean air,
she knocked lightly on the cabin door.

When no one answered her first knock, she peered through
the small, square, stained-glass window shaped like an anchor
that decorated the center panel of the door. The dark-tinted
glass prohibited her from seeing much of the interior, but it
appeared to be even darker, or perhaps more dimly lit, than
her own accommodations. She opened the door just a crack
and called softly, "Captain Fitzhugh, it's Anna. Are you in
here?"

She scanned the cabin for some sign of the captain and was
just about to leave when she heard the squeak of the pedestal
rocker of a high-backed desk chair that faced a long trestle
desk. She could still see nothing of the captain, but the slight
movement of the chair told her he was in the room. A feeling
of unease pricked the nerve endings of her skin as she asked
hesitantly, "Captain, should I come in?"

"Yes, Anna, do" came the whispered reply.

She entered the cabin and shut the door behind her. When
her eyes adjusted to the low light, she could see that Kevin
O'Toole had been right about one thing—the room was incredibly plush compared to her own meager cabin. A full bed covered
with a thick patchwork quilt was nestled in a sturdy platform
that raised the mattress at least three feet off the floor. A
pair of plump white feather pillows rested against a headboard
carved with leaping porpoises and sea nymphs. A low-lit kerosene lantern attached to the headboard illuminated their play.

Above the bed and spanning two walls were shelves with
dozens of pigeonholes for charts and maps, and larger niches
for navigational instruments. At the foot of the bed sat a sea-
man's chest painted on the front with a sailor dressed in a
Shetland wool jersey and cap. A bureau and wardrobe occupied
the third wall of the cozy quarters.

Anna might have been content to spend a comfortable evening in Captain Fitzhugh's inviting quarters if she had not become first surprised and then angered by the dining arrangements the captain had set up in the middle of the cabin. Far from being a friendly conversational atmosphere, the intimate little table for two with its single candle, two cut-crystal goblets, open bottle of wine, and gleaming silverplate platter and cover appeared to be a perfectly orchestrated scene for a planned seduction. Hers!

Though the room was lit only by the candle and bedside lamp, Anna saw enough to know that she would rather spend a hungry night in her own dreary cabin than one more minute in the clutches of Captain Fitzhugh. How could she have been so misled by the jovial captain's demeanor before the *Seahawk* sailed? And worse, now he had the nerve to intimidate her by hiding behind that desk chair, waiting to pounce like a panther on its prey.

She grasped the brass door handle behind her and spoke to the back of the chair. "Apparently there has been some mistake, Captain. You must have been expecting someone else for dinner."

Turning abruptly to open the door, she heard the metallic hiss of the chair as it swiveled toward her and the low, throaty command, "Don't go, Anna."

She stood paralyzed as recognition penetrated her consciousness, and her knuckles turned white on the door handle. It was the same sultry voice that had haunted her all that afternoon, the low, sensuous tone that she feared time would erase from her mind. She was too frightened to turn around, afraid that voices had the power to taunt and tease like the apparitions of her dreams.

"Don't go, Anna," the voice urged again. "You promised to stay for dinner."

"Philip," she whispered, and turned slowly to face him.

He raised himself from the chair, but remained across the room, watching her with eyes like molten pewter, powerful enough to hold her immobile in their warm gaze. His long, slim legs were braced slightly apart and encased in meticulously tailored black gabardine, and his arms hung at his sides, the fists clenching tensely at the ends of the ruffles of the full white shirtsleeves.

"What are you doing here?" she asked timidly, for she hadn't yet convinced herself that he was real, that the candle-light wasn't deceiving her.

A grin split the shadowed contours of his face, and his gaze sparkled with mischief, as if he were finding some subtle enjoyment in a scheme that left her feeling awkward and child-ish and unprepared.

Her skin warmed to the roots of her hair. The knitted shawl suddenly felt scratchy and heavy, and she let it drop from her shoulders to lie dangling from her elbows. Her face flushed with the heat of . . . what? Anger? Confusion? Desire? The three emotions warred within her.

"What am I doing here?" he repeated with a wry grin. "Well, after all, Anna, it's my ship."

If he intended his little quip to be amusing, he had made a serious mistake. Yes, he looked wonderfully handsome. Yes, she was definitely confused. But overall, she was suddenly as angry as she had ever been in her life.

She picked up the nearest object to her, a bottle with a carefully crafted four-masted brigantine in its clear belly, which she pulled out of its protective niche on the wall and held over her head. "It's your ship!" she spat back at him. "How dare you do this to me? It's not enough that you admit you don't love me; you're not even honorable enough to let me go! I suppose next you'll tell me it's your ocean as well . . ."

"Gulf, Anna," he corrected with measured calm. "We're not on the ocean . . . in fact, we're not even in the gulf yet, technically." He was thankful he was still several feet away from her, because he sensed that if he had been closer, the flames broiling in her eyes could have somehow seared his skin.

"Don't play games with me. You are not the king of the seas, *Captain Brichard!*" She flung the title at him as if it were a weapon while she wielded the bottle threateningly above her head. "And you're not the king of *me,* make no mistake about it."

"Anna, put the bottle down, please." He advanced toward her. "Bernard spent a lot of time making that thing; it's one of his treasures. You'll break his heart if you destroy it."

"Then he'll have *you* to thank when it's in splinters on this floor!"

Philip rushed to grab a pillow from the bed and held it out to her as a trade. "Take this," he said, reaching for the bottle with his other hand. "Do whatever you want with the pillow, but give me Bernard's model."

She drew back her arm and nearly hurled the bottle at him but stopped at the last second as her eyes darted to the encased brigantine and quickly perused its painstaking details. Even in her anger, she couldn't destroy a man's delicate handiwork. She set the bottle back in its cupboard again, but the concession only seemed to fire her anger more. She grabbed the pillow with a powerful yank and swung it at Philip's face. He managed to duck, but she found her mark with her return swing and he staggered backward.

Continuing his efforts to dodge her assaults, he asked breathlessly, "Anna . . . do you mind telling me . . . just one little thing?" When she paused for a brief moment, keeping her eyes firmly on her target, Philip quickly added, "Why are you so angry? I thought you'd be glad to see me."

"You thought? You *thought!*" She ran shaking fingers through her tousled hair. "I can tell very clearly what you thought. Dinner on *your* ship in *your* candlelit cabin with *your* obvious temptations on the table. You had every intention of continuing where we left off this morning."

Dropping the pillow to the floor, she stared at Philip with a penetrating glare she hoped would convey her anger, if anything could. "You know, Philip, you have one serious character flaw . . . you don't know the meaning of the word 'no,' but you're just going to have to learn, because you can feed me . . ."

She stepped to the table and raised the silverplate cover off the platter with a flourish designed to make a point, but she wasn't prepared for the sight of a delectable roast surrounded by plump, browned potatoes. Her mouth watered as she inhaled the fragrant aroma and she sighed, ". . . roast rib of beef."

Her anger took a brief but unexpected plunge in favor of a stronger need. Just the sight of the food made her stomach growl, and she felt almost weak from hunger when just a few minutes ago she had sworn she couldn't eat a bite. She leaned into the tantalizing steam before forcing herself to replace the cover so she could resume her attack on Philip.

"You can keep me prisoner on your ship. You can even take me to your coffee-bean island instead of Boston, if that is your intention, but that will not make me subject myself to your manipulations." Putting her fists on her hips, Anna faced Philip squarely and fixed unblinking eyes on his, which still glinted with a maddening display of mirth. "No is just *no*, Philip," she stated defiantly. "That's all there is to it!"

He pulled out the chair nearest her and gallantly swept his arm toward the seat. "Anna, please sit down." When she balked, he stepped back and held his hands up in a gesture of surrender. "I'll keep my distance, but let me at least serve you your dinner. You must be starved."

He was right, but she couldn't bring herself to trust him so easily. To further persuade her, Philip revealed the dinner again and wafted the delicious aroma toward her with the silver dome. It was her downfall, and she moved slowly toward the chair he held for her.

He poured deep red wine into two glasses and gave one to Anna as she sat. Then he carved a thick slice of rib roast and put it on her plate along with several buttery potatoes covered with a dark rich broth. Last, he buttered a crusty slice of bread and offered it to her.

She ate several bites of the meal and wiped her mouth with her napkin before allowing herself to look at Philip across the table. "This is really quite good," she conceded.

"I'm glad you like it," he said, taking a long draught of his wine and leaning back in his chair to look at her. "Are you more inclined to have conciliatory feelings toward your dinner partner now? If not, I suppose I could give you this wine bottle to pummel me with. At least Bernard wouldn't care so much."

Anna couldn't hide a smile as she brought the fork to her mouth once more. "I said I was enjoying the meal; don't jump to any conclusions that might include you." She sipped her wine and regarded Philip seriously. "Why *did* you come, Philip? We said our good-byes, as difficult as they were, and surely you know me well enough to know that I wouldn't change my mind about . . . well, the situation in my cabin before we sailed."

"Oh, yes, I do know you well enough," he said, smiling fondly at her. "My mother always said I should be able to recognize a stubborn streak when I see one." He looked down at his plate and cut off a juicy piece of beef for himself. "You may not believe this, but I had not planned to sail with you today, and I did not come aboard to continue my attempts to make love to you, as appealing as that might seem to me at this moment."

Try as she might, Anna could not maintain her desire to see Philip black and blue. At the same time, she practically abandoned all thoughts of eating. All her senses were suddenly centered on his warm gaze, and she let it wash over her like a comforting blanket. "Then why?" she asked in a voice scarcely above a whisper.

"I came to a conclusion about you . . . about us, rather, and I decided to offer a proposition to you." He leaned forward, took another swallow of wine and rested his elbows on the table. "I want you to know that I understand how you feel about going to Boston. Not that I agree with your going, but I can sympathize with your need to discover your background, your *identity* as you called it last night in the *garçonnière*. This need seems to be extremely strong within you."

She had to be careful. She was actually beginning to trust him again.

"I'm wondering if you think it would interfere with your quest to discover yourself if you arrived in Boston with an identity slightly different from the one you now have."

"I don't understand," she said.

"Would you still be able to find the Connolly you are looking for if you suddenly became a Brichard?"

Anna was too stunned by his words to move. Her lungs felt

compressed against her pounding heart, and she scarcely had the power to draw a breath. She was certain she had heard his question correctly, and its implication seemed absolutely clear, but she wasn't about to make a fool of herself in front of Philip again by assuming more than he intended.

If he meant what she prayed with all her heart he meant, then he was going to have to say it clearly, and precisely, with no hidden meanings, and no subtleties. Hearing only her own wild heartbeat, Anna grabbed hold of the edge of the table to steady her nerves. Then she answered with a question designed to make him believe she was not taking him seriously. "Are you thinking of adopting me, Philip?"

He leaned temptingly close, and a broad smile split his face. "Oh, Anna, no wonder you are on my mind night and day. The idea of having a slew of little Brichards running around the yard at Frenchman's Point does enter my mind when I think of you, but believe me when I say my interest in you is not the slightest bit fatherly." He reached across the table and took her hand. "I think you know perfectly well what I mean, dearest Anna. I'm asking you to marry me . . . right here, right now."

She leveled her gaze across the table at him, assessing the depth of his commitment in his eyes while she was content to feel his thumb massaging the palm of her hand. She was very close to taking the leap of faith needed to believe that his proposal had indeed come from his heart. But had it really? After all, she was the same girl he had left on the *Seahawk* this morning, with the same problems and uncertainties facing her. Why, then, had he changed his mind, and would he change it again?

Moments passed, and Philip shifted in his chair and ran his hand through his hair. "Aren't you going to say something?"

"Why?"

"Because I've just given you a marriage proposal, that's why!"

"No, I mean why do you want to marry me? This morning you didn't even love me."

He stood up abruptly and pushed his chair under the table to provide more pacing room for his long strides. "Obviously

I did love you this morning, Anna," he said as if it were a fact anyone should accept at face value. "Otherwise I wouldn't be here now."

"Maybe . . . but maybe I just want to hear you say it."

He braced his hands on the back of his chair and fixed a flinty gaze on her, as if he were accepting a challenge. "Fine. I love you. There, I said it. You heard it. It's true. I suppose you hear violins heralding the pronouncement and see cherubs fluttering about in the air . . ."

"Yes, I do," she said, her eyes filling with tears, "and it's absolutely beautiful."

His eyes lost their spark of steel and softened to the gray of a dove's wing. "Anna Connolly, you are enough to make any man a believer in miracles." He came around the table and drew her up and into his arms. "I guess I still have a lot to learn about love, but I hope I will have you to teach me. So, in the midst of this roomful of violinists and chubby angels, will you please say that you'll marry me?"

Anna wanted nothing more than to throw her arms around him and accept his proposal with all the love that was in her heart, but she drew back from his embrace, wiped the moisture from the corner of her eye, and looked at him with grave determination. She had to know that he had considered all aspects of his decision. "Philip, what if Henri fails in Cape de Rive? What if we can never return to Frenchman's Point?"

"I have faith in my brother, Anna, but even if he doesn't clear your name, it doesn't matter. We will go somewhere else until we can return."

"But what if—"

"Anna, stop." His eyes pleaded with her to trust him. "Nothing is going to change my mind. Can't you accept that? I told you I want to marry you right now . . . tonight."

She wanted desperately to believe him, but how could he mean what he just said? "That isn't possible. We couldn't be married tonight."

He gripped her arms, urging her to stand still. "Stay right there, Anna." He crossed to the cabin door and flung it open wide. "Bernard, Bernard!" he called.

The captain of the *Seahawk* appeared at once and waited on the threshold of the cabin. "What is it, Philip?" Then, remembering his manners, he tipped his cap at Anna. "Good evening, miss."

"I told you earlier to have something ready when I asked for it," Philip said. "Would you mind telling Anna what it was?"

"The book of maritime law, and I have it handy on the desk in the navigator's quarters. Shall I get it?"

"Yes, you shall, and bring young O'Toole as well. Tell him to wash behind his ears and put on a clean jersey. He's going to be a maid of honor, and you're going to be a priest!"

Fitzhugh grinned delightedly, and rushed off to accomplish his errands. Philip closed the door, turned toward Anna and said, "Is that what you want to wear? It's lovely, of course, and you look beautiful, but then, women have such definite ideas about these things . . ."

"Philip, you don't mean . . ."

"Oh, but I do. It's all perfectly legal. When Fitzhugh pronounces us man and wife, it will be as binding as if the pope himself had suddenly washed up on deck to do the honors."

She no longer questioned his sincerity. The depth of his love and honesty of his commitment shone in his eyes. "All right," she said, laughing. "I'm convinced that you want to marry me, but let's wait. I want my grandmother to be at my wedding. She's my only family, and since my mother . . . well, I think I'd like to have Ophelia stand up with me."

He kissed her quickly and nodded. "Then that's what we shall do, and you shall have a new gown and a proper wedding with a proper priest. But, Anna, never doubt for an instant that I want to marry you, because I have no doubts at all."

Anna grabbed the back of a chair to steady herself. Everything she had dared to dream about was actually happening. "All right, Philip. I believe you," she said, and it was true.

He flung open the door once more. "Bernard! Forget everything I told you. There will be no wedding this evening!" Then he shouted a last dictate. "And Bernard, unless the *Seahawk* is sinking, don't bother us any more tonight!"

Closing the door, Philip slipped the lock into the metal latch with a soft click. Then he leaned against the door panel and looked at Anna, his eyes caressing her face feature by feature, almost as if he were touching her. "So, since I assume I have your 'yes' answer, what do you want to do now?"

She sank down in the chair, feeling delightfully dizzy. Of course there were still many problems she would have to face, but now, due to the most wondrous of miracles, those problems no longer seemed insurmountable. "I think I'd like another glass of wine," she finally said.

Philip went to the table, refilled her glass and held it out to her. His dark gaze intent on her face, he said huskily, "I am your humble servant, my lady . . . my love."

She reached for the glass, and her fingers laced with his. Neither one of them moved as they held the glass between them, their eyes meeting over the shimmering burgundy contents caught in the glow of the single candle.

When her hand began to tremble, Anna took the glass and raised it to her lips. Over the sparkling crystal rim, her gaze rested adoringly on the man who had come to accept her for who she was . . . the one person who had changed her fear into hope and her grief into happiness she'd never thought possible.

Philip's eyes glittered like mercury under his chiseled brows, and his hair fell onto his forehead in thick raven waves. Anna longed to part his open shirt until she could place her hands on the soft mat of curls visible at the V of his collar.

She did not resist when he came around the table, took the glass of wine and set it down. Placing his hands on either side of her face, he whispered tenderly, "God help me, I couldn't let you go. I love you, Anna. I realize now that I always have and I will never stop."

"Oh, Philip, I have dreamed of hearing you say that . . ."

The rest of her words caught in her throat as Philip's mouth covered hers. With the first gentle pressure, she gave herself up to the pleasure of his lips. His mouth slanted on hers and his tongue moved insistently, urging her to open to him. Her lips parted willingly, and he plunged inside. She arched her back to receive him, and he explored the recesses of her mouth, circling her tongue with his. She reached around his neck and pulled him close. His hands crept down her face to linger over the sensitive areas of her neck and chest. She felt the heat of her own skin tingling warm under his touch.

Desire throbbed in Philip as his need deepened the kiss, spiraling his passion upward. How could he have considered ever letting her go? He laid his palm above the gathered bodice of her dress, and let the warmth of her skin flow through his veins. When he slipped his hand inside, her heart beat against his palm, and hunger swirled into his groin.

He kissed her eyes and cheeks and earlobes, nibbling the soft flesh with teasing bites. He wanted to taste every part of her like a starving man who had long been denied what he needed most.

One hand rested against the side of her face, and while his mouth was busy elsewhere, his thumb caressed her lips. With his other hand, he loosened the buttons of her dress, slowly, one by one, letting his anticipation build. No longer was he playing the part of the forceful, desperate lover, eager to take what she let him have as if one time would be all he would know of her. His only thought now was to love Anna for a lifetime, slowly, sensuously, making her first experience one to treasure for all their years together.

When the last buttons came loose at her waist, he coaxed the dress over her shoulders and hips. It fell in a rippling puddle at her feet.

He reached for her hands and let his gaze move over her possessively, lovingly, the most intimate parts of her now only covered by her translucent undergarments. She stepped free of the dress, and came so willingly into his arms that her unconditional trust nearly shattered him, increasing his resolve to cherish her and love her, slowly and tenderly.

His lips sought hers again, and he kissed her with an urgency guided by the force of her passion. She wanted him as much as he wanted her. He felt it in the sweet trembling of her lips and the total surrendering of her body to his. The knowledge filled him with awe, and an overwhelming desire to be worthy of the trust she placed in him.

"You're not afraid, Anna?" he said. "Don't be afraid."

While he watched, she slipped the straps of her chemise from her shoulders and pulled the garment over her head. "No, I'm not afraid."

He gazed at her breasts. They rose and fell with each shuddering breath she took. Philip traced a nipple with his fingertip, then grazed it with the pad of his thumb. He lowered his head to the puckering tip and let his lips feed. Anna leaned back, giving him access to her breast, and a low groan, wild and needy, came from her throat.

He kissed her again, thoroughly and completely, as desire pooled inside him. "My God, you are so beautiful," he whispered. Her eyes, like shimmering sapphires, beckoned him. He cupped her breast, sending new tremors through her body. Then, in one swift movement, he lifted her into his arms and carried her to the bed.

Anna sank down into the softness of the thick quilt on Philip's bed. While he removed his clothing, she let herself float on the wave of desire he'd created within her. A pulsing need centered itself between her legs and radiated to all her extremities. Everywhere Philip had touched her, the nerve endings sang, like tight strings of a violin.

When he came to the bed, his erection was full and throbbing, but Anna reached for him without hesitation. She wrapped her arms around his neck and urged him down beside her. With slow, languorous movements Philip explored every inch of her. He touched and caressed until every cell in her body cried out for some vague, mysterious completion.

He found the most sensitive part of her and stroked her with his hand. The feelings that had been building slowly erupted with a force so powerful and unstoppable that behind her eyelids, Anna saw stars, great, shining, dazzling stars that seemed to arc through her bloodstream.

When at last he parted the warm, wet opening and slipped his finger inside, Anna arched up from the mattress. A low groan came from her lips. She gripped his back, kneading the bunched muscles of his shoulder blades.

"I don't want to hurt you, my darling," he breathed into

her ear as he continued to prepare her. "But there is always a little pain the first time."

"It's all right," she murmured, urging him on, needing a fulfillment she didn't quite understand, but knew for certain only he could give. "Don't stop." She felt herself rising higher and higher to a plane she never knew existed. She was only sure that she wanted desperately for this man to take her there. For now there were no more nagging doubts. There was only Philip and the feelings he awakened in her.

He parted her legs, and slowly, gently, slid inside her. She felt herself wrap around him, pulling him in, while in her core she experienced a strange, wild spasm of delight.

"I love you, Anna," he whispered into her ear. "You are mine now and forever."

She reached for his nape and pulled him to her for a mind-numbing kiss that seemed to break the restraints Philip held on his desire. He plunged deeply into her. There was a quick, sharp stab of pain, then a velvety glide, in and out, a warm, silken journey of joined bodies.

Something wild and intuitive pulsed through Anna's veins. She clung to Philip, freeing her mind and body. Their hearts raced in the frantic climb to a place Anna had never been. When she convulsed with a white-hot explosion and cried out, he poured himself into her and answered her cries with his own.

For sweet, long moments afterward, Philip cradled Anna in the protective curve of his arm, planting sweet kisses on her forehead and lazily stroking her arm. "Are you asleep, Anna?" he asked.

She snuggled against him, savoring the sound of his voice. "Actually, I was just wondering, Captain. Are we going to Boston, or are we really headed to the island of your coffee beans?"

"Neither place is nearly as wonderful as where we have just been, my love," he said, "but in eight days time we will sail into Boston Harbor."

"You're going with me to my grandmother's?"

"My lady, I consider it an honor to make your quest my own."

She raised his hand to her lips and kissed his palm, gratitude swelling her heart. But all at once, a strange unsteadiness came over her, as if she were centered in the midst of a billowing cloud being moved forward on powerful gusts of wind. "What's happening?" she asked, leaning up on her elbow.

"That's right," he chuckled, curling his arm behind his head and gazing at her with teasing eyes. "In spite of what has just happened between us, you are still a virgin sailor, aren't you, my love?"

"There it is again!" she said, grabbing his arm in alarm. She definitely felt the bow of the ship dip down in the sea before returning to a steady equilibrium.

"The sails are being unfurled, that's all," Philip explained. "We must have reached the gulf and Bernard is pressing for speed."

"Let's go on deck and watch! I want to see what's happening."

"Then you shall," he said, "just as soon as I remind you what waits for you when we return." He cupped her face in his hands and settled his lips on hers for a torturously long kiss of such urgent tenderness that Anna could scarcely open her eyes when it ended, unwilling to break the spell he cast over her.

They dressed quickly and went on deck. Philip pulled the shawl from Anna's shoulders and draped it over her head. Her hair fanned out around the edge and blew back from her face like a silken halo. He turned her around and pulled her against his length as they both looked up at the three masts of the *Seahawk*.

The skilled crew unfurled the remaining sails of each mast one by one, turning and angling each to catch the best of the breeze. As the sails filled, the *Seahawk* drove through the blue-black water with greater and greater force, its iron hull meeting the demand of increased speed with bold confidence.

Philip wrapped his arms around Anna's waist and she settled her hands on his. "It's breathtaking," she said, watching the practiced movements of the *Seahawk*'s crew as they released lines and pulled them tight once again, refastening them when the time was exactly right.

"It certainly is," he said, lowering his gaze until he could see the top of her head. "I quite agree that something inexplicably wonderful has taken my breath away."

Despite his arms around her, despite his exclamations of love, Anna suddenly shivered in his embrace. It wasn't cold that gripped her senses. It was fear, unwelcome and unbidden.

The night was black around them. The sea swelled dark under their feet. And Anna's past came like a ghost from the grave. She gripped Philip's hands tightly and tried to push the images from her mind. What if she were caught and taken back to Cape de Rive? How could she bear to lose the happiness she'd finally found? Try as she might, she couldn't stop the intrusive doubts from haunting her once more. Her troubles were far from over. *Not now,* she pleaded to the visions in her mind. *Please, not ever!*

CHAPTER FOURTEEN

The *Seahawk* slowed to a crawl, propelled by only the main sail as it maneuvered among a maze of vessels seeking harborage at the bustling pier appropriately called Long Wharf. Anna and Philip stood on deck watching the substantial old brick buildings along the shore take form as the ship edged closer to the center of the city's heartbeat, Boston Harbor. With his arm around Anna's shoulders, Philip pointed out landmarks.

"It's a completely different world here," she said, marveling at the huge warehouses and commercial buildings flanking the wide harbor. When the booths comprising one of the largest markets in the world came into view, she exclaimed in delight, "I'll bet you can buy anything there!"

Convinced that Jake Finn or other bounty hunters wouldn't be looking for her in Boston, Anna persuaded Philip to let her wander amidst the noisy, jostling crowds bargaining with the merchants in the market. Her years of peddling with an uncle who had grown up next to this same harbor had taught Anna well, and she came away with an armload of expertly bartered treasures. Philip, who would have bought the brightest star in the heavens and laid it at her feet if he'd been able, looked on in rapt admiration.

When they left the market, Philip hired a cab to take them to Beacon Hill, while Anna surveyed the waterfront with a mixture of curiosity and sadness. She learned that the huge gray stone buildings that lined the docks housed hundreds of tiny flats. She could picture a honeycomb of narrow hallways and confining little rooms inside those cold granite walls where families eked out meager existences in a struggle to survive. It occurred to her as she scanned the bleak faces of the buildings with their dingy, dark windows that she might actually be looking at the flat where her father and uncle were raised by the proud Seamus Connolly, her grandfather.

No wonder her father had worked long hours at the brass foundry in St. Louis to provide her and her mother with the small but cheerful little house they occupied near the city limits of St. Louis. And no wonder her uncle Mick had much preferred the open road and a life of freedom to a future tied to the docks and hemmed in by those oppressive gray walls.

"What's the matter, darling?" Philip asked when he came up to her. "You look troubled. Are you having second thoughts about finding your grandmother?"

"No, it's not that. I was just remembering my father and my uncle, and I think I'm suddenly beginning to understand the Connolly brothers a little better. This is where they came from, right here, by the harbor, and being here makes me miss them so. I know that time has passed, and I shouldn't be so sad." She looked up at Philip and tried to hide the sense of longing that had gripped her. "After all, I have you, and that's more than I'd ever hoped for."

Philip wrapped his arms around her waist and locked his hands at her back. "I know you, remember. You told me about your past. Anna, I understand."

She had told Philip a great deal about her past during their long, languid days on the *Seahawk*. She had described her father, the dashing Thomas Connolly, and her mother, the beautiful heiress, Kathleen, who had stolen his heart. Philip knew about the fire that had taken her parents' lives when Thomas tried to rescue his ailing wife from the blazing house.

Perhaps Philip really did understand Anna's feeling at this

time. As they stood together at the scene of her heritage, he
told her he shared her grief and pain and knew what this trip
to Boston meant to her.

"I can tell you one thing, Miss Anna Rose," Philip said.
"There are three men in recent history who are very fortunate
to have known you, and I count myself as one of them. And
it's not so strange to imagine that the spirits of Thomas and
Mick linger along this wharf, probably watching out for you
at this very moment. I hope they approve of me and know that
I will love you and care for you all my days. These feelings
you're having, Anna, they're why you came here, aren't they?
To understand once and for all what it means to be you?"

A feeling of astonished wonder washed over Anna, and she
marveled again at her good fortune to have found Philip. "I
guess you learned more than just facts and figures in *l'école,*
didn't you? You learned how to be wise and say just the right
thing."

"I should remind you that you haven't always believed that
to be so," he said with a good-natured grin. "I'm just glad
that you've been able to see that there is a good side to me."
He took her hand and led her toward the cab waiting at the
curb. "Now, our coach is ready. The question is—are you?"

She took a deep breath. "As much as I'll ever be."

"Remember, love, you don't have to stay," Philip assured
her. "You can come with me to the island. St. Sebastian is
beautiful this time of year with its crystal water and white sand
beaches. In fact, I can picture you wading in the warm surf
with the Caribbean breezes in your hair."

She gave him a sideways look. "You're not playing fair,
Philip Brichard. I have to at least give Beacon Hill a look."

"Yes, and I have to supervise the loading of barrels of
coffee," he admitted with a resigned nod. "You would be a
certain distraction, Anna, but that doesn't keep me from wanting
you there."

Once her purchases had been stored on the *Seahawk,* and
Philip had brought their overnight valises, they climbed into
the waiting carriage and left the harbor. Anna watched the
changing scenery as the cab wound through narrow Boston

streets. Soon they were on a much broader avenue which led
up an incline to a row of elegant multi-storied residences.
Across from the dwellings, on the other side of the avenue,
was a lush public garden with many varieties of manicured
shrubs and a bright array of colorful flowers blooming in well-
kept beds. Standing guard over all this splendor, and bordering
a large pond, were dozens of magnificent weeping willow trees,
their long branches sweeping the carpet of soft grass at their
roots.

Several brightly painted and lavishly decorated carriages for
hire stood by the entrances to the garden. The idle drivers
nodded in their seats while their horses nibbled grass at the
curb. Anna was awestruck by the splendor of her surroundings.
"Look at this magnificent garden. Where are we, Philip?"

"This, my love, is Beacon Hill. It's time to stop and inquire
as to the whereabouts of the . . ." Philip stopped abruptly as a
puzzled look crossed his face. "I just realized, I don't even
know who we're looking for. What's your grandmother's
name?"

Anna resumed staring out the window at the homes along
Beacon Hill, deciding that each one seemed grander than the
last. She glanced briefly over her shoulder and said, "Ophelia
Sullivan. My grandfather was Patrick Sullivan."

Philip leaned forward to ask the driver to stop for directions
when he suddenly wheeled around and grabbed Anna's arm.
"Anna!" He pulled her attention away from the panorama of
beautiful mansions. "What did you say your grandfather's
name was? Did you say Patrick Sullivan?"

She nodded, confused and alarmed by the shocked expression
on Philip's face. "Why? What's wrong? Have you heard of
him?"

"What business was he in?"

"I'm not sure exactly. I remember my mother telling me
that her father traveled a lot, to foreign places, perhaps like
you do. He always brought my mother a trinket when he
returned from a trip, and she had them all stored in a trunk in
our attic. There were porcelain dolls and animals carved of
wood and wide-brimmed hats with paper flowers all over . . .

Philip, why are you staring at me like that? You're beginning to scare me.''

The shock on Philip's face was transformed to a beaming grin as he grasped her shoulders and peered into her face. ''I knew him, darling, I knew your grandfather! He was a shipper and dealer in artifacts, porcelains and such from as far away as Europe and the Orient. Our paths crossed a couple of times in the Caribbean, and I remember thinking that I was grateful we didn't trade for the same commodities. He was a very shrewd and successful businessman, Anna.''

''Well, I guess so, to live in a place like this!'' she agreed. ''I can't believe that you knew him, though it makes sense now that I think about it.'' She felt relieved at first to learn that Philip had known her grandfather, but that relief was quickly overshadowed by a nagging doubt, and she asked warily, ''He wasn't a very nice man, was he?''

Philip waited several moments before answering, and when he did, his response was restrained. ''Some thought Pat's personality was a bit dour, and I've heard he managed his crews with harsh discipline, but I could never fault his ability to make the best deal. He was honest and followed a strict code of ethics, from all I could tell, and he was respected. But nice— I can't truthfully say that I'd use that word to describe him.''

''That's what I thought you would say, if you were being honest. Did you ever meet my grandmother?''

''No, I only saw Pat in foreign ports. In fact, I've only been to Boston one other time in my life. But I have a hunch you'll like her. Imagine . . . this grandmother I once doubted even existed, is Pat Sullivan's wife! Something tells me the woman's a saint!''

Anna laughed. ''To have put up with him, you mean.''

Philip shrugged noncommittally, though his mouth pulled up at the corners in a wry grin. He asked the driver to pull over to the sidewalk. Then he called out to a passing pedestrian, an elderly man sporting a bowler and walking with an ebony cane. ''Pardon me, sir, we're looking for the home of the Sullivans, Patrick and Ophelia.''

''Old Pat's gone, you know,'' the elderly gentleman said

through a thick Irish accent. "Been dead these many months now."

"I know, but could you tell us where he lived . . . where his widow lives?"

"I might be able to do that," the old man said, his eyes twinkling with mischief, "if you can follow the tip o' my cane." He twirled the walking stick under his arm and pointed the black onyx tip at the house directly behind him. "You're sittin' in front of Old Pat's right now. I'm surprised you can't hear his ghost bellowin' out the window!"

Philip glanced at Anna. She was covering her mouth to keep from laughing out loud. "Thank you!" Philip called. "Good day to you."

Telling the driver to wait for instructions, Philip assisted Anna from the coach, took her elbow, and they walked up the brick path to the front entrance.

Anna wasn't close to laughing now. In fact, her body stiffened with anxiety, and she covered Philip's hand with shaking fingers.

"You're so pale, darling," he said. "You're not going to back out now, are you?" He increased the pressure of his hand on her arm.

"I'm just a little nervous," she admitted, stopping in the middle of the walkway. "No, that's not true. I'm scared to death!"

"Of Ophelia or the bellowing ghost of Pat?" he asked as if it were a completely logical question.

It brought about the intended reaction, and Anna giggled. "I'm not sure."

Philip turned the bronze chime on the door, and within moments it was answered by a maid in a black dress covered with a starched white pinafore that stretched across ample breasts. A small mobcap with a black satin ribbon entwined in its ruffle sat atop her head, doing a very poor job of containing a riot of frizzy red spirals that stuck out around her face and neck. Her eyes, which were painted with garish hues of blue and lavender, peered at her guests with blatant interest, especially Philip.

Anna didn't like the way the maid's red mouth curled up in a provocative grin, or the way her eyes brazenly roamed down Philip's long length. This woman hardly seemed an appropriate maid for her grandmother!

"Well, what 'ave we 'ere?" she boldly asked in an ill-concealed Cockney accent.

"We're here to see Mrs. Sullivan," Philip said, seemingly oblivious to the maid's flirting. "Is she home?"

"She might be, if I was to know 'oo's callin'. Why don't you leave your card, ducky?" She picked up a silver tray from a hall stand and extended it to Philip. "It's the way the grand lady likes things done around 'ere."

Philip forced an indulgent smile. "I don't have a card, miss. Please just tell her that Philip Brichard from New Orleans and Miss Anna Rose . . ."

"New Orlenz!" the maid shot back. "I've always wanted to go there." She eyed Philip through artificially thick blue-black lashes and toyed with the pinafore ruffle above her breast with a long fingernail that hadn't seen many house chores. "I've 'eard it gets 'ot and steamy in the summer."

"Look, miss . . ." Anna could tell that Philip was fast losing patience with the saucy maid.

"What's going on, Myra. Who's there?" The refined voice coming from inside the house drew everyone's attention to an elderly woman dressed in a fashionably tailored violet silk day gown. Panels of beaded ivory satin covered the woman's flat chest, and delicate lace ruffles stood up against her neck where a tiger's eye brooch rested under her chin.

"It seems you 'ave comp'ny, Mrs. Sullivan, unexpected as they might be in the middle of the day."

Ophelia Sullivan came to the door and looked over the threshold at her guests. Her milky green eyes gave Philip a quick approving perusal. Before he could introduce himself, her gaze swept to Anna and remained fixed on her face. A quick flash of recognition sparked in Ophelia's eyes, and her thin lips parted in a startled gasp. "Kathleen," she breathed. Her hand came to her throat. "My God in heaven, it's you."

"Please, Mrs. Sullivan," Anna said, reaching for the woman's hand. "I'm not Kathleen, though I've heard we look alike."

"Of course you aren't," Ophelia amended at once. She struggled to maintain a semblance of dignity as she studied the familiar face before her—the face so like her daughter's. "You can't be. My Kathleen died many years ago." Her pupils paled with moisture. "But who are you?"

"I'm Anna, Mrs. Sullivan, I'm Kathleen and Thomas Connolly's daughter."

Ophelia scarcely had the breath to speak, and her words came out in a choked rasp. "Oh, my darling granddaughter, come here to me."

Anna allowed Ophelia to enclose her in an embrace. She felt the woman's tears on her cheeks.

When Ophelia stepped back, she held Anna's hands and admired her, shaking her head in obvious delight. "My, but you are a beauty, just like my Kathleen was. Do you remember your mother, dear?"

"Very well, Mrs. Sullivan. She was beautiful and so kind. I loved her very much, and I miss her still."

"Don't I know what it is to miss Kathleen," Ophelia said sadly. "I have lived with the heartbreak of it for years." Then as if seeing Philip for the first time, she held out a thin hand to him, "Oh, my, where are my manners? Who is your young man, Anna? I know he's not old enough to be that ornery Mick."

Anna smiled and put her arm through Philip's. "This is Philip Brichard, ma'am. We're going to be married."

"Married! Isn't that wonderful. Come in, both of you. We have so much to talk about." Ophelia stepped between them, looped her arms with theirs, and took them to her parlor. "When did you get to Boston?" she asked. "Are you staying long? Where are you from, Mr. Brichard?" Having apparently chased away the melancholy of painful remembrances, she immersed herself in the joy of getting to know her granddaughter and her handsome fiancé.

"Now, where is that flighty maid Franklin had me hire?" Ophelia took her guests to a pair of elegant brocade settees.

"That girl's never around when I need her. Myra! Myra! Bring us refreshments! So, Anna dear, where is that rascal Mick? I have to thank him for sending you to me."

"There is so much to tell you, Mrs. Sullivan," Anna said, knowing that if Henri were not successful in Cape de Rive, she would have to tell Ophelia the whole truth about Mick and her own troubles. "I hardly know where to start."

"Start by calling me 'grandmother,' won't you?"

Before accepting Ophelia's offer of tea and biscuits, and to give the ladies a chance to get acquainted, Philip went outside to dismiss the hired coach. While he was paying the driver, another carriage pulled up in front of the Sullivan home, and a solidly built, well-dressed man, some years older than Philip, climbed out of the cab. The uniformed driver drove the carriage around the side of Ophelia's mansion. Without noticing or at least acknowledging Philip on the curb, the man went directly to the house and entered without knocking. Finding this slightly odd, Philip followed him in.

"Oh, Franklin," Ophelia trilled from the parlor. She rushed out to the foyer to meet the man and drew him back inside with her. "The most wonderful thing has just happened . . . a miracle really."

Philip watched the scene from the foyer as Ophelia ushered the man to Anna. "Look, Franklin, my granddaughter has arrived. You know I'd given up hope that she would, but she has. This is Anna. Anna, my dear, this is Franklin Danvers. He was vice president of your grandfather's shipping company, and one of our dearest friends, and now he's . . ." Ophelia blushed like a schoolgirl. "Well, he and I are engaged to be married."

Anna responded appropriately by congratulating the stoic Franklin Danvers and planting a kiss of good wishes on her grandmother's cheek. "There will be two weddings soon, then, Grandmother," she said. "Philip and I are thinking of being married in Boston."

"Really, dear? That would be wonderful, but Franklin and

I won't be getting married for a while yet. Heavens, no. In fact, my time of mourning won't be over for another two months. Oh, but did you hear that, Franklin? I can help Anna plan her wedding!'' She clasped her hands under her chin and practically giggled. "I don't remember when I've been so happy.''

"How did you happen to arrive in Boston, Anna?'' Franklin asked after he'd gone to the mahogany bar and poured himself a drink.

"I brought her,'' Philip said, stepping into the parlor for the first time since Franklin arrived. The two men faced each other, and Franklin appraised Philip with stern scrutiny before extending his hand as Anna made the introductions.

"I've met Pat Sullivan on several occasions,'' Philip said, "but I don't remember ever meeting you, Mr. Danvers.''

"I'm afraid I didn't get around much like Patrick did. He preferred I stay in the office.'' Philip detected a touch of resentment in Franklin's voice, but in light of Pat Sullivan's reputation, he wasn't surprised. Philip doubted that any of Pat's employees liked him much.

"What are you drinking, Philip?'' Franklin asked. He poised his hand over a selection of decanters and glasses.

"Actually, tea was being kept warm for me, I believe.''

Franklin turned away from the ladies and indicated a decanter full of brandy. "I think we can do better than a cup of tea,'' he said in a conspiratorial voice, and Philip nodded his agreement. "What business are you in?''

"Shipping. The same as you, I guess, though with different ports and goods if you're handling things as Sullivan did.''

Franklin's hand trembled. Drops of amber liquid spilled out of the decanter onto the marble surface of the bar. "Oh, look what I've done,'' he muttered. Regaining his composure, he handed Philip a glass. Then he slipped a long finger under his starched collar as if it had suddenly become uncomfortably warm. "Everything's just as Pat left it,'' he said. "Why would I change a good thing?'' He relaxed, and his face became the picture of amicability.

After a few more minutes of polite conversation, Franklin

pulled his pocket watch out of his waistcoat and frowned. "I'm afraid you'll have to excuse me. I have some business to attend to in Ophelia's study."

"Oh, Franklin, it's always, business, business, business with you," Ophelia scolded. "Do come back as quickly as you can, dear."

Franklin smiled at his intended bride. "Of course, Ophelia, but some things are too urgent to be let go."

Watching his retreating figure, Ophelia whispered to Anna, "He's a good man, but he takes life much too seriously. I've already had one husband like that. But then, Franklin's sense of responsibility and attention to details were my mainstay after poor Patrick's accident. He insisted on relieving me of the unpleasant burden of seeing to Patrick's funeral, and since then he has capably taken over the reins of Sullivan Shipping and has all but taken over the management of the household. I am so grateful to him, even if he did insist on hiring that dizzy little London woman, Myra Manchester."

Ophelia paused and breathed a sigh of contentment. "But I will say this, for the first time in my life, I am truly a lady of leisure, Franklin has spoiled me so."

"So you're happy, Grandmother?"

"Why, who wouldn't be, dear?" Ophelia chirped gaily, then quickly corrected her breach of decorum. "Considering that we are still in a state of mourning in this house, of course."

"Excuse me, Mrs. Sullivan," Philip said, "but may I ask how Patrick died?"

"It was a dreadful accident in the warehouse, and, ironically, it was Patrick's own fault. He had been told by his doctors and by me several times to avoid climbing on ladders. He was prone to light-headedness as he got older. Thinning blood, I suppose. Well, as your mother may have mentioned, Anna, he was a stubborn man, and his obstinacy was his downfall . . . literally! He was checking inventory late one night, alone, and it has been surmised that he was on the top of a ladder when a tower of cartons tumbled down taking poor Patrick with it. He was crushed under the weight of dozens of Staffordshire porcelains. It was ghastly!"

"I should say so," Anna agreed, noticeably moved by her grandfather's tragic demise.

"Amazingly, not one statue was broken," Ophelia added with a curious smile.

Franklin Danvers marched through the kitchen door with a purposeful stride. As soon as he entered the room, Myra Manchester jumped out from behind the door with a feather duster in her hand. When Franklin walked by, she brushed the duster playfully against his nape. " 'Ello, luv," she said.

He pivoted around, swatting at his neck. "Quit playing games, Myra," he scolded. "I've been looking for you." Sometimes he wondered why he ever put up with this chit.

" 'Ave you now?" she said, a suggestive grin pulling at her full, luscious mouth. He remembered why he put up with her.

"I'm going to the carriage house. Meet me there in five minutes, and for God's sake, Myra, make sure no one sees you leave the house!"

"No problem, luv. It's as good as done."

"Frankie! Frankie!" Myra croaked in a loud whisper as she crept among the assorted carriages that belonged to Ophelia. It was dark in the carriage house, and it bothered her that Franklin hadn't even lighted a lantern to help her see her way in the lengthening dusk. "This isn't funny, luv," she said nervously.

A hand reached out from the backseat of an elegant phaeton and grabbed Myra's wrist. "Shut up!" Franklin hissed, pulling her roughly into the coach. As soon as she was inside, he drew all the curtains closed. "You'll bring the house down on us!"

"Well, you could've lit a light, Frankie. You're darn lucky I forgive you most all yer bad manners." She leaned into him, her wiry curls brushing his face. Her lips found his rigid mouth and crushed over it.

"Not now!" Franklin grumbled, pushing her away and swiping at the trace of lip color she'd already managed to smear on him.

"Then what'd you want to see me for?" Myra asked, dumbfounded by his reaction to her usual advances.

"Just listen for once! Do you have any idea who those people are who came to the house today?"

"Certainly not," she said, still stinging from his rebuff. "Listenin' at doorways is not part of my duties."

"Well, that's about to change. That young woman is Ophelia's granddaughter, and her fiancé is owner of Brichard Shipping in New Orleans. I can't imagine two people who could mean more trouble for me."

Myra was suddenly interested in what Franklin had to say. "What do you mean, *trouble?*" She was clever enough to know that trouble for Franklin certainly translated to trouble for her.

"Don't be obtuse, Myra, the girl's an heir, a direct heir to Patrick's business and fortune, and she's already begun wheedling her way into Ophelia's affections. And the poor addled woman seems about as lovestruck as a mother who's just seen her first babe. If we were already married, I wouldn't worry. My lawyer would have already drawn up airtight contracts that would have put Sullivan Shipping unquestionably in my name. But this damnable mourning period and Patrick Sullivan's longlost granddaughter are going to spoil everything! To top it off she's brought with her a fiancé who's more than likely licking his lips to get his hands on the business himself."

Franklin's eyes shone with such fierce intensity that Myra crouched away from him. She didn't like this side of him.

"I deserve Sullivan Shipping, Myra . . . I've earned it! I didn't wait as long as I did pandering to Patrick and work as hard as I did to get him out of the picture to have it all taken away now."

"O' course not, luv," Myra agreed sympathetically. She knew that when Franklin's temples pulsed as they did now and when his eyes blazed with such fury that anything she said might enrage him more. "What do you want me to do, Frankie?" she ventured meekly.

"Brichard's leaving tomorrow for the Caribbean, but I have a hunch the girl will be staying. Watch her, Myra. I want to know where she goes, who she sees, what she says to Ophelia, everything! Do you understand?"

" 'Course I do, luv. You know you can count on me."

Franklin grabbed her hand with the force of a drowning man and held it up to his lips. "That's right, Myra, because if we fail, you know where you'll end up, don't you? Back at Skully's with the rest of the girls if you're not in jail. You don't want that, do you, Myra?"

She nodded frantically, the circle of bright curls bouncing around her face. "O' course not, luv."

Franklin drew her index finger into his mouth and began sucking it. Now we're getting down to business, Myra thought. Then, without warning, his teeth sank into the soft pad of her fingertip. She gasped with the pain and tried to pull away from him. "You didn't have to hurt me, Frankie," she whimpered. "I'll do what you tell me, you know that. I'll come to you with anything I find out."

Franklin pulled her finger out of his mouth and held it up. Even in the dim light, she could see a dark trail of blood dripping down her knuckle. "I knew I could count on you, Myra," he said, "but there's one more thing . . . don't arouse suspicion. Be everywhere, hear everything, but, for God's sake, don't make a spectacle of yourself. Be discreet. Know when to keep your mouth shut!"

"I'll be careful," Myra promised, staring at her finger. "The ladies will 'ardly know I'm around." She watched Franklin close his lips around her finger once more and slowly begin drawing on the tip. Her fear was forgotten as a quiver of excitement raced up her spine. She sidled close to him and ran her hand over the thin hair slicked back over his head. "I love you, Frankie, I'd do anything for you."

He dropped her hand and pulled her to him, crushing her breasts against his chest. "You're like a disease with me, Myra, you know that, don't you? You're in my blood."

She wriggled against him and reached for the buttons on his trousers. "Maybe so, luv, but in yer pants is where *I* want to be."

Franklin leaned back in Ophelia's phaeton and let Myra do what she did best.

Ophelia decided over dinner that Anna and Philip would both stay as invited guests in her home that night, and she would hear no argument to the contrary. They would, of course, stay at opposite ends of a long corridor on her second floor, as was only proper, but due to Philip's leaving the next day, Ophelia could see no reason to separate the young lovers by sending him back to the *Seahawk*.

After all, Ophelia conceded with a matronly blush, Franklin Danvers often stayed in his own suite of rooms at the Sullivan mansion instead of going to his quarters in Copley. And Ophelia made her desires explicitly known that she hoped with all her heart that Anna would stay with her while Philip tended to his affairs in St. Sebastian.

Later that night, when Philip walked Anna to the door of her room, knowing he was going to have to leave her on the threshold, he asked what she had decided to do. "So, my darling, do I send your trunk over in the morning, or will you be coming back with me to the *Seahawk?*"

She had only just made up her mind, and already she was imagining the pain of missing him. "Promise you won't be disappointed?"

"My love, if I had to go into New Orleans for the morning, and you chose to stay at Frenchman's Point rather than accompany me, I would be disappointed, even if I knew I would see you at dinner. So don't ask me not to be disappointed that you've chosen to stay with Ophelia." But he smiled down at her with such a measure of understanding in his eyes that Anna knew he would accept her decision in good humor.

"I don't know how I'll be able to stand being away from you, Philip, but I've just met her, and she's promised to tell me all about my mother when she was a little girl and about the 'breathtakingly handsome but brazen Thomas Connolly' she calls him, who showed up more than once on the Sullivans' doorstep. She has photographs and momentos and wonderful stories to tell me, and I feel starved to know it all.''

''I know, and I understand that learning about your background is why we came here after all. Just so you don't decide to stay,'' he said with forced good cheer. ''I'll bring you back whenever you like to visit, but remember, my love, that your home is with the husband who loves you.''

''I feel as though it already is,'' she said honestly. ''Besides, though it might seem like half a lifetime, you'll only be gone twelve days—that's what you said, isn't it? And while you're away, Ophelia has agreed to help me plan a wedding.'' Anna gave him a flirtatious little smile. ''Consider yourself forewarned, Captain Brichard . . . when you return, prepare to be a groom.''

''I'll look forward to it,'' he said with a wicked grin. ''Especially to the wedding night.'' He pulled her into his arms and rested his chin on the top of her head. Then he peeked around the doorframe to her room. ''Are you sure we can't . . .''

''Philip, certainly not! I have a hunch my grandmother might take a broom to you, and as closely as that red-haired maid has been watching us tonight, I fear we would have an audience.''

''She is a curious girl, isn't she?'' Philip remarked. ''But for all her strange behavior she seems harmless enough, and quite attentive to you, as a matter of fact. And I feel better knowing a man is in the house most of the time. Danvers is far from the jovial sort, but he seems hardworking and capable and devoted to Ophelia. It's easier leaving you knowing he'll be here to watch out for your welfare.''

Anna raised her face to his and grinned. ''And who will watch out for yours I wonder?''

''Who else? Bernard Fitzhugh. He's almost as excited about this match as I am, so he'll see to it I return all in one piece.'' Philip brushed his lips lightly over hers and murmured huskily, ''I've been dreaming all day of having you alone for a moment, and now that it's actually happened, all I can do is wish you good night. Well, my love, I hope that this is one good night you'll remember for the next twelve days!'' His mouth lowered to hers, and if she had planned to say anything else, she quickly forgot what it was.

CHAPTER FIFTEEN

Ophelia was still consoling Anna long after the breakfast dishes had been removed from the table. "There, there, dear," she said, patting Anna's hand, "he'll be back before you know it. Twelve days isn't so long. Patrick used to be away for weeks at a time, and I got along just fine without him, wonderfully well, actually."

Anna couldn't help smiling, especially when she envisioned the way Philip would have reacted to Ophelia's statement. She could easily imagine his stifled laughter, and for a moment she could almost convince herself he was in the room. "You're right, of course, Grandmother, and I'll be fine. It's just that in the short time we've known each other, we haven't been apart for even a day."

"Ah, the blossoming of true love," Ophelia sighed. "It's a beautiful thing to be sure—memories to treasure after the blooms have faded." She leaned back in her chair, and her eyes dimmed with a faraway dreamy quality as if she were remembering a special time from her own past. But she stoically pulled herself out of her reverie and regarded Anna with renewed energy. "I've just thought of the perfect plan to chase away all your blues, my dear . . . shopping! As soon as your trunk arrives, you'll dress in all your finery and powder your nose, and we'll head to Downtown Crossing. How does that sound?''

"It sounds wonderful," Anna said, trying to share her grandmother's enthusiasm. In truth, she was grateful for Ophelia's suggestion to leave the house, since she knew that, first thing, she had to send a telegram to Henri at his office on Chartres Street. "I hope you won't mind, but I need to go to the nearest telegraph office before we shop. It shouldn't take too long."

"Whatever you want, dear. This is your day to do whatever pleases you." A jangle of silverware made Ophelia glance over her shoulder to the enormous serving buffet that occupied one entire wall of the dining room. Myra Manchester was bent over the breakfast chafing dishes with her back to the ladies.

"Myra, for heaven's sake," Ophelia scolded, "you've been fussing over those servers for almost an hour now. I can't believe you haven't cleared away the dishes yet."

Myra clattered a large serving spoon against a silver platter, creating the impression that she was indeed very busy. Then she faced her mistress. "Nearly done, missus," she said. "There's more than the usual tidyin' what with the extra guests and all."

"Very well, but do hurry, please. I want you to watch for Anna's trunk to arrive, and as soon as it does, ask Mr. Hines to bring it up to her room. Then go out to the carriage house and tell Lloyd to prepare the phaeton and bring it around to the front of the house."

"Oooo, the phaeton is my personal favorite of all your carriages, ma'am," Myra gushed. "I'll bet a girl can get quite a ride in that luvly buggy." Myra's shoulders shook with what appeared to be a shiver of pure delight. After a moment she asked casually, "Where might you ladies be off to this morning, Mrs. Sullivan?"

"We're going to purchase some things for Anna. She's going to be married soon, you know."

"Isn't that luvly," Myra said, her hands working continually over the dishes.

"She'll need a complete trousseau, won't you, dear?"

Ophelia said to Anna. "And a wedding dress and night clothes and linens, and, oh, my, there's so much to think of!"

"Will you be going anywhere else after yer buyin' spree?" Myra asked without looking up.

"I don't see that it's any concern of yours," Ophelia answered.

Myra scooped up a tray of silverware and headed for the kitchen. "I beg your pardon, ma'am," she said. "I was only askin' in case Mr. Danvers came 'ome in the afternoon as he often does these days. 'E might very well ask me where you are, and I only thought to spare him worry as to yer location."

Apparently mollified by Myra's explanation, Ophelia nodded. "Very well. Anna and I won't be late, and I'm quite sure we will return before Mr. Danvers does, so you needn't concern yourself with him."

"Yes, ma'am." Myra backed through the kitchen door carrying the tray. Once in the kitchen, she set her burden down, leaned her hands on the large scrub table and heaved a great sigh of relief. "Watch it, girl," she scolded herself. "If you don't remember to be more subtle-like, you'll 'ave the 'ole lot of 'em on yer back!"

An hour later, Anna stopped at the telegraph office and sent a message to Henri informing him of Ophelia's address. She satisfied Ophelia's curiosity by saying she was merely telling Philip's family that she and Philip had arrived safely. Since Anna felt secure away from the Mississippi River, and since she believed rumors of her deeds would never follow her to Boston, she decided not to tell her grandmother anything about her troubles in Cape de Rive, unless she was absolutely forced to by unfortunate circumstances. Perhaps when everything was settled, after Henri had cleared her name, she would be able to confide in Ophelia, but not yet, not when the two of them were just beginning to form a bond of kinship.

Anna was both surprised and gratified that she was already experiencing a familial closeness with her grandmother, and she didn't want anything to affect their developing relationship. In fact, Anna was finally allowing herself to feel hopeful about many things, including Henri's trip to Cape de Rive. Maybe he actually could convince the authorities she was innocent.

It was Myra Manchester, however, and not Anna, who received Henri's answering telegram when it arrived at the Sullivan mansion later that same day. She opened the door and peered across the threshold at a delivery boy in uniform. "What is it?" she asked anxiously.

"I have a telegram for Miss Anna Connolly," the boy stated, indicating the envelope attached to his clipboard.

Myra immediately recognized this bit of good fortune as an opportunity to put Franklin Danvers in her debt. "I'll just 'ave it then."

The boy clutched the clipboard to his chest. "My instructions are to give it to Miss Connolly personally."

Myra fixed him with a hard stare. "That'll be a little 'ard to do, considerin' Miss Connolly ain't 'ere right now. I'll give it to 'er myself when she returns."

"Well, I don't know about that. Like I said . . ."

What a twit this boy was. "Now look, laddie," Myra said, flashing him the smile that had made her one of Skully's favorite employees, "this 'ere's the Sullivan 'ouse, and all sorts of important personages cross through this door. They can't be expected to wait for their telegrams accordin' to yer whim of when to bring 'em back, now, can they? Give it to me now, and I'll see it goes directly to Miss Connolly the minute she returns." She held out her hand, palm up, and waited while the delivery boy fidgeted on the doorstep.

After an exasperatingly long standoff, Myra reached inside the neckline of her dress and down into her camisole. She pulled out a dollar bill and waved it in front of the boy's face. "See 'ere, you're still gettin' yer tip, if that's what yer fussin' about, prob'ly more than the likes of you are used to."

The messenger stared at the dollar. Seconds later, he handed over the telegram, and Myra smiled in triumph. Before he could change his mind, she shoved the dollar at him and slammed the door in his face. "You thievin' bugger!" she muttered out the window at the retreating figure. "You'll darn well give me back every red cent, Frankie, and more!" Then she hurriedly squirmed out of her pinafore, ripped off her mobcap and replaced it with the straw hat covered with peacock quills she wore outside the mansion. She called down the hallway to the kitchen, "Hines, I'm leavin'! I got an errand to run."

Without waiting for Hines to acknowledge her message, she dashed down the steps to the sidewalk and hailed a coach waiting across the avenue at the public garden. She climbed in and settled back against the cushy seat. "Fleet Street and Atlantic," she called to the driver. "Drop me at Sullivan Shippin' Comp'ny."

Franklin Danvers pulled Myra into his office and closed the door quickly behind them. "For God's sake, Myra, have you lost your mind?"

He had been at his desk when she came into the warehouse, and he had immediately run out to corral her before she could talk to anyone who might question her presence there. "How many times have I told you never to come here?" He drew the shades on his office windows and glared at her. "This is an outrage, and frankly I don't know why I continue to put up with you."

"Don't you now, luv?" she responded with a flirtatious lilt to her voice. "Perhaps you'll be glad you put up with me when you see I've brought a message delivered today for the 'igh and mighty duchess 'erself." She pulled the yellow envelope out of her pocket and held it temptingly in front of Franklin's eyes.

"What? A telegram for Anna?" Franklin grabbed it and turned it over in his hand. When he saw that the seal was still secure, he said, "She hasn't seen it then?"

Myra gave him an exultant grin. "You'll be privy long before the duchess is. She and yer right proper fiancée are out shoppin' at Downtown Crossin', not payin' any mind at all to telegrams and the like.''

Franklin took a stiletto-style letter opener out of his desk drawer and carefully maneuvered the sharp tip into a corner of the envelope seal. Slowly and methodically he slid the point across the telegram to loosen the adhesive without destroying the flap. He unfolded the message inside, saw that it was sent from New Orleans, and read to himself, ''Leaving immediately on fastest steamer to Cape de Rive. Will advise with results of investigation as soon as possible. Regards, Henri.''

''Cape de Rive, Cape de Rive,'' Franklin muttered. He tapped the letter opener on his leather desk blotter. ''Where have I heard of that town?''

''It's in Illinois, I believe, Frankie,'' Myra offered. ''I've 'ad a few acquaintances go there to find work. At one point I'd 'ad 'alf a mind to go there myself, but I'm glad I didn't.'' She plopped down on Franklin's desk and stroked her long legs with painted fingernails.

''By God, Myra, you're right,'' Franklin proclaimed, ignoring her sexual preening. ''It is in Illinois, and, as I recall, that town has a reputation for having a seamy underbelly. You don't suppose our little Miss Connolly is involved in something less than savory, do you?''

''You mean she might 'ave broke the law?'' Myra's red lips rounded into a circle of surprise. ''What do you 'spose she might 'ave done?''

''I haven't the faintest idea, but if we're lucky we'll discover that she's been posing as a long-lost relative of wealthy widows.''

''Now that would be a bit o' good fortune, wouldn't it? The queen wouldn't take too kindly at that!''

''Exactly.'' Franklin took a sheet of paper from his desk drawer and began writing: ''To: Constable of Cape de Rive, Illinois: Am inquiring about one Anna Connolly. Please respond with any pertinent information you may have regarding same. Franklin Danvers.''

''Take this to the telegraph office, Myra, with return requested to the shipping company address. Maybe I'll get some answers as to why Ophelia's darling showed up when she did. I have a feeling she's hiding something, and if she is, I'm going to find out what it is and hopefully stumble on a way to get her out of our lives.''

Myra pointed to the envelope still on Franklin's desk. ''What should I do with that there telegram, Frankie?''

He moistened the flap once more and managed to seal the envelope well enough that no one would be likely to notice it had been opened. ''Give it to her, Myra. She's no doubt expecting it, and we wouldn't want to arouse her suspicions.''

He sat back in his chair, and clasped his hands on the back of his head. ''I feel good, Myra,'' he said. ''It's just possible that Miss Connolly will turn out to be only a momentary annoyance. All I need is one dirty little secret, and my prim and proper Ophelia will drop her dear granddaughter like yesterday's slop.''

Myra walked around the back of Franklin's chair and began kneading his shoulders with expert fingers. ''I'm 'appy as a kitten in cream that you feel good, Frankie, but I can make you feel ever so much better.''

He grabbed her hands to stop her. ''Not now, Myra, not here. We'll have plenty of time to celebrate later and hopefully for the rest of our days.''

When he returned to Ophelia's later that afternoon, Franklin was polite and cordial. He admired the ladies' purchases and chuckled at their stories of fittings and shopkeepers. He even pretended a serious interest in Ophelia's ideas for Anna's wedding.

''Isn't it wonderful,'' he said as he escorted Ophelia into dinner that evening. ''You have your lovely granddaughter here to occupy your days. She truly is a godsend, isn't she, my dear?''

The constable in Cape de Rive received Franklin's telegram after learning that Stuart Wilkes's widow had raised the reward for her husband's murderers to ten thousand dollars. Within minutes, he called Jake Finn to his office.

"I'm about to do you the biggest favor of your life, Finn," Constable Petrie said. "I know you've been looking for that Connolly girl all up and down the river with an eye on the reward money."

"It's ten thousand dollars now," Jake reminded Petrie unnecessarily.

"Well, I know where she is," Petrie said smugly, "and for five thousand dollars I'll tell you where. You can go get her, and we'll split the reward."

Jake Finn considered the proposition and decided it was a fair enough deal. He and the constable sent a telegram to Franklin Danvers in Boston the next morning telling him that Anna Connolly was wanted for an undisclosed crime in Cape de Rive, and to keep a close eye on her until 'Deputy Jake Finn' arrived in a few days by train to fetch the fugitive. They reminded Mr. Danvers of the importance of his cooperation, thanked him for his civic duties, and warned him that Miss Connolly was a dangerous criminal, and he should not attempt to capture her himself.

Petrie and Jake did not overly concern themselves that afternoon when they received a slightly suspicious response from Mr. Danvers. He indicated that he would, indeed, keep a close watch on the criminal until Jake's arrival, but his own identity was to be kept strictly confidential. At no time was Miss Connolly or anyone associated with her to hear the name Franklin Danvers in connection with her apprehension.

"So what if he wants to lay low?" Constable Petrie muttered to himself as he watched the east-bound train depart from Cape de Rive with Jake Finn aboard. It was no concern of his who this Danvers character was or why he wanted to remain anonymous. In fact, his secrecy just might eliminate the possibility of having to split the reward into thirds. After all, the important thing was that a desperate fugitive would soon be captured and brought to justice, and the streets would be safe again from the likes of Anna Connolly.

* * *

A strong southerly wind had brought the *Seahawk* within a few miles of the southeast Florida coastline in just over three days. Philip was thankful for the speed with which the clipper was making the journey to St. Sebastian. Bernard Fitzhugh was an able captain, and Philip had given him free rein to command the ship since they left Boston.

Likewise, when they reached the island, he intended to let the capable Fitzhugh make speedy preparations to outfit the *Seahawk* for the return sail to Boston while Philip tended to the purchasing, lading, and shipping of the coffee. A second Brichard schooner was due to meet them at the island harbor and return the cargo to New Orleans. If everything went as Philip hoped it would, they would be back in Boston in less than the predicted twelve days, he would be reunited with Anna, and the coffee would arrive at the Brichard warehouse on schedule.

With the late-afternoon sun warming his face, Philip stood on the deck, his foot propped on a thick coil of rope. He held a telescope up to his eye and leisurely scanned the barren Florida shoreline.

Suddenly Fitzhugh called to him with an edge of alarm in his usually calm voice. "Philip, you'd best come over here and have a look. There's a ship just south of us, and her crew is dumping cargo into the sea."

Philip joined Bernard on the bow of the *Seahawk*, and with his naked eye he could discern the hulking shape of a large four-masted clipper, which was bigger even than the *Seahawk*. It was drifting in the calm waves, its masts barren of any sails.

"She's a giant," Philip said, raising the telescope for a closer look. "In fact, she appears to be one of the English ships made in the forties to carry large cargos from Europe and the Orient. I can't imagine what she's doing in these waters."

"Well, if they dump another sack in the ocean, I think you'll see what she's doin'," Bernard said ominously.

Philip watched through his lens as a long oblong-shaped bundle wrapped in canvas was dumped off the starboard side of the ship into the sea. "Good God!" he cried. "It looks like a body!"

"That was my opinion exactly," Bernard confirmed.

Philip swept his telescope along the side of the ship, searching for any signs that might identify its registry. When he reached the elongated bow, he was able to make out the design of a serpent jutting out over the water from the projecting prow. "Scan to the west," he said to Bernard. "What do you make of the figurehead?"

Bernard squinted a sharp eye against his own telescope and came up with the same observation as Philip. "It's a snake of some sort, though I can't see any identifyin' colors."

"Who used the serpent on his ships?" Philip asked, experiencing an overwhelming sense of dread. "Wasn't it Sullivan, Bernard? Didn't old Pat use the serpent?"

"Aye, he did at that, but Pat hasn't used one of those old tubs in a long while. Long before he died he switched to the faster clippers and schooners like we have. That vessel there's a relic of the past and ought to be fightin' off wood worms in a museum."

"Unless . . ." Philip couldn't take his eyes away from the ominous serpent on the prow of the ship. "Unless . . ."

"What is it?" Bernard prompted. "What are you thinkin'?"

"Unless the man who's now running Sullivan Shipping had a cargo so large that it wouldn't fit in a faster schooner. Unless he wanted to deliver a bigger shipment and make fewer trips, and speed was not as important. Then maybe he'd pull this monster out of dry dock."

Bernard eyed his friend with sober curiosity. "Just what do you suppose they've got in that hold?"

Philip slipped his foot between the ship's rails and propped an elbow on his bended knee. With his eye still focused sharply on the large clipper, he said gravely, "Bernard, have you ever heard of a German fellow who's known as the kaiser?" Out of the corner of his eye Philip saw Bernard shake his head. "He lives in the marshlands of Florida, land infested with snakes and alligators so big that very few whites choose to live there. It's inhabited mostly by Indians.

"This man, the kaiser, has established a kind of dynasty deep in those wetlands. He grows sugarcane, and it's almost time for the back-breaking harvest. He always needs laborers badly. I hope I'm wrong, but I have a terrible feeling that this ship might be delivering human cargo to him. I know I'm going to find out. I think I've figured out how we can board that vessel."

Just as Philip ordered his navigator to sail toward the large ship, its captain must have spotted the *Seahawk* and guessed its intended path. A flurry of activity began on the deck of the serpent ship as her crew climbed to the yardarms to man the riggings. One at a time the sails of all four masts were unfurled, and the old clipper began pushing through the sea, away from the *Seahawk* at a steadily increasing rate of speed.

"We'll catch her!" Bernard called to Philip as he rushed to give instructions to his own crew. Soon the *Seahawk* was in swift pursuit.

Despite her elegant and graceful name, the cumbersome *Winged Eagle* was not able to outrun the *Seahawk,* and within an hour Philip was close enough to shout across open water to the *Eagle*'s captain. "Ahoy, Captain! Heave to!"

After several attempts to get the clipper to slow down, Philip executed a plan he hoped would work. He held up a scrolled piece of paper bound with a leather strap and waved it at the *Eagle.* "I've come with special orders from Sullivan Shipping! From Mr. Danvers himself!"

This ploy brought the captain of the *Eagle* to the starboard-side rails. He shaded his eyes and peered across at Philip. "What's that you say?"

"Franklin Danvers sent me to intercept you. I have his orders right here."

The captain leaned far over the rail, as if by doing so, he could somehow read the writing on the scrolled paper. For a moment, Philip even feared that the portly man might actually fall into the sea.

"And just where might you have seen Mr. Danvers?" the captain shouted to Philip.

"I saw him only three nights ago in the home of Pat Sullivan's widow. He confided in me what your orders are, and when he found out I was headed for the Caribbean, he asked me to look out for you.'' Philip held up the improvised ''orders'' once more. ''Let me board and you'll see Danvers's message for yourself.''

Philip waited anxiously, hoping his scheme would work. After several long minutes, he saw the crew of the *Winged Eagle* furl their sails, and the vessel slowed to a crawl. Obviously the captain's fear of defying Franklin Danvers outweighed his mistrust of Philip.

Bernard cut the sails on the *Seahawk,* and soon the two ships were anchored side by side. Philip lowered the *Seahawk*'s dory into calm water, and he and Fitzhugh rowed the few feet separating the ships. They secured the dory to the *Eagle* and climbed to her deck while the remainder of the *Seahawk*'s crew stayed inconspicuously on deck according to Philip's orders.

The stocky captain of the *Eagle* demanded to see the paper in Philip's hand. With a flourish designed to keep the man's attention on the paper and not on his right hand, Philip unrolled the blank message while at the same time he drew his Colt pocket pistol out of his belt. ''Begging your pardon, Captain, but I'm afraid I misled you. While I did indeed see Franklin Danvers in Boston, he did not instruct me to intercept you. In fact, I have a hunch he will be quite unhappy that our paths have crossed.''

''Now, looky here,'' the captain blustered, as his gaze remained fixed on the pistol, ''I don't know what kind of game you're playing here, but you've boarded Sullivan Shipping property under false pretenses, and, according to the laws of the sea, the crime is punishable by making the offender food for the sharks.'' He waved his hand behind his back to alert his crew to be ready to attack the trespassers.

''I wouldn't advise that,'' Philip said calmly. He signaled to the *Seahawk,* and, in moments, all twelve members of his crew were posted at the rails with rifles and pistols at the ready.

The *Eagle*'s captain scowled at Philip, and his narrowed eyes glinted with sparks of rage. ''You've got no right to board my ship . . .''

"Perhaps not, but just as you make up your own laws of the sea, so do I, and this pistol aimed at your belly gives me all the right I need. Now, open your hold, sir."

The captain hesitated while a scarlet flush of anger crept into his cheeks. Finally he gestured to his mate, who unlocked the hatch cover.

Philip stepped to the edge of the open hole and looked inside. His worst fears were realized. Dozens of pairs of terrified eyes stared up at him from the stench-filled hull as brown-skinned natives from one of the islands stood huddled together in confusion and fear.

Philip's rage was palpable as the pistol shook in his hand and the muscles in his jaw clenched. A bone-chilling fear snaked its way to all his nerve endings as the horrifying consequences of his discovery became clear. He turned back to the captain with a menacing look that made the heavyset man shrink away from him.

When Philip spoke, his voice was as cold and hard as the barrel of his gun. "Since I'm sure you know that slavery was abolished in our country, Captain, then these men must be bound for the kaiser in the Florida swamps."

"Every one of them signed on legally," the captain boasted, squaring off against Philip. "I've got all their X's on the log in my quarters."

"I'm sure you do," Philip said, seeing through the pitiable defense. "As if these poor souls have any idea what kind of a life they're headed for, working in those miserable cane fields."

"They'll be paid wages for their labor."

"A paltry amount, and you know it. I've heard how this despicable system works. These men are brought from isolated villages and persuaded to go to Florida with false promises of a better life for themselves and their families and higher wages than they've ever heard of. But none of their money ever returns to the wives and children left behind, because it's all spent just to keep food in their bellies on the cane plantation. Most of these men won't ever see their families again, and many of them won't live six months in the brutal conditions of the kaiser's camp."

"Look, all I'm doing is taking these poor blokes where they want to go. I don't know what happens to them when they get there. I'm just a man doing my job."

"And being paid handsomely, no doubt, by Franklin Danvers for delivering your miserable human cargo. Tell me, Captain, is that how Danvers persuaded you to take a job no honorable man would accept?"

Philip edged close to the trembling man and grabbed his collar. He sputtered and choked when Philip twisted his hand around the fabric and squeezed it into a hard knot against his neck. "Just how much is each of these men worth to the kaiser? How much is Danvers being paid?"

"I . . . I . . . I don't know." The captain tried unsuccessfully to wriggle out of Philip's grasp. "That's the truth. Danvers doesn't confide in anyone about his business dealings."

Philip released his grip, and the captain stumbled backward, colliding with a stack of half-empty food crates. He landed on his rump in the middle of rotting garbage.

"Well, now," Philip said, "that's because any honest shipper won't have anything to do with him now, isn't it? Just one more question. How many island men did you sign on for this trip?"

Rubbing his aching hips, the captain squinted up at Philip. If he thought of lying, he abandoned the notion with a grimace of pain and the thought of more of the same. "One hundred and eighty-two."

"How many men are presently in the hold?"

"Well, I couldn't tell you the exact count today."

Remembering the mysterious bundles he and Bernard had seen jettisoned from the side of the *Eagle,* Philip trembled with anger. "I saw today what happened to two of them."

The captain sat up, trying to muster the last of his fading bravado. "It wasn't nothing I did to them that killed them. They was sickly when they signed on." When Philip took a threatening step toward the man, he cringed into the protection of the broken crates. "What are you gonna do?"

Getting down on his haunches, Philip glared at him. "I wish I had the time to do all I want to do to you," he said, "but

I don't. Besides, these men are only hours away from their destination, as miserable as it may be. You're going to continue on your way, because I fear that many of these people wouldn't survive the journey back. But I'll make you a promise, sir. You will be coming back for them, every last one. Each man in that hold will have the opportunity to cancel his contract with the kaiser and be returned to his island. And whether or not those orders come from Danvers or from me, I suggest you take them seriously!''

Philip left the captain and crew of the *Eagle* and climbed down to the waiting dory. Once back on board the *Seahawk,* he heard the *Eagle*'s captain give the order to set sail. Within moments, the big clipper was under way toward the coast of Florida once more. Philip turned to Fitzhugh and declared, ''Turn the *Hawk* about, Bernard, and pray for a strong shift in the winds. We're heading back to Boston!'' His only thought was that he had left Anna in the hands of a scoundrel and he needed to get back to her as soon as possible.

''Aye, Philip, our thoughts run the same course,'' Bernard said as he went to issue orders to their crew.

Philip looked up at the heavens where the first stars were just becoming visible in a clear sky. His lips moved in a silent prayer for a powerful headwind to carry them swiftly north against the current. *Surely Danvers won't do anything to Anna,* Philip tried to convince himself. *He doesn't even know we've intercepted the ship.* ''Old Pat may have been a cold bastard,'' Philip muttered, ''but he would never have contracted to do the devil's work! Who knows what his successor might do!''

CHAPTER SIXTEEN

Three days after the *Seahawk* abruptly changed course and headed back to Boston, Franklin Danvers was sitting at his desk in his office at Sullivan Shipping. He was bent over long columns of numbers checking his accountant's figures to make certain the man wasn't cheating him. This was the one responsibility of being the head of a company that old Pat Sullivan had taught him, and Franklin continued to check up on all his employees as Pat had done. "Too bad the old boy didn't check more carefully on me," he mused.

A large shadow suddenly crossed the green ledger paper on his desktop. He looked up to see a big, barrel-chested man in a rumpled ill-fitting suit staring at him from the doorway. The man had a thick stubble of dark beard on his chin and cheeks, though it was barely distinguishable from the grimy dirt that streaked the rest of his face. His hair hung in limp, greasy strands across his gray collar.

"You Danvers?" the man asked in a gruff voice.

Franklin anxiously scanned the faces of the few employees in his warehouse at the early-morning hour. Surely there had to be a security guard nearby. Seeing none, he demanded, "Who the devil are you?"

The man entered the office without an invitation and lifted a flap of his dusty jacket to reveal a five-pointed metal star pinned to his vest pocket. "Deputy Jake Finn. You're expectin' me, ain't ya'?"

Relieved, Franklin jumped up from his chair and came around his desk. "Yes, yes, of course. Thank heavens you're here." Several days' accumulation of dirt enveloped Finn in a haze of dust motes, and Franklin hesitated before offering him a seat on one of the priceless antique tooled leather chairs that flanked his desk. He finally decided it would be best not to rankle this crude man by expressing his own personal disgust at his appearance. "Sit down, please," he said.

Jake sat heavily and rested his elbows on his knees. "So where is she?" he asked, wasting no time.

Franklin leaned back against the edge of his desk. "She's at the home of my fiancée here in Boston. I'll give you the address in a moment, but first, I have to know something. What has Anna done?"

"She murdered a poor sorry bastard," Jake responded without emotion.

"What? Come on, now, Mr. Finn. As much as I distrust the young lady myself, I find that hard to believe. I've been in Anna's company for days, and I don't think she's capable of murder."

"Cold blooded."

"Do you have proof?"

"Thought you might ask me that," Jake said. He took a poster from his suit coat and showed it to Franklin. It listed Anna and Mick's crimes under their pictures. There was no doubt they were accused of killing a man named Stuart Wilkes.

Franklin read every word greedily. "Anna told me her uncle died a few weeks ago," he said.

"If that's the case, then there's a passel o' Illinois lawmen lookin' for a dead man, includin' yours truly," Jake announced with a raucous laugh. He stretched his big legs out toward Franklin, leaned his head against the back of the chair and folded his hands over his belly as if life was really good when you were a deputy.

"Then she *is* a dangerous criminal!" Franklin exclaimed. "Why the devil didn't you tell me this in your telegram? This girl has been in our midst for days now!"

Jake blanched at this direct question. He was obviously a man who didn't take well to explaining himself. "Well, sir," he began, "we didn't tell you because . . . well, because you're not trained to handle a situation like this. You ain't a lawman, and you mighta made a mistake and let the fugitive get away. Besides, we've only known this gal to murder rich folks."

"I assure you, Deputy, my fiancée and I qualify," Franklin clarified, miffed by Jake's implied assumption that Franklin was part of the underprivileged working class. "We've been in danger all this time!"

Jake leaned forward and stared into Franklin's face. "Then give me the address and let me go get her."

"All right, but remember what I said in my telegram . . . you are not to mention my name or say that I had anything whatsoever to do with her capture."

"I'm not stupid, Mr. Danvers, now, where—"

"Wait a minute!" Franklin interrupted. "I just realized something. I'm missing a perfect opportunity to assist you and come across as a hero to Ophelia at the same time."

Jake squinted his tired eyes at Franklin. "What are you tryin' to pull, mister?"

"Nothing, nothing at all. In fact my idea will work out perfectly for both of us." He glanced at his watch. "Anna ought to be gone from the house by now. She had a dress fitting or some such nonsense. Ophelia will be home alone. I'm going to show her this poster. Besides changing her opinion about her dear, sweet granddaughter, I'll earn her undying gratitude for saving her from the clutches of a criminal. Come with me, Mr. Finn. I'll drop you a few blocks from the house, and you can wait for me in the gardens across the street."

Jake rose from his chair and stuck his face within inches of Franklin's. "Now just a doggone minute . . ."

Franklin was getting tired of this oaf. Who did he think was in charge here, after all? "Do you want your fugitive, Mr. Finn?"

"It's why I'm here, ain't it?"

"Then do as I say. My carriage is just outside. I'll only be an hour or so, and then I'll meet you in the gardens." Franklin grabbed his hat from the hallstand and went to the door. "You'll get your prey, Finn, but Anna's not going anywhere until I give you the okay to go get her."

"You'd better not keep me waitin' too long, Danvers. I'm a busy man." Before preceding Franklin out the door, Jake opened the humidor on the desk and took out a cigar. He bit off the end and spat it onto the Aubusson carpet, oblivious to Franklin's sneer of disgust.

Ophelia!" Franklin called as he entered the house on Beacon Hill. "Ophelia!"

She came down the hallway from the kitchen and looked at him in alarm. "For heaven's sake, Franklin, what's the matter? What are you doing here in the middle of the morning? You look as though you've seen a ghost."

He grabbed Ophelia's arm and drew her into the parlor, sliding the pocket doors closed behind them. "Where's Anna?" he asked, maintaining the same agitated tone he had perfected on the way over.

"She's at the dressmaker's, why? What's wrong with you, Franklin?"

"Sit down, my dear. What I'm about to tell you is going to come as a shock."

He led Ophelia to a chair while she continued chattering. "You're beginning to scare me, Franklin. Now, stop it and tell me what's going on!"

"It's about Anna," he said, trying to infect his voice with sympathy. "I'm afraid she's not the sweet child we believe her to be."

"That's nonsense," Ophelia said. "What are you talking about?"

Franklin took the poster from his pocket and handed it to Ophelia. "I was just given this by one of the guards at the warehouse. Apparently it was distributed by the crew of a schooner that docked yesterday afternoon.'' He waited while Ophelia read the details, then knelt beside her and patted her hand affectionately. ''I know this must hurt you terribly, my dear.''

''I'm not in the least hurt, Franklin,'' she said. ''I'm angry, and completely and totally dumbfounded!''

''I know, I know,'' he commiserated, ''as was I . . . to think that Anna could have so brutally murdered . . .''

''Oh, hogwash, Franklin!'' Ophelia snapped. ''You don't believe a word of this, do you? I'm only shocked because this ridiculous poster is being circulated!''

Franklin shrank back from her as if she'd suddenly become a stranger to him. ''But, Ophelia, it's all there in black and white. It's Anna's picture, and I would assume that's Mick. Obviously he didn't die unexpectedly as Anna told us. He's very much alive and could be prowling our streets at this moment! You can't possibly tell me that you aren't taking it seriously?''

''Yes, I can. I don't believe any of it!''

''But you have to!'' Franklin exclaimed, his voice rising in panic. ''We have to call the authorities! This woman must be removed from our . . . *your* home immediately!''

''We'll do no such thing!'' Ophelia declared emphatically. ''Anna has been here over a week now, and she and I have been inseparable. I know her, Franklin, and she is no more capable of this crime than I am.''

''You mean you're just going to ignore this?'' Franklin grabbed the poster and rattled it in front of Ophelia's face. ''That's just plain foolish, Ophelia!''

''No, of course I'm not going to ignore it. I'll show it to Anna, and ask her to explain. If she is in some kind of trouble, then we'll help her, that's all.''

''That's all?'' Enraged at Ophelia's misplaced loyalty, Franklin resisted the urge to strangle her on the spot. ''How can we possibly help her? She's wanted for murder!''

''Maybe so, but she didn't do it. I'll hire a lawyer, a whole team of them if I have to! We'll put our resources behind Anna and clear this mess up.''

Franklin saw Sullivan dollars slipping through his fingers, and he nearly exploded with rage at Ophelia's naiveté. He certainly hadn't expected this reaction from her. In just one week Anna Connolly had so completely wrapped herself around Ophelia's heart that now she threatened to usurp his own carefully executed position with the old lady. He certainly couldn't let that happen!

Suppressing his anger under a guise of compassionate logic, he tried one last time to reason with Ophelia. "My dear, I hate to appear callous, but you are letting your infatuation with this dangerous, though admittedly charming girl, affect your common sense. Surely you must know that Anna represents a very serious threat to you ... to us! Who knows what she is capable of right under your own roof. Why, we don't even know for certain that she is Kathleen's daughter ..."

"That's enough, Franklin!" Ophelia bellowed, rising from her chair. "I won't hear another word of your unfounded suspicions. Certainly I know my own granddaughter!" As she faced Franklin, Ophelia's normally soft eyes were lit with the fire of her indignation. "I'll handle this in my own way, Franklin, do you understand? You are to stay out of it. I don't want you telling anyone about this, not your security personnel, not the police, not anyone! If you feel threatened in this house, then go back to Copley, but Anna stays!"

Franklin quivered with rage, and his fist automatically clenched into a tight ball, but he somehow managed to control his actions. He turned away from Ophelia until he had calmed himself enough to face her. "All right, my dear," he finally said, reaching for her hand. "I see that I've upset you, and I certainly didn't intend for that to happen. Of course I'll do whatever you wish. I'm only concerned for your welfare. Naturally I have no desire to return to Copley. I want to stay here and do what I can to help you and Anna. I shouldn't have to tell you that I've become quite fond of her. Surely my actions must have shown you that."

Ophelia allowed him to hold her hand, but her eyes still held a wariness. "I thought you had, Franklin, and if you do care about her, as I do, then we both must do whatever we can for her, and the first thing we must do is talk to her, find out how these horrible lies got started. We'll speak to her this evening.''

"Yes, of course, whatever you want, Ophelia. You know I'm on your side." He bent to kiss her cheek, but she pulled away from him. "Go on back to work, Franklin," she said. "There's nothing to be done until Anna returns."

"If you wish, dear." He crossed to the parlor door and slid it open just enough to slip into the foyer before closing it behind him again. He almost bumped into Myra Manchester, who stood next to the door wringing her hands and moving nervously from one foot to the other.

"Murder, Frankie! She's a murderer!"

"Shut up!" Franklin said. "I don't know if she is or not, but I do know that she's trouble, and I've got to get rid of her. You've seen the last of Anna Connolly, Myra!"

"Oooo, I 'ope so. She scares me, Frankie, she really does!"

"Don't be absurd," Franklin said with a derisive snort. Then he stormed out of the house and walked two blocks down the street before crossing over to the public gardens. It didn't take him long to find Jake Finn. The big man stood out like an ape from his position under a tree.

He intercepted Franklin as soon as he stepped through the iron gates to the gardens. "Well, did you take care o' business, Mr. Danvers?''

"She's yours, Finn. Take her as far away from Boston as you can, and don't let her ever see Beacon Hill again."

Jake grinned with satisfaction. "She ain't likely to see anything at all with the hangman's hood over her head. You just point me in the right direction."

"She'll be back any moment and will be riding in a black-and-silver phaeton pulled by an Arabian mare. They will pull up two blocks down the street in front of the two-story red brick mansion with the gray wrought-iron fence at the sidewalk. Make sure you nab her before she gets to the walkway, and for God's sake, don't let her cause a scene."

"She won't squawk with this shoved in her ribs." Jake showed Franklin the butt of a pistol protruding from the belt under his jacket. "And I got this on my side, too," he added confidently, tapping his deputy's badge. "Ain't nobody gonna help her escape from the law! I won't disturb your quiet little neighborhood, Mr. Danvers."

"See that you don't ... and Finn, remember, you never heard of me, you never saw me in your life."

Jake's grin broadened, revealing a smattering of stained teeth. "I don't even see you now, Danvers."

"Don't fail in this matter, Finn," Franklin threatened. Then he returned to his carriage and headed back to his empire at Sullivan Shipping, which he once again felt was secure.

A half hour later, Ophelia's driver pulled up in front of the Sullivan mansion. Anna got out of the phaeton and let the driver proceed around back of the house. She had just opened the front gate, when, out of the corner of her eye, she saw a man running toward her from the gardens. She whirled around to face him. There was no mistaking the bulky frame of Jake Finn.

Suppressing a scream, Anna ran across the street to where a carriage for hire waited for a fare. She jumped inside and shouted instructions to the driver. "Just drive, and hurry!" she said frantically, as, out the window, she saw Jake coming dangerously close. The driver cracked a whip over his horse's back, and the carriage lunged away from the curb.

"Faster!" Anna cried. She watched in horror as Jake waved his arms to get the driver's attention. Thankfully the driver was more concerned about his fare than about the half-crazed man he nearly ran over in the middle of Beacon Street.

"Where to, miss?" the driver asked as soon as they'd turned a corner and were safely away from the gardens.

Anna tried to think clearly as a riot of questions tumbled about in her head. How did Jake find out she was there? Was he in Boston alone, or did he bring other bounty hunters with him? Most importantly, where could she go that she would be safe? Her legs trembled, and she wrapped her arms around her knees to gain control. She had to remain calm.

Finally she reached what she believed was the most logical

solution to her predicament, and she ordered the driver to take her to the harbor. She would find Sullivan Shipping Company and ask Franklin Danvers to help her. She would be safe with him at least until Henri contacted her from Cape de Rive with news that she could come out of hiding.

It was lunchtime when Anna told the carriage driver to stop at the harbor a couple of blocks from where she remembered Franklin telling her his offices were located. She felt safer approaching the warehouse on foot so she could look around in all directions. Besides, since she didn't know if Sullivan Shipping was being watched, she didn't want to draw attention to her arrival in a colorful garden carriage. When she spied the offices, she looked around carefully for any suspicious bystanders. Not seeing any, she hurried inside.

She was relieved to see that the warehouse was practically empty, since most of the employees were outside having lunch. She found Franklin's office, and sighed with gratitude when she saw him inside at his desk. She opened the door and stepped in, leaning heavily against the nearest wall as she tried to catch her breath.

Franklin looked up from his work at the unexpected intrusion, and his mouth gaped open in surprise. "Anna! What are you doing here?"

Even in her agitated state, she noticed a strange, almost menacing spark in Franklin's eyes ... a rather exaggerated reaction to being disturbed. But she couldn't worry about Franklin's feelings now; she had nowhere else to go. "I'm sorry, Franklin, but I need your help."

He went around the desk to her, at last showing some concern. "Here, Anna, sit down. You look as if you've been through a terrible ordeal."

"I didn't know where else to turn, so I came here. I'm in trouble, Franklin. It's a long story, but I need to hide here for a couple of days. Please, just trust me."

"Of course, dear, of course. What's the problem? What kind of trouble are you in?"

"There's a man ... he knows something, at least he thinks he knows about something I did. But I didn't do it. He's a very bad man, Franklin, and he's trying to find me. He's here in Boston. I saw him in front of Ophelia's. You've got to help me hide until we hear from either Philip or his brother, Henri."

"Calm down, Anna," Franklin urged. He seemed distracted, as though he heard her, but she still didn't have all his attention. "Let me think," he said, rubbing his hand under his chin. His gaze kept darting to the warehouse area outside his office. Anna sensed a mounting agitation in Franklin. In fact, in a strange way, he seemed almost more worried than she was.

"Franklin, I know everything will be all right. I can stay here, so if you're worried about Ophelia . . ."

He glared at her. "Shut up, Anna. I can't think with your ridiculous chatter."

Suddenly the door to his office burst open and Jake Finn strode in, cursing his bad luck. "The damn biddy got away from me, Danvers! Hightailed it in a hire cab before I could stop her." Jake stopped dead at the frantic look on Franklin's face, and he followed the imaginary line from Franklin's eyes to the object of his distress—Anna.

"Jeezus!" Finn shouted. His eyes popped open and his jaw dropped to his chest. "She fell right into our pot before we even got the water boilin'!"

"You idiot!" Franklin ground out. "Do you realize what you've done!"

Anna rose to her feet and stared at first one man then the other. She was just about to identify Jake as her pursuer when the meaning of his brief conversation with Franklin became startlingly clear. These men knew each other! Her breath caught in her throat and her heart pounded in her ears at the terrifying conclusion she was forced to draw. "It was you," she hissed at Franklin. "You told Jake Finn I was here!"

"There's really no point in denying it, now, is there?" he responded flatly. "If I weren't so angry at Finn's failure to capture one pitiful little female, I might even find some ironic amusement at your choice of refuge, Anna. As it is, now you've put me in a difficult position with dear Ophelia. Unfortunately, Anna, you've become inordinately bothersome, and, thanks to Finn here, I'm forced to deal with you myself."

Anna made one desperate attempt to break out of the office, but Jake's beefy arm stopped her cold. "No way, little hen," he said gruffly as his hand closed over her arm. "You're not gettin' away this time."

Anna glared up at him in disgust before she turned the full force of her vengeance on Franklin. "How could you do this? What about my grandmother? I know she couldn't be in on this."

"She's my biggest problem," he said, "next to you, of course. You've completely wrapped Ophelia around your little finger, and I just can't convince her you're the dangerous criminal the rest of the country knows you to be. She wants to help you, Anna, even if it means throwing away half your grandfather's fortune to do it."

She struggled against Jake's firm grip, but he only tightened his hold until she winced with the pain. "No one's going to have to do anything about me, Franklin. Or spend any money. Philip's brother is an attorney, and he's in Cape de Rive clearing my name right now."

"There ain't no way he's gonna be able to do that!" Jake exclaimed. "I know for a fact that you pushed Mr. Wilkes out a window!"

"He fell! And anyway, it was self-defense. He would have killed me. You know that, just as you know he killed my uncle in cold blood."

Jake grinned with swaggering confidence. "Ain't no proof of that, 'cause ain't nobody ever found a body. I'm afraid that's an idea that just won't float, missy." He chuckled to himself as if he'd just told a joke.

"All of that really isn't the point anyway," Franklin said. "The damage as far as I'm concerned has already been done. Ophelia will know that I've been disloyal to her and to you, Anna, and she will be most displeased. I can't afford to disappoint Ophelia or she'll tighten her purse strings. You can see, Anna, I've got much too much to lose."

"You are despicable! I don't know why my grandmother hasn't seen through your charade."

Franklin polished his fingernails along the front of his jacket. "Love is blind, they say."

"What are you going to do with me?" she said. "Are you going to let this lying bully take me back to Cape de Rive? You can't do that, Franklin!" When Danvers didn't respond to her question, Anna assumed he intended to do just that, and she threatened with false courage, "I'm going to scream as loud as I can, Franklin, and bring everyone in this warehouse into your office."

"I wouldn't do that, Anna." He opened his desk drawer and took out a steel letter opener. He tapped it in his palm while Anna stared at it, imagining what terrible things he could do with the menacing instrument. "We're going for a little walk. I need time to think." Franklin motioned for Jake to stay on one side of Anna, and he went to her other side. He pressed the tip of the blade against her rib cage.

"I can run this through you so quickly that you won't have time to utter a sound," he threatened. "So you'd better come quietly."

"I will not! I won't go anywhere with you," she declared, struggling against both her captors. The tip of the letter opener ripped through the light fabric of her summer gown, and she felt its cold edge against her skin. Then a quick stab of pain shot through her, and she looked down at her side. A small pool of blood grew increasingly wider along the narrow slit in the dress.

"Just that simply, Anna," Franklin said with a twisted smile. "You won't have the lungs to draw even one more breath, much less scream. Now I think you'd best cooperate. It's just a short walk across the way to another warehouse. You'll be quite comfortable there while Mr. Finn and I gather our wits. We'll let you know what we decide."

The trio drew no attention from the few people outside the Sullivan offices as they walked across an alley to another building. Once inside, Franklin took Anna past stacks of crates and barrels to a smaller storeroom in back. He used a key to open the padlock on the heavy steel door and shoved Anna inside. "This is where we keep some of our more valuable goods," Franklin said mockingly. "It should flatter you that we've chosen this particular room for your accommodations tonight."

While the door was still open, Anna looked around at the articles in the room, hoping to find an object with which she could defend herself. Giant Oriental palace urns and garden seats decorated with fierce Japanese warriors were piled among ferocious-looking porcelain dragons and snarling lions and tigers with sharp white teeth. There was nothing in the room she could even lift, much less use as a weapon. And the one thing she had hoped to see, but did not, was a window. Once the door was shut, she knew she would be in total darkness.

As if he read her mind, Franklin hesitated before closing the door. He picked up a kerosene lantern that was used in the storeroom and set it inside on the floor. Then he carelessly tossed in several matches from his vest pocket, knowing she would have to scramble around on the floor to find them. "Keep your eyes open, Anna," he said mockingly. "Who knows what eight-legged creatures arrived with your Oriental companions. One of the more common pests is the scorpion. We're always on the alert for those annoying insects buried in the packing straw."

"Franklin, don't do this!" Anna cried, rushing to the door as the beam of light from the warehouse narrowed to a sliver. "Please, won't you listen . . ."

Her words were silenced as Franklin pushed the door into place and secured the padlock once again. Then he turned to Jake. "Come on, Finn. She won't go anywhere until we've decided what to do with her."

Jake stood rooted to a spot beside the door. "I'm not leavin'," he declared. "It took me long enough to find her, and I'm not about to let her out of my sight now."

Franklin considered arguing with the big man, but he remembered the pistol hidden under Jake's jacket and thought better of it. He needed time to decide how best to handle the bumbling Mr. Finn. He'd have to make sure Jake wouldn't present any more obstacles to the future success of Sullivan Shipping. "Suit yourself," Franklin shrugged. "I'm going home."

A beefy fist clamped down on Franklin's shoulder as he started to walk away. "Wait a minute, Danvers. Give me the key."

"Not a chance, Finn. If I did, I'd return tomorrow to find an empty storeroom and no trace of you or Anna."

"You're interferin' with a lawman tryin' to do his job, Danvers. That's a crime."

"You're no more a lawman than I am, Finn! My guess is you've worked out a deal with the honorable constable of Cape de Rive, and you're splitting some sort of reward for Anna's return." When Jake's face turned white under all the grime, Franklin grinned knowingly. "I thought so. And I suggest you remember that I know the truth about you in case your trigger finger gets itchy during the night and you're tempted to blow that lock all to hell."

From the defeated look on Jake's face, Franklin knew the "deputy" wouldn't try to break Anna out of the storeroom. "Tell me something, Finn," Franklin said now that he knew Jake had very few principles he lived by, "do you have to bring Anna in alive?"

"That's the way Wilkes's widow wants it."

"Too bad. It would be so much easier. Well, I'll think of something. You just settle yourself against that door for the night, then, Finn, if you're determined to stay."

"I'll just do that, and Danvers . . . don't double-cross me. I've worked too hard and traveled too many miles for this hen. I ain't about to let her go, and I ain't about to let you trick me neither."

"How could anyone trick you, Mr. Finn . . . at least twice in the same day," Franklin mocked. "See you in the morning."

When Franklin arrived at Ophelia's that afternoon, he found his fiancée upset and frightened. "Anna never returned to the house, Franklin," she told him. "I checked with Lloyd, and he said he dropped her in front after the dress fitting, but she never came in. Where could she possibly be?''

"That is strange, my dear," Franklin sympathized, "especially considering that today those vile posters were distributed around the city."

"You don't think she's been apprehended, do you?"

"I hardly think that happened, Ophelia. She surely would have contacted you for help if she'd been taken to a police station."

"Yes, I would think so, but what other explanation can there be? I'm so worried about her." Suddenly Ophelia grabbed Franklin's arm. "The hire cabs across the street! If Anna didn't come in the house, perhaps something scared her and she took a hire cab! Let's go talk to the drivers!"

Franklin definitely did not want Ophelia to learn that Anna had hired a cab to take her to the Sullivan warehouses, but he couldn't prevent her from running across to the gardens. He trailed after her as she questioned several drivers until she finally found the one who had driven Anna. The driver said he had dropped the young lady at the harbor. She seemed nervous and upset, but she didn't mention why.

When the driver could provide no further information, Franklin took Ophelia back to the house. She was crying when they went inside. "The harbor, Franklin, why would she go there?"

The driver had unknowingly given Franklin the perfect opportunity he needed to discredit Anna. "I'm sorry, dear, but it looks as though Anna has fled. She's probably aboard a ship right now miles out into the ocean. As much as I hate to admit it, I'm afraid Anna might have been guilty of the crime on the poster after all. Otherwise, why would she have run away?"

"Oh, I don't know, I just don't know . . . I can't believe it," Ophelia wept.

"There, there, my dear. Everything will be all right." Franklin dutifully fussed over his intended all evening long, though Ophelia was quite inconsolable. Myra brought hot compresses for her head, and winked playfully at Franklin as soon as the cloth covered her mistress's eyes.

Franklin tried to get Ophelia to drink cups of tea or soup all evening until he finally convinced her to retire from her sofa to her bed.

"You won't leave, will you, Franklin?" she asked before going to her room.

"Of course not, dear, I'll stay the night," he said comfortingly as they walked passed Myra on their way from the parlor. Franklin pretended not to notice the maid as she leaned in close to him with a suggestive grin on her face. "Later, luv," she mouthed, and Franklin nodded so just Myra could see.

CHAPTER SEVENTEEN

Ophelia fell into a deep sleep shortly after retiring, induced by the sedative Franklin mixed in her last cup of tea. He needed some assurance that he could pursue his own interests without fear of being discovered. It was the middle of the night when he left Myra's bedchamber next to the kitchen pantry and returned to his own suite of rooms. He slept fitfully for two hours and then rose well before sunrise and dressed quickly in the quiet house.

Franklin truly didn't have the stomach for murder. It was usually messy and difficult and required extreme care to conceal. Therefore, he dreaded what fate had dictated he must do in the next hours. But a man had to protect what he had worked for, didn't he? He must be the guardian of the investment in his future, and sometimes that involved some unsavory acts.

Murder had been surprisingly easy, however, as Franklin recalled the circumstances of old Pat's demise. He had waited in the dark, silent warehouse for Patrick Sullivan to enter. He hadn't wanted to kill Pat, but there had been no other solution. The man threatened to live forever, fed by his bad temper and his desire to inflict misery on others, and Franklin had to stop him, no matter how unpleasant and drastic the means.

With the ultimate reward foremost in his thoughts, Franklin had pushed—not even with a great deal of force, it was practically a gentle nudge, almost as if it had been done by a capricious gust of wind instead of by his own hand—and the crates had toppled over. And then the next stack had fallen, and the next one as well, as easily as a row of tumbling dominoes feeds upon itself.

Thinking about it now, he might not have had to shove the crates at all, but, just to be sure, he had moved down the line, upsetting the balance in Patrick's regimented life until the old man lay buried under a mountain of potential riches. Only his hand, with its fist clenched in rage and fear, stuck out from the piles of wooden boxes, making it easy for Franklin to check the pulse to determine the old man's blood had stopped pumping. And, Franklin thought with a dismissive grin, no one had really even mourned.

But now he was faced with another threat to his well-planned future, and he was forced to act again. And again, he didn't want to. He would much rather that his plans had continued to move along as he intended—as they had until that girl showed up. He didn't want her here, he hadn't invited her, but now he was compelled to eliminate her, and that low life Jake Finn as well. And no one must ever connect Franklin with their tragic deaths.

He doubted that anyone would grieve too long over Finn, but Anna's fiancé and Ophelia could insist on thoroughly investigating her demise. Therefore, her death had to look like an accident caused by her own hand. How fortunate that Franklin was good at causing accidents.

It was still dark when he looked in on Ophelia. She was sleeping soundly, as he knew she would be. He returned to Myra's room and shook her awake.

"What is it, luv?" she asked drowsily, blinking his face into focus. " 'Ave you come back for more?"

"You're a disgraceful wanton, Myra," he scolded. "What I want is for you to listen carefully. I'm going to the warehouse."

"What, now? Whatever for?" she squealed.

"Hush, you foolish girl. Let's just say that I'm taking care of a nagging problem—one that could hurt both of us. That's why I need your help."

"You're gettin' rid of the duchess, right?"

"Just listen carefully. I want you to get up and stay close to Ophelia's room. If she stirs and asks for me, tell her I was so distraught over the events of yesterday that I walked the floors until quite late. Tell her I left instructions that I shouldn't be disturbed until breakfast. I'll be back by then. And Myra, under no circumstances are you to let her knock on my door, do you understand?"

She nodded, bringing tight coils of frizzy red hair into her eyes. Brushing them off her face, she threw the covers back, revealing the plump mounds and curves Franklin had buried himself in a few hours before. When she stood up, Franklin's gaze swept her naked body. "You really have no shame at all, do you, Myra?"

"About as much as you do, luv," she answered smartly. "We make a good team, you and me, Frankie, so don't you worry. I'll keep yer bird away from yer nest till you get back." She was reaching for her robe when Franklin left.

A short while later, he opened the warehouse door and picked up the lantern he had lit in the alley. As he entered, its low light cast elongated shadows between the stacked crates and pallet boxes. He picked his way to the storeroom in back and looked down with disgust at the unkempt body propped against the steel door.

"Some deputy you'd make, Finn," Franklin sneered, careful to keep the direct light away from Jake's face. He was determined not to disturb him, knowing that it would be so much easier if Jake passed to the great beyond without ever waking up.

Unfortunately, however, Franklin's intended target reacted to the muffled commotion in the warehouse and awakened with a start. "Wh-what the hell?" he stammered, staggering to his feet and swinging his fists wildly. Franklin dodged a poorly aimed blow as Jake adjusted his bleary eyes to identify the face of his visitor.

"Oh, it's you, Danvers," he mumbled, leaning back against the wall. "What time is it anyway?"

"It's almost sunrise," Franklin said, fighting off his disappointment and setting the lantern on a box. An alert Jake Finn made his plan slightly more complicated. "I want you to take Anna out of here before anyone arrives and sees you."

"Fine by me," Jake said, reaching for the pistol in his belt.

Franklin placed his hand over Jake's to stop him from removing his weapon. "What do you need that thing for?"

"I've got to take the hen in alive. You know that, and I don't want her yakkin' and drawin' attention to what we're doin'. The gun here's just a little insurance that she'll keep her mouth shut."

The last thing Franklin wanted was for Jake to have a loaded gun in his hand. Besides giving him an unfair advantage, a gunshot blast would bring everyone near the harbor rushing to the warehouse. No, a gun was not a good idea.

"Wait till you open the door at least," he said. "I would bet that a hot night in that storeroom has already convinced your hen that she should cooperate. Besides, you needn't worry any longer about Anna talking and revealing to anyone that you and I are working together. My fiancée knows all about it." The lies were coming easily now. "Mrs. Sullivan is quite content to see her granddaughter taken back to Cape de Rive."

When Jake's hand was safely away from the pistol, Franklin said, "So are you going to open that door and take her out of here, or are you going to leave her in there until she dies of starvation?"

"Oh, I'm ready. I'll have her outta here as fast as the beat of a fly's wing." But instead of acting swiftly, Jake tugged at the waistband of his dirty trousers, providing extra room between his legs. "Jus' let me go out back and take care o' bizness," he snickered with a brown-toothed grin.

"For heaven's sake, hurry up!" Franklin said, becoming more and more nervous with each delay. "The sun will be up in a few minutes."

When Jake returned a moment later, he was grinning broadly. "I can practically feel the Widow Wilkes's gratitude now, Danvers," he snickered. "Just let me slip the cuffs on that hen and be on my way. I'm lookin' forward to the taste of good likker running into my gullet for a change. You gimme the key, and go outside and find a coach that'll take me and the fugitive to the train station."

Franklin tossed his key chain to Finn, and watched as Jake went to the door, looked at the padlock, and fumbled with the various keys to find the right one.

This was the opportunity Franklin had been waiting for. He picked up an ax he'd left in the warehouse the day before and crept up behind the unsuspecting Jake. With two hands, he lifted the heavy tool over his head and swung it down with all his strength. The ax connected with Jake's back, the sharp edge lodging at the base of his neck.

Jake's mouth contorted with the need to howl his outrage, but no sound passed his damaged vocal cords. Only strangled gurgles came from his open lips. Blood flowed freely down the ax handle, making it sticky and hard to grip as Franklin struggled to loosen the blade from between Jake's shoulders. Finally it pulled free, and Franklin stepped back from his victim.

Jake turned around. His eyes blazed with a glassy fire, and his mouth opened and closed with each constriction of his throat. His arms extended in front of him, and his hands dangled at shoulder height, like a nightmarish scarecrow. He came at Franklin clenching his fists in a stranglehold.

For a moment Franklin could only watch Jake's threatening approach with horrified awe, for he could not comprehend how the big man managed to stay on his feet. Jake's arms swayed in the shadows of the eerie lanternlight like leafless, gnarled tree branches in the wind, and with each step, his hands came closer to Franklin's throat.

Then, remembering the weapon hanging from his fist, Franklin raised the ax again and targeted Jake's chest. The blade entered Jake's sternum, and he clutched at his heart. Still he advanced several steps toward Franklin before he finally fell, mortally wounded.

"What kind of a beast are you?" Franklin asked, his voice quivering with exhaustion and disgust. He looked down at Jake's face and shivered at the animal-like snarl on the dead man's lips. And Jake's eyes, staring lifelessly up at him, were etched with a glossy vengeance that made Franklin cringe.

He leaned against a large pallet box to catch his breath. He must calm down. His work was not yet finished. Thank goodness his plan for Anna did not involve an ending as messy as Jake's. Franklin looked down at his bloodstained hands and wiped them on his spattered trousers. He longed for a cleansing, warm bath. He'd had enough of blood.

With a grimace of distaste, he gripped the sticky ax handle once more and swung the blade into a metal drum filled with kerosene. The slit was sufficient for the liquid to start oozing out and down the side. "Perfect," he muttered. "Now no one who investigates will question how the fire started." Then he picked up his key chain from the floor and opened the door to Anna's prison. He had to hurry. It was almost sunrise.

When the heavy door was pushed open, Anna woke from a numb drowsiness and crawled out of its path. Her lantern had run out of fuel hours before, and she had sat in the dark with nothing to do but wonder what creatures inhabited the room with her and to ponder what Franklin had in store for her. And, of course, to think about Philip. Knowing she might never see him again, that her time with him might be ended so soon, was worse than facing the menacing presence on both sides of the door.

"Good morning, Anna," Franklin said. "I trust you slept well."

She squinted into the beam of light from Franklin's lantern until her eyes adjusted to his form in the doorway. She could not see any details of his face, only his body outlined in the gold illumination.

"It's time to come out, Anna," Franklin said. "I want you to see what you've done."

"What I've done?" she repeated, her voice scratchy, distant.

His words didn't make any sense. She was exhausted from lack of sleep and weak from fear. She shook her head to clear her mind. "Let me go, Franklin," she pleaded. "I didn't come here to hurt you . . ." Now fully aware, tears of hysteria gathered in her eyes. "I only wanted to meet my grandmother."

"And you have, my dear. Your mission has been accomplished; now you can move on . . . or up." He glanced upward as though at the heavens and chuckled. He kicked the door, and it slammed against the interior wall of the storeroom. Anna choked back a cry of alarm. "Now, come out! I want you to witness the carnage you wrought during the night."

She walked slowly through the door into the large warehouse. Franklin held her arm and raised the lantern so the body of Jake Finn was clearly visible. Anna's stomach lurched violently when she saw him. She shuddered and turned away from the blood and gore.

"It's not a pretty sight, I'm afraid," Franklin admitted with a contemptuous edge to his voice, "but he was so hard to kill. I'm quite amazed that you could do it. But then, an ax in the hands of even a small child could be a deadly weapon."

What was he talking about? Anna's mind reeled with the effort of trying to make sense of his accusation. She couldn't look at the body on the floor any more than she could the arrogant sneer on Franklin's face. "Why-why did you do this, Franklin?"

"Because you and this ill-bred oaf were going to ruin everything I've worked for. But not anymore." Franklin spun her around to face him. "Too bad, my dear, for it seems that you and I are cut from the same cloth . . . neither of us will stop until we get what we want, even if it means murder."

"But I didn't murder anyone . . ."

"Spoken like a sinner on the gallows, Anna. We are all innocent when we're about to face the unknown. But those of us who knew you will remember you for what you really are. Ophelia, the constable from Cape de Rive, even your lover when he returns from the Caribbean and learns of your demise—we will all know that you killed Jake Finn as well as that unfortunate man you booted out the window in Illinois."

Anna's blood raced through her veins and pounded in her ears as terror seized her, blocking any logical thought from her mind. She shrank back from Franklin and clawed at his hand around her arm. "Let me go!" she cried. "Don't do this!"

He only increased the pressure of his hold and set the lantern on the floor. His eyes glittered red in the flickering light, and his face was a mask of unflinching determination. "I can't let you go, Anna. You know that."

At last she battled back. She kicked at her target, the toe of her shoes connecting with Franklin's shins. He hollered and backed away from her in a crazy jig that gave her the opportunity to wrench her arm free from his grasp. But she hadn't taken two steps when he caught her again, grabbing her wrist and drawing her roughly back. Then his hands were on her throat.

He was through toying with her. His hands tightened around her neck, constricting her air passages. The room spun around her in a crazy spiral, like a carousel out of control. Franklin's thumbs pressed down on the hollow of her throat. Her knees gave way under her, and she sank to the floor.

Still she clawed at his hands, her efforts becoming weaker as he squeezed harder. The last sensation Anna felt was her eyes rolling upward, away from the hideous grimace of strain on Franklin's face. The light in the warehouse mutated from gold to gray and finally to black.

The deed accomplished, Franklin stood up and shook his fingers to relieve an unpleasant cramping. He took several deep breaths to check his raging emotions. Glancing up to the high narrow windows in the warehouse, he saw the first gray rays of sunrise, and he knew he must complete his duties quickly.

He placed Anna next to Jake and laid the ax close to her hand. He would make certain the drum of leaking kerosene was near the scene before he left. It had to look like one of Anna's blows had missed its human target and landed on the barrel. When the investigators searched through the rubble of ashes, all the clues would be evident. Anna had killed the man who had been pursuing her, and a fire had broken out while she was trapped inside with her victim. Franklin scurried about, setting his macabre stage. There was still so much to do.

The *Seahawk* slipped into Boston Harbor just before sunrise. It had taken the clipper a few hours longer on the return trip to Boston, but it had seemed like days to Philip. He waited impatiently at the deck rail until he was close enough to toss the mooring lines to a harbor attendant. Before the lines were even secured around the pilings, Philip jumped clear of the ship and landed on the dock.

"Hold on, Philip!" Bernard Fitzhugh called. "You might need help. I'll come with you."

"Thanks just the same, Bernard, but I'd rather you'd stay here. We may have to be ready for a quick departure." Philip raced toward one of the few hire cabs at the dock at that hour and called back over his shoulder, "Besides, I can handle Franklin Danvers myself . . . in fact, I'm looking forward to it!"

He shook the shoulder of the dozing cabdriver who awakened quickly. Then he barked the Beacon Hill address. The coach raced down the empty streets to the home of Ophelia Sullivan. There was an ashen, predawn sky over the trees lining the avenue when the coach careened down Beacon Street, startling the few citizens out for their morning strolls. Philip ordered the cab to wait while he ran to Ophelia's door and pounded with his closed fist.

Upstairs in the Sullivan mansion, Myra Manchester bolted upright from her position against Ophelia's door where she had been maintaining her guard. Confused thoughts tumbled in her head as she tried to decide what she should do—answer the insistent pounding at the door or stay at her post. She didn't have long to wonder, because Ophelia opened the door to her room and stepped into the hallway, practically bumping into Myra.

"What's going on? Who's at the door?" Ophelia asked, hastily wrapping her robe around her. She appeared dizzy and uncertain, probably due to the strong sedative Franklin had given her the night before. She braced one hand against the doorframe.

Before Myra could answer, Ophelia's eyes suddenly shone with alertness and a look of immense joy crossed her face. "Anna! Anna's come back!" She ran down the stairs, gripping the wooden banister to steady herself.

It better not be the duchess, Myra thought, trailing after her mistress and making plans for a hasty escape if it became necessary.

Ophelia swung the door open and emitted a cry of alarm. "Oh, my God, Philip!"

"Where's Anna, Mrs. Sullivan? I've got to see her now!"

"I don't know. I don't know," Ophelia clutched the lapels of her robe and stared at him with wide, frightened eyes.

Grabbing her arms, Philip forced her back from the door and into the nearest chair. When he spotted Myra nearby he snapped an order. "Bring some water!"

The maid scurried down the hall.

"Mrs. Sullivan . . . Ophelia! Listen to me. Where's Anna?"

"She's gone. She left," Ophelia sobbed.

"What do you mean? Where did she go?" Philip fired the questions at Ophelia, hoping to bring her out of her disoriented state, but he received no coherent answer.

Myra returned with the water, and Philip put the glass to Ophelia's lips. When she had drunk a little and calmed down enough to be rational, he asked her again, "Tell me, please, what's happened to Anna?"

"You don't know, do you?" Ophelia cried, casting pitying eyes on Philip. "You don't know about those vile posters? Anna's run off because of them."

Panic constricted Philip's lungs, and he shook off the numbing dread that had seized him. He had to think clearly. How did the posters get to Boston? "Yes, yes, I do know, but they're lies, Ophelia. Anna didn't hurt anyone. You know her. She's not capable of murder."

Ophelia drew a long, trembling breath. "I knew it," she said. "I knew Anna could not have murdered that man."

"That's right," Philip confirmed, nodding his head like he might to a small child. "Anna didn't do it. My brother is a lawyer, and he's in Cape de Rive proving Anna's innocence right now." Ophelia nodded with him. "Now tell me, Ophelia, where is she?"

"I wish I knew." Another round of tears spilled down her cheeks. "She should have known I would help her, but she didn't give me a chance. Franklin brought a poster home and showed it to me. I told him it was nonsense, but he said Anna might have done it."

"Franklin? Where did Franklin get a poster?"

"He said someone gave it to him at the harbor. He thought we should turn Anna in to the authorities, but I said no. I think he was angry with me."

"What did he do?"

"It was the way he looked at me—I was frightened. I told him to leave Anna to me, that I would talk to her later, but she never came home. A cabdriver at the gardens said he took her to the harbor. Franklin says she's run off to avoid being arrested." Ophelia grabbed Philip's shirtfront. "We've got to find her!"

The veins in Philip's temples throbbed his alarm, and fear wrapped icy fingers around his belly. "Where is Franklin now, Ophelia?" he asked.

"Upstairs in his rooms, I guess."

"Will you get him for me?"

"Of course."

While Ophelia climbed the stairs, Philip paced in the small foyer. Catching a glimpse of the maid in the hallway to the kitchen, he asked, "Do you know anything about this?"

"Me?" she responded in a high-pitched squeal. "Whatever would I know? I'm just the lowly maid around 'ere. Nobody tells me nothin'." With tiny sidesteps, she began moving away from the foyer. She had just neared the entrance to the kitchen when Ophelia called from the second floor.

"He's not there! Franklin is gone, too! Myra! Myra, did Mr. Danvers tell you he was going out?"

Like an actress hearing her cue, Myra darted into the kitchen. "I'm sure I don't know, ma'am," she called over her shoulder. Philip watched her disappear into a room next to the kitchen, then heard the door slam.

Ophelia came down the stairs. "That doesn't make sense," she said. "Myra must know something. She's been up for hours."

Philip raced into the kitchen in time to see Myra's coattails flying through the back entrance of the mansion. He grabbed a handful of coat and pulled her, kicking and struggling, back inside. "Going somewhere?" he asked.

"Get yer 'ands off o' me!" she hollered, stomping her feet angrily. "Yu've got no right to keep me 'ere if I want to leave!"

"Where are you off to so early, Myra?" Both his eyes and his hands pinned her to the wall of the kitchen.

"For a walk is all!"

"This household is in an uproar, and your mistress is near hysteria, and you're going for a walk?"

"All that mess is yer doin', not mine!"

"You know what I think, Myra? I think a lot of what's happened here *is* your doing, and I think you have a good idea where both Mr. Danvers and Anna are."

Myra leveled her haughtiest gaze on Philip's face. "Even if I did know where they are, which I'm not sayin' I do, why would I tell you? You're not a member of this family!"

Philip tightened his grip on her shoulders, and she shrank against the wall. "Myra, listen carefully to me. If you have done anything that has hurt Anna or resulted in her arrest for a crime she didn't commit, I will see that you are sent back to England without a penny, do you understand me?"

"You can't do that."

"I can and I will. Anna is missing, and I think you have information that will help me find her."

"You're crackers, you are," she blustered, but the darting of her quick little eyes told Philip her haughty confidence was slipping.

The maid was worried, and he knew for certain she held the clue to Anna's whereabouts. Just a bit more pressure and he'd have her confession. "Myra, if anything has happened to Anna, you'll be charged in a court of law as an accomplice to Franklin Danvers. You'll go to jail for many years, do you understand that?"

"I ain't goin' to jail for no bloke," she said. "And I ain't goin' back to England, either."

"Then tell me what I need to know," Philip said in a tone meant to chill Myra Manchester to her bones. "And I'll know if you're lying to me. I don't like people who lie any more than I do those who consort with the devil, and I believe you've been doing that right under this roof!"

She narrowed her eyes at Philip, weighing the sincerity of his threats. Then, with a last saucy toss of her fiery curls, she said, "So if I was to tell you where I think yer duchess is, you'd leave me be, right?"

He didn't blink. His unflinching gaze held hers in a hard, cold stare. "No lies, Myra. Where is she?"

"Franklin said somethin' to me this morning about goin' down to 'is warehouse. It was quite early, and 'e made me swear not to tell Mrs. Sullivan."

Philip loosened his grip on her shoulders, and she released an anxious breath. He turned away from her and crossed the kitchen in three long strides.

"Of course I would 'ave told Mrs. Sullivan," Myra called after him. "I 'ad planned to all along, I did. You won't let 'er fire me, right, sir?"

Myra's pleading was drowned out by the pounding of Philip's heartbeat. He passed Ophelia in the foyer, patted her arm and managed to give her a slight smile of encouragement. Then he raced out the door to the waiting carriage.

In the warehouse at Sullivan Shipping Company, a wide, bright river of kerosene covered the floor in a ring around the two bodies lying side by side. Standing beside the split drum he had just emptied around the makeshift funeral pyre, Franklin Danvers stood back to allow himself a brief, satisfied look at his creation. "So, Miss Connolly, you have already joined your loving grandfather in the hereafter. I'm sure you'll discover that Pat Sullivan cares no more about you in death than he did in life.''

He took a last look at the pallets of merchandise which would soon be reduced to ashes and shrugged. "What is insurance for, after all? Poor, misguided Patrick—you never realized the potential in Sullivan Shipping, surrounded as you were by these baubles. Oh, you made a modest fortune, but nothing compared to the profits I'll bring in with my new ventures. I'll recover the loss of this merchandise with only two shiploads of my Caribbean trade.''

Striking a match against the sole of his shoe, Franklin held the flame in front of his eyes for a moment. He considered saying a few ceremonious words about the dearly departed, but erased the notion with a malevolent chuckle and tossed the match into the gleaming liquid. A tower of flame leapt up and began dancing a jagged trail around the victims. "Bon Voyage,'' he said as he made a hasty retreat to the warehouse door.

The first thing Franklin noticed when he exited was that the sun was now hovering above the eastern horizon, and he commended himself on a job well executed with time to spare. When the docks were once again teeming with life, he would be on his way back to the Sullivan mansion where he would join his fiancée for breakfast and bask in her sympathy for his sleepless night.

And he would pretend to be as shocked as Ophelia when they learned of the fire and Anna's brutal murder of Deputy Jake Finn. Franklin would then have little trouble convincing his grieving fiancée that Anna brought her tragic death on herself. He pushed the heavy door closed and sighed with contentment. It had been a successful morning.

When the door clicked into place, Franklin turned with a start toward the sound of a coach speeding around the corner of the alley. He pressed his body against the exterior wall of the warehouse, fully expecting the coach to race by. He was astounded when the driver jerked back on the reins, bringing the horses to a rearing halt. Through the settling dust, Franklin saw Philip Brichard jump down from the cab.

Seeing Franklin about to bolt, Philip closed the distance between them in seconds. He gripped Franklin's arms with his fists, preventing his escape. "You're not going anywhere, Danvers," he said. When he saw reddish stains on Franklin's clothes, Philip's blood ran like ice in his veins. "Where is she?"

"Get your hands off me, Brichard!" Franklin shot back. "Have you lost your mind?"

"You'll lose much more than that if you don't tell me right now where Anna is."

"How would I know where that murderess is? She's run off without a thought for you, apparently!"

Philip's fist connected with Franklin's mouth, and an agonized growl came from the man's split lips. "I'll have you locked up for this, Brichard!" Franklin threatened as he swiped at the blood dripping down his chin.

"Open the door!" Philip ordered, shoving Franklin toward the warehouse entrance.

Franklin planted his boots in the gravel road and resisted enough for Philip to know that the warehouse did, indeed, hold the clue to Anna's disappearance. "Open it!" he demanded again, twisting Franklin's arm around his back and tightening it until the man was almost brought to his knees.

"She's not in there," Franklin gasped. "I tell you I don't know where . . ."

"Open the door!" He increased the pressure on Franklin's arm.

"Go ahead and open it yourself. It's not locked."

Philip let Franklin go and grabbed the door latch. At the same time, Franklin reached under his pant leg, drew out a boot knife, and targeted Philip's chest.

Philip responded to the unexpected movement beside him and dodged the first thrust and then the next, letting Franklin tire himself. The plan worked, and Franklin was soon panting and perspiring heavily. Philip, however, could only think about the precious minutes ticking away.

When a poorly executed plunge left Franklin unbalanced for a moment, Philip took advantage of the opportunity to subdue his opponent. He charged headlong into Franklin's stomach, and the two combatants landed with a thud in the alleyway.

Franklin's knife flew from his hand **and** skidded across the road, but he continued to battle with his fists. They landed ineffectually around Philip's head and shoulders while Philip pummeled Franklin's face mercilessly. A last effective blow to Franklin's cheek snapped his head back against the ground, and his struggling ceased. He lay unconscious in the alley.

Philip jumped up and flung open the warehouse door. Heat from the inferno inside forced him back a step, but he quickly overcame his shock and charged into the interior, shielding his eyes from flames shooting to the ceiling. The fire was contained in the center of the room, but small flames licked at surrounding pallets threatening to engulf everything in sight. The heat was intense as Philip maneuvered himself as close to the ring of fire as he could.

Then he saw Anna, lying inside the core of the blaze, and he reacted instinctively. Bounding over the flames, he gathered her into his arms. With a joyous sense of relief, he saw her eyelids flutter and felt her move against his chest. One quick glance at the man he recognized as Jake Finn told him there was nothing he could do for the bounty hunter. He bent his head to cover Anna's face and ran back through the fire. Sparks landed with stinging fury as fingers of the blaze clawed at his skin and clothing.

Once he had cleared the ring of fire, Philip headed for the door only to be stopped by a dark shape blocking his path. The light behind him in the warehouse was so brilliant he could just make out the outline of Franklin Danvers against the entrance. Momentarily stunned, Philip stared at the figure blocking his exit, swaying back and forth as if dancing to some hellish tune in his sick mind.

Franklin's lips parted, revealing the gleaming white of his teeth, bared in a snarl. He reached for a drum of kerosene.

Then, with what seemed to Philip superhuman strength, and with a howl of vengeance, Franklin lifted the drum over his head and aimed it at Philip and Anna.

There was no escape. The fire behind him, the menacing presence of Franklin Danvers in front, Philip clutched Anna to his chest and prepared to take the impact of the drum. Suddenly, a metallic clickety-clack made Philip look at drum. The oddest twist of fate almost brought a smile to Philip's lips. The drum cap had fallen off, and it rolled along the cement floor of the warehouse with a bright clatter. Meanwhile, a glistening stream of liquid ran down the side of Franklin's body and snaked its way to the outermost flames of the ring.

Franklin teetered crazily with the shifting weight of the barrel. His arms locked above his head. He was unable to set the barrel down, and unable to look away from the burning trail of kerosene.

It happened instantaneously. The stream of liquid from the barrel met and joined the fiery circle, and a blindingly intense flash lunged toward Franklin, illuminating his grotesque face for one horrifying second when he realized his fate was sealed. The last thing Philip saw before he charged out the door was a burst of fire engulfing Franklin's body.

Philip dropped to the ground several feet outside the warehouse and covered Anna with his body. When the fire reached the barrel over Franklin's head, the eruption inside the warehouse swelled with a deafening rumble. A brilliant effulgence of light burst through the warehouse door.

A searing heat singed Philip's head and back, and he choked on acrid smoke. As soon as it was safe to move, he lifted Anna and stumbled out of a black cloud to find the waiting carriage. The driver struggled to hold the reins of the terrified horses, but once his passengers were inside, he skillfully turned the rig around and raced down the alley. Philip cradled Anna on his lap and stroked her hair, listening to the harbor fire bells clanging a strident warning through the air.

CHAPTER
EIGHTEEN

Anna awakened to a dim awareness before the carriage reached Beacon Hill. She hovered in a sensation of safety and comfort before she consciously recognized the strong, soothing voice that reassured her and the gentle hands that stroked her face. She tried to speak, but her throat burned with a smarting pain, and Philip urged her to remain quiet. She opened her eyes briefly to convince herself she was not dreaming and then closed them again after placing her hand over the one of Philip's that rested on her cheek. She smiled as she drifted back to sleep.

Philip instructed the coach driver to pull around to the back of the Sullivan house to avoid being seen by any street traffic. He dismissed the driver with an ample reward for his masterful driving and carried Anna to the open rear entrance where Ophelia waited anxiously.

"Thank God you found her. Is she all right?" Ophelia asked, before becoming fully aware of Anna's appearance. She clamped her hand over her mouth when she saw the soot and grime on Anna's dress and the bruises on her neck. "What's happened to her, Philip?" she asked through trembling fingers.

Ophelia trailed after Philip as he carried Anna upstairs. He rattled off a cursory explanation of what had taken place at the warehouse, stopping when he reached the part about Franklin's grisly death. He laid Anna on her bed and faced Ophelia. In a much gentler, softer tone, he told her about Franklin's fate, leaving out the most unsavory details.

Ophelia sank into the nearest chair and shook her head. For a moment Philip thought she hadn't heard him or that she refused to believe what he'd told her.

When she finally spoke, Ophelia's words were tinged with a deep regret. "He was a sick man. I don't know why I didn't see it. Anna could have been killed. What a foolish old woman I am."

"He fooled me, too, Grandmother," Anna whispered from her bed.

Ophelia went to the bedside and took Anna's hand. "Oh, my dear, I'm so sorry for what Franklin did to you."

"It's not your fault. No one could blame you."

Philip brought a pitcher of cool water and began washing Anna's face. He asked Ophelia to bring a nightdress for her, and began removing her clothes. At first, he had thought that Anna's injuries were limited to the bruises on her neck, and smoke inhalation. He assumed that the blood on her dress was from Jake Finn, who had obviously spilled pints of it on the floor. But when Philip saw the slit in the side of Anna's dress and the congealed stains on the fabric, a new fear gripped him. "Anna, you've been cut. How did this happen?"

"It's not so bad, is it, Philip?" she answered. "I think he only punctured the skin."

"No, I don't think it's too serious," he said, though he was not convinced of the truth of his statement. He drew Ophelia away from the bed and whispered, "I'm concerned about infection, and I want to get Anna to a doctor. I'm worried about those damn posters, Ophelia. Do you think it's widely known in Boston that she's wanted for the crime in Cape de Rive?"

"I don't know. Franklin said he got a poster from someone

at the docks, but he could have been lying. Let me try to clean the wound first. I know what to do, and we don't want to take any chances.''

Philip hesitated, considering their options. Anna's health was certainly the most pressing consideration, but he didn't want to alert the authorities to her whereabouts. Ophelia's plan seemed the wiser choice. "All right, but we have to hurry," he said. "We must leave Boston as soon as possible. I've got to get Anna away from here before they begin to investigate the fire."

"Oh, I almost forgot," Ophelia said. "A telegram was delivered for Anna early this morning." She pulled the envelope out of her pocket and handed it to Philip. "It's from Cape de Rive. I hope it clears this whole sordid mess up, and you won't have to leave so quickly."

While Ophelia tended to Anna's cut, Philip read the message from Henri. When he finished, he went to Anna and smiled. "Henri's encouraged that he can clear your name this morning, love. He's advised us to wait for his next telegram. Hopefully this nightmare will be over soon."

"Good," she whispered, flinching while Ophelia applied an antiseptic solution to the wound. "Because I don't feel like leaving this bed for a good long while, unless it's to go to the kitchen!"

A small crowd gathered in the early-morning dawn beside the lake outside of Cape de Rive. Included in the nervous group were Constable Petrie, Jake Finn's partner, Sam Fletcher, who had insisted on coming, two of the men who had played poker with Mick Connolly on the day he was killed, and a few men with ropes and nets. This group had been hired by Henri to conduct the search for Mick's body at the bottom of the lake.

Henri knew it was a long shot, but a gut instinct that the methodical Brichard brother rarely relied on told him that Anna's uncle would be found in this watery grave. Further, he was encouraged by the fact that the spring season in Illinois had been unnaturally cool, and a quick test of the lake water indicated the temperature was well below normal for this time of year. If Mick had sunk to the bottom, the chances were fairly good his body hadn't decomposed to a great extent in the natural refrigeration.

Henri had insisted that the Cape de Rive citizens accompany him to the lakeside to try to identify the body, if one were found, since the remains would deteriorate rapidly exposed to the air. "All right, gentlemen," he said to the waiting dredgers, "you might as well begin."

Two hours later, one of the netters called to the crowd, "We've found something and we're bringing it up!" The rest of the party quickly moved to where a body was being hauled to the bank.

Henri stared down at the amazingly preserved, though slightly bloated, body of a man he felt certain was Mick Connolly. He recognized the red plaid shirt Anna had described to him. The shirt was perfectly intact except for a hole in the chest area, marking the entrance of Stuart Wilkes's bullet.

While the members of the identification party gawked with morbid curiosity at the remains, Henri studied the corpse with an analyst's eye, matching the body's physical description with the one Anna had given him of her uncle. The soft tissue around Mick's eyes and lips had been nibbled by bottom-feeding creatures in the lake, but, overall, his facial features were recognizable.

Henri unbuttoned Mick's shirt and revealed the fatal chest wound, which would turn a reddish-brown color after the body began to dry. Now it was a clearly defined white-ringed area that had obviously been produced by a bullet fired at close range.

"Gentlemen," Henri said, "I believe we have located Michael Connolly, the man half your town swears killed Stuart Wilkes—the same man some of you are searching for in an attempt to earn the reward money."

Sam Fletcher backed away from the throng, and his face blanched. Henri watched him with a critical eye. Perspiration glistened on Sam's forehead and he wrung his hands nervously. "There ain't no way you can say that's Connolly," he blustered.

"He's half eat up from crabs and parts of him are covered with mud."

"That's algae, Mr. Fletcher," Henri corrected, "and easily removed." He swiped at Mick's jaw, and the brownish substance came off on his fingers. "What do the rest of you think?" Henri asked, turning to the men who had been at the poker game. "Is this the man who bested Stuart Wilkes at the Lucky Chance?"

"It certainly *could* be, Mr. Brichard," one of them said. "As I recall, Mr. Connolly was wearing a red shirt. If I had to say for sure, I would be reluctant, but it appears that this is Michael Connolly."

"Y'all are bein' railroaded by this slick lawyer!" Sam Fletcher protested. "I still say you can't look at this here corpse and call it Mick Connolly!"

"I'm afraid Sam Fletcher is right," Constable Petrie agreed, a little too readily in Henri's opinion. "We would have to have more concrete evidence that this man is Mick Connolly."

Henri took a leather pouch from his vest pocket. He was now ready to take the biggest gamble of all and reveal to the crowd that he had been in contact with Anna Connolly.

"Unfortunately, the one person who could identify this man positively is hiding out from bounty hunters anxious for the reward offered by Mr. Wilkes's widow. That person is, of course, Anna Connolly, this man's niece."

"Then you know where she is!" Petrie declared, eagerly pointing an accusing finger at Henri, and nodding at his fellow citizens.

"At this particular moment, no, I haven't a clue as to where she is, but I do have something that will offer conclusive proof in her absence." He spilled the contents of the pouch into his hand as everyone stared in rapt attention, then picked up a button and held it between his thumb and forefinger. "I'd like you all to examine the buttons on the dead man's shirt."

One by one, the spectators leaned over the body and scrutinized the etched whalebone buttons Anna had sewn on Mick's shirt the past winter. Henri nodded at the button in his hand. "This button was given to me by Anna Connolly. It was practically all that was left of her belongings after her uncle was killed and their wagon was burned to the ground somewhere along this shoreline. I think you will agree that the scrimshaw design on this button is an exact match to the ones she herself sewed on her uncle's shirt and which you have just examined. This *is* unquestionably the body of Michael Connolly, gentlemen.''

A low murmur of agreement spread among the crowd, and Henri pursued his advantage. ''I think, too, gentlemen, that if we proceed around the lake, we will find traces of burnt wood or singed metal fittings from Michael Connolly's wagon, offering further proof that Anna's account of what happened that night is the accurate one. Stuart Wilkes was the murderer among you, not Michael Connolly, and certainly not my client, Anna Connolly.''

Heads began to shake in accord with Henri's conclusions— all but one. Sam Fletcher's mouth opened and closed several times until he finally blurted out in a high-pitched voice, ''Now just a damn blasted minute—''

''No, you wait a minute, Mr. Fletcher,'' Henri interrupted. ''I should remind you that you are implicated in what happened here that night, and I am an attorney. At this time Miss Connolly has only identified Mr. Wilkes as her uncle's murderer, but if you interfere in these proceedings I promise you that I will prosecute you to the fullest extent of the law for your part in the criminal activities that resulted in Mr. Connolly's death and the destruction of his property. And,'' Henri added, ''if you recall hearing of my brother's encounter with Mr. Jake Finn in New Orleans, then you know that a threat from one of my family is meant to be taken seriously.''

Sam Fletcher's mouth clamped shut.

''What about the reward money?'' one of the dredgers asked. ''What d'ya suppose Mrs. Wilkes is gonna do?''

''Well, if there isn't a case, Andrew, there sure isn't likely to be a reward for solvin' it, now is there?'' Petrie shot back angrily. ''I'm sure Mrs. Wilkes will withdraw that offer quick enough. She won't be too keen on advertisin' the particulars of this occurrence based on what we discovered today.'' Then to Henri, the constable added, "I'm recommendin' to Judge Swenson that this case be dropped, Mr. Brichard."

"Thank you, Constable. I think that's a wise decision. Now, if a couple of you would like to earn a little extra today, I'd like you to go into town and bring back a wagon and a coffin. My family would like to give Mr. Connolly an honorable burial."

When Henri's follow-up telegram arrived at Ophelia Sullivan's home later that same day, several things happened within the next few hours. Bernard Fitzhugh left Boston to attend to business in St. Sebastian without Philip Brichard. A doctor was summoned to the mansion to examine Anna, and he proclaimed her to be in good health despite her ordeal. Philip talked with fire investigators about what happened at Sullivan Shipping Company, and, with Ophelia to back up his story, no further inquiries were necessary.

True, the insurance company would refuse to pay damages for a fire that was deliberately set by the acting president of Sullivan Shipping, but Ophelia was much too happy to worry over such "trifles." She had extracted two solemn promises from Anna and Philip that made her future seem brighter than it had in many years. Philip agreed to work during the next few days with the remaining hierarchy of Sullivan Shipping to establish policies for the company's future success. He also agreed to assume the role of president, acting in Ophelia and Anna's behalf, since he would be returning to Boston often with his wife.

"How lucky I am to have a ready-made merchant and shipping magnate brought into my family as my grandson-in-law," Ophelia gushed over tea that evening.

"Please, Ophelia, don't give me more to live up to than I am able," Philip laughed, though he was honored to be the recipient of the glowing praise in Anna's eyes.

The promise that Anna made her grandmother was that she and Philip would still be married in Boston, and while the fate of Sullivan Shipping was important to Ophelia, it was wedding plans that she thrilled over all that afternoon. Anna and Philip

soon gave up urging Ophelia to "keep it simple," and not tire
herself with unnecessary details.

"Don't be silly," she chided. "You've given me ten days
to plan this wedding. But if I had to, I could do it in half that
time!" By evening, messages had already begun to fly from
the Sullivan mansion to florists, caterers, and musicians.

Ophelia had a lovely garden in the back of her house, and
that was where Anna and Philip finally retreated at the end of
the day. They sat together on a birch swing suspended from a
lattice trellis covered with morning glories and English ivy.
Anna tucked her feet underneath her and laid her head on
Philip's shoulder. He kept the swing moving at a steady, gentle
pace while he stroked her arm.

Philip sat up and peered down at the top of Anna's head
when he heard her laughing softly. "What do you find so
amusing, my love?"

"I suppose I should thank you for saving my life," she said.

He knew exactly what she was remembering, and his mind
flashed back to the dusty street of Cape de Rive and the time
he pulled her away from Stuart Wilkes's speeding brougham.
She had made the same comment that day. "Well, the thought
had crossed my mind," he said, using the same words to answer
her.

Anna turned in his arms and looked at him, and Philip's
breath caught in his throat at the love he saw reflected in her
eyes. She reached up and brushed a strand of dark hair off his
forehead and smiled. "Thank you, Mr. Brichard, for saving
my life . . . and asking me to share yours." Her lashes lowered
over glistening eyes as his mouth descended to hers.

EPILOGUE

Beyond the grove and the *garçonnière* at Frenchman's Point, a meadow carpeted with high grass and delicate small-petaled wildflowers stretched to where live oak trees shaded a rise in the normally flat landscape. It was to this gently sloping hill that Anna Rose Brichard went on the evening she and her husband returned home.

The warm breeze from Brichard rice fields and the bayous further on ruffled her hair, which hung down her back in thick waves. She entered the gate in the white fence surrounding the family graveyard that had been situated on the pleasant hill for over one hundred years. Anna had no trouble finding the newest grave from among the dozen others where Brichard ancestors were buried.

A shamrock was carved into the speckled marble front of the gleaming tombstone, and underneath its four leaves was the name, Michael "Mick" Connolly. Anna knelt beside the profusion of spring flowers that covered the grave and placed her hand on the low mound of earth that marked the final resting place of her uncle.

Several feet away she saw the larger monument to Claude Brichard, and the thought that her uncle was buried so near the revered patriarch made her smile. "Who would have thought, Uncle Mick, that we would end up with those very same 'New Orleans blue bloods' you talked about when we met Philip in River Flats. You were right about him then. He was our twenty-dollar gold piece, and he has become everything to me since. And, though you must know how hard it is for me to admit this, one of your plans actually worked this time.

"It happened just like you said it would, although not quite as easily. I met Ophelia, and she opened her heart to me just as you predicted. And I found the most wonderful man to love me and take care of me. Everything you dreamed for me has come true. Now I just wish I could hear you say 'You see, Anna, I was right, wasn't I?' just one more time.

"But I'll visit with you here every day if I can. In fact, I think the little walk up the hill will do me good." Anna covered her tummy protectively. "I think I'm going to be a mother. Remember the 'lady talks' that Laura and I had by the fire that winter I turned thirteen when you hid your face in a book and pretended not to listen? Well, I think it's all happening to me, but I haven't told Philip yet. I want to be sure.

"I promise I'll tell this little one all about you and about how you were my best friend when I needed one most and about the special love we had. I'll make sure he knows you almost as well as I do, though he can never understand how much I loved you. That will always be special just between us.

"You rest, Uncle Mick, and don't worry about me anymore. I am happy and very much in love. My heart is filled with Philip Brichard and his family, but there is still a big part of it where you will always be."

Anna turned toward the rustling of the grass behind her, and she saw Philip coming up the rise to join her. She ran her hand over the smooth letters of Mick's name on the tombstone and rose to meet her husband. When he opened his arms to her and she walked into his embrace, she was smiling.

About The Author

A native of the Midwest, Cynthia Thomason now lives in Davie, Florida, with her husband, teen-aged son, black Persian cat and Jack Russell terrier. When she's not writing historical romances, she is an auctioneer and estate furniture buyer for the auction company she and her husband own. Cynthia would love to hear from you at this address: PO Box 550068 Fort Lauderdale, FL 33355

WATCH FOR THESE ZEBRA REGENCIES

LADY STEPHANIE (0-8217-5341-X, $4.50)
by Jeanne Savery
Lady Stephanie Morris has only one true love: the family estate she has managed ever since her mother died. But then Lord Anthony Rider arrives on her estate, claiming he has plans for both the land and the woman. Stephanie soon realizes she's fallen in love with a man whose sensual caresses will plunge her into a world of peril and intrigue . . . a man as dangerous as he is irresistible.

BRIGHTON BEAUTY (0-8217-5340-1, $4.50)
by Marilyn Clay
Chelsea Grant, pretty and poor, naively takes school friend Alayna Marchmont's place and spends a month in the country. The devastating man had sailed from Honduras to claim his promised bride, Miss Marchmont. An affair of the heart may lead to disaster . . . unless a resourceful Brighton beauty finds a way to stop a masquerade and keep a lord's love.

LORD DIABLO'S DEMISE (0-8217-5338-X, $4.50)
by Meg-Lynn Roberts
The sinfully handsome Lord Harry Glendower was a gambler and the black sheep of his family. About to be forced into a marriage of convenience, the devilish fellow engineered his own demise, never having dreamed that faking his death would lead him to the heavenly refuge of spirited heiress Gwyn Morgan, the daughter of a physician.

A PERILOUS ATTRACTION (0-8217-5339-8, $4.50)
by Dawn Aldridge Poore
Alissa Morgan is stunned when a frantic passenger thrusts her baby into Alissa's arms and flees, having heard rumors that a notorious highwayman posed a threat to their coach. Handsome stranger Hugh Sebastian secretly possesses the treasured necklace the highwayman seeks and volunteers to pose as Alissa's husband to save her reputation. With a lost baby and missing necklace in their care, the couple embark on a journey into peril—and passion.

Available wherever paperbacks are sold, or order direct from the Publisher. Send cover price plus 50¢ per copy for mailing and handling to Kensington Publishing Corp., Consumer Orders or call (toll free) 888-345-BOOK, to place your order using Mastercard or Visa. Residents of New York and Tennessee must include sales tax. DO NOT SEND CASH.